Advance praise for Lee and Miller's *Low Port!*

"I always said Barsoom and Dune had too many warlords and God-Emperors and not enough street cleaners. LOW PORT tells the stories of those who *don't* live at the top of the heap. An important anthology that tells some important—and always overlooked—stories. Good stuff."—Mike Resnick

"*Low Port* is an excellent idea, wonderfully executed. I loved reading about real people for a change. *Low Port* proves that there's more humanity and spirit in a regular person than in a bevy of wealthy princes and swashbuckling heroes."—Jerry Oltion

"It's hard to get a handle on the kinds of stories you'll find in *Low Port* by simply reading the title. Depending on your tastes, this could be a double-edged sword. What you won't find in *Low Port* are stories about the larger-than-life characters that seem to populate so much of today's popular fiction. What you will find, however, are stories about the characters that normally get only a passing mention or the unlikely heroes that get completely overlooked.

"Overall, this anthology is entertaining and has some thought-provoking stories that will keep readers on board in order to see what kind of odd scenario or character they will encounter next. Recommended for readers of any genre who appreciate a well-told story."—Jason Brannon, *SpecFicWorld*

"The 'low port' may be the lower decks of the space ship, the kitchen or the dungeon of a castle, the homeless of society, or even an orphan. They can be the lowest on the rung, but it doesn't always mean they are the lowest of the low or the bottom of the barrel. Everyone has their pride and their dreams and that is what I find most admirable about this anthology.

"This is an unusual and interesting group of stories by authors old and new, authors tried and true. Be sure to check out these stories. It may be about the lower level characters, but it is high-level adventure."—Barry Hunter, *Baryon Magazine* 91

"The characters of *Low Port* are the beings that keep the world going while royalty dances among the stars. And the stories of these survivors have a flavour that is uniquely their own.

"Consider the very different niches and needs of the notorious outlaw in John Teehan's "Digger Don't Take No Requests" and the deadly Trelayne, Douglas Smith's "Scream Angel." Neither quite on the right side of the law, but both desperately needed for life to go on and a balance to be struck for their fellow citizens. And everybody in *Low Port* knows the cost of survival and balance, whether they are willing to make the sacrifice or not.

"All is not gloom and despair in these well-chosen stories, however. A wry humour radiates from the garbled world in Joe Murphy's "Zappa for Bardog," with a lead character that is lovable, if untouchable, and a refusal to give up among the rebellious beings. And, title aside, "Lair of the Lesbian Love Goddess" shows off Edward McKeown's sly and clever mastery of the joke left unsaid.

"These are the "commoners" though, and life is never easy for the ones holding up the rest of the pyramid. The conclusion of Ru Emerson's "Find a Pin" brings on as much of a tear as a smile, with its tale of loss and of the possibility of a better future for Lisa Marie. For the Haps, the Canes, and the far more complex creatures feeding in "Angel's Kitchen," every moment is a battle to stay alive and to keep the amazing secrets Chris Szego has hidden within.

"...if you turn away at that point you will be cheating yourself out of one of the best-written and most carefully crafted anthologies to come along in quite some time. And these are all characters you should know remain just outside the bright glow of ship exhausts and gala balls, just waiting to be discovered."—Lisa Dumond, *Black Gate* Magazine, MEviews

Low Port

edited by

Sharon Lee

&

Steve Miller

Meisha Merlin Publishing, Inc.
Atlanta, GA

This is a work of fiction. All the characters and events portrayed in this book are fictitious. Any resemblance to real people or events is purely coincidental.

LOW PORT

Published by Meisha Merlin Publishing, Inc.
PO Box 7
Decatur, GA 30031

Editing & interior layout by Stephen Pagel
Copyediting & proofreading by Teddi Stransky
Cover art by Christian McGrath
Cover design by Kevin Murphy

ISBN: Hard Cover   1-59222-012-6
        Soft Cover   1-59222-013-4

http//www.MeishaMerlin.com

First MM Publishing edition: September 2003

Printed in the United States of America
0 9 8 7 6 5 4 3 2 1

Low Port

edited by

Sharon Lee

&

Steve Miller

Table of Contents

Introduction

What you have in your hands is a tangible example of the classic science fiction question "What if?"

That question is usually seen as the start for a single story, but it came to us over dinner as we discussed a Liaden Universe® project in which Solcintra's Low Port was mentioned (and which eventually became the story "Phoenix" in the SRM Publisher chapbook *Loose Cannon*).

"What if?" we asked, we could interest Stephe Pagel, our long-time publisher at Meisha Merlin, in an anthology that dealt with the people of Low Port. Not *our* Low Port necessarily, but the prototypical Low Port that must exist across universes...That of course would mean dealing with strange heroes, odd protagonists, not with the usual iconic heroes of our genre—swashbuckling swordsman, square-jawed astronaut, magic-flinging wizard or witch, world-saving physicist—but with the other people you might expect to find in a world, the people who lived with the results of the swashed buckles, the new satellite, the saved world.

Stephe had already shown a willingness to try new things in his collaborative editing of the *Bending the Landscape* anthologies with Nicola Griffith, and certainly Lee Martindale's *Such A Pretty Face* anthology for Meisha Merlin showed more evidence of the same.

The idea stayed at the dinner table a few days as we finished projects in hand and planned our next series of novels; it peeked out from under the napkins and around the salt cellar, and over the course of a month or so it burst forth three or four times along with the daily minutiae of a writing household—"have we got enough toner to print three copies of that thing?" "Oops, the inkjet is low on color," "Ach—are we out of dollar stamps, again?" and many ceteras.

The idea mutated from dealing with the average people of the world to dealing with the fringes—the down-and-outers, the people who lived really on the edge, the people who lived over the edge—and took on more of the port aspect. As it mutated the idea became more tangible. It swooped across the dinner table, it interfered with us while we were reading magazines, and it insisted that it be written down on the long "Talk To Stephe Pagel" list we keep on the table beside the to-do list.

A few nights after we put the idea on our list, Stephe Pagel called to check up on some arrangements for an upcoming convention and we put him on the speaker phone so we could gang-up on him—oops, so we could both talk to him at the same time—and eventually got to the bottom of the list and whispered back and forth (quietly, we thought) about actually asking him about Low Port.

"All right, all right—I hear you guys conspiring over there. What's going on now?"

Discovered, we mentioned the idea, hurriedly.

"Did you say anthology? Antho? I dunno, guys, I mean, anthologies are just such a hard sell..."

There was a pause then, and he said, "Can you run the idea by me again?"

Which we did, in two-part harmony, pointing out that so many stories these days seemed to be about the grand schemes, the rich and famous, the...

"OK, hold up. Why don't you give me something in writing? I mean a lot of people can talk a good anthology—and I'm not sure I'm in the market for an anthology right now—but if you can put together a proposal I can at least see if there's something there that we can work with..."

In the way of such things, the proposal took longer to write than we expected. We'd never done a print anthology before, so we researched how others did it, we compared our notes with what people sent to us, we refined the language, and then we shipped it off. In the way of such things, it took longer for the publisher to look at the proposal than we'd expected and then longer to get an answer.

In fact, we'd been thinking about the project for over a year—and we'd just about given up on anything happening—when were asked to be panelists (along with Stephe Pagel and Lee Martindale and several others) at ConQuest 32 in Kansas City on the subject of editing. Stephe, with his publisher's hat on, was explaining the kind of determination and focus it took to put an anthology together, the difficulties in selling anthologies to readers, the necessity of having a good, clear concept. Then he spoke of how pleased he'd been to work with Lee Martindale on *Such A Pretty Face*, and how he was looking forward to working with Sharon and Steve on *Low Port*, which proposal he'd just accepted.

Wait a minute! That's us. Could've knocked us over with a feather.

So now, several years later, you're seeing *Low Port* as envisioned by writers you know and writers you will know, brought to you as science fiction, as fantasy, as magic realism, as noir of this or that kind, as comedy and tragedy, as original visions come to life by writers eager to take the challenge—"What if there was a Low Port?"

We hope you'll be as amazed, and as moved, by the diversity of answers to that question as we were.

Sharon Lee and Steve Miller
October 2002
Unity, Maine

VOYEUR
Eric M. Witchey

ANDRÉ'S PALM WARMED. His subsistence credit adjustment had arrived.

He closed his fingers around the status bead embedded in his hand. Squeezing the hard lump in his fist like it might keep the money from leaking out, he sucked in the rank air of his quarters and held the breath. He glanced at the dingy white shelves of his empty galley. A starving roach skittered across a shelf and fell into the yellowed sink.

Silently, he prayed the status bead glowed green. He swore if it did he would never again pay the dwarf, never again go into the world's darkest places to stare through the tiny window.

He opened his palm.

In the center of his grimy lifeline, the dirty bead glowed dim green. He exhaled his relief. The adjustment had raised his credit rating enough to buy food. The thought made his belly heave and growl as though it were angry over three days of emptiness.

André's quarters were at the fringes of the world, the dark warrens where outsiders lived out slow deaths away from the eyes of productive insiders. The fringes were the last places. Stale air came there only after the rest of the world had breathed it. Sickening yellow water trickled from the faucets, its last stop on the way to recycling. Whores, addicts, and outsiders all eventually found their way to the fringes to hide from debts, from their own shame, and from the judging eyes of the productive. In the end, they too went to the recyclers, or they rotted, forgotten, wrapped in their paper blankets inside tiny, stained steel quarters until another tortured soul cleared away their remains and moved in.

André hated himself for living there, for having fallen so far that he could go three days without food. But the same poverty that starved him made the dwarf turn him away. He hadn't sat in the rickety chair at the tiny window for two days.

If he could stay away from the window for two days, he could stay away for three. If three, then four. He'd be an insider again, a productive citizen.

He rummaged through the louse-infested rags covering his floor until he found a tattered shirt and a pair of pants that mostly covered. He put them on and used collected lengths of twine to tie down the loose folds around his emaciated frame. He left his quarters determined to own and eat a fifty-gram tofu ration. A shining white block of extra-firm would be his sacrament of salvation.

Barefoot, he plodded along the curving corridors of the fringe until he came to the straight, bright halls where insiders lived. At the first inside hallway, he stopped. A few people, clean and brightly dressed, busy with meaningful lives, paused in their strides to stare. One woman, pale-skinned and dark-haired, gasped and covered her mouth and nose.

He had once reacted to outsiders that way, afraid of stench and disease. He reached out to touch her, to calm her.

She ran.

"Bitch," he said, but there was no venom in the word. He would eat. If he ate, things would change. As an insider, he could touch a woman and she might touch him back.

The straight hallway before him was the shortest path to food. The distribution center was a five-minute walk along that hall then across Alpha Park. André had once been a groundskeeper in Alpha Park. He knew that direct sunlight and open spaces scared people, so that way lay fewer judging eyes and faces. Of course, that was also the way to the blackberry patches that hid the hatch to the tunnels, the entrance to the dark labyrinth that hid the albino dwarf and the perverse little windows that had stolen André's soul.

The hallway angling off to his left joined Main, the grand corridor that ran the length of the world and passed between the boundaries of Alpha Park and Beta Park. Main would let him stay among insiders and far from the secret tunnels, the twisted little man, and the window.

Faster is better, he thought. The more judging eyes he saw, the more he would want to hide from them. The more time he had to think, the more likely he would fall to the dark call. The freshest air was in the parks. The sun would feel good on his wasted face. He would walk fast and be past the bushes without so much as a glance.

When the corridor spilled him out onto the green lawns of Alpha Park, he paused and looked up. The yellow ball of fire hung in the sky midway between him and the distant greenery of Park Epsilon on the opposite wall of the world. Sweat beaded on his forehead and trickled into his eye. The sting made him wince.

A breeze carried the scent of berry blossoms. He looked across the park's groomed lawn. Maybe a hundred meters away, the berry bushes, a bright clump of green covered in pink-white blossoms, guarded his dark secret. Long, thorny tentacles stretched up toward the sun. The new groundskeeper had neglected their trimming. They seemed to sway, to beckon. The hole in his world called to him through the bushes.

He looked away. To burn the darkness from his mind, he stared directly into the sun.

He no longer wondered how many people knew where the tunnel entrance was. When he had found it, he thought it a great secret. Exploring the labyrinth was an adventure that broke the boredom of his life. He had thought others would want to go with him. They did not. Now he knew it was something unimportant that the world had chosen to forget. He cursed his discovery for separating him from the rest of mankind, for turning him into an outsider.

The sun was too bright. He closed his eyes against it. The image of a woman appeared on the backs of his lids. His wife.

He brought her here once, he confessed to her and showed her the hatch beneath the bushes. She left him.

The bright image cooled and faded. Her name was...

It didn't matter. It was a small thing long forgotten. It was like the memories of taking joy in his hands clasping cool pruning shears or pressing into sun-warmed soil. Her name was no more or less than any paled memory of his life before the window. She was the tiny echo of lost feelings.

Hunger grinding at his belly was now and real. He opened his eyes. He looked past the calling bushes. He locked his eyes on the far entrance to the hallways leading to food. He managed a step. He managed another.

Then he was under the bushes, fighting the thorns and pulling up the hatch. Then he was in the darkness, slipping along low tunnels he wished were not familiar. Down a tunnel, hand on the left wall. Down another, hand on the right. Down a ladder, another tunnel, another ladder. Every heartbeat took him further from food and salvation.

He decided to turn back ten times. Twenty. Thirty. Finally, under muted red light, he watched his hand unfold before the scarred face of the albino dwarf guarding the tiny rooms, the ancient chairs, and the windows. The light made the dwarf's skin pink. It made his pink eyes seem empty and ancient. André knew the little man had grown old taking the money of lost souls like him.

The dwarf passed his extractor over André's palm. The status bead cooled and dimmed. André found his viewing room, settled in the warped spindle chair, reached behind him, and closed the door. Absolute darkness and the stink of urine and sweat engulfed André.

He didn't care. Only the moment when the metal blind slid away from the window was important. His heart beat faster, anticipating the obscene bliss that would wipe away his hunger and shame.

It was obscene. It was the worst of addictions, a sickness that would kill him. He had tried a thousand times, and he couldn't stop himself. That tiny, round window was his reason to live. He couldn't remember when the worn wood of the spindly chair had become more comfortable than the sofa in his living room or when the vision beyond the glass had become more exciting than his wife.

He touched the cold wall and found the metal blind and the circular window frame. He cupped his bony hands around the steel frame. He knew he wouldn't see faster because he was closer. He knew there was no light in the room to reflect the old chair and his bony frame. Still, he pressed his forehead to his cupped hands.

Even squinting in the darkness waiting for the window to open, he told himself he could get up, turn away, and walk back inside. He could still go back where men and women lived lives that mattered. The tofu ration was lost, but he didn't have to be an outsider.

Deliberately, he put his hands on his knees as though to stand.

"Stand," he said to the darkness. "Stand like a man. Go back inside."

The hand trick never worked.

He found his hands back at the little window trying to shield out distractions that came more from the darkness within than from the darkness surrounding him.

The metal blind slid away.

André pressed his face to the glass, trying to fill himself with the sight beyond, trying to pour himself out between his hands into the infinite space between a billion stars.

"Stars," the dwarf chanted when they first met. "Galaxies, nebulae, the secrets of the universe can be yours if you have eyes that can see."

The dwarf had told the truth.

André stared into the mind of God. His mortal thoughts streamed outward into sublime forever. A chill of blissful awe shook his frail body. Infinity flooded his mind and washed away the guilt and shame of looking outward.

DIGGER DON'T TAKE NO REQUESTS
John Teehan

Four years, 8 months, 23 days

So I'm flatpicking up a bit of "Foggy Mountain Break-down", enjoying the hell out of it, and finish with a trademark Doc Watson run. Got lots of people gathered around me by the observation deck; touries, techies, goonies and moonies on their way back and forth between here and the Concourse. Good crowd, and there be a couple of touriefems giving me a friendly eye. It's while I'm considering the possibilities that I click on this one nervous little moonunit in a sloppy jumpsuit hanging around the edge of the crowd. I can spell the trouble with this unit.

S-p-a-z-n-i-k.

I do a little patter about the Old Man on the Moon and how I met him my first week Up Here and how he taught me this next song which is nothing more than an old whaling song with some of the words changed. One grinning tourie recognizes the tune and whispers something to his ladyfriend. I send them a wink before the end of the song to let them in on the joke and figure the guy'll drop an extra dollie or two in the tin for making him look clever in front of his lady.

Never hurts to let the paying public feel good about themselves. Hell, it's the very soul of busking. Okay, the money is the heart of it, and the fun is in playing, but the soul is in the way people gather around and just gig.

I pick through and finish up another song to a scatter of applause, little kids jumping high over their parents heads to see me—enjoying the hell out of the lighter gravity—when I catch a cough from a uniformed loonie goon by the passageway entrance. They don't mind me playing, but the crowd's getting kind of dense and it's time to move along.

I give a little bow to thank and amuse whilst passing the tin around. Not bad. Some loonie dollies and some meal tickets. And a button. Ha! I love kids. Where'd they find a button Up Here?

The crowd disperses (as do the touriefems, alas) and up comes my nervous little spaznik in the sloppy suit.

"You Digger?" he asks. He looks something Asian. About a meter and a half tall and stick thin. He blinks at me through a tangled mass of black hair and seems a little unsteady.

I count up my takings and divide it among many pockets. "Be me. Who you?"

Like some newbie, he sticks his hand out, "Kimochi Stan."

Shaking hands is a Down There thing to do. It's nothing personal—you touch friends, even some acquaintances of good reputation, but you never know when some newbie with the sniffles slips by the Quarrines. Still, the kid looks like he could use a friend so I take his hand and pump it all gregarious-like.

"Cool sobriquet," I tell him, "something like 'feels good' in Jappongo, right?"

He looks embarrassed. Most of us who end up bumming around the Concourse pick up these little nicknames. Sometimes they're given, like Ice Cream Lou's or Amazing Gracie's, or we make them up ourselves. Instant notoriety. No crime. Kimochi must be American or Canadian-born though. Japan doesn't fool around with travel visas to the moon; and my new pal Stan doesn't seem to be weighed down with an accent.

I tune up the guitar by touch, muffling the homemade strings with my fingers. "So what's up, 'Feel Good'?"

"I want to go home," he says like his heart is about to freeze up and shatter. Poor kid shivers before me. Lunar fidgets we call it. Like homesickness, but a hundred times worse. Maybe the good feelings he came up here with pffted out into vacuum. Hope he don't bawl on me. Tears ain't good for business—not unless you're playing real skinned-knee bluegrass. I wonder how long it took before Feel Good's fidgets started settling in. Sometimes takes a month. Sometimes they start as soon as the shuttle docks. Poor little breast-fed babies.

"Shouldn't be a problem," I tell him. I stow my guitar into its carrybag and lean it against a wall. "You got a return chit. Sooner or later they gotta send you back."

"No, I want to go home now. I can't take it here anymore," he stammers and twitches like a jumping bean. "Tattooed Lydia said you could help me out."

Lydia, oh Lydia, say have you met Lydia? Lydia the tattooed lady? Nice girl—looks like a living picture book. Real friendly too, if you get my drift. And she sends a lot of business my way.

The orb of Earth had long-since ceased to be a *gollygee* sight, but the observation deck was still milling with eager-eyed touries. I look around for goons—both kinds—the loonie goons with the uniform stripes on their arms, and cheesehead goons, the muscle for Concourse queens like Amazing Gracie. The loonie goon from before is gone, and no other two-legged security in sight. Plenty of cameras in a public place like this, but cameras don't bother me. Brahe City Security isn't who I'm concerned about.

"Maybe. Maybe not," I tell him. "How good is your chit?"

He reaches under his shirt and pulls out a gray plastic tag on a thin chain. Along the underside is a magnetic strip. "It's got two and a half months left. I need to go home tomorrow."

Survived two whole weeks Up Here, eh?

"Cool your jets, buddy-guy," I say. "You think you're booking a jump to Las Vegas? Best I can do is a berth to Mexico City in a week." That much is almost true. Let's see what else he's got. With only so many spots available on transports going Up and Down, even charity has its bounds. And it's not like he can just walk up to Lunar Authority and say "take me home." They got iron-sphincter schedules with every seat going up *or* down booked well in advance of some poor moononit with the fidgets. You can buy whatever kind of visachits you want—Down There—but to book an early passage downside, you need an expiring chit saying you've used up your prepaid welcome. No Travelers Aid around here. Not yet anyway.

The best Kimochi Stan can do if he wants to bug out is either fake an illness—which will land him in the Quarrines for a spell—or do something to get tossed into Facilities for an undetermined amount of time until Lunar Authority decides they might have some cargo space available. Doing crimes got you put in jail Up Here, but once you got sent Down There you spent even more time in jail. The only smart way to get back to Earth before your time is to get hold of an expiring chit and grab the seat assignment before the shuttle takes off. Most touries know this. It's the moonunits who think they can just wing it without a plan.

"I can't make it another week," says Stan, all distressed and the like—more *warui* by the second. Total spaznik. He pulls a handful of meal tickets from his pocket. "I have three week's of meals. Genuine!"

They better be. Getting caught with phony meal tickets gets you nothing but bread and water with the loonie goons until they kick you home for more of the same. I sling my guitar bag over my shoulder.

"Follow."

I set a loping pace, wide-leaping, low-gravity strides, but— you know—*controlled and graceful*, and take a public tunnel leading away from the Concourse and crowds. I don't think anyone is following us, but there's no sense letting Amazing Gracie or her crew spot me taking a spaznik to a hideyhole. At the end of the tunnel I jump up a level and pull an unscrewed access panel from the wall. I motion Kimochi inside and pull the panel closed behind us.

Boxes of control switches, circuits, and pressure gauges line the walls and insulated pipes crisscross the ceiling. Things get more cramped in these rabbit holes, so instead of the arcing strides that pass for walking up here, you have to sort of pull yourself along, single file, bracing your hands against the walls while keeping your head low.

Even in enclosed quarters, there's no sense in giving Kimochi Stan enough time to gig on the path to my hideyhole. In the techtunnels, there are no conveniently placed glowstrips to show touries the way to the food court or gift shops. The walls and circuit boxes aren't numbered and coded in any sequential order, but if you know how to look at them—and I do—they make spiffy-skiffy landmarks. Two years ago I did some sly work for this one claustrophobic techie and got the lay of the land. Learned a lot about the ins and outs of just about every rabbit hole in Brahe City.

We take so many twists and turns, paths that double back, and others that look like dead-enders unless you squeeze past another loose panel, I figure I've got Stan lost enough where if he tries to branch out on his own, he'd be dead lost. Not that I want him to, mind you, but I didn't get by for four years Up Here by being the fool. If any of Gracie's crew grabs him and beats my hideyhole loc out of him, I'll be all done. Busted flat. Game over and sent downside.

I weave through the maze for another fifteen minutes, until I'm abso-smoothly sure I have Kimochi thoroughly scroggled. Judging from the bitty whimpers, he's just about there. I quit the runaround and cut across a little courtyard where eight tunnels all join together. I pick the leftmost one on the far wall and head toward my hideyhole. Well, one of the several I got scattered hither and yon.

We reach the end of the last tunnel where I switch on a battery lamp taped to the wall. I can't really call it home; but it's a place to sleep and sometimes just hole up. A sleeping bag sits on the floor and some boxes for clothes and incidentals lean against a wall. It's a cozy as it's going to get, a lost little place that only me and probably Security knows about. But like I said, this is just one of several, and Security can't be sure which one I'd be using and when.

Not that they care much.

I swivel toward Stan and point, "About face," I tell him. He's looking worse and worser. Real fidgety. The Concourse is a nice big open space, like a mall, but even then it can feel real small to a lot of earthworms. The rabbit holes, by comparison, are as tiny as wombs—or coffins—depending on how you look at things. My pal Stan is not in a good state of being, but he doesn't question me. He just nods and turns away until I say otherwise.

I put my guitar down and pull a box away from the wall. A single strand of hair sticks out from between two panels right where I left it. I push on a corner of a panel then pry it off. Inside, sitting on a plasteen pump control housing, is a chip scanner I once fished out of recycling and fixed. I grab it, replace the panel, and push the box back.

"Give me your chit," I say, standing up.

Stan turns back around, pulls the chain over his head and hands me the chit. He looks around at my little refuge—pure envy on his face. Brother, this didn't come easy. It took a long time before I had enough tricks to stake out a safe hideyhole in the belly of the base. Learned from those who came before me, but none of whom lasted so long. As for Stan, he probably curls himself up in some communal corner each night, hoping not to be robbed by another spaz. He doesn't look the sort to have the dollies for a comfort room. I run his tag through a slot in the scanner and check the length of time remaining in his pre-paid stay. Not exactly eight weeks, but close enough not to make a big stink about it.

I hold up his chit. "With this and your meal slips, I'll trade you a berth to O'Hare in three days."

What happens next is totally my fault.

Stan launches himself at me and shoves me up against the wall. If he had taken more time to brace himself before his lunge, he might have had more luck. As it was, I've lived on the moon for nearly five years and *I* know how to move my body. Stan has only been here a couple weeks and moves as clumsy as a toddlerbabe.

Of course it don't pay much to be overconfident. I twist and tumble him to the floor, which at one-sixth gee doesn't hurt him much. Of course I forget how weirdly desperate these spazniks can be. Stan kicks up his legs and tangles them with mine in a clumsy sort of judo then pulls me down with him.

He rolls atop of me and sneaks in a good clip, hitting my jaw, making my teeth click and thankful that my tongue isn't between them. Again, this guy forgets just where he is. It doesn't take Samson to throw a guy off your chest around here. I shove him away and scramble back before he can grabble at me again.

He gets up and tries for another launch, but this time I'm ready for him. Poor spaz. I crouch on the floor and wait for him to move. Stan braces himself against the wall, then launches himself at me. I bounce to the right and rebound behind him where I grab him by the collar and yank him back. His head smacks against the wall. Whammo!

That's all it takes.

I didn't even slam him very hard—him being a potential customer and all—but that doesn't stop old Kimochi Stan from breaking down into bawls. I let him go and he crumples to the floor, hugging his knees to his chest and boohooing.

I could give him a good kick right there, and probably should. But I don't. I remember my first couple of months Up Here. It can get edgy. "Want to tell me what that was all about?" I ask.

Stan just sits there for a minute, then lifts his head and winces. "I thought you might be holding out on me and had a return chit that left today," he says.

I look at him, not really surprised. "That desperate?"

He nods glumly.

I sigh. Just a dumb spazzing cheesehead who slipped through the psyches. "A smart loonie doesn't keep his chits all in the same place. Maybe you should stay up here longer to learn how things is done, dig?"

"No..." he moans.

I grab my scanner which got dropped in the scuffle. It looks no worse for wear—at least this isn't Earth gravity. I toss Stan his chit back. He looks at me all worried-like. He should be. After a stunt like that I should leave him in the deepest, darkest, most remote tunnel in the Belly. I'm sorely tempted, but even an idiot like this might have gotten savik enough to let someone else know where he was going. And if he doesn't reappear, living and breathing, sometime soon, word would get out that dealing with Digger gets you a stone-cold corpse. Bad hoodoo.

"Look, Stan. No hard feelings, but don't try that shit again. Listen to older brother instead. Tomorrow, you meet me in the Concourse by Ice Cream Lou's Rent-a-Room with your chit, your meal tickets, *and* two fully charged batteries. I'll give you a chit for O'Hare leaving the next day. If you can't find the dollie for some batteries, then it's Mexico City in a week. Until Lou's, I don't want to see your face. Got me?"

He nods and curls himself up tighter. If the kid behaved himself maybe I'd have gotten him to O'Hare without the batteries, but I *hate* getting jumped—fidgeting spaznik or not.

"You're not going to go lunar on me again."

He nods again and mumbles something. I can't hear him but he sounds properly contrite.

"Good. Now get up."

I grab him by the collar and push and pull him along with me. I take a different route back to the Concourse and exit from a different panel than the one we entered. I make him repeat back the deal we struck, then send him on his way. He's still choking tears and he looks a mess. I hope anyone who sees him will be able to figure out the story for themselves.

After I send Stan stumbling on his way I recede back into the tunnels and go around the Concourse to another hideyhole some fars aways. This one has the treasure trove hidden *inside* the pump housing and I check my supply of extra chits and dump my takings from the day. I got a good amount squirreled away Up Here in hideyholes spread across Brahe City. Nest eggs. There be rumors percolating about that Project Burroughs is going civvie *Real Soon Now*. Visa rules are gonna be tough, tougher, toughest for Mars, but money talks. I still got a ways to go to raise the funds, but without real credentials up here, I'm stuck playing the hallways for change.

Consider, brothers and sisters, there's no work to be had up here; not unless you wrangle a contract before you blast off—and those are tough to get. The United Nations Space

Agreement guarantees anyone the right to travel to the moon,
but they don't encourage immigration. Aside from the visa
chits, there are meal tickets to use in the food court and loonie
currency for incidentals and souvenirs from the tourie shops.
Lodging costs extra too, from cheap comfort rooms to posh
suites with private observation ports overlooking the dusty,
dry lunar surface.

Other than to work for one of the UN tourie businesses, or
in one of the research labs at the other end of the station, there's
not much left to do. You're given some passes to a few historic
sites like the Eagle landing site or the Artemis wreckage, but
after that you have to pay. Fine for a tourie on a week's holiday.
Sucks for the rest of us, but we make do.

Most of the units who come up are your average touries.
Here for a week to two, then gone back to the bosom of Mama
Earth. Then there are the techheads and service folk and such
who hang on from six to eighteen months then go home. Finally there are the squatters, like me. Not destitute or slovenly
or anything. We're more like moon groupies who come up for
the atmosphere (ha!), but many of whom also come away with
disillusions.

But not me.

I love the moon. I love it Up Here and Out There. But I
know it's not for everyone. You see, the trick is to find a niche
and hang on tight.

Take Amazing Gracie (please!) who owns a big slice of the
black market. Then there's Ice Cream Lou who provides the
playspace for the boys and girls who turn exotic sixth-G tricks
for bright-eyed touries. Tattooed Lydia sells one-of-a-kind skin
souvenirs—each one unique and guaranteed not to fade away
for at least five years. There are others. Lots of others. Opportunity is where you find it.

Those who can't hack it Up Here trade us their chits for
ones that will send them home early. As for yours truly, I do
what I can to ease their burden—be it a song, a story, or a good
trade—all the while working on my own grand plan.

I stop outside the food court and look to see if I can't add yet a few more dollies to my stash and maybe some meal tickets to sell later. I play and I sing and I do my thing while staying out of the way of the loonie goons. I'm no beggar. I work for a living thank you very much.

You try singing in a public place. I dare you.

Four years, 8 months, 24 days

"Howdy Gracie," I say. *Lordie, but she's a big woman!*

"Digger," she smiles nice and outer-space cold-like. Gracie and two of her goons—the Beach Boys, big, blond, and musclely—grab me on the Concourse and 'escort' me down a service tunnel. Fuck. "Word's out you picked up another two months. Food too."

I give her my best grin. Poor Gracie. She's never going to outlast me Up Here. "Maybe…then again…maybe."

"He should have been mine. I wouldn't have ripped him off like some dusty scavengers I know." Gracie looks pissed.

"How now?" I ask with all the innocence of a newbie. "He's getting an early trip downside—just like he wants. And I get another couple of months of air and some extra slop."

"Plus two of my batteries," Gracie adds. She cracks her knuckles.

Uh oh. "Don't know nothing about that."

"Fool me, fool?" she says. Damn, she's seriously pissed. "That spaznik was near to breaking so you held out for something extra. Got him itching, so he jumps Seraphim Sally when she's coming out of the toilets and snags two of my batteries out of her bag."

I shrug, totally unsurprised now, but I didn't tell him to go and do something like that. "Why cry to me? You know who he is. Finger him."

"Oh yeah, like Security is going to help me grab back batteries I stole from them to begin with. Cheesehead. The spaznik's gone underbelly and you were the last person to talk to him."

Underbelly, has he? Hope he don't get lost. Spazniks come in two flavors. Some manage to secure an early homecoming, then party off what little few dollies they have as noisily as possible. You'd be surprised how many times they change their minds about leaving, but by then it's too late—the loonie goons always seem to know.

Then there are ones like Kimochi who will never be described as 'people-persons' and go into hiding as soon as they get their return ticket for fear of getting robbed by folken as desperate as them. Chances are, ole Kimochi Stan won't show his face again until boarding time—if he doesn't get himself fatally lost.

"I didn't tell him to steal anything," I tell her.

"Dammit, Digger," Gracie bounces me against the wall then grabs me by the shoulders, lifts me off the floor, and pins me. "I want those batteries back or they're going to find you stinking up the ventilation shafts." Her goons grin real nasty-like.

Man, I so hate people trying to whale on me. Maybe I can wriggle free, but not with the Beach Boys right behind her. Nor with Amazing Gracie outweighing me by a max factor. And let's not forget her amazing army. She sucks about half the long-haul transients up here into joining her racket, and a good chunk of the other half are at least on retainer. No place to run to, Digger. No place to hide.

"Deal?" I offer. What the hell. Beats becoming a smear on the wall.

"It better include two batteries, dustmite," she says, "and while we're at it, shake your pockets loose." Off to the left I see three more of her bully boys, Huey, Dewey, and Frank (where do they come up with these names?) turning the corner. Anytime she wants, she can pulp me even without her bruisers tagging along. Gracie has a very 'hands on' personality, but the goons make for serviceable camouflage against the cameras. Oh, this is not good. Security won't waste their energy for a simple rough-up. Maybe if Gracie kills me, that'll put a dent in her long-term plans—but I'll be long past caring. With goons covering her back, no one sees nothing.

Calmly, calmly, I push my hands inside Gracie's elbows and she grudgingly lowers me back to the floor. Where am I going to go?

"Look, batteries are long gone," I say. "Traded those an hour after Kimochi uploaded them to me. And you know how things work, they change hands a double-dozen times by now. Hell, someone in your network probably has them." That's not entirely true. One is sitting in a hideyhole, but I'm not about to tell her that and be forced to take her there.

"That doesn't mean you're getting off," she says. Her goons are crowding behind her now. Covering us up real nice now. Crap-squared.

I reach down my shirt and pull out a tag. Unlike all the plain gray ones, this one has a gold-colored strip running down the back. I watch her eyes as I take it out. *Oh good Gracie; I have you now.* "Seven months left," I say.

She loosens her grip on me and doesn't even notice I shrug the rest of the way out. Her jaw goes something slack as she stares at the chit. "That's not real," she says. Her goonies are just as gawking.

"Sure 'nuff 'tis."

"No tourie gets a year-long visa. You gotta be pro to get one of those. It's a phony."

I smile, "This spaz was a university fellow who blew his funds at Lucky Dick's. I tripped over him the first week he got here and he was already on the road to ruin. He must have blown more than money at Dickie's because he was a bloody mess when I found him. An act of mercy got him to the infirmary and he somehow, accidently, must have swapped this chit for a monther that was almost up."

"Fuck, Digger. Why not wait until he was dead before you robbed him?"

"Professionalism." I turn the chit over and let her see the hologrammed logo next to the strip. "You got a reader? Good for seven more months."

She jerks her head and a tall blond beach guy with a reader slung around his neck comes around. I put my hand around the chain and lean forward to let her run it through the reader. They machine beeps cheerily.

Gracie frowns. She's suspicious, sure as spit, but that don't matter. It's real, and I got her hooked. "Why you giving it up?" she asks.

Shrug. "Got more chits. Figure I give you this and you call your goons off, plus I get a couple of free rides."

"Your ass."

"My ass is purty, thank you. You take chit, free and clear, and you and your goonies don't hassle me for seven months."

"And if we just take it from you?"

I yank the chain back, pop the chit in my mouth and set my teeth against it. She knows I can ruin the codes on the strip if I start grinding my teeth together, but if she gives her word, she'd has to keep it. That's how she got to be Amazing Gracie—mean and ugly as she is. If it got out that her word was as good as a holed spacesuit, she'd be without her army and probably downside within a week. That's just how things work. Nobody likes a dishonest crook.

Grace spits on the floor and nods to the other goon. Spit flies funny at sixth-G, in case you didn't know.

The other blond guy comes forward and pulls the chit off over my head, "Seven months, dustmite, then you're dead," he says.

I smile all pretty-like. Gracie sends her goons back and then smiles back at me. Not a pretty smile—she don't have many of those left for anyone. She growls through her teeth, and leaves.

Easy, Digger.

I relax and lean back against the wall. My own freaking fault. My best chit. Granted, I got more, but still—that was my best chit. When Kimochi gave me the batteries, I knew he must have done something that would send Gracie gunning for me. I should have never made him an offer for a quicker ride home in exchange. Stupid is as stupid does.

But no worries. I got more chits, and I can wrangle more when the need arises. Digger has lots of tricks still.

I whistle, straighten my jumps, and pick up my guitar. Time to get to work. I head out the corridor and make my way toward the observation decks.

"Spot check."

I turn my head. A loonie goon with a blue stripe on his arm stands there by the exit like he was waiting just for me. "Pardon?"

He looks at me and taps a shock stick against a gloved hand. "Spot check, Digger. You know the rules. Transients got to have a valid visa chit on their persons at all times or are subject to deportation following a term in Facilities."

I know the routine, and realize Gracie must have 'lerted me out at the very first chance to this slap-happy goon. No time for games, so don't even grin. I just reach into my leg pocket and take out a dull gray chit and hand it over.

The goon frowns, but sets the chit into his belt scanner. *Beep!* Digger is kosher! He hands it back to me with a grunt.

"I hope you enjoy your final week with us here at Brahe City." His voice is nice and sarcastic-like.

Ha! Yeah, my emergency backup's got a week left—almost ready to pass off to the next spaznik I see in trade for a fresher chit. But with what I've got back in my hideyholes, I'm covered for at least another three months easy. No way am I going back Down There.

I got other plans.

Four years, 8 months, 25 days

Word's out. Brahe City Security is looking for me. Tattooed Lydia heard it from Lucky Dick who got it from a goon. Don't know why. Don't care. I figure to dive deep into the tunnels for a few days.

I hear assailants-unknown jumped Kimochi Stan before he could make his shuttle home. My name is mentioned, which is so not good. He'll be at the infirmary for about a week and then on his way home whenever Lunar Authority thinks it has room on another shuttle. Poor sap.

As for yours truly, I can't be too worried. If Security really wants me, they'll figure out a way to get me. That they don't flush out the rabbit holes might mean they know I had nothing to do with Stan. And I'm legal, but hey—discretion and so forth. I low profile it for awhile and just haunt.

Four years, 8 months, 28 days

Rumors that Project Burroughs is going civvie are true—only now it's called Barsoom City though it can't be more than a couple of domes. We got a whole mess of folken up here making ready for a torchship heading to Mars. Between the techies bound for Mars, their friends and family seeing them off, and distracted loonie goons, I lose myself in the crowds and restock my food.

Four years, 9 months, 2 days

Still no word on why Security is looking for me, if they still are. Can't be because of Kimochi. Even if he didn't see who jumped him, why would I want to rough him? I take a chance and grab my cleanest, freshest chit and play for the Barsoom City-bound crowds and make more money in one day than I have all month! Still have a long way to go though before I can get off this dusty rock. From the skinny I hear on Barsoom, the cost of the passage is more than I expected and the visa rules stiffer. Thankfully, I've got patience and time to build up my stake and wait for the rules and regs to lighten.

Mars or bust, man! Just you see.

Four years, 9 months, 5 days

A torchship went out to Mars the day before yesterday and another one goes off tomorrow. Brahe City Security seems to have better things to do than chase down innocent little moonunits like me, so I keep playing and making my way.

Later I cross the Concourse and see the Beach Boys giving me the evil eye, then start following me. They aren't supposed to give me any trouble for a while to come, but maybe they're running rogue. Either way I don't like their look and lose them through the food court.

Outside, I bump into Stan who looks better than I expected. Battered and bruised, but not fidgety or nothing. He looks surprised to see me though and says something about having to wait another three weeks before Authority will send him home. I give him some meal tickets and he shuffles away too quick to thank me.

Some people, you know? Well, at least he's alive. Maybe he'll have better luck back home.

I decide to head towards the science dome to see if any of the techheads are on break and in the mood for some music. With all the hubbub in Brahe City these days with the traffic and all, they must be looking to unwind.

I turn a corner and run right into loonie goons. *Crap.*

My chit's good, but they don't even check it as they hustle me on to Facilities. We pass right by Amazing Gracie's corner where she and the Beach Boys are busting their guts laughing.

My chit's good! It's good! No fucking way is this going down.

Four years, 9 months, 6 days

I spend the night in Facilities pounding the walls. The loonie goons took my guitar and emptied my pockets so there's no mucking about with the locks. I get a cold sandwich and bug juice at some point, then this big bruiser of a goon shows up to take me to see the Boss.

Boss Mead.

This is the big cheese, head of Brahe City Security. A no-nonsense, cheerless heavy who ain't never had a good word for the moonunits or anyone else who skates on this side of legitimacy. Bet he's tone deaf too. We come to an office and I sit in a chair and wait. The big loonie goon stands by the door and keeps a watchful eye on li'l ole me.

Man, this is like being sent to the principal's office—triple-squared. Maybe Mead's not a bad guy, I tell myself. Maybe he's got a wife and kids and spends quiet off hours playing board games and the like. He might read poetry to puppies for all I know. But hell, the door opens and in he comes all gleaming in his blues 'n whites and looks at me. I don't see Major Mead the family man, I see Boss Mead, the hardass who's gonna bounce my ass downside for no good reason.

Shit.

End of the line, Digger, old boy. You kept your nose clean and you didn't make a nuisance of yourself and you helped out from time to time and it's still gonna end with the big dump on the wrong side of the gravity well.

Mead sits behind the desk and calls up something on a datapad, reading all quiet like there is nothing major happening at all. I've been up here for almost five years. Five! And he's acting like deporting me is as routine as deciding whether he's going to have the pudding or the pie for dessert.

Oh sure, I think of jumping out of that chair and dashing out. If I could make it through the Concourse, maybe I could evade for a week or three with a sprinkle of hope that if I stay under their radar long enough they'll forget all about it as a bad job and we could go back to normal.

Yeah. That'd be the thing.

Except I've got this big-ass uniformed goon stationed at the door behind me, ready to break me in two if I sneeze without warning. Yeah, sure.

Fuck it. If I gotta go, let me go with style. Make some kind of raised-middle-finger gesture to the Man and to hell with the rest. I get this crazy idea. Fucking insane and start undoing the fastens on my jumpsuit. Maybe a little creative streaking is in order.

"What the hell are you doing?" barks Mead, looking up from the file. From behind me, big meaty hands clamp down on my shoulders.

I force myself to relax under the grip and continue working on the suit. As soon as big boy lets me go, I can slither out of it soon enough. "Getting naked. Why not? You're going to boot me out no matter, like a baby from the womb, so why not indulge?"

The hands grip my shoulders tighter and the goon leans on me real hard, hard enough to even make a difference Up Here. Mead just stares at me, this totally dumbfounded expression on his pugly. He looks at me for about half a minute, then sits back and shakes his head. He waves a hand at the goon who hesitates, then releases me and leaves the room. I start to shuck out of my suit.

"Stop that," snaps Mead, like I'm a child. Well, duh.

And suddenly sure I feel all foolish and the like. I'm making no great claims to rational thinking at this time. Futile dumb toddlerbabe gestures can't be the best I can do. I'll skip the tantrums and go with dignity, boy. But whatever the hell is going to happen, I'm still going to make him work for it. I refasten my suit and sit there.

He puts down the datapad and folds his hands. Then he looks me over with a disapproving kind of frown.

"Rough day?" he asks.

Okay, so I'm rumpled and wrinkled. You'd be too. And I'm a little irked. "Rough week. What's the story? You can't toss me. I got valid chits."

Mead sits back and presses a button on the desk. A computer screen flashes on. "Joseph Dagwood Hill," he reads, "born in Syracuse, NY. Attended Brown University. Majored in engineering, but dropped out midway through junior year. Formed a band called Diaspora then disappeared from the music scene a year later. You reappeared at Brahe City under the name Joe Hill but go by Digger while on the Concourse. You've been here for over four years and nine months which makes you the longest-lasting civilian transient on the station."

I lean back and tangle my fingers behind my head. Kind of relaxed, you know, but a forced relaxed. So he has a file on me. No fears. "All the air I breathe is paid for. All my food is kosher."

"And you don't go panhandling," Mead adds, "and you don't steal—directly, at least. You don't bug the guards when you get picked on by other moonunits."

"So I've done nothing wrong."

Mead nods, though it looks like he's agreeing only on the technicalities.

"I've done a lot right too," I tell him.

"How do you figure?" he asks.

"A lot of folks come up here not prepared for the more subtle differences between getting around Down There and getting around Up Here," I tell him, all serious-like. This is serious business. (Do me a favor and forget that getting-naked crap.) "I help them adjust. I show them how to handle their food tickets so they don't overdo it or trade them in for dollies for the tourie shops without getting ripped off. I play a bit of music from home for the homesick and add a bit of local color to the Concourse. Many's a time I've given directions to touries and techies alike without asking for anything in return."

The Boss tilts his head to one side. Oh he's suspicious all right. He's suspicious. "So what are you getting at?"

"I've even pulled the odd techie chore or three," I tell him, "under the roses, so the speak. I think if there's a job for a guy like me Up Here, I should get it," I tell him. There. Now it's out. A real job would mean real dollies and the sooner I could raise my stake for Mars.

"Well there isn't," he says.

"Then what are you going to do? Kick me off?"

"Yep."

"You can't. I broke no laws. You've said so yourself. I'm not a nuisance to any of the staff or touries, and I pay my own way. I can raise a stink at the UNSA and then come right back Up Here and start all over."

"You scam your own way. Visa chits were never meant to be used as currency for bums."

"So the lunar commission is boohooing over the fact they can't reap off of other people's paid air?" Now I'm more than pissed. They can alter visa policies Down There if they get the votes, but I'm so grandfathered in I got whiskers that reach the floor. They can't change the rules on me this late in the game.

He holds up his hands and shakes his head. "We're getting off track. Yes, it's my intention to put you off the moon, but you don't have to go back to Earth. How does Mars sound?"

I almost fall out of the chair. Ouch.

"Bullshit," I tell him.

"No bullshit. We tried to find you for the first ship, but you kept moving around and I've had my hands full enough with all the new folks arriving and passing through. We were lucky, *you* were lucky, that Gracie's boys spotted you and tipped us off. The second ship leaves later today. Barsoom City needs a support staff with the Project Burroughs personnel pulling out. Trouble is, the only personnel we have so far who will be able to hack life on Mars are the scientists and technicians. We don't have a shortage of them, but we do have a shortage in another area." He looks at me curious. "Are you too proud to push a mop? Or handle some laundry or cooking?"

This is unreal. "No," I say. Hell, I've held down worse jobs in college.

"You sure? You weren't too far from a degree in engineering at one time. And most of the initiative you've shown up here has been self-serving. Can you serve others is my question. You'll actually be working, not loafing around with a bunch of other bums."

"I wasn't a prodigy student, even at my best," I admit to him. "My grades would have gotten me nothing more than a cubicle Down There, not a techslot on the moon. But I can make a good grunt. I can even do some tech work when it's needed. Ask around. Sign me up." *Sign me up now, before you change your mind.*

"You don't want to hear about pay or benefits?"

"You covering my air and food?"

"It's part of the package. The food won't be much better than the slop we give ticket holders here at first—not until the greenhouses and protein processors are online—but you'll get what the science and tech folks get."

"Sign me up." I tell him. *Yes. Yes. Yes!*

"Not so fast. You ready to take on a two-year long contract?"

"Earth years or Martian years?"

He chuckles and looks a little pleased with himself. "Martian, of course. That's about four Earth years. Give or take."

I think about it for only the briefest of moments. Nearly five years on the moon, four years on Mars. Who knows? Maybe out past Pluto before I'm sixty. And hey, people are living longer. The technology is only getting better.

"And of course you get a free ride back to Earth when your contract is up," he tells me.

"No," I say.

"No?" The guy looks a little surprised. He leans across the desk and gives me his best darkly-type scowl. "Look son, I can't make you take the job on Mars, but if you think you're going to continue coasting Up Here any longer—"

"No, I mean I don't want to go back to Earth."

"You'll want to stay on Mars? Don't speak too soon. It's not all it's cracked up to be."

"Neither is the moon—but going forward beats falling backward. When the contract is up, I want berth to any other colony settlement that will take me. If there's nothing ready, I'll sign up for another Martian year until something *does* turn up."

"You're kidding," he says, staring at me all curious-like. "Son, Barsoom City isn't a big dome, although it'll get bigger in time. If you think you'll find better a better life on Ceres or someplace, you've got more than a few years of waiting."

"They'll need dishwashers on Ceres too. If not now, then eventually. And if not Ceres, than Callisto. Or on a deep space explorer or comet rocket."

How did Columbus get all that crew? They weren't all sea-dogs and convicts. There must have been a few dishwashers who just wanted to see how far they could go, how many horizons they could cross. For a lot of folken, the ties to Mama

Earth are too strong, but I was ready to be spaceborn the first time I opened my eyes and saw them twinkling lights in the sky. Brahe City was just the first small step. One small step, baby, and it's the stars—our destination. *Don't try to stop me now.*

I look at Boss Mead and he ain't so bad seeming right now. I think of how Gracie laughed as I was dragged by, and now who's laughing? Mead and I talk some more, then he cuts me loose with a butterscotch-colored chit, "Be at dock H in twelve hours. I'll forward your guitar to the ship. Use the rest of the time to gather your personals, but no contraband. Now beat it. And good luck."

And it's off I go.

I hit all my hideyholes, one after the other, and grab my stash. Of the chits I got left, I head out to the Concourse and give them to Tattooed Lydia and tell her to keep what she wants, give the rest to whomever. Same with the chit scanner. I also tell her to describe for Gracie the chit I'm wearing, but not to tell her where I've gone. Let her stew for a bit until she gigs it out for herself.

Lydia closes up early and we go shopping. I'll need some new jumps for Mars. Buy some books maybe and vids and geegaws and gimschiffles to trade. Even scientists and techies need toys. What's left over I put into an actual bank account, courtesy of a butterscotch chit which makes me too official for words. Lydia and I feast on the rest of my meal tickets then hit Big Lou's for a spot of comfort time before I blast off.

I told you she's the friendly sort.

Brothers and sisters, listen well to the one who went before. Keep your eyes open. Keep your ears open. Be patient, but know an opportunity when it slaps you upside the head. Until then—make your own opportunities and be not afraid.

Who knows what's down the road, but I aim to find out.

THE GATE BETWEEN HOPE AND GLORY
Holly Phillips

NO QUESTION THE rider was dead.

The repair crew, all four of them, stood on the rim of the cargo pod's airlock staring down at the body huddled against the pod's stained white tiles. Not the first hitch-hiker to attempt the trip up to the station from the planet in an atmosphered pod, and probably not the last. Chouss and Awandi dropped a ladder into the pod and climbed down to deal with the remains. The pod's interior was slightly warmer than the maintenance pit; Chouss pulled off her gloves to unclip the harness that held the rider against the cargo restraints.

She—the rider was a she—had done everything she could: breather tanks, forged worker ID so the robot cargo handlers would ignore her, even a skin-tight insulation suit under the gray coveralls to keep her skin from freezing. But without a vacuum suit and helmet no one could survive the total loss of atmosphere from the maintenance pump.

And anyone taking a vacuum suit down to Glory didn't get to leave again.

Chouss reached bare-handed to remove the useless breather mask from the rider's dead blue face.

"Chouss!" Awandi said, shocked. "What if she's a denanos?"

Chouss gave her a pitying look. "Denanos don't leave Glory."

"Oh."

"Anyway, she can't bite me if she's dead." She slipped the mask free and smoothed the fine black hair off the rider's face. Awandi had never seen the crewboss so gentle with anyone alive. "Look how pale she was."

All Awandi could see was the slate blue of the cold vacuum dead, the same color as the corpses displayed on station news after the company ended the strike by venting gamma spoke's atmosphere. Cousins, neighbors, friends. Blue strangers, their agony frozen stiff on the screen behind the company spokesman's serene brown face.

Wen lowered a line and they hooked the rider to the winch, raised her up to the catwalk where Soje had a bag ready. They handled the corpse matter-of-factly, even kindly, having nothing against any of the poor bastards who tried to escape from Glory.

Soje handed the breather and mask over to Wen as salvage, then carefully straightened the limbs, looking surprised at how flexible the joints were. "Must have lasted until the pump," he said.

"They're moving fast down at docking ring," Chouss said. "Getting set for the backlog when the next ship comes in, on account of gamma being off line."

Off line. Awandi winced at the euphemism, thinking *vented*, thinking *vacuum*, thinking *murder*. But Soje—her brother Soje, who had been in with the strikers, who had been lucky to escape the decompression of the station-wheel's gamma spoke and the arrests that followed—Soje only nodded, folded the rider's small hands across her chest and reached for the zip.

"Huh," said Chouss, already heading for the com to call authority. "She looks even paler up here, hey Wandi?"

Awandi looked again, and swallowed. "She is paler."

Soje glanced up at the tone of her voice. "What do you mean?"

Awandi crouched down beside him, holding his wrist to keep him from closing the bag. "She's getting even paler. Look!"

Slate blue faded to a light cyan, lavender about the lips, deathly color draining away beneath the pale skin. Black lashes marked the curve of eyelid, black brows like brushes of ash over the violet-shadowed orbits. Awandi stared. She had never seen anyone so pale outside a history text. She had never seen anyone dead change color, either.

"What are you doing?" Chouss demanded from the com panel.

Black eyelashes fluttered, thin white nostrils flared. Awandi fell back onto her ass. Soje froze. Chouss came crossly over.

"Ever heard of a schedule? We got six repairs lined up after this one for the bottom of the watch, you want to find out what the bosses think if we don't—" She broke off. "Mother suck me dry!"

For the rider was breathing. The rider was alive.

Soje looked from her face up to Chouss. "You call authority?" She shook her head, numb.

"Don't," he told her with all his old, pre-strike command.

Chouss frowned down at him, crewboss even in the presence of a miracle.

"Chouss, please," he said, and command fell like a mask from his guilt. "Please. I can't let them take anyone else." His eyes fell away from her look, back down to the rider. "Please," he whispered.

The rider stirred. Opened brown eyes and gazed into Soje's hard, dark, sorrowful face.

"Hello," she whispered. "Why can't I move?"

"You're in a body bag."

She blinked, looked past him to Awandi. Laughed.

They still had a schedule to keep. Soje helped the rider down to the cubby where the crew took its breaks and left her curled on a bench asleep, wrapped in the body bag for warmth while the rest of them went back to work. They had lost almost an hour and had to scramble, but that didn't stop them from talking.

"Some miracle, yeah?" Wen said to Awandi. "What'd the bosses give to find out how she survived, you think, cousin?"

"How about what will they do to us if they find out she did?" she hissed back. "We've got to turn her in!"

Wen paused with the pod's airlock telltale half disassembled to give her a sober look. "We give nothing to the bosses."

"But —"

"Nothing." He turned back to the telltale, forcing her to return to prying at the compromised seal. "Listen, my cousin.

You're afraid that if the bosses, who already think your big brother is a unionizer, find him with unauthorized personnel they maybe won't bother with a shuttle when they send him dirtside, yeah?"

"Yeah," she miserably replied.

"With the rest of us along to keep him company. So. What d'you think they'd do if we called them to come get her? What do we say when they ask how come she's not dead, how come she's in this pod, in this pit, on our watch?"

"Well, how *come* she isn't dead?" Awandi glanced around, making sure Soje wasn't near. "Wen, what if she's a denanos?"

"So, well, she hasn't bitten anybody yet." He glanced up with a grin. "Cousin, denanos never leave Glory. I thought everyone knew that. Why should they? Better to rule in hell than be a leper anywhere else, yeah?"

"It's not just a disease, Wen. A disease cripples you, okay, kills you maybe. It's not a disease that turns you into an alien damn monster that can't die—"

"Awandi. Save the ghost stories till after work, yeah?"

"But how else did she survive?"

He shrugged, broad scarred hands never pausing in their work. "Broken seal, bad pump, good skin suit and a quick ride up from dock ring. Plain dumb luck."

"But—"

"Hey," Chouss called from the catwalk. "Wandi, aren't you finished with that seal yet? We got another pod on the way."

Glue weld, new seal, voltmeter to check the weld was true: "Green," Awandi yelled, just as Wen ran the final test on the new telltale unit. "Green," he said, and the pod was moving even before they'd skipped back onto the walk. Then there was no time for anything but work.

Soje took the rider home with him, trusting her fake ID to fool residential section's monitors. Foolish trust, Awandi thought, and refused to ride with them in the lift. Even if the security monitors didn't catch the interloper, some snitch among the workers would spot her startling white skin and report her. Report Soje, who thought he should anyway be dead.

Awandi remembered her brother the way he had been before the strike: smart, confident, full of fire against the company's contempt for the workers that kept it alive. "Workers control the means of production," he used to say, his face alight as he quoted some ancient text.

"But we don't, do we?" their mother had said, not long before she died. "Denanos and the poor convicts under them produce the goods. And the workers in AuFen and Shirrea who make the ships and pods. What's left for us to control? How dirty or clean the pods are?" A long speech for a woman whose lungs had been seared by a chemical leak.

But Soje had just glowed all the brighter, living for the argument. "If Glory's Gate Company can't meet Commonwealth shipping regulations on cargo pod maintenance and repair, they lose their trading license. It wouldn't even take a CW inspector to shut them down, no starship is going to risk unlicensed pods. Not even the independents, not when the cargo is biochemicals from Glory. All it would take is twenty watches of refusing to work and the company would be eating out of our hands!"

Their mother hadn't been impressed, even dying from a treatable injury the company would not cover in the medical plan. (Striker joke: "What's the worker's medical plan?" "Plan your funeral now and avoid the rush.") No, their mother hadn't been impressed, but others had. He wasn't alone in his union ideals. But he was the first to contact maintenance crews in other spokes, the first to risk exposure by company spies to spread the word. It had sounded so simple—not easy, maybe, no one was that naive—but simple, yes. Refusal to work. Strike.

The bosses' response was simple too, and easy as pressing a switch. Emergency venting, they called it. A shame those fool rebels were mad enough to trigger the decompression sequence and too incompetent to stop it in time. Empty lies. Empty spoke. Two hundred fifty-three workers dead.

Should have known, people said. Maybe they should have. A company too cheap to provide its workers with emergency decompression equipment obviously didn't much care one way or the other. But they hadn't known: none of the strikes in Soje's illicit history texts had taken place in space.

"Now we know why," he had bitterly said, before descending into his silence.

Silence the rider had broken. When Soje turned up for work their next watch, Awandi thought she caught a glimpse of the old spark in his eyes and grew cold with fear.

"Her name's Izu. She's a convict," Soje told the crew. He was running a diagnostic with one hand and eating a ration bar with the other: two AuFen farfreighters had arrived last watch and the growing backlog of pods didn't allow for meal breaks. "She got sent to Glory because her family was part of a squatters' colony and she resisted when the landlord's hired goons tried to remove them. Can you believe it? Sent to Glory because she didn't want to leave the only home she'd known."

Awandi shrugged. Sure she believed it. Why shouldn't she?

"She's been there four local years." Soje shook his head. Awandi was amazed at how quickly he seemed to have taken up another cause. But the light in his eyes couldn't hide the wider darkness behind them.

"She say what it's like?" Wen asked.

"Hell." Soje's grin twisted like he had a bad taste in his mouth. "You know what they call the station down there? Hope Gate. Some joke, huh?"

Chouss snorted, nine-tenths occupied with a valve repair. "But wait till you hear why she came up." She had gone with them to Soje's quarters in the off watch. When Awandi had asked her why she took such a risk, she had said, "Same risk either way, girl. Your big brother goes down, we're all going with him whatever we do. Anyway, it's my damn crew."

Now Wen asked her, "What d'you mean, why she came? She's escaping from Glory, what more reason does she need?"

But Chouss was frowning again over her valve. Soje said, his mouth still twisted, "The denanos want to apply for colonial status in the Commonwealth."

Wen burst out laughing. Awandi stared. "They what?"

This time Chouss answered. "They say even if the convicts lost all citizenship rights in the Commonwealth—"

"—which maybe they haven't, since they were condemned by company courts, not CW ones—" Soje interjected.

"—the first denanos never gave up theirs. The planet was only quarantined, officially, and only became a prison because the companies started using it that way, not because it was law. And because they can support their population—"

"—or could if the companies gave them full value for their goods—"

"—they should have colony status, with a member at Parliament and all the rights of citizens, including Forces intervention to uphold those rights."

Wen was still laughing. "Denanos. In the legislature." He slapped Awandi's arm, urging her to enjoy the joke. She ignored him, a sudden vacuum in her gut.

"So she is one," she said.

Soje and Chouss both gave her looks of disgust. "She's human as you and me," Soje said. "She's sleeping on my floor, you think I wouldn't notice she was drinking my blood?"

"They don't really—" Chouss started, then shrugged and went back to work.

Wen wiped tears from his cheeks. "So how is she planning on getting to Parliament? Take one damn big breather tank to get her from here to there in a pod."

Soje looked around them, as if a boss could have sneaked into the pit while they were talking, then leaned forward and said, "They hired an independent farfreighter to take her as a passenger. Bribed them with contraband bios. All she has to do is get in a pod slated for that ship's hold."

"Oh, is that all," Awandi said.

Chouss said, "Not so hard. Maintenance com can call up pod manifests, schedules and shuttle loads to and from the planet, farfreighter loading and departure priorities. All you need is to be quick and smart."

"And lucky," Wen added.

"And have a maintenance crew all ready to help," Awandi said with a hard look at her brother.

But he just shrugged and smiled that thin, twisted smile. "I get her gone, maybe she'll take me too."

In the end, despite her reluctance, it was Awandi who researched the schedules, she having the best feel for the ornery station com. And at the end of watch, aching with weariness—they had repaired eighteen pods, more than she'd ever seen go through the pit in one watch—instead of going home to her cubby she followed Soje back to his, both of them picking up ration packs on the way. It turned out the rider's—Izu's—fake ID wasn't quite good enough to feed her, which figured. With 253 fewer residents the station could afford to overlook an extra body or two, seeing as it could make its own air, but food and drink were imports, and always precious.

Soje had said Izu was still suffering from her rough trip up from Glory, but when he opened the cubby she was sitting up, his contraband library pad propped against her knees. Hard for anyone that pale to look exactly healthy, Awandi reckoned, especially when her lips and eyelids were still faintly blue, but she was alert enough. She looked tiny and frail next to Soje's muscled length, so Awandi reluctantly shared her dinner ration, as Soje did, while she told them about the schedule.

"So," Izu said when she was done. "It is likely to be fifteen watches from next when my freighter loads?"

"Sure," Awandi said. "But it's easier to figure the order ships will be loaded than it is to figure which pods'll be used. Always plenty of pods in the bays, and which pods are used from which bays depends on a lot, including maintenance crew efficiency and which section of docking rim the ship is assigned. The pod bays are in the feet of the spokes," she added at Izu's bewildered look, "and the pods are taken from the bays at either end of the given dock section."

Izu's confusion didn't lift very far. "But you can get me to the ship, yes?"

Awandi stifled a sigh. "Our crew can only get into delta spoke's pod bay. The chances that one of our atmo pods will be assigned to your ship are not all that good."

Izu looked from Awandi, to Soje, to her hands. Awandi couldn't decide if the look on her face was one of desperation or determination, but it was fierce.

"We'll get you to your ship," Soje said. Ignoring his sister's look, he went on, "If the pods assigned aren't from delta, we'll take you through the repair and supply shafts to whichever spoke—"

"Soje," Awandi said, aghast.

"The other crews will help us," he said earnestly. "When they know why she has to go—"

"Soje, do you seriously think anyone gives a fart about whether a bunch of denanos get a colony? You're asking them to risk a one-way trip to Glory for—"

"It's not just for the denanos," he began.

"Oh, right, how could I forget the criminals?"

"Will you just listen?"

"How can you ask anyone to listen to you after what happened the last time?"

Silence. Soje stared at her in shock, as she stared at him, horrified by what she had said yet unable to let it go. He swallowed, the muscles working in his throat, but before he could find anything to say Izu spoke.

"Awandi. Forgive me. Your brother has told me about the strike and its tragic end. I grieve for your people. But it has occurred to me that if I could take a message from your union to the Commonwealth, I might be of some use."

"A message," Awandi echoed without taking her eyes away from Soje.

"Or a messenger," he said. "If a union representative makes a complaint against the company, the Commonwealth will have to intervene."

"Soje, Soje." Awandi rubbed her hands across her face. Her voice was gentle when she spoke again. "Soje, the union died when gamma spoke blew. Don't you see? There is no union. I don't say it to hurt you. You're my brother and I love you. But you have to see, you're only going to get yourself killed." She spread her hands. "And for what? A CW observer? What on or off of Glory makes you think they'll care?"

"They will care," Izu said, eyes dark in her pale face. "They will care when they find out about the illegal biochems the company has been extorting from Glory in return for the supplies the CW is paying Hope Gate to transport. Commonwealth authorities take their contracts, and their laws, very seriously."

"What are you talking about?"

"Illegals left off the shuttle manifests," Soje said. "Company's been stockpiling them, shipping them out on the company personnel transports." He grimly smiled at her look. "You're not the only one who knows how to use a com."

"It is true," Izu said. "Even if the Commonwealth cares about nothing else, the traffic in illegal biochems will bring them. If we can prove our case, they will be forced to take over operation of Hope Gate."

"And once we're CW territory, we're eligible to join the IntraCommonwealth Alliance of Space Workers' Unions," Soje said, his eyes once more alight. "Which means that if the CW doesn't give us what we want, the whole damn system goes on strike. There's no way we can lose."

Awandi looked at him. At them both. "Unless the company blows the whole station into vacuum, along with all the evidence," she said.

When neither of them had an answer to that, she went home.

Despite every argument Awandi could bring to bear, Soje began spreading the word, first to the crews in delta spoke, then beyond. He was feverish, desperate, alive. With Izu's transport arriving within a few watches he had no time to waste on secrecy. He just spoke to crew after crew, in mess halls, rec halls, passageways, lifts. Risking severe penalties under the post-strike regulations, he even went to other pits in his off shifts, helping crews with the added workload, wearing himself to the bone. And although Awandi heard a few faint echoes of her own misgivings, they were all but drowned by the chorus of approval and support.

"They're crazy," she said to Wen one off watch in the rec hall, watching Soje in the midst of a group like a star in the center of its system.

"Crazy to hope?" he said.

She stared at him. "You think he's right?"

"What I think, cousin, is that I'd rather be blown out an airlock trying to live free than be worn down and burned out like your mother and mine. In fact," he added with a grin, "I'm not sure I wouldn't rather be on Glory." And he went to join the group around her brother.

After a watch that had seen seventeen cargo pods, two of them major repairs, all Awandi wanted was sleep. But she had spotted Soje heading for the inter-spoke transport, and so she went instead to his cubby to talk to Izu.

"You are afraid," Izu said, and gestured Awandi to sit beside her on Soje's bunk. She was smiling, but it was hard for Awandi not to see her pale face as a mask hiding lies.

"You aren't afraid?"

Izu lifted a hand in a kind of shrug. She was so small and her gestures so graceful she made Awandi feel the size and shape of a pod. She said, "One is always afraid, on Glory." Then she smiled. "Even more afraid in the cargo pod. When I woke up wrapped in a body bag, it seemed as if the worst had already happened. I've already died and gone to hell; even if it didn't quite happen in that order, it's hard to see what there is left to fear."

"Easy for me," Awandi said. "I have more than just my life to lose."

"You imagine I do not? Should your company cease to transport the CW supplies, no one on Glory will survive."

"Not even the denanos?"

Izu studied her a moment, a smile hovering at the corners of her eyes. "They are surprisingly human. They need food, and air, and love, the same as everyone else."

"But they can survive on Glory, even outside the catacombs, can't they?"

"The nans can cope with a great deal, it's true. Yes, the denanos can survive in the open for short stretches of time, but—"

"What about injuries? It's dangerous on Glory, isn't it? The dust storms and the criminals and the quakes. I bet they can heal pretty good, too, huh?"

Izu swallowed. "It depends on the injury, but yes, they—I mean, I understand they can—"

"What about decompression?" Awandi interrupted. "Can they survive that?"

Izu's eyes flickered, then dropped to her folded hands. "Perhaps. For short periods. They—" She broke off at a thump on the cubby's door, relieved.

So, Awandi thought. But then, *she* was relieved to open the door, to have an excuse to put space between herself and the other woman. Relief died a quick death, though. The instant she saw Chouss and Wen, and the battered, blood-soaked man that hung lolling between them.

"Move, girl," Chouss said, low and fierce, and Awandi stepped belatedly aside. The five of them crowded the cubby, even once Chouss had lowered the man to the bunk. It was Soje.

"What..." She couldn't make her voice work.

"He was in alpha spoke," Wen said, lifting Soje's feet to the bunk. Chouss was checking his pulse, her frown like a chasm between her brows. "Somebody put him on the transport," Wen continued, sitting wearily by Soje's feet. "Just luck I found him."

"How is he?" Her voice still wouldn't rise above a whisper.

Chouss said without looking up, "Not good. Weak pulse, cold skin, bubbly breathing." She sat on the floor by the head of the bunk and propped her head on a bloody hand. "Not good."

Wen leaned his elbows on his knees. "Got the shit kicked out of him."

"Who? Security?"

Wen shrugged. So did Chouss after a minute. "Them or scabs."

"Well. Did you call medical?"

Again just a couple of shrugs. Awandi started to shake. Instead of venting her rage on them, she turned and called medical, careful to press the buttons gently instead of pounding them through the wall.

EMS. State the nature of the emergency.

"My brother. He's injured."

Name and location.

"Aramin Soje, delta spoke, residential section four, cubby number eight-one-three. Please hurry." Her voice started to die again, trapped like her heart in her throat. "Please hurry."

The faint hiss of an open line. Then a different voice said, *Repeat that name and location.*

"Soje. Aramin Soje. Delta spoke, residential..."

But the light on the com panel had died. The line was dead.

"So much for medical," Wen said, and put his face in his hands.

Awandi sat on her brother's bunk, holding his hand and watching him die. He had their mother's hands, as she did. The same long bones and big knuckles, the same calluses and scars, the same sharp line between the brown of the back and the pink of the palm. The hand she held lay slack in hers, cold as the rest of him. All his energy was in his lungs, trying to breathe. Trying to breathe.

Weary with grief, she asked Chouss, "Isn't there something you can do?"

Chouss propped her graying head against the cubby wall and closed her eyes, her only response.

"Wen?"

He rubbed the back of his hand across his eyes, shook his head. No.

No. Awandi lifted her head, feeling the pull of the station's spin, and looked at the pale woman from Glory standing in the corner, arms wrapped around her chest as if she were cold. It was hard to ask. "Izu? Isn't there something you can do?"

Izu looked at her, at Soje, breathing pink froth through his shattered mouth. Slowly lifted her hand to cover her eyes. "No."

As if she hadn't spoken, Awandi said, "I'll help you get to your ship. I promise. Even if it...Even if it doesn't work."

"Wandi," Chouss said. "Don't. She's as helpless as the rest of us."

"No she isn't."

"Let her be."

Awandi let go her brother's hand and stood, noticing again how she towered over the other woman. "Please," she said. "Please, Izu."

"Wandi," Wen said painfully. "Let it go."

"No."

Izu was staring at her, eyes wide and fixed.

"It was because of you," Awandi told her. Just one step and they were face to face. "I don't say that to lay blame, Izu. It was his choice. He did it for his own reasons. But still. If you hadn't come."

"Damn it, Awandi," Chouss said, climbing to her feet. It was her crewboss voice. "Back off."

"He would have saved your people and mine," Awandi said, the words somehow apart from her, cold and calm, separate from the hot black star of grief in her gut. "He would have. Your people and mine. And you won't lift a damn finger to help him?"

"Awandi," Chouss said, putting a hand on her shoulder.

"I am so sorry," Izu said, white as the paint on the walls, lips blue as a bruise. No pretense she didn't understand. "I am so sorry, Awandi. But I cannot. I cannot."

Awandi's fist, like her voice, seemed disconnected from the rest of her. It lifted and swung out with the power of scores of watches in the pit and smashed Izu's jaw.

"Damn it, girl, that's enough!" Chouss said, hauling her back against the door. Wen was on his feet, between Awandi and the Glory woman. There was hardly enough room for all of them to stand. Soje's breath wheezed and bubbled into the silence.

Awandi met Izu's eyes over Wen's shoulder. "Show them," she said quietly. "Let them see."

Izu slowly took her hands away from her face.

"Sweet Mother," Wen said, stepping back onto Awandi's foot. On the side of Izu's jaw, where Awandi's fist had connected, a black stain spread and grew, lifting the skin from underneath. A black swarm rising to repair the damage, biochem mechanicals, alive and not alive, colony of strangeness under the human skin. Even though she'd been expecting it, Awandi rubbed her sore knuckles on her shirt, skin crawling.

Chouss gripped her shoulder hard enough to leave a bruise. "Denanos. By the hard bitch of vacuum, Wandi, you were right."

"Well," said Izu. The black swelling shifted as she spoke. "Now you know. But I still can't help Soje."

"Why not?" Awandi demanded. "You said denanos could survive injury—"

"He isn't denanos."

"But you could make him one, couldn't you? Can't you? Isn't that why they quarantined you in the first place, because it's so damn contagious?"

"Is that what they tell you?" Izu shook her head. Already the black stain was beginning to shrink. She appeared to feel no pain.

Awandi shoved Wen's back to get him off her foot, then squeezed around him to sit back down on the bed. Soje's hand seemed even colder than before.

"What do you mean?" Chouss said. "Why else did they quarantine you?"

"Why?" Izu smiled, her subtle fierceness returning to her eyes. "Why would the Commonwealth be afraid of a race of people who are hard to kill and take a long time to die, who can live and work in environments that would kill a cockroach, who can invent drugs and poisons in their guts—why? You tell me. Are you less afraid of me now than when you only thought I'd drink your blood and give you a nasty disease?"

Awandi rubbed her brother's hand, trying to instill a little warmth. "Should we be more afraid? Do you want to take over the universe?"

Izu folded her arms. "All I want, all any of us want, is to live the way we choose, where we choose, in peace."

"Same as us." Awandi looked up with a thin smile. "Right Chouss? No different than us."

But Chouss was frowning at the denanos. "It's not contagious?"

Izu sighed. "Yes, of course it is. But not *that* contagious."

"So you could give it to him. You could save him."

"Awandi." Izu threw out her small hands in a helpless gesture. "There is no guarantee that my nans would survive his immune system, or that his genetic profile is close enough to mine for them to reproduce in his cells, and even if by some miracle they did, there isn't time. It takes sixty hours at least for the nans to establish themselves to the point of being able to heal, and he doesn't have that long."

"He's a stubborn bastard, in case you hadn't noticed," Wen said. "He'd hang on."

He might not have spoken. "And even if all that weren't true, which it is, I still couldn't infect him."

"Why not?" Awandi said like a threat.

Izu hugged herself and said, "Because if any denanos infects any human without that human's direct, explicit and informed consent, the whole race will be in contravention of the quarantine act which allows us to live on Glory. We'd be criminals for real, without the faintest hope of colonial status, or even another, less deadly home. More to the point, we'd be without protection from all those out there who'd kill us, or use us as drug factories, or both. I sure as Glory didn't come out here to do that to my people."

"You sure as hell aren't going any further than the Gate if we don't want you to go," Chouss pointed out.

Izu studied Chouss' face, then Wen's, then Awandi's. "Someone else will come," she said, but she sounded a long way from certain.

"This is the Gate," Wen said, sounding like Soje. "Who do you think holds the key?"

"No denanos is going anywhere the crews don't want them to go," Chouss added, just to make it absolutely clear.

Izu looked at them all again, for the first time with real desperation. "But you have to. My God, don't you see? This isn't just my people, it's yours, too. Awandi, tell them," she pleaded, before a look crossed her face as if she remembered that maybe Awandi wasn't the best advocate she could choose.

But Awandi said, "I don't have to tell them. They already know. Isn't a worker on this station doesn't already know by now, thanks to Soje."

Silence. Soje breathed, a faint liquid wheeze.

Then Wen said, "Listen, Izu. Only thing that's holding you back is this legal problem, yeah? You'd help him if he was awake to say he wanted help?"

She passed a hand over her eyes. The black stain on her jaw had faded to a dull blue-gray. "I guess. If I knew he wanted me to."

"Soje? Hell, he's done just about everything else, I guess turning into a denanos wouldn't stop him."

"Wen!" Chouss said, shocked.

He looked up at her. "You don't think? If it were the only way he could get out of here, take his message to the Commonwealth?"

"Someone else can go," Chouss said. "I'd go, if it came to that."

"But Soje would still be dead," Awandi said with her brother's twisted smile. "Right Chouss? Even if he survived this beating, there'd be another, and another. Unless it was an airlock failure, or a chem tank leak, or..." She shrugged, still trying to warm Soje's hand with hers.

"She's right. Anyway," Wen added with a taut grin, "the way things stand now, I reckon we must make up a union quorum between the three of us, and if two of us vote him union rep to the Commonwealth he pretty much has to go."

Chouss opened her mouth to respond, but Izu broke in sharply before she could. "I don't remember saying I'd infect him. I won't. I can't."

"Well, hell, woman, who's going to say he didn't ask you?" Chouss all but shouted.

"Couldn't even if we wanted to," Wen added. "Seeing as how he just said he wanted you to make him a denanos." Looking from one woman's stare to the next, he grinned and added, "Didn't he, Chouss?"

She snorted, rubbed her nose with a work worn hand. "Well sure he did. Didn't he, Awandi?"

His hand was so cold. "Yes."

Izu put her hands over her eyes. The skin over her jaw was once more a clear, pale ivory. "Do you realize what you'd be doing to him? He wouldn't be your crewmate anymore, or your brother, he'd be a denanos. There aren't many places he could live except for Glory."

What had Wen said? "Better to rule in hell than to live as a leper anywhere else," Awandi said.

Izu looked suddenly tired. "You think so? Nobody named the planet for the color of its sunsets."

Awandi didn't even know what a sunset was. "If it turns out he'd rather die, he can always step out the nearest airlock. I suppose space would kill him eventually?"

Izu swallowed. "Quicker than eventually. But it's not just Glory—"

"Izu, damn it!"

"No. Listen to me. *Somebody* is going to make an informed decision. The nans could mutate, especially since they aren't tailored to his gene code, and it's an ugly way to die. The only work he could get off Glory would be in brutal conditions, in the employ of people who cared for his well-being even less than your company does for yours. He couldn't have children: denanos are made, not born. Whatever the Commonwealth decision about Glory and the Gate, he'll almost certainly not be able to come home again. Ever again." She looked hard at Awandi. "Know what you're asking me to do to him. He would be an object of hatred to millions."

Awandi swallowed, looking away from her brother's face. The memory of her own fear was bitter in her mouth. "Chouss?"

Chouss rubbed at the crease in her forehead. Nodded.

"Wen?"

"You know my vote. I wouldn't put it on him if I weren't willing to do it myself. If it were what I had to do to survive."

Awandi looked again at her brother's battered face. Better to rule in hell...She looked up at Izu, swallowed bile, and said, "Do it."

Eight watches later, the independent farfreighter *Pardis* clamped on to the station's docking ring. Two watches after that, the order for cargo pods began registering on station com. Fourteen pods were being shifted out of delta bay. Three of them were atmosphered.

Izu nodded, calm, when Awandi brought her the news. The denanos had scarcely slept since infecting Soje with her black, nan-thick blood. Within a watch he had ceased to breathe through pink froth, but he still hadn't regained consciousness.

But he hadn't died, either.

The middle of the crew's off watch saw the three of them stagger red-eyed to his cubby, each with a duffel containing gear that would get them an automatic trip through an airlock if security came along. However, security had lately been staying clear of the workers' quarters—most noticeably since Soje's beating: word had spread. Someone took the temperature of the crews and decided to turn down the heat a little. No one had any doubts that it was only a temporary measure, though, and the brutal pace of maintenance and repairs continued unabated.

Most brutal of all for Awandi, Wen and Chouss, since they dared not report Soje's "death" until he and Izu were safely gone; they were in the meantime working short two hands. They could only keep company supervisors out of the pit and out of their hair if they kept up their efficiency rating. Chouss fell asleep against the wall while Awandi and Izu wrestled Soje's slack limbs into the insulation skin, and Wen fought to keep awake to check the breathers. Then they staggered off again, Soje suspended between them in a body bag/duffel of Wen's design, praying the unconscious man would not moan the way he sometimes did. To the personnel lift and down the spoke to the rim, sharing the space with workers who carefully showed not the least interest in the party and their burden.

Out of the lift and into the cargo pod bay. They were barely able to keep Soje from dragging in the higher pseudo-gravity of the station's rim. He did groan once or twice, but the sound was lost in the clamor of the pods being readied for transport. More intensely uninterested workers toiled around them, a backdrop of gray figures into which they could blend and disappear while searching out the right pod. An AuFen inert atmo pod, vast orange egg, it could have been the one that had brought Izu to the station.

The small customs inspection lock was just big enough to send Izu and Soje through one at a time. Maintenance workers cool and efficient at their tasks, Chouss and Wen opened the lock and helped Izu in with her breather, while Awandi unzipped Soje's bag to make sure his mask was secure. It was. Also, his eyes were open, the right one stained with red-and-black blood.

"Hey," she said softly, numb with hope, pulling the mask aside.

"Hey," he said, hoarse and slow. "Why can't I move?"

She had to grin. "You're in a body bag."

He grunted and closed his eyes.

"Soje. Soje? It's okay, you're going to be okay. Soje, open your eyes."

Swollen lids drifted open, blinked. "Thought I was dead," he said, as if confirming the thought. Wen and Chouss had closed the inspection lock and were cycling Izu through.

"No, you aren't. You're going to be okay. You're going to Parliament with Izu." Tempting to leave it at that, but she couldn't do that to Izu, or to him. "Izu saved your life, Soje. She made you a denanos. Soje? It was my idea, I made her. So don't blame anyone but me, yeah?"

He blinked, wet his torn and bloody lips. "No blame." He seemed beyond surprise. "Denanos, huh? So that's how...she survived."

"Yeah. Seems the nans can keep your blood from boiling in a decompression. Handy, huh?"

"Huh." His eyes drifted closed. Then: "It isn't going...to turn me white...is it?"

Awandi laughed in spite of herself. "She swears it won't."

Chouss turned from the lock and said quietly, "He ready? Izu's through."

Awandi reached for the breather mask. Soje opened his eyes. He seemed more alert this time. "Wait," he said.

"Got a schedule to keep, cousin of mine," Wen said.

"Wait." Soje licked his lips again. "Denanos...can survive decompres...sion?" Another pause, then, on an apparently unconnected thought, "Am I contagious?"

"Yes, and yes," said Wen. "Come on, man, we got to put you through."

"If we were all denanos...we could strike."

It took a second to sink in, then all three of them froze.

"We could strike," Soje said, "and we could win."

Awandi looked at Wen, at Chouss, a chill in her gut. The racket of the pod bay filled in around them like a protective shell.

Wen said, voice thin with uncertainty and surprise, "If it were what we had to do to survive?"

Awandi said, "But what about what Izu said, how denanos have to live?"

"If we held the station," Chouss murmured, barely audible. She licked her lips. "If we held Glory's Gate, and controlled the denanos trade..."

A long moment while no one spoke. Then: "If it's what we have to do to survive," Wen said, uncertainty gone.

Soje took a careful breath, then said softly, "Give me...a kiss good-bye...little sister?"

Awandi looked at them both, her crewmates, her family. Looked at her brother watching her with his black-and-red stained eyes. Awandi wiped her damp cheeks and whispered, "What we have to do to survive."

But what she was thinking was, *What we have to do to give you a home to come back to.* She bent down and gave Soje a kiss, filling her mouth with the taste of his inhabited blood.

RIIS RUN
eluki bes shahar

"BUTTERFLY, ARE YOU sure this is going to work?" Paladin asked me.

"Trust me," I lied.

We was sitting dead an drifting at marginal power in the middle a the never-never, waiting for *Fortune's Girl* to show up at the rondaytik.

"I do trust you," my partner said. "That's why I'm worried."

Whiles before, was dicing with a kiddy hight Elory Dace an losing, but there's nowt else t'do on Coldwater when you're waiting to lift, an that's certain truth. Sides, I was in the way an for t'kill him soon's I figured out how, me being in the way a doing Oob's hard jobs for him somewhiles, which same Elory should'a known an didn't, so I guessed I'd see my credit again soon enough.

We was both hot pilots for Oob, which meant waiting around on Coldwater for the office now and again. Name's just plain and fancy farcing, cause the last time there been liquid water here was some time afore there been an Empire, which is some whiles even with fancy Imperial accounting. Nothing but ice now. And snow.

I been running cargoes for Oob long times—he put me in my first hull, an now I owned my own, ship *Firecat*. I was still here because I had lots a good reasons for not wanting to attract major attention from the rich an famous, which main desire ran to working for a wiggly nightbroker who'd sell me out the moment he saw percentages in it, Darktrader's Guild or no. Before Elory, Yours Truly Butterflies-are-Free Peace Sincere was the only one a Oob's leggers what ran even close t'Chernovsky main, an that not very, as any scanner'd be happy to tell you. You don't belong along one a the main B-Pops on the Chernovsky scale, you don't even get t'take a swing at the

Imperial Phoenix. You get to be your plain an fancy "client race," an from where I sit, even being a dicty-barb has more upside. Us they just shoot when they catch us outside our pro-scribed Imperial bought long time gone Interdicted hidey-hole.

So when Elory walks in a hundred days ago looking like a new minted citizen fresh from Grand Central an saying he's looking to herd skyjunk in the never-never, it don't fadge. Main-line clean-scan humans does not go crawling to wiggly nightbrokers for plenty, even if they is spinning fantasy. Whether his Tickets a Leave was forged or no, he could herd skyjunk, an he hit what he aimed at. He could talk Trade, flashcant, patwa, an Interphon well as I could. Our boy Elory had what you might call your basic job skills a the Outfar. So Oob thunk the obvious thought, an sent him on a silk run with a troublekick he didn't mind losing.

Elory came back, him an his ladybird. *Fortune's Girl* was a sweet piece a high-iron, just what she ought to be: not too pretty, not too clean, a old Falke-Starhauler built for four an jerryhammered for one. Where she came from weren't nobody's bidness but his.

Oob kept sending him, an Elory kept coming back, so Oob did what any bright kiddy with a mind on longevity'd naturally do. He told me off for to send young Elory on the Long Orbit.

There's ninety-nine simple ways to let a sophont out a life, an I'd used lots a 'em oncet at least. But it don't pay in my line a work to leave unanswered questions on your backtrail, an Elory was six a those. So along of killing him, I wanted a look inside his hull, me an my partner both, which made things a little harder, 'cause that weren't something we could rig whiles there was people around t'see. Plus, I couldn't just shoot him exactly, even if on Coldwater nobody'd care. I wasn't all that slow with a heavy, but I'd never seen him draw surprised. He might be faster. An a short fast career a being dead weren't in my life plans.

So I was dicing an losing an thinking, three things Pally says I'm not good at, an two a which I tend to agree with him on somewhiles, while I tried t'figure out how t'ghostwhack Elory Dace an *Fortune's Girl* an live t' keep quiet about it. It didn't hurt airy a'tall that if I could do it clean his hull would be mine to sell, neither.

Terreckly I'd come along of a plan, an Oob'd liked it when I sold him the pony. Pally hadn't. He's the nervous type. But he didn't get a vote—at least not out where Oob could see—cause nobody can know about Paladin.

I found Paladin on Pandora back before I got my first hull. He got me out of a tight spot then, an a lot more since, so we're partners. On Pandora he'd been a box a junk for so long he didn't even know we had a Emperor, an me, I come from so far outside Mainstream I never even heard a High Book—that's Chapter Five a the Revised Inappropriate Technology Act a the Nine Hundredth an Seventy-Fifth Year a Imperial Grace to you. Why it matters is cause what my partner Paladin is, is a fully-volitional logic. A Library.

It took the two a us about six minutes Prime t'find out what kind a laws there is against Old Fed artifacts like Paladin after I woke him up, but if anybody knows what Libraries is (other'n "a machine hellishly forged in the likeness of a human mind," says the talkingbooks) or why they all has to be destroyed, they isn't talkin'. All I know is the head-price on him—an on me for havin' him—has been reliably reported to be enough to buy you outta any crime in the Imperial Calendar, even being a dicty-barb away from home.

But you don't sell out your friends.

"He won't be expecting me." We was waiting on Elory, Pally an me. I was improving my partner's nerves. "Thinks he's waitin' on somethin' t'fall off'n a Company ship." An Elory wouldn't see us, because he wouldn't be looking. True fact. Pally alluz worries too much.

"And while he is, you're just going to walk up to him and shoot him with that quaint revenant. While I admit it has the virtue of simplicity..."

I try to not listen oncet Pally starts talking like a learningbook, because it means he's mad. But what I had in mind ought t'work. I had the suit I use for hullwork an a variable-generating compkey, an I didn't need nothing more'n that t'get me into *Fortune's Girl.* An oncet I was in an Elory was dead, I could cozy *Firecat* up to *Fortune's Girl,* hook Pally in t'her computer an let him find out everything she knew.

The hull-suit most stardancers use is a step up from an evac bag, but not by much. I stripped an got into mine, because Elory should be here soon an there wasn't no point in waiting around for late-breaking current events. Far as Oob knew, he was as punctual as he was pretty, an that meant he'd be early.

I put my loose toys in the hotlocker an hooked everything I was taking onto my belt, then sealed the helmet into place. Paladin popped the lock, an *Firecat's* loose air went on vacation in a plume a ice. He cut lights an power, an my Best Girl disappeared so far as I could see. It got colder. I hung in the hatchway, looking at stars.

Not for long. *Fortune's Girl* made Transit in a flash a light, close enough t'see her actual shape, which meant we was right on top a her, maybe a dozen-many kliks away. His sweeps'd find *Firecat* in a tik or so, but with no power nor come-hither on her it'd take him whiles to puzzle her out. I didn't wait around. I kicked off from my hull.

If I was using power, he'd a spotted me sure, but I was kyting on gas-jets: pure mechanical energy, no power-suck to tickle his ship-eyes. It looked slow, but I knew better than to hustle. In Market Garden I saw what happened to kiddies as tried playing fast an loose with inertia. I had time. He wasn't going anywheres until he had what he came for, nevermind it weren't here.

Neither was I, by what he knew.

I landed on his hull soft an sweet as a first kiss an walked forward till I reached the main access hatch. He'd hear me coming—it was too much luck to hope for to think he wouldn't—but I had the edge.

I hoped.

The comp-key got me through the lock. I left my helmet an jetpack there. If I needed them, I'd be dead already. The other things I kept with me.

Shipped stock from High Mikasa, the Falke-Starhauler's got a cockpit access hatch. Most stardancers junk it in the strip-down for nightworld running, an everyone else I know keeps it locked back, cause a alla the roundaboutation you got t'do when you're short-crewed.

But Elory, bright lad, liked the exercise. Or else he was born worried. It was in place. An it was locked. Not a problem.

Most folks in my line a work are specialists. Stardancers herd skyjunk. Hardboys do wetwork. Priggers an shimcribs take care of actual valuta liberation, providing always the valuta's on the heavyside. If your kick's on a ship, an the whole ship's being taken, what you got is your genuine, honest to *Thrilling Wonder Talkingbooks* Space Pirates, which I guessed I now was.

All a which is a roundabout way a saying that in a Empire full a one-hit wonders, I can manage a little bit a everything. It took a little more farcing than the outside hatch, but not much, an I was through.

The hatch peeled back. Elory was waiting.

"It's you," he said, getting up.

He sounded disappointed, like he was maybe expecting someone taller. I didn't wait for the color commentary: he had a ship's axe in his hands an looked ready to use it. I fired.

Nobody but a damn fool carries a blaster inboard a ship in space. Rupture your hull, damage your fields, an there's nothing between you an the streets a Angel City but hope an good wishes. That's why pirates wear armor when they board a ship, an why they teach swordplay to Highliner an Company crews. Plasma weapons ain't safe inboard, an a stunner will fry tronics as well as organics. But where I come from, they ain't never heard a neither blasters nor spaceships, an I was born a blacksmith's daughter. I'd had time t'plan an make what I needed.

I was carrying a crossbow.

The first bolt took him in the shoulder, an the second one in the chest. By then I was out a ammo, but Elory Dace was outta time. He dropped the axe, took a step, an dropped to his knees.

"Why?" he asked.

He was bleeding in a way it'd be hard t'fake, an I could see both his hands, so I risked going close enough to touch. There wasn't any fight left in him, not even for revenge. He went all the way down whiles I was getting there, an I caught him, easing him onto his back. Crossbow bolts is short—piece a metal long as your hand an thick as your finger—an these had gone all the way in. He was coughing blood in the sincere way that don't encourage you to plan ahead, so I guessed I owed him the truth.

"Oob don't like things what don't make sense, che-bai."

He smiled, like he thought that was funny. All of a sudden he looked worried, like it'd just occurred to him he was taking the Long Orbit.

"Promise me...I was going to Riis...pick up a package. Take my run."

Riis is a Restricted World, furs, drugs, gemstones, an a damfool sense a their own importance. It'd be a tight fit, his cargo in *Firecat*, but I couldn't see the harm.

"I promise," I said. The Clearances would probably be in his comps, if he hadn't just been stargathering for bloodlack, an I'd know that soon enough.

Then he was dead, an I'd earned my bonus.

I slid into the Mercy Seat an dialled back the gravity long enough to make it easy money getting Elory-as-was down to the lock. I was glad to see he hadn't passworded his boards or any other such damfool talkingbook nonsense: it was enough t'worry about his comps. Down at the lock I sealed up my suit again an cycled through with Elory. There was some safety-lines in the lock an I took one an hooked him to the hull with it. Oob was going to want me to bring back proof, an he'd be easier to cut up if he was frozen.

Then I went back to the cockpit an flashed the lights. I saw an answering star as Paladin lit *Firecat* up, an then I went down t'Main Cargo for t'unspool the Transport Tube an wait.

Most ships has a cargo bay an a cargo hatch. *Firecat* don't. Ships with bays an hatches—like *Fortune's Girl*—is set for to make transfers in caustic or airless environments, hence the Transport Tube.

Hooking it up was going to be the fun part, because no matter what they tell you in *Thrilling Wonder Talkingbooks*, no ship ever stops dead in space. *Fortune's Girl* was moving, an *Firecat* was moving, an the money trick was going t'be matching relative velocities close enough t'hook up the Tube an keep both ships under pressure. Pally's not a Jump pilot, but he could jink my Best Girl's attitude jets enough to bring her in for a kiss.

Or bobble it—even a good pilot can—an kill us both.

I watched her come in close, hoping I hadn't come up with the one-hundredth way to die that stardancers always talk about. Finally *Firecat* was close enough so's I could see her clear in *Fortune's Girl's* running lights an count every separate peeling patch a hullseal on her skin. Time to go.

I popped Elory's lock—mine now—an held on while more atmosphere bled to space. When the pressure equalized, I went about the business of sealing the two ships together.

It's easier if you got a partner with hands. It's easier if you got a heavier suit with powered jets. It's easier with lots a things. But it got done, an the two ships was breathing together, fields synched. I went over to *Firecat*, shucked the suit, an got dressed again.

"Elory wants me t'go to Riis," I said where Paladin could hear. "Got a cargo waiting, he said."

"And?" Paladin asked.

"Figured I'd go," I said. "Iff'n you can find his Clearances." I was looking for the connect cables an not finding them, which was damsilly foolishness on account of I'd looked 'em out special on the way here.

Paladin didn't say anything in that noisy way a his.

"*I* don't know why!" I said. "Who knows why dead people do anything?" I found the cables an dragged them out, then had to wriggle around under the Mercy Seat to get one end hooked up to Paladin.

"Where do you want to sell the ship?" Paladin asked instead.

"I dunno. Wanderweb. They don't ask lots a questions in a Free Port." Like how one person could get two ships into orbit. Free Ports can be useful that way. I actually hadn't thought things that far along; I might have t'stash *Fortune's Girl* somewhere nearby with a salvage beacon on her an hope she was there when I got back, but if she weren't, I'd only lost credit I hadn't invested too much in, an I'd still have the headprice.

I got the rest a the cable over my shoulder an went walking back up to *Fortune's Girl's* cockpit.

Whiles Paladin farced the comps, I tossed the ship.

Elory was a tidy lad, an something was wrong.

I'm good for secrets, but in my experience, most people is damnfool sloppy. Elory weren't. There weren't airy more t'find from his cabin than he was a kiddy who liked hottoys an held onto every credit he'd pulled on every run he'd made for Oob, seemed like.

That, an the fact that the co-cabin was locked up very tight indeed. My comp-keys wouldn't budge the hatch, an that was downright peculiar. They'd opened the cockpit, which should be the second-best lock on any ship.

"Butterfly."

Paladin's voice came over Ship Main Speakers. He didn't sound happy. "I've found something you aren't going to like."

That made two, which was two too many.

I went up to the cockpit where Paladin could see me.

"The ship's computer system is surprisingly sophisticated for a vessel of this size," Paladin began, taking the scenic route through his explanation. "There were a number of safeguards against tampering. Downloading the Riis clearances was to have wiped the rest of the system and started a self-destruct mechanism that would have appeared to be a simple engine malfunction. It took me some time to disarm the safeguard systems and access all the files."

"Je?" Wasn't no point in trying to hurry Paladin when he was in a mood to lecture. I sat myself in the songbird seat an regarded infinite space.

"Elory Dace was not who he appeared to be, several times over."

"True-tell?" says me.

"Officially he was working undercover for the Trade Customs and Commerce Commission."

The TC&C is what makes a darktrader's life such a home delight out here in the Outfar, but usually they waited till you put a kick on the heavyside somewhere to bother you. "An plus?"

"The Office of the Question."

Was good thing I was sitting down already. Nobody wants to meet the Tech Police. *I* double didn't want to meet the Tech Police with an Old Fed Library sitting in my hull.

"He didn't know about us," Paladin said, answering the question I was too creebed to ask. "His superiors had a rumor of a technology brokering ring operating in the nightworld. Dace— or to be more correct, Millanuran Nanath—was sent to investigate. All inappropriate technology is proscribed, not just the technology of the Old Federation. It might even have been something new."

Because a machine that can think for itself is so damn useful that nobody will leave it alone, an who knows what they're doing in the Confederacy or the Sodality?

"There's a locked cabin. Get me in."

Behind the hatch was the rest a Brother Elory-or-Nanath's life. Full grey Teaser uniform with all ID. An in a locked case—one my comp-key did open, this time—his Tech Police uniform.

I picked up the helmet. Full-face. Want t'scare you to death before they ruin your life, forbye. Pretty black uniform an cape. Heavy blaster with a stunner piggybacked on, automatic Class D warrant for civilian possession, which it was just too bad I couldn't think of any good way to take it with me, because a Military Heavy is a very discouraging word in the circles I run in. But I couldn't take the chance of someone wondering where I'd got it, or it maybe having a talk-back on it that Paladin couldn't catch.

I went out again.

I thought about things while I farced Elory's Best Girl of useful valuta. He kept a nice galley, an his housekeeping inventories was up to date an all found. It was almost enough to take the edge off what I had to do next.

I couldn't keep *Fortune's Girl.* Couldn't sell her, either. Somebody'd trace her back to me, an the numbers was on the side a somebody figuring out something hadn't gone the way their boy planned it to. An there was no way I could'a arranged that without high-tech help, so people'd come looking. Tech Police people.

Fortune's Girl had to go, just like Elory planned.

When I was done an putting the cables back, I told Paladin. He wasn't happy, but he had to admit I was right for oncet. He couldn't put the comps back the way they'd was. I'd have t'jink the goforths myself.

I suited up again an untubed *Firecat*, then went t'take care a the rest a the light housekeeping. No matter what the former Elory did in his spare time, Oob still wanted his head. An I wanted my bounty.

He weren't near as pretty after having been freeze-dried, but I'd seen worse an done some of it. I sheared off his head with my vibro an put it in a carrybag, then went down to the Black Gang see what I could do for his ship.

Stardancers alluz say as there's ninety-nine ways t'die, an one a them is getting your goforths up to Jump an leaving them there, specially if all the safety overrides happen to go walkabout first

so she can't step down. Not hard t'farce, mainly for that nobody
in his right mind'd ever want to do it. When I was done, every
tell-me was showing red. I flipped more switches, calling up everything she had. *Fortune's Girl* started to wake up. More lights
went red. Some started to flash. The girl had a lot of legs.

Time to go.

I put my helmet on. This time I'd borrowed a set a jets
from *Fortune's Girl*. I got back to Firecat quicktime. I didn't
know how long we had, but it wouldn't be hours.

Paladin started moving us as soon as the hatch closed. I
peeled off the suit once there was air an dropped down into the
Mercy Seat to watch the show.

We was far enough back that there was nothing to see, but
Firecat's sensors showed *Fortune's Girl* big an hot. About a tenth
of an hour later she went over. The canopy went black as the
hard particles came through, but I watched it all on filters. I
walked *Firecat* through the debris cloud afters, just to make sure.
All over but vain regrets.

Then I pulled over the comp. Permits an clearances for
Riis was there, all neat an legal, just like Pally'd said. I started
farcing a tik.

"What are you doing?"

"Covering our trail." Riis was a reach, but we'd make it.

Pally didn't say nothing a-tall.

"Think. I ice Brother Elory. He gives me his Riis Run, the
deadman on his Best Girl which somebody's got to know back
at Teaser Home and Mother. Why don't I take it, somebody
wants t'know?"

An if I didn't take it, if I did anything other'n what a poor
but honest darktrader what didn't got an Old Fed Library in her
hull would do, there'd be questions, soon or late, oncet people
found out young Elory weren't breathing no more, which they
would, *legitimates* being the chatty kiddies they is.

Somebody's alluz looking, certain truth. An secret's only
secret if no one looks, so you can't never do nothing t'make
them see you.

More silence.

"When you got the good numbers you tell me, ne, che-bai?" I muttered. The numbers read out clear. I pulled the angelstick for the Jump.

Riis is Closed World, which means all visitors is strictly restricted t'Port an City. It's warmer than Coldwater by a not very. You need permits to land, permits to lift, permits to trade. According to his tickets-a-leave, Elory Dace-as-was's bidness here was t'pickup a paid cargo to lift for a destination unspecified. Not unusual in our line a work. It could be true, or just more farcing, but I was supposed to believe it.

I did spare a braincell t'wonder who he'd actually been expecting to show up an kill him back at the rondaytik, seeing as it weren't me.

But talking kytes no kick, as my dear old freight-factor alluz said. I got *Firecat* into a ring on the heavyside an hooked up, jacked Pally into the main banks to pull news an weather, an went looking for my maybe fantasy kick.

It was snowing in Riisfall. My Coldwater gear kept me warm enough.

My first stop was Port Services office. The Portmaster wished me a pleasant downfall, an asked what cargo. I showed him my tik. He suggested I try the Guildhall to see what they was holding under that number.

I went to the Guildhall an called for the cargo, but I weren't surprised to find it was all vaporware an computer glitches. I hung around whiles, letting whoever was watching get a good look. Then I went off to somewheres quiet to let them find me.

Bidness as usual. If it was handled all aboveboard an proper, they wouldn't call it darktrade.

I never been to Riis, but didn't have no trouble a-tall finding the kind a place I wanted. A nice dark dockside bar an bathhouse, just off the Port, Intersign glyph outside for 'stardancer.' From the look a the place, I wouldn't have t'worry about running into Companyfolk here: just Gentry

an leggers an gypsies an Celestials. Peaceable folk what mind
their manners. I found a booth in the back an ordered something hot.

Along of when I was on my third round an thinking about
finding a bath an room, I got company.

"Elory Dace usually makes this run," my new friend said
chattily.

He was muffled up in a young ransom a Riis furs, native
cut, but he talked Interphon like a cosmopolite.

"He retired an left me the run," I said. I had my hand on
my blaster under the table. Both his hands was in sight, but he
could have anything up his sleeve. This was where I got t'find
out how far Brother Elory's deadman switch ran.

My new friend passed me a sheet a thermofax, folded small.
"This has your information. Your payment's with the cargo."

He left. I waited, then unfolded the sheet. It gave me address an time, the usual amateur encouragement not t'be seen
arriving, an everything but the important things: how much an
what the cargo was. Maybe they thought I knew.

The time wasn't for whiles yet: well as I could work the
conversion, local dark meredies. More proof, not like I needed
it, that this was strictly amateur night.

I went back to *Firecat.*

"The address is for a hostelry at the far edge of the Port City,"
Paladin said, back from a jaunt through the Port computers.
"One frequented both by natives and by visitors to the city."

"Not furs." I hadn't really thought it was.

"Do we leave now?" Paladin asked.

I thought about it. "Not yet. But I'm going t'get there
early. An so are you."

I took a small but useful bag a tricks an left for the Accommodation of Useful Virtue—by which name my meet-
cute went. Once I was off-Port an in Riisfall, I did my best to
look less like what I was an more like a simple—though
offworld—grubber. The coldweather gear helped. It was still

snowing. The Riisfallin kept the Port clear with sweeps and shields, but not one meter beyond.

Paladin'd pulled the name an particulars of a guest at the Accommodation what might reasonably be expecting a delivery, but nobody stopped me at the front. Riisfall City makes what you might call your uneasy adjustment to Imperial technology; there was stairs, not dropshafts. I took them.

The doors uplevel was Imperial standard, easy to open. Wasn't nobody there, even though the cubie was rented an standing empty. It's amazing what information you can pull off even a dumb terminal, which same high-ticket bennie of Imperial civ all the cubies at the Accommodation had.

An I intended to make sure it was wide awake an ready to be helpful.

First I pinged *Firecat*. Paladin would make sure there was no record a that. Then I took the casing off the terminal an hung a few bells an whistles on it to make sure the call couldn't be disconnected short a ripping the set out a the wall. If anyone tried to use it for anything, Paladin wouldn't be noticed. But he'd have full ears.

It wasn't much in the way a backup. But it was all we could manage.

I put it back together an looked for a nice place t'hide whiles my host showed up. Aside from the door an the terminal, it was standard Riisfall subtech: windows that opened, a stove for heat. The stove wasn't on. The cubie was cold. I found a likely closet an made myself comfortable.

About an hour before I was supposed to arrive, I heard voices. A roomful.

"I thought it would be Captain Dace." An older man, fussing.

"Imperials are all alike. All she wants is the money. She'll do the job." My friend from the bar. I'd pegged his type now. An inbetweener. You wanted something done, he'd help. For a fee.

"But can she be trusted? I've heard they sometimes...dump their cargo." A woman this time. She sounded soft an scared.

"No!" The first man again. You'd a thought I was about t'space his pet goldfish.

"Ser Emeth, Sera Emeth, the woman is Guild-bonded and reliable. Captain Dace vouches for her. She'll take the cargo safely to Kiareth," the inbetweener said. I wondered why he'd brought what sounded like citizens to the handoff. For that matter, I wondered why he'd come himself.

But I'd heard enough. There was a cargo. Nobody was planning to shoot me. An they had a wholly-unreasonable destination in mind. Kiareth is in the Outer Midworlds, a place I don't go. I could get whatever it was there if I had to, splitting fees with another darktrader. So it was time to see the pony.

I drew my blaster an came out.

Ser an Sera Emeth was native Riisfallin—tall, blond, looked like they wrestled the native wildlife two falls out a three before breakfast. They was both covered in furs.

Sera Emeth squealed, clutching a small ambulatory bundle a furs. Apparently this was a family affair.

"You're early," my contact said.

"Promptness is a virtue." Paladin says that lots. I kept my blaster pointed at all four a them.

Nobody said anything for whiles.

"Where's the package?" I was getting impatient. "An my fee."

The inbetweener gestured to Ser Emeth. He reached into his furs—slow, so I wouldn't shoot him—an brought out a fist. He opened it.

There's three things you can take off Riis. This was gems. Five ice-diamonds, big as my thumb-joint an clear as water. Enough to make up for losing *Fortune's Girl.* Enough to buy her twin sister stock out of High Mikasa.

"This is the package."

Sera Emeth unveiled the short bundle. It was a girl, blond, undecided in the looks department. Maybe a little younger than I'd been when I ran away t'see the wicked city. Frail.

There's always people who ain't happy with the bennies a Closed World status, an *kiotes* who, for a fee, will show 'em the stars. Looked like Elory'd been running *kiote* off Riis. I wondered how that fit in with either a his other lives, but not very much.

"I don't run live freight."

Possible for Elory, in *Fortune's Girl*. Not for me, in *Firecat*. With Paladin.

"You have to take her!" Sera Emeth pushed her at me like she was offering her up for sale. The kinchin goggled an clung to her mam, which made her smarter nor anyone else here.

Ser Emeth took a step toward me. I discouraged him some with my blaster. He stopped.

"You can't be serious," he said.

"My ship. My rules. *Ja'i* kinchin. Think about it."

"But...we had a deal." He looked at the inbetweener. He shrugged.

"She has the right to refuse the cargo."

"But you can't!" Ser Emeth wanted to argue, him being a citizen what thought talking could change facts. I wanted to get out a there without fuss. I figured he'd wind down sooner if I let him air his lungs.

"Captain...you don't understand what life is like here, on a Closed World. Captain Dace said he could arrange things. We're not Interdicted. I have sponsors waiting for her outside. All I have to do is get her there. I want to give Helwys a chance at a better life."

I had a better idea than he knew. There's plenty of Imperial tech available on a Closed World if you're willing to pay darktrade prices for it, and from the look of the Emeths, they could afford to pay for plenty.

"Give her a chance, then. Keep her here. There's ninety-nine ways t'die out there." An his "sponsors" might be slavers or organleggers, depending on what deal Elory was working. But I didn't want any part a it. I'd been a slave. I knew.

"You don't understand. She's dying *now!* She needs medical treatment—the Empire—"

The Empire wouldn't care. I knew that for certain truth. They'd throw her away, less'n keeping her livealive bought them something they wanted.

"Everybody dies. Find someone else." I slid along the wall, heading for the door.

"*Do you want more money?*" Sera Emeth sounded shrill. "We'll get it! We'll—"

Helwys started to cry, clinging to her mam.

I pointed my blaster at her. That shut them all up.

"Sera Emeth. I give you one word for free. No matter what you think, yon kinchin's better off dying here than going out there. Whatever your friend there told you ain't true-tell. Maybe there's a sponsor. Maybe Helwys gets sent up contract warmgoods to pay her freight. One way an another she don't come home again for ever."

I reached the door an got out.

I thought they might be fool enough to drop the whistle on me, like gigging my hull would buy them something they wanted to keep, nevermind I could do them more harm than they could do me, by what they knew. But I got no trouble the whole way back to the Port, aside of the snow.

It used to snow that way back home, sometimes, in the winter. Probably still does.

Paladin was waiting for me when I got back to *Firecat*. Where else would he be? He had the heat turned up full. I peeled out of my gear and went looking for something hot.

"We have the first available clearance, Butterfly, but it won't be for some hours," Paladin said.

"I couldn't take her. Not even as far as Coldwater." Not in a ship barely big enough for one, with an Old Fed Library blackboxed into the hull.

"We'll be gone by horizonfall."

"Only inventories for one. And say to Oob, true-tell? Probably wasn't nobody on Kiareth, neither, forbye." Or if there was, could be they'd bring rude questions t'ask about the late Elory Dace.

"Undoubtedly the Emeths will not heed your good advice, though with Elory Dace's disappearance, Chenling Elm's scope of operations will become severely limited. They will almost certainly try again, and almost certainly fail."

"The diamonds would'a been nice, though."

"Butterfly, are you listening to me?"

I looked up from my hotbox. "We're kyting at horizonfall." And Helwys Emeth was going to die, but maybe, if she was lucky, without knowing about all the worse ways there was t'go outta life. "Wake me when it's time."

I got up and started pegging out my sleep-sling.

Was quiet tik home. I'd backtrailed Elory Dace far as needful. No profits, but no losses neither. With what I took outten his hull, I was covered for the Riis Run. I could bring Oob Elory's head, collect my headprice, an tell him no more but what he needed to hear. Why Elory'd been running *kiote* weren't my problem. A man's darktrade bidness is his own, specially if he's dead.

But I didn't think I'd ever come back to Riis, not for any money.

And I was starting to get tired of snow.

BIDDING THE WALRUS
Lawrence M. Schoen

EGGPLANT JACKSON WARNED me about Clarkesons, back on the first day of my apprenticeship. I remember him sitting me down and saying in his best mentoring tones, "Gideon, never take a contract from a Clarkeson. They might look mostly human, but they're not. Every one of them is a colony creature, a mass of self-aware micro-organisms walking around and talking like an individual. They don't think the way we do, chaos can erupt around them when you least expect it." Okay, maybe thirty years of memory has prettied it up some. Mentoring really never was Eggplant's strong suit. What he probably really said was that a deal with a Clarkeson had a way of coming back and biting you in the ass. Like many lessons from my youth, I remembered Eggplant's warning too late.

Randolv Greyce walked into the front office of Gideon Cybernetics within a minute of my opening the door for business. He asked to speak with the Walrus, pronouncing it with the clipped Hindu vowels I associated with tourist sleep learning. He held up a credit voucher with enough digits to lure back all three of my ex-wives. That was my undoing. Money, especially large sums of money, has that effect on me.

"I'm Walrus," I said, and raised a hand to quickly groom my mustache. I tore my eyes from the voucher to give him a quick study. He was dressed in a striped jumpsuit riddled with polka dots. Raspberry hair stuck out from his head like a wreath, made brighter by the contrast with his dead fishbelly complexion. He looked more like a clown than a customer, except that the clown suit wasn't clothing but a decorative sheddable skin produced by an epidermal committee. Randolv Greyce wasn't an individual, he was a colony being. He was a Clarkeson.

I hadn't yet checked the morning mail from the station's bid board, but the Clarkeson had. He handed me his copy of a bidding contract naming Gideon Cybernetics as the second party. Miraculously I'd managed the winning bid on a customized micro-bot job, undercutting my competition throughout the rest of Loophole Station by a good five percent of the cost and promising delivery in a tenth of the time. I remembered the contract from earlier in the week; I'd put in a bid at the start of the five day window. I always bid, but a small operation like mine rarely wins. I manage to snag enough jobs to keep the business afloat. Barely. I hadn't known from the bid board that Greyce was a Clarkeson, only that he managed a matrix of industrial properties. He leased short and long term manufacturing shafts on a Jovian moon back in Sol system and needed a flexible and discrete means of handling industrial sabotage to keep his tenants happy. The bid was for writing and producing tiny smart-bots armed with EMP pellet launchers and a typicality-feature matching expert system—something far short of a true AI to keep it within the regs for Sol system—with enough smarts to disable invading spy-bots without harming authorized hardware.

I'd written a similar decision package for a Tunisian agribiz before coming to Loophole, my masterpiece which ended my apprenticeship to Eggplant Jackson. I had the source code in archival storage. Instead of writing fresh code, I could just adapt it to the current particulars, graft a pellet launcher to the standard mini-bot blueprints, and give Greyce what he wanted faster than anyone else on station.

I took the Clarkeson's voucher and told him to come back in two days. Then I transmitted acknowledgment of the bid win to the station board. Seconds later my balance statement reflected a hefty deposit. I pulled the old design from the archives, slapped it onto a flim, and stepped into the second of GC's three rooms. Weird Tommy, my sole employee, sat at his console, humming to himself while he played some game involving fibonacci sequences and countable infinities with a color

palette that would make an A.I. sweat. I cut the console's power
to get his attention and gave him the good news. He beamed
like a happy puppy, took the flim, and immediately set to splicing in the specs Greyce required. I could have done a cleaner
job of it myself, but not as quickly as Tommy. I had some business with a couple angry creditors that morning and left him to
work. I came back hours later with an armload of Tommy's
favorite nutrient bevs and flavor-impregnated soys. He hadn't
budged; Weird Tommy's entire world had become the code I'd
given him. I doubt he even knew I had been gone or come
back. I watched him for a bit, the bright and broken son I never
had. I couldn't help but wonder if Eggplant had ever felt a
similar affection for me. Then I simply left the food within arm's
reach. Once Tommy's blood sugar dropped low enough, his
subconscious would make a grab for the goods.

The next morning he'd finished the code, streamlined it,
and patched the thing into an idiot savant breed-bot. Gideon
Cybernetics had two breed-bots, out of the seventeen on all of
Loophole Station. They were the reason I managed to win the
few contracts that kept me in business.

Most bids come down to materials, talent, and time. On
Loophole, all the contractors have the same costs for materials,
so that falls out of the equation except for the really big jobs.
Talent I've got, and so does Weird Tommy; we're the tops at
program and design. The snag is always time, combining the
talent and materials quickly enough to give the customer what
he wants. I built our breed-bots myself, and there's nothing better when it comes to small scale manufacture. They could throw
together anything I could design, adapting their own programming on the fly. Any breed-bot is intelligent, but I prided myself on the quality I'd built into the twins. Even so, Loophole
officials came by to check them, as they did all the station's
breed-bots, every two weeks. I couldn't fault them for wanting
to verify that the savants were still idiots, fragmented personali-
ties with tightly defined expertise and little else. Not even station law would allow full capacity A.I.s in human space.

My breed-bots finished a gross of Greyce's smart-bots by late afternoon and the Clarkeson showed up to claim them himself. He signed the paperwork and a union dock worker carted the hardware away to his ship while Greyce made the balance of his payment in genuine solar dollars. Even with the conversion fees I'd come out well ahead.

The Clarkeson beamed at me. "Walrus Gideon, we must celebrate," he said.

"Celebrate?" I'd never had a customer pay me and then ask for a party.

"Absolutely, to commemorate our successful transaction. Come, I have time before I need to depart this station; permit me to purchase beverages of joy to commemorate our mutual satisfaction. Is that not the custom?"

"For some, I suppose. I don't mind having a drink or two with you. Give me a minute." I triggered the palmlock on my office safe and stowed the solars. Moments later we were catching the station rail in search of libation.

We ended up halfway around Loophole, near to his docking port, and sat in the bar of the station's second fanciest restaurant. Greyce was buying. The actual number of drinks rose from two to something closer to eight. Eggplant had never mentioned the Clarkeson tolerance for alcohol, or maybe Greyce was just a special case. By the fifth glass of hydroponic corn-squeezings I had dropped my guard. Greyce and I were old buddies now. I spent the better part of an hour trying to explain what a walrus was, and he drew pictures on several dozen cocktail napkins attempting to depict similar mammals unique to Clarkeson worlds. When we finally staggered out of the bar, we were arm in arm, laughing and singing.

We found our way to his docking tube. A stationmaster's sticker on the panel confirmed his shipment had been stowed and he was cleared for lift. The Clarkeson fumbled with the keypad and almost fell inside as the hatch retracted, but I caught him at the last moment.

"Walsie," he said staring up at me like some infatuated mooncalf, "I can't thank you enough. I thought I'd have to spend a month waiting for someone to custom build those smart-bots."

I propped him up and shook my head. "Randolv, don't give it another thought. Your payment is all the thanks I need." And I meant it. The two day job had brought in more than I'd made in the last six months. Who needed more thanks than that?

"No, no, you've really come through for me. Let me give you something. Hold on." He stumbled inside and out of sight. I waited on the gantry, leaning against the dock wall and thinking of all the ways I could spend those solars.

Greyce returned carrying what looked like a chrome puppet under one arm. He shoved a knobby control ring at me, all angular crystal and interlacing microcircuitry. I was so drunk I immediately slipped it on my right index finger without hesitation. I twitched once as it zapped me with a micro-voltage jolt and implemented its calibration sequence. Human tech had nothing like it. I recognized it, a wearable one-way interface. I'd worn one once before, while supervising the initial run of a salvage module I'd scripted for asteroid scavengers. That ring had given me telefactor supervision over a dozen spidery robots carrying out the routines I had written.

"Randolv, I can't accept this," I said. "Even unlinked a control ring is way outside anything I could afford. It's worth half again what you already paid me."

The Clarkeson waved away my objection. "It's not unlinked," he said and handed me the metal puppet. "It's linked to this, which is why I can't take it into Sol system. So you might as well have it."

The puppet's burnished surface felt cool to the touch. I held it up and found myself squinting into cobalt colored lenses. Biomagnetics pulsed through the ring and the puppet's eyes flared briefly. "What is it?" I asked. "And why can't you bring it into Sol sys?"

"It's an Arconi homunculus with a personality index slaved to the control ring."

The words hit me with a jolt. "Personality index? You mean it's got an A.I.?"

"No, no, not really, only a limited A.I." He gave my arm a reassuring pat. "The Arconi go a bit further than humans with their idiot savant A.I.s, but even they won't make one that's autonomous."

I frowned. I'd heard of Arconi devices but never seen one. "So this isn't independent?"

Greyce shook his head. "It's as harmless as a human being," he said, "as safe as anyone wearing the ring. Limited, like I said, but just try explaining that to Sol customs! Those agents won't care about the limitations, they'll hear 'A.I.' and turn me right around. I'd planned on selling it before I left station, put it up on the bidnet here. Even with the five day wait I thought I'd have plenty of time. But you were too fast, Walsie, and between the port charges and the money I'll save getting to Sol system sooner than expected, it's cheaper to just give it to you and be on my way. Think of it as a bonus."

"But what does it do?"

Greyce laughed at that and stepped back into the tube. "Anything you'd do," he said, and waved at me as the hatch slid shut again.

I shook my head and stared at the puppet. It resembled a miniature Arcon, a meter tall rendering of an attenuated, hairless human. I shrugged, tucked it under my arm, and wove my way to the rail station. Ten minutes later I was back at Gideon Cybernetics. In the middle room Weird Tommy was curled into a ball on his cot, eyes darting furiously with some of the fastest REM cycles known to man. I dropped the puppet on the workbench, and breezed on through to the backroom which I euphemistically referred to as my apartment, and aimed myself for the bed. I felt exhausted but sleep eluded me. I lay there in the near dark and stared at the control ring on my finger. Intermittent microbolts of neural lightning coursed through the lump of crystal as I imagined the possibilities the addition of a limited A.I. would have for Gideon Cybernetics and the additional contracts I could bid on. Visions of sugarplums and solar dollars danced in my head and somewhere in the process I fell into a deep and dreamless sleep.

Next thing I knew it was noon and my head was pounding out a message to remind me that alcohol, despite all its seductive ways, remained a potent toxin. I'd already lost the morning, but resolved to salvage something of the day despite my hangover. I slathered my head, cheeks, and chin with a thick dollop of peeler gel and wiped myself free of the stubble, leaving only my trademark bristle brush mustache and gleaming scalp. A fresh shave always makes me feel like a new man, and I stepped into the middle room whistling like a happy capitalist on his way to market.

Weird Tommy sat in his scoobie chair, humming tunelessly. Both his arms plunged deep into the rests on either side. A pair of micro waldoes rose from the front of the chair and tinkered in the guts of some shiny silver bot on the desk in front of him.

A year ago I'd been desperate for help and pulled Tommy out of the psych pool. His coronal tattoo had branded him as a borderline-functional schizophrenic with an obsessive-compulsive component that made him a natural problem solver. The station saw him as a potential hazard. I saw a scared kid with other kinds of potential, and he's been working for me ever since. Even with medication the schiz wanks his attentional filters, and I knew he wouldn't notice me in the room until I interrupted whatever he was concentrating on and made him shift his focus to me. I came up behind him to see what he had the waldoes into. It wasn't a bot; it was the Clarkeson's puppet. Or maybe not. Two other identical looking chrome figures were strewn across the desk as well. I placed a hand on the armrest's override pad and made myself known to his closed off world. Tommy jerked up with a start. His eyes focused on me, and I felt the gaze of his absolute attention.

"Boss," he said, "we got a problem."

My mustache twitched at the remark. It took a lot to worry Tommy. Most times, only the dead are more laid-back.

I slapped a remote on the wall and the office bot scuttled into activity, flash-brewed a cup of coffee and brought it to me. I peered more closely into the guts of the thing Tommy was tinkering with.

"What's the problem?"

"When I woke up this morning the number two breed-bot was churning these things out."

"Churning?" I said. "How many is churning?"

"Half a dozen at least. They were in the front room, working all the terminals. They'd opened up the outer door and were running the shop."

I sipped my coffee, trying to make sense of this. I saw the control ring on my hand and it all fell into place.

"Son of a bitch," I said. "Those bots think they're me."

Weird Tommy blinked back at me. "Boss?"

I held up the ring for him to see and he stared into its depths. "That's Arconi tech, boss. No wonder I can't find an imprinted source module in this thing. You're the source."

I nodded. The Clarkeson had said the puppet was a homunculus. An odd word, and in my inebriation I hadn't thought about it. Now it was clear, the homunculus's personality was slaved all right, slaved to the personality of whoever wore the control ring. While I'd slept it had integrated its new persona and awoken as a miniature version of me, Walrus Gideon, eager entrepreneur.

I laughed. "Don't worry, Tommy. It's not really a problem. The thing's just trying to help our business, doing the things I'd do, boosting our efficiency."

Tommy considered this and nodded, "Right, so it fed its own specs into the breed-bot to replicate itself and crank things further."

"Makes sense in its own way," I said. "Give me a hand rounding them up. One of me is more than enough for this station."

"We can't, boss. They're not here any more."

"Not here? Where are they? Why'd they leave? Where'd they go?"

Tommy swallowed hard and pointed toward the front room. "Like I said, I found them using the terminals. They were hooking into the bidboard, just the way you do every morning. They were putting out bids on jobs."

That stopped me. "They were bidding? How? The board wouldn't let them on without a contractor's code."

"They used yours," said Tommy. "They logged on with your codes and started putting out bids on different jobs. When I tried to stop them they scattered. I grabbed a launcher from the job we just did, and managed to zap three of them with EMP pellets, but the rest got out."

That was sharp. I didn't think I'd have thought of the pellets. They were hardly standard issue on Loophole. "So where are they?" I asked.

He shook his head. "I don't know. But they keep accessing the station board and bidding. I've got a program running, trying to track them to whatever public terminal they're using, but they keep switching. Near as I can tell, they're all over the station, at least three of them, maybe more. But boss, that's not the problem."

Tommy's weird. I'm used to that, but it croggled my mind to think that a bunch of alien homunculi robots scrambling around the station acting like me wasn't a problem, and that something else loomed larger.

"Okay, Tommy, what is the problem?"

"I've gone over some of the bids they put in, boss. They're good bids, vacuum tight. You couldn't do better yourself. And they're competitive too, we'll probably score thirty to forty percent of them."

I laughed at that. "How is that a problem, Tommy? Most weeks we're hungry for business; we're lucky to win one in ten. We can use the work."

"Yeah, boss, but most weeks you only put in five or ten bids. They've logged over a thousand."

"A thousand? How can three bots have already put in a thousand bids?"

"They're quick," said Tommy, and offered nothing more.

"I'm ruined. There's no way we can handle winning that many jobs. My god, if I tried to withdraw that many bids the penalties alone would bankrupt me!"

I whirled into the front room and slammed into the nearest terminal, relying on long habit to guide my fingers through the sequence of logons and protocols that eventually connected me to my account on Loophole's bidboard. According to station records I had one thousand eighty-five outstanding bids. I skimmed the first few and came to the same conclusion Tommy had. The bids were good, too good. In five days' time when the pool closed, contracts would be issued to the winners, and Gideon Cybernetics would be inundated with several hundred times the business it could handle. As the horror of it sank in the data display refreshed. One thousand eighty-six.

"I've been munged by a Clarkeson," I swore. I called up my preference file for the station's board and began the sequence of code phrases that would allow me to alter my password and cut the homunculi's access. They could still follow the action on the bid board, but they wouldn't be able to place any new bids. Then I slumped back and tried to figure what to do next. The control ring still glittered on my finger. I tore it off, wrenching a knuckle in the process, and strode back into the middle room.

"Tommy, what can you tell me about this?" I said, tossing the ring onto his bench. "What kind of a control ring doesn't give the wearer control? I'm not getting anything from this thing, not the tiniest bit of feedback."

Tommy caught the ring on the second bounce, tearing his eyes from it with obvious effort. "I think you're outside of their range, boss." He gestured to the gutted puppet on the bench. "It's not very much. The receiver I found in this one probably couldn't recognize a signal beyond half a dozen meters."

"Then why didn't they shut down when they ran out onto the concourse? The Clarkeson said the homunculus wasn't an autonomous A.I."

"Well, technically it isn't. It's an autonomous A.Y."

"A.Y.?" I said.

"Artificial You. Each of them is operating with a reduced version of your personality, knowledge set, and skills. That's what the ring does. It lays down the initial template and index."

I took the ring from him and slid it onto my finger. "They have to be stopped, before they do any more damage. How can we get them back here?"

Tommy shrugged. "I don't know, boss, what would bring you back to the office?"

That stopped me. One of the perks of Tommy's hyper-attention is the way it cuts through to the heart of things. What would bring me back to the office? There wasn't a good answer. We had no other contracts to work on. The Clarkeson's had been the first job GC had seen all month. I didn't have a lot on my calendar.

The breed-bots had been inspected three days ago. I'd finished all pending off-station correspondence two days earlier, and spent yesterday making the rounds of my creditors. Other than the thousand and some new entries from the Clarkeson's puppets, I had only a single outstanding bid that could come through today, a multimedia chip design for a hybrid cryogenic organ delivery vendor. I was fairly certain Scully Picasso over at Cubist Cyberdreams had underbid me by at least five percent, which was two percent below what I saw as my cost. Not surprising; Scully had done the last upgrade for the cryonics firm and could do the job in half the time it would have taken GC, in much the same way I'd been able to grab the Clarkeson's contract. I actually had nothing pressing today, prior to the homunculi. Unless...

"Tommy! What's the status of that cryo chip bid? Has the deadline passed?"

"No, boss. Bidding ends at thirteen hundred, but the Cubists probably snagged that one. Why?"

I glanced at the wall clock, rushed back to the front room and sat down at a terminal. It was still a quarter hour before

A week later, when the chaos finally ended, we had completed all three-hundred and eighteen contracts from the homunculi's winning bids, more than half of them ahead of schedule and earning bonuses. GC made more money in that week than I expected to see in my entire life. I put it all in the office safe, and then Weird Tommy and I dismantled every one of the homunculi before the station inspectors came by to recertify our pair of breed-bots and asked any embarrassing questions. Sure, the Arconi puppets weren't real A.I.s, but I still didn't want to have explain to any station officials. Besides, we still had the specs and could manufacture them again if we ever had the need. I didn't think we would though. One of me is plenty, and the galaxy just isn't ready for dozens of Weird Tommys.

THE GIFT
Laura J. Underwood

CAER ELENTHORN HAS too many scars, Rhys thought as he walked the back streets of the area known as Broken Wall. Here and there, rubble of stone and timbers still littered the narrow streets, forcing one to step cautiously, stark evidence of how the Hound and his Haxon horde had once swept out of the mountains of Carn Dubh and torn apart this great northern city. Folk came back once the Hound was defeated and tried to restore their lives, but it was not easy when homes were little more than ruins.

A pair of urchins scuttled about the streets in pursuit of a small dog. Shadows were growing long. Some citizens of these grim dwellings had already closed their shops and barred their doors. No one in their right mind walked these streets after dark. Even thieves and murderers and drunks were less prevalent once the sun had set, for some of the leftover pestilences spawned by the Hound's dark power still roamed at night. Rhys was not afraid. He was mageborn, and these sometimes-intangible remnants of the Hound's invasion tended to avoid his kind.

That didn't stop him from being a cautious man, for possessed of the power to use magic as he was, Rhys also knew that mageborn flesh was still mortal. He had been but a child of seven when the Hound turned his life upside down. A part of him was still that small boy hiding in the secret cupboard as Haxons butchered his parents. That was where the healers found him cowering, and it took more than one of their number to haul him out of his small sanctuary that day. They comforted him and took him to their Temple of Diancecht. There they trained him in their arts...at least until the magesign had manifested in him, forcing them to send him to Caer Keltora and the mage school at Dun Gealach to learn to manage his emerging power. How often had he lain in his narrow cot, praying to Diancecht to take the mage power from him and give him the touch of a True Healer instead?

Alas, for all his prayers, he was still mageborn. In spite of that, he called himself Brother Rhys, and went back to the healers to complete his training before returning to the lowly place of his birth...or what was left of it. Here, he had set up shop, and offered what knowledge of herbs and potions he had to the people who needed it most. The lower layers of humanity, as he heard one of the nobles at Dun Gealach call them. Rhys set bones and stitched wounds and even birthed children when no midwife could be found.

Which was where he was heading now. One of the whores at Tosher's Hole was about to drop another babe. Tosher had sent his potboy to ask Rhys to come and deliver the child. The whore in question was his wife Lena, or so Tosher claimed. Rhys didn't care. He was a healer.

But not a True Healer, he thought with a sigh of resignation.

His mage sight revealed the door of Tosher's Hole in the shadows of the dead-end alley where it stood. Frankly, Rhys could have found it with his nose alone, for it stank of hops and sweaty men and overcooked meat and garbage. It was a wonder to Rhys that the King did not order such vermin-infested quarters burned to the ground.

But then why would the King of Elenthorn bother to come here? Wasn't he safe in his brand new fortified palace on the other side of the river? Part of his "great restoration" plan had been to bring back his city. But rather than clean up and rebuild what was, the King chose to take over the good farmland and meadows and forests on the other side and start his great city anew with the help of mageborn, while leaving the old city to languish into ruins.

This meant that places like Broken Wall thrived as a haven for rats of all kinds. In fact, one of them stood at the door of Tosher's Hole even as Rhys approached. Only this one was the

size of an ox and about as slow of wit. Liam was his name, and
he was the bane of many locals. He took whatever he wanted,
by whatever means necessary. Rhys had tended enough of
Liam's victims to know this.

At the sight of Rhys, Liam's hooded brows drew together
over his thick nose. He stood a good head taller than Rhys and
was thrice as wide. Yet as Rhys approached the door of Tosher's
Hole, Liam hesitated then stepped aside. Rhys managed not to
laugh aloud. It seemed absurd to him that a monster of Liam's
temper and proportions would be wary of a thin, brown-haired
man dressed in a simple tunic, shirt and trews who looked decades younger than his true age, thanks to the magic in his blood.
But then Liam didn't like pain unless he was inflicting it, and
while Rhys was not one to exploit his mage skills, for his own
sake he had been forced to hit Liam with a mage bolt—a tiny
one—just to make the behemoth think twice. Then again, Rhys
mused; it would be amazing for Liam to think once.

Rhys put a hand to the door and pushed it open. Inside,
Tosher's Hole was dark, and the air was heavy with the smoke
of an ill-attended fire and cheap oily candles. The tavern was
thick with bodies too. Tosher served the cheapest ale and the
cheapest whores, which made his place popular with many locals. A few heads rose suspiciously, but most of these people
knew Rhys on sight and ignored him.

He wove his way across the room, and was almost to the
bar when a commotion broke the usual chatter. Rhys turned,
glancing towards the source.

"Ow! Let go of me!" Flesh smacked flesh. "Ow!"

The noise came from Liam's general direction. Indeed, the
big man reared back a hand and snarled, "You behave yourself
or I'll take a tawse to ya!"

Before him cringed a lass of no more than thirteen. Her
figure was starting to show under the thin linen blouse that had
seen better days and the long skirt that looked like a cast-off.
Her feet were bare and quite dirty. In fact, she looked as though
she had not known the luxury of a bath in a number of months.

Bits of her long brown hair spilled out of an ill-kept braid and fell in her dark eyes.

"Let go," she protested and slapped a hand at Liam's grasp, for all the good it would serve. He gave her a hard shake that spilled her into the corner by the door and reared over her as though about to strike again.

"Liam!" Rhys called.

Liam stopped and glanced over his shoulder and frowned at Rhys. "Stay out of this, Brother," he said. "She's mine to do as I please..."

"Yours?" Rhys said.

"Won her in a game of High Ladies," Liam said.

Rhys frowned. "Slavery is illegal, Liam," he said. "Were I to report you to the watch, you would go to the King's dungeons..." He noticed a number of locals were now inching back and leaving Liam plenty of room. They had seen him trounce men for less.

"Ain't no business of yours or the King," Liam snarled. "I won her and she's mine and—"

Rhys saw the lass move like quicksilver. She seized a jack of ale from the nearest table and earned a squawk of protest from the previous owner. With a shout, she turned and swung it in an underhand arc. The jack struck Liam squarely in the crotch and splattered ale up his breeches.

Either the blow did not hit as true as Rhys thought, or Liam was too thickheaded to notice. He bellowed like a maddened bull and swung at the lass. She threw herself past him, only to trip because one of the locals stuck a foot in her path. The motion sprawled her at Rhys' feet. She looked up at Rhys, dark eyes full of fear. Liam turned with her and surged across the empty space, still roaring his rage.

Think fast, Rhys told himself. Unless he wanted to be trampled. He threw up a hand, sifting bits of essence from the lives around him and hissed, *"Adhar clach!"*

Liam ran into a solidified wall of air with enough force to knock him out cold. The room went quiet for a brief moment as he hit the floor and shook the foundations of Tosher's Hole. Then as if they were actors responding to a cue, the locals began to guffaw. Whether they were laughing at Liam or the fate he would plot for Rhys was uncertain.

Rhys sighed. "Forgive me, Blessed Brother," he whispered under his breath, then leaned down to offer the lass a hand. She took it hesitantly, glancing back at Liam with a genuine look of concern...

"Is he...?"

"Not dead," Rhys said, though he did flick out with mage senses to be certain.

Her dark eyes rose to Rhys. "I feel...ill," she said.

"I can imagine," Rhys said. "If I were you, I'd get home as fast as I could..."

Rhys was about to head for the bar, but she caught his arm. "Don't have a home," she said. "Guess I'm yours now..."

"Mine?" Rhys looked stunned at the declaration. "Oh, Blessed Brother no, child," he said and shook his head. "No one owns you..."

"You do now," she insisted. "He won me from Old Nance's brothel, and now you won me from him..."

"No," Rhys said and moved away. His mind was still trying to fathom how she could be so comfortable with the knowledge that she had come from a brothel. Then again, Old Nance's place was not much better than Tosher's Hole was, and the whores there kept their daughters around because they could help turn a profit. "Look. I don't own you. No one owns you, child..."

"But I got no one else," she said. "And if you don't let me come with you, Liam will just beat me when he wakes up..."

Rhys frowned and glanced over at the still prostrate form of Liam. True enough. Rhys sighed.

"All right, you can come with me until I find a place for you to stay," Rhys said. "But for now, I must tend to Tosher's wife."

"I can help," she said. "I seen little 'uns born at the brothel..."

Rhys took a look at her filthy hands and the scraps of her clothes.

"Only if you wash first," he said. "Come on."

She followed him like an eager pup. He continued towards the bar where Tosher stood shaking his head.

"If you're wise, Brother Rhys, you'll sell her to the first man you meet on the street and be done with the trouble. Liam might not be as forgiving about this..."

Rhys made a face. "Which room, Tosher?" he asked.

Tosher shrugged towards the stairs. "End of the hall," he said. "Mind the hole..."

Rhys nodded and made his way up the stairs. The lass was still at his heels.

"Do you have a name?" he asked.

"Old Nance used to call me Moth," she said.

"Moth?" Rhys repeated.

"On account of she says I flitter about like one." Moth smiled.

"Moth," Rhys said, and remembered the old saying about their attraction to flames. Then pushed it aside.

The upper floor reeked of blood and at the far end, the wretched whimpers and moans of a woman in pain filled the air. Rhys raced towards the end of the hall, mindfully stepping around the aforementioned hole, just as the door open and two women came bustling out. Rhys recognized them as two of Tosher's older whores. They wore worried faces under their thick cowls of greying hair.

"Oh, Brother Rhys," one of them said. "We was starting to wonder where you be. She's not doing well at all, I fear..."

The smell hit Rhys before he even entered the chamber, a certain stench that accompanied infection. *Oh Brother, no,* he thought and rushed on in. Lena lay on the bed, bolstered by birthing pillows. There was a great deal of blood, but no sign of a child. Two more women were clutched Lena's arms, and Lena bit hard on a bit of wood wound with thick leather. She writhed back and forth.

"It don't seem to want to come," the whore added.

Rhys hurried across the room. *Blessed Brother!* There was no reason for so much blood.

"It's not coming out right," one of the women said.

Indeed. As Rhys examined Lena, he could see toes. Horns, the babe was coming out breach. "How long has she been in labor?" he asked.

"Since midmorning," the oldest whore said.

"Midmorning?" Rhys said and glared. "Why was I not summoned earlier? The child is likely dead!"

"She's never had trouble before," she retorted. "I birthed her last one myself..."

Rhys shook his head. "Hot water and fresh linens, if you have such a thing," he said, and began to draw herb packets from his satchel. Fretfully, he cleared a space on a small sideboard and opened each packet in turn. The whores returned with the required items, and after pouring some of the water off into a cracked mug, Rhys washed his hands. He set some of the herbs to brewing in the small cup and hurried over to the bed.

The light was not as good as he would have liked now, but he was certain that the toes on that tiny foot looked blue. With careful fingers, he worked his way around the limb. Lena continued to writhe and moan. Rhys felt like slapping her into silence, but knew it would do no good. So he probed until he was sure the babe was not wrapped in its cord. It was not in a good place for him to turn it around, so he was forced to take hold of the limbs and pull. While the women squawked encouragement at Lena, he dragged the baby free.

A boy and it was not moving. Frantically, Rhys cut the cord, cleared the little mouth and rubbed the small chest. When that did not work, he upended the child, attempting to get the baby to draw a breath...but it would not, and Rhys felt hope abandoning him like a tide.

"Give him to me," Moth said, suddenly at his side.

Rhys looked at her face and saw a peculiar mask of calm. Her eyes were luminous and dark as eclipses and she held forth her hands. He saw that she had made an attempt to clean them, for water ran tracks through the filth of her arms.

"Please, give him to me," she said.

His instinct was to push her away, but there was something in that look that he could not ignore. Swallowing, he placed the child in her outstretched arms. She drew it to her breast and closed her eyes...

Rhys felt the power of the god Diancecht as it flowed into the room and bathed both the girl and the child with a golden light. His own breath stopped in his throat as he watched her stroke the newborn's chest. Was that the light, or did those small ribs rise and fall? A pitiful little cough and then an infant's wail filled the room.

The whores rushed forward with cries of joy and took the child to clean it. Lena gasped for air between sobs and laughter.

Only Rhys had yet to breathe. He stared at Moth who looked down at the stains of blood and mucus now mixed with the filth of her robe. Then quietly, she looked up at him. "Was that the right thing to do?" she asked.

Oh, Blessed Brother, the child is a True Healer! Rhys thought. All his life, he had prayed for such power, and been denied, and now here was a whore's daughter blessed with the gift he had coveted for so long.

"Did I do it right?" she asked again. "It felt right...and I stopped being sick when I did it."

"Sick?" he repeated.

"Aye, every time I get around someone who's bad off, I feel sick," she said. "And sometimes, the sickness goes away if I touch them, and they usually get better. Was it right?"

Right? he thought. *Of course, it was right you silly little gyte. The Blessed Brother is telling you there is a need and...* But the look on Moth's face assured him that she would not understand such a tirade. And why should she? The girl had never been trained. He was willing to bet she couldn't read or write.

Rhys sighed and nodded, looking back at the bed. Lena cooed over the lad now wrapped and cleaned, and she smiled and shoved one of her tits into his mouth. Slowly, Rhys gathered his herbs and glanced at the brewing cup. It had been a sedative for the mother, in case everything went wrong. He picked it up and drained it into the reeds at his feet. Then quietly, he headed for the door.

Moth followed as though not sure what else to do. Rhys climbed down the stairs where noise continued to ring.

"What is it?" Tosher called.

"You have a son," Rhys said and continued on his way. Behind him, congratulations flowed. He left Tosher's Hole, eager for the air of the night.

On the streets, he realized Moth was still following him, but now she looked about with unease at the shadows.

"Aren't you afraid of the Swallowers?" she asked.

"The what?"

"Them black things that come out of the shadows and swallows you," she said.

"They're called Darklings," Rhys said. "They rarely come into cities anymore, and besides, they don't like light." And to prove it, he whispered, *"Solus."* The warm glow of magelight drove the shadows away. Moth hurried up beside him, looking relieved to have the light. "So where is your home?" he asked.

"Where's yours," she said and ducked her head. "I belong to you now..."

"Child, you don't belong to anyone," Rhys said and started on.

"Can I still come with you?" she ventured. "I've no place else to go."

Rhys merely nodded. He had no intention of leaving her on the streets. Liam would probably find her, and she'd be back under his unworthy thumb.

He took the path back to his shop, drew out a key and unlocked the door. Inside, the smells of the herbs wafted with their familiar odors...a scent he loved. Moth slipped in behind him as he stood for a moment, breathing the sweet air. Her warm odor overwhelmed his nose.

"You need a bath," he said. "And perhaps some fresh clothes."

"All right," she said, and before he could even close the door, she started to disrobe...

"No! Wait, not here!" he cried and quickly shut the door and drew the shutters. "Go in there!" He pointed towards a curtained niche.

Reluctantly, she obeyed, still stripping off her clothes. Rhys took a deep breath to gather his wits, then rushed about to fetch a few items. Lavender in her bath would make her sweeter. He found some old clothes of his own, still wearable, and thrust those at her, along with a towel. She sat in a corner, wrapped in the towel as he quickly used magic to heat the water of her bath. He threw in the lavender and glanced over at her.

"Now get in and scrub every part of yourself," he said.

He hurried out of the niche. The sound of her easing into the water filled his ears, then the splash of liquid. Rhys busied himself, preparing tea and warming some of the oatcakes one of his customers had left as payment for a poultice. *Horns, if I had her skills, I would not have to rely on the herbs and commonsense. I could touch them and cure their ills.* He shook his head. No good would come of envying this gift.

But it galled him to think that Diancecht would give such a special skill to such an ordinary, filthy...

The niche curtains parted, and she slipped into the room, dressed in one of his old nightshirts. Clean, she had a fair complexion and a face that bore some resemblance to that of a fox. Her hair had a red sheen, telling him that the original color had been dirty. She looked much younger now, but the light he had placed in the bathing niche behind her made her womanly shape visible through the thin linen. Rhys swallowed. Healers did not take vows of chastity. *She's a child,* he warned his body and turned away.

"Here. Come have some of these. I'll go up and fix you a bed in the front room."

"I can sleep with you..."

"No," he said. "You...cannot."

She looked just a little disappointed as she came over and helped herself to the oatcakes and tea he placed on the table. While she fed, he went upstairs to the front room. It was actually an examining room, but there was a pallet in the corner that he used for patients who needed to lie down. He took his time arranging fresh bedding and fluffing a pillow for her. By the time he got back downstairs, she was dozing with her head on his work counter, half an oatcake still clutched in one hand. Nor could she be rousted when he touched her hand and called her name. So in the end, he slipped arms under her thin, budding frame and carried her up the stairs. He placed her on the pallet and drew the covers to her chin. Then he went back downstairs to brood the night away.

"Why her?" he whispered. "Why not me?" What possible motive could the Blessed Brother have to give so precious a gift to a simple child who did not even have a sense of her own value? *And why let me find her?* The questions bored into his brain, adding to the already heavy conflict he dealt with every day of his life. He had a power he would rather deny, and coveted a power he could never have. Not since the Great Cataclysm when the Old Ones joined their magic blood to that of mortals to produce the mageborn—and possibly True Healers, according to some scholars—had any ever possessed both these gifts.

But magic is not a gift, Rhys thought as he finished his tea and oatcakes and seated himself before the fireplace. *It's a curse.* Mortalborn viewed mageborn with different eyes after the Last War. The Hound of the Blackthorn saw to that. He showed the world what wickedness could be done with even a little magic, and left a bitter taste on humankind's tongue. Now, only the healers and especially the True Healers were respected.

I am a trained healer and herbalist, but I am not a True Healer. Instead, I am the pariah they fear...

One had only to look at the ruins of Broken Wall to understand why.

Exactly when Rhys fell asleep in the chair, he did not know, but there was a fist on the door, and an old woman's voice calling, "Brother Rhys, come quick."

He pushed himself upright with a moan and stumbled over to the door. The knocking persisted. "All right," he mumbled and fumbled with the locks.

The door opened rather abruptly, catching him in the side of the face and throwing him back. He was aware of bodies, and the sour smell of men who had drunk too much ale. As he tried to get back on his feet and opened his mouth to call a spell, a fist slammed him back down. The blow split his lip and pain temporarily stunned him. Rhys heard Moth cry out, first in anger, then in fright, but he was too busy with the pain to realize that her voice faded with the distance.

Besides, he saw the malicious grin and broken nose of Liam's broad face rear over him. Then something harder than a fist clouted Rhys and made the world disappear for a time.

He opened one eye to a shaft of sunlight and the sight of two urchins crouched warily at the open door of his shop, holding a small dog between them. His face felt like he wore a mask or a mushroom where his left eye once held court, and gentle probing with his fingers revealed that the skin around the cheek was broken and the eye merely matted with a crust of blood. He sat up gingerly, aware of pain and the ringing in his ears.

"Shoo, get back," a woman's voice said. "Brother Rhys? Oh, dear..."

He looked around in time to see the entrance of two Sister Healers from the Temple of Diancecht across the river. Sometimes, they brought charity and supplies to his door. He'd forgotten it was that time of the month again. The oldest of the pair was Sister Helena, and she had looked old when Rhys was a child taken in by the Temple. She had mentored and trained him even after his magesign manifested. Now, she looked positively ancient to him, though she moved with the ease of a spry young lass.

"Well, aren't you a sight," Helena said with a shake of her head. She left her younger companion, Sister Bredda, to deal with the urchins and came over to his side. "What manner of malice brought you to this?"

"A very large brute named Liam who thinks I stole his whore child," Rhys said and crawled to his feet. Helena put a hand on his shoulder to steady him when he swayed like an old drunk.

"Did you?" she asked.

"No, she followed me home," Rhys replied and caught his breath when he realized how absurd and juvenile that sounded. Especially when her eyebrows rose to form an arch over her accusing smile. Rhys sighed and shook his head.

"Well, whatever the case, you should sit down and let me deal with that before it gets any worse. What did they hit you with?"

"I have no idea," he said. He was of half a mind to refuse the offer and deal with his own wound. But he rather doubted Helena would allow him to get away with that. Better to surrender to her ministering. Rhys seated himself on the nearest bench and allowed her to clean and dress what turned out to be a rather long cut up under the hairline. He bit his tongue as she stitched it. Helena was not a True Healer either, but she was good and had taught Rhys well. Once she was finished, he willingly took the willow bark tea Sister Bredda brewed. Several sips of it worked quickly to ease his pain.

"So, tell me about this whore child who followed you home?" Helena asked as she put away the rest of the bandages.

"Her name is Moth," Rhys said. He glanced towards the stairs. "I found her at Tosher's Hole. Liam was beating her, and I stopped him..." He hesitated, not sure he wanted Helena to know he had fallen back on magic. "At any rate, she...has the Brother's gift. She revived a newborn infant I gave up for dead."

Helena looked thoughtful as she seated herself. "Why do I get the feeling you are not pleased to know this?"

Rhys looked away. Even she knew how he had longed for this gift himself.

"If what you say is true," she went on. "Then we have a duty to find her and bring her to the Temple to be trained. And since the Brother in his wisdom led you to her first, I think perhaps it is a sign that you are meant to find her."

"Broken Wall is a large place," Rhys said, "and a brute like Liam knows every rat hole in it. It could take me weeks to find her, and by then, Liam is just as apt to have sold her or killed her or..."

Helena's hand touched his forearm, arresting his patter. "You and I both know that you could find her much more quickly."

Rhys felt his face go cold. "I..." He could not force the words easily across his lips. "I cannot use magic that way..."

"Cannot?" Helena said. "Or will not?"

Rhys closed his eyes.

Helena sighed and patted his arm as she rose from her seat. "I cannot force you to do what you feel is wrong," she said. "But ask yourself if the Brother would think it right before you choose to let this child's life be wasted, Rhys. Come, Sister Bredda. We've charities to deliver."

He stayed where he was, listening to the footsteps of the two women as they closed the door and walked down the broken cobbles. Horns, he thought, covering his face with his hands. It would have been so easy to drink the willow bark tea, lie down and forget this little incident. To pretend that he had never seen Moth or known of her gift. But Helena knew, and would never allow him to live peacefully with himself.

Helena? he thought. *What about my own conscience?*

Yes, he was jealous, and yes, he would give anything to have the gift Moth possessed. But in truth, he could not abandon her to Liam and the dark life of a whore's child.

Slowly, he rose and climbed the stairs to the room where she had slept. Her blankets were thrown back as though she had come running when Liam and his cronies broke through the door. Briefly, he stared at the rumpled pallet, and then with a sigh he stretched his hand.

Healer he might claim to be, but it could not change the magic legacy that he so denied. Rhys closed his eyes and stretched mage senses, letting the tendrils of his awareness slip into the very cloth and seek her essence. Everything in the world possessed essence of one sort or another, and human essence was the life force that lived in flesh and bone and blood. He touched the faint wooly essence of the blanket and found Moth's warmth. It shone in his mind's eye like a brilliant flower of silver and gold. The essence of a True Healer.

He tasted it with his senses and memorized it until he could fix his awareness to any tangible hint of its power. Then quietly, he rose, pulling a plain cloak on over his simple clothes and left the room, following the essence like a hound follows spoor. On the stairs, it was stronger. Not unusual, since she had been frightened, and as he made his way to the ground floor, he sensed the terror in her. She had not wanted to leave with Liam. The brute's essence was there too, dark as Arawn's heart and cold as winter on a mountain. Rhys locked onto it as well, knowing where he found one, he was likely to find the other.

Rhys picked up his pace and hurried out onto the street. He wind whispered a spell to make the essences sing to him as he followed them. The path was not so straight as it was sure. Liam's pace had been quick, and Moth had been fighting him all the way. Rhys detected the essence of fire. Liam had carried a torch to keep Darklings at bay.

The path eventually took Rhys into the Quays, the remains of river docks long ago abandoned. The only cargo that came here was of a variety the king would never allow—assuming he knew of it at all. In fact, the sort of men and women who inhabited the Quays made the folks of Broken Wall's darker corners seem right pleasant and charming.

Here, the streets were muddy and one walked on planks to avoid sinking in the sticky mire. Rhys carefully picked his way along. The stench in the air was enough to take one's breath away, and his stomach heaved in protest as he realized all he had in it was the willow bark tea. Rhys pushed on, trying to ignore the odors and his own queasiness. The temptation to turn back was too strong at the moment.

No, he would not abandon Moth. He should have taken her straight to the temple the moment he realized what skill she possessed. Instead, he had given into apathy brought on by his jealousy. *Who am I to decide that what the Blessed Brother wills is wrong and unfair.* Rhys pushed on.

At last, he found an inn along side an old pier that had once been a thriving port for travelers. Abandoned after the war, it was now a thieves' den. Rhys drew closer, stepping past drunks and whores who stumbled about the narrow boards, having slept off last night's activities. It was a dance to stay out of the muck and the pools left by the river's last spring flood. He managed it though, and still remained focussed on the essence of the girl and the man. When he reached the door, he could see broken windows, and smell dirty bodies and badly prepared food and ale that resembled piss water.

Rhys slipped inside and found a shadow to stand in for a moment. Mage eyes quickly adjusted to the dark, revealing a number of men and women slumbering on the floors. The innkeeper yawned as he put a small effort into wiping the filth off his counter. Rhys whispered a spell to make the man look elsewhere then stretched mage senses again and followed the tangle of Liam and Moth. It led up the stairs and along narrow halls that Rhys followed with caution in every step until he stood before a door.

There were spells, he was once told by the mageborn who trained him, that could put an entire room of people to sleep. Rhys wished he knew that spell now, but it had been one of those lessons he balked against, not because the spell was useless, but because he had felt the need to rebel at everything that had to do with magic. It had not stopped him from learning what to do with the skill he did possess. But a small part of him wondered if even those skills would be enough.

Liam would, no doubt, expect trouble. And he would do what he could to stop Rhys from casting spells. Rhys had only to touch the swollen edge of his mouth to know the behemoth had been told precisely how to break a mageborn's concentration. *Just my luck!*

Rhys sighed and stretched mage senses. He felt Moth and Liam and three others. The girl's aura indicated that she struggled against whatever Liam had used to bind her. Rhys could tell that the others had only just awakened. He could hear the splatter of urine.

This was not going to be easy. He would have to do something all-inclusive. Something frightening enough to put them off guard. To distract them so that he and Moth could flee. Hopefully, he would be able to reach some place where he could open a spell gate to the Temple of Diancecht without getting caught or disturbed.

Fire spells came to mind, but he quickly put those thoughts out of his head. No use in risking a multitude of lives, for the building would likely catch flame like dry tinder.

Illusions, then. Bend the shadows. Make them look like a Darkling. That might work. He took a deep breath, drew essence from the air, and whispered the words of the spell. Around him, the shadows swarmed and shifted and drew into a hideous form. They became a blanket of darkness with glowing eyes, razor teeth and scrabbling claws. The conjuration was so real, Rhys had to suppress a shiver as he reached through it and scratched the wooden surface of the door.

"What the..." A man's voice—not Liam—rumbled from the other side. The trod of footsteps crossed loose boards. The door opened, and Rhys willed his illusionary Darkling to charge through the gap.

And it worked, he was surprised to notice. Or rather, it had the effect he desired. The man who opened the door cried out and fell back in fright. Liam and his companions cursed and dove towards the nearest exits as the shadowy creation swelled to fill the room. Moth screamed in terror as the men ran like rats for the window and the door. Rhys barely stepped aside before Liam and one other barreled through and thundered down the hall, shouting for help.

Rhys quickly stepped into the chamber, resisting the urge to retch when he smelled the vile odors within.

"Moth, it's me," he said and rushed into the corner where she cowered and struggled. Liam had bound her at ankles and wrists. She jerked in fright when Rhys touched her. "Moth, please, I've come to help you..."

She stopped struggling and looked at him in disbelief as he drew his small dagger and cut her bonds. Her arms went around his neck as he pulled her to her feet.

"Be grateful later," he chided, working himself free of her grasp and pushing his dagger back into its sheath. "We must hurry before Liam gets his tripes back..."

Too late. Rhys could hear the clatter of heels on the stairs. He knew he could not open his spell gate swiftly enough. And when Liam's huge bulk filled the doorway, a torch in one hand, the need to escape became all the more apparent.

Blessed Brother, what should I do? Rhys thought.

Moth made that decision for him. She seized Rhys' arm and tugged him towards the window. "Come on!" she cried.

Liam roared, "I'll kill you for this, healer!" And charged across the floor.

Moth was already half out the window when Liam grabbed Rhys by the shoulder. The torch came arcing through the air, aimed at Rhys' head. Instinctively, he threw up a hand and shouted, *"Adhar clach!"* The air hardened into a shield, and the torch bounced off that invisible surface, splattering fire and oily bits mere inches from his face. Bits of flame were thrown into the reeds, which took fire.

"Come on," Moth practically screamed.

She pulled Rhys out the window. Liam bellowed in rage. The loose shingles of the roof beneath Rhys' feet slanted more sharply than he liked. Moth ran down it as though crossing a flat plain. Rhys was less graceful, and he lost his footing as he followed the girl. He sat down hard and slid to the bottom, grateful for the large chimney that kept him from going over the edge. He didn't think he could have spoken a levitation spell in time to save himself otherwise.

Moth had already shifted directions. She seemed to know where she was going. Rhys followed and hoped it would lead them to some place flat and safe where he could open a gate. A quick glance back over his shoulder revealed smoke billowing out of the window of the ramshackle inn. Flames were eating their way through the higher portions of the roof. *Blessed Brother, no!* Men and women surged out of every opening like rats fleeing a flooded bilge. And Liam squeezed his ox-like bulk through the window in mad pursuit of the healer and the girl.

From the streets, a hue and cry arose. Folks gathered buckets, running for the puddles and the ponds, and even heaving the wet mud itself in a desperate attempt to keep the fire from spreading to their own homes. *Blessed Brother, I should conjure water to assist them.* But that would mean stopping, and Liam was coming too hard and fast on Rhys' heels to risk it. Guilt rose, and Rhys half-heartedly pushed it aside, and promised to return to help those in need as he fled.

Moth skittered to a halt, looking over an edge. Rhys stopped beside her and realized there was no place to go except down into the river. It looked too murky and shallow to be safe. Moth hesitated only a moment, then shouted, "Come on!" as she leapt from the edge. Rhys watched in horror as she hit the surface and sank below. Panic filled him when she did not emerge right away.

But he had no time to wonder if she had hit the bottom or drowned. A tremendous roar of rage sounded at his back. He had barely turned before a huge body slammed into his own. Hands grappled for his throat. All Rhys was aware of was the dizzying moment of being airborne, and of drawing one final breath, before he slammed the surface of the water on his back. Pain lashed every nerve as he sank under the surface, pushed down by Liam's greater weight. Rhys beat fists against the man, his own lungs screaming for air. He kicked at Liam as well, barely able to make out the big man's enraged features in the murky depths where their thrashing stirred the silt.

Liam refused to let go. That murder was his only intention could not be denied. But Rhys did not want to die, not this way. *Brother forgive me,* he thought as he drew his short dagger and plunged it into the man's side. Liam jerked in pain, and that was enough for Rhys to break free. Limbs beating the water, the healer surfaced and drew a breath of air.

By now, the embankment was lined with onlookers. A few motioned towards something on down the way. Rhys swam to the nearest dock, grabbed on and turned. Draped in his old shirt, a familiar shape floated face down on the surface of the river.

"Moth!" he screamed in agony and plunged back into the water. He swam fast as he was able, seizing her and flipping her over on her back so he could drag her to the shore. Several hands helped them from the river. Moth lay motionless on the creaking, damp boards.

"Oh Brother, no," he whispered and touched her throat to seek a pulse. But he shivered hard from the chill of the river and the wind, and she was so cold. "Moth, please, open your eyes...please..."

My fault! Rhys closed his eyes as remorse welled in his chest. *I should have taken her to the Temple last night.* Instead, he had allowed his jealousy of her gift to prevail, and now, he did not possess the power to heal her.

"Hey, she ain't streaming, young sir," one of the onlookers said. "Give her a shake."

Rhys opened his eyes again and blinked as his thoughts rapidly cleared. Not streaming meant there was no water in her lungs...He lifted her, shook her, patted her face.

"Moth," he said. "Moth, please, wake up. Open your eyes, child..."

She stirred and coughed and moaned in his arms, and her eyes fluttered opened. Blearily, she looked up at him and muttered, "I feel sick..."

Rhys was torn between joyous laughter and serious contemplation of what she meant. Then several of the men hauled a bulk out of the water. Liam stumbled when he tried to stand, then clutched his side where blood and water mixed. He sank to the boards and moaned. His face was white with pain and shock.

Moth looked at Liam, then at Rhys.

"What must I do?" she asked.

Part of Rhys thought that Liam deserved to die of his wound. That Broken Wall and its poor denizens would be better off without this cruel bully in their midst. But that was not what the healers had taught him. Even as a child, when Rhys cursed the Haxons for stealing his parents' lives, Sister Helena would chide his angry words with her own. *"All life, no matter how lowly or disdainful, is precious to the Blessed Brother whose will we serve with our hearts and our vows..."* Now, it occurred to Rhys that perhaps his prayers for the healer's sacred touch had not been answered because in his heart, he still had much to learn about forgiveness. Such a precious gift did not belong in the hands of one who thought ill of others...

Oh, Blessed Brother, now I see that I have a place, even without your gift. I belong here in Broken Wall, ministering to the poor to the best of my humble ability.

Moth, however, did not belong in this place. She belonged in the Temple of Diancecht where she could be trained to use her gift that it might truly benefit those in need...

He sighed and cupped Moth's chin in one hand, and offered her a wistful smile of reassurance. "You must do whatever the Brother wills," he said.

Rhys helped her over to Liam's side. The big man watched both of them, wary as a fox, unable to hide his fear from those who surrounded them.

"We're going to heal you," Rhys said, and with skilled hands, he pulled back the torn clothing to expose the wound. At his instructions, the locals brought clean water with which to wash the injury. Then Rhys guided Moth's hands to the wound, and told her how to pray for Diancecht's bounty.

Moments passed, and Rhys marveled that no one moved or even drew a breath before Moth was done. And even Liam stayed where he was, staring dumfounded at the scar that now graced his ribs.

Moth looked tired but relieved as Rhys quietly helped her to her feet and led her away from the river and its denizens. No one stopped them when Rhys opened a spell gate and took Moth to the Temple of Diancecht where she rightfully belonged.

THE DOCK TO HEAVEN
L.E. Modesitt, Jr.

INFOSNARK—THAT'S ME. Mom called me Mario. Dockers call me Snark 'cause if there's info to be found without tags, no one does it better than me. Highport's a big place. Ships come from everywhere—Old Earth, Xianth, Clarkburg, Alpha Felini, Sansalibre, D'Ahoud, Melinia. They got ships, and they come to Highport 'cause it's the only way you get to Heaven. Angels insist it's got to be that way. Least, that's what Lorico told me. He may look diablo, but never piloted me wrong.

Twodays are slow. Always have been. Slow isn't always bad, but it's fastbeam to trouble. Times busy, people swirling around, the patrollers don't bother if they see you, so long as you're not doing something brightflared wrong. Slow times, they look deeper. For us snarks, their looking deeper isn't good.

Was coming back from the farwest concourse lines on the low guideway. Slower, but cheaper. Farwest's mostly Sandurco space. Was wearing the greensilver dumper suit and scanner access pins. Lorico does 'em well, and they'll take three-four scans before they flare red. Costs a cred for each pin, but you can't snark if you don't know where the weak points are. Screens and channels don't show everything. Even if they do, so much noise you can't find the signal.

Sandurco had space on the *Elept* to Purgatory. Eight full cubes. Problem was that the space was reserved for a transfer. Iron-bound, cold steel contract. Inbound was from Xianth. Inbound wouldn't make transfer before the *Elept* needed to translate. But Sandurco was bound not to make known the space was available. That's where I came in. Needed to find an instalast cargo, have it ready to upload just before translation. Most of the creds would go to Sandurco and the shipper, but be a small shower of creds—and favors—for me.

Came out of the scangates, under the high ceilings that show the images of Heaven sky, blue with clouds sculpted into cities, and turned to the guideway. Saw something below the entrygate, off to the right. Dark and shiny. Hard. Wanted to run, 'cause it just screamed creds. Didn't. Ambled, like always, looking around, being the scrounge most take me for. Easier that way. Most at Highport don't know what I do. Suits me fine.

Jumped down and scooped it up. Slipped it inside the greensilver dumper jacket, and jumped back up on the strip beside the guideway, flashing a cred-token.

Hadn't taken two steps when Saalmo was on me. Sleaziest patroller on the west end.

"What you got there, Snark?"

"Cred-token. Some angel dropped it. Didn't want to get dirty." Lied, of course. Nowhere in the Port's dirty. Outside, on the ramps, or in town, that was dirt. One reason why I tried to stay inside as much as I could.

"You sure?" Saalmo oozed more slideless than a guideway mech.

Flashed the cred-token at him, close enough for him to see, but not grab. Real Angel token. Gotten it along with my fifty creds from Derdri a stan earlier for tipping her to a half-cube on the Cherabims' *Celestria*, outbound to Clarkburg. Would have been a hundred for an inbound.

"You got fast fingers, Snark. Thought what you got was darker, bigger."

Belted the cred-token and pulled out my mem. "This?"

Saalmo shook his head. "Better watch it. I heard tell that the Seraphim are going to sweep the whole Port." He laughed. Ugly laugh, the kind that said he knew something, and wouldn't tell me. "Pretty soon, they won't let you move around like a dumper. Dec orbit to nowhere for snarks."

"You've been telling me that for years." Slipped my mem back into the underarm pouch. "We're still here. Need us."

"Not so much as you think, Snark." He shrugged. "Don't listen to me. You never do." He turned and walked to the guideway out to the fareast concourse. He went high-level. Patrollers don't get charged.

I was glad to see him go. Wanted to see what I had, but didn't dare look in the brightzone. Buzzed the accesslock, and took the maintenance ramp. From there walked to the dropshaft—cargo level. Nerod just nodded, let me ride down with the used formulator paks.

Forced myself to wait till I'd made it clear, in the dead alcove under the midbridge. Space two meters by three at the end where the scanners don't reach. Five I'd found over the years that no one else knew about. More than twenty everyone knew. Always keep a scan for the deaders no one else knows.

Took out the dark and shiny case, not much bigger than my palm. Creds wasn't the flame for it. Oligari top comm. Enough netcreds and tools to access every net and portsys. Break anything with my routines.

Entered the owner self-code script. Oligaris got one. All units do. Small holo flared up. Showed an angel, but with short silver-gold hair, and luminous green eyes. Tall, I guessed, but a guess 'cause size doesn't show on the image, and angels are always tall. Nothing special, not for angel. Bothered me. Owner of an Oligari ought to be special, even an angel. No name. Just a code. Smart, that way. Unit lost, and you still couldn't trace her, except through the code.

Figured I could use the comm-breaker, maybe to shoot the stuff for the Sundurco bit—*if* I could find someone who needed eight cubes to Purgatory.

Keyed in the schedreqs, then linked the Oligari into the Portsys with the owner's codes.

Couldn't help grinning. Had every spare cube in Highport flaring into my new toy. Stored the stuff, and transferred it to my mem. No telling how long I could keep the Oligari. Then I headed back the underway to Lorico's. Star-rain was falling outside Highport—big drops. Turn to stars when they hit the permacrete. One flash, and their light's gone, just dull water running over the gray stone. Port's fields do that, but it's still star-rain.

Passed Noryset's. Front parlor looked empty. Always was in mid-day. Dockers don't look for women till they go offshift, and townies aren't welcome. Water seeped over everything. Rains harder in town. Highport fields throw the extra rain at everything around.

Lorico's place is one room, back of Gheratt's. Gheratt does mech-maintenance, the underlevel stuff, at the port. Some in town, too. Lorico's his cousin.

Lorico could pass for a diablo. Pale white skin, square face, red lips, black hair, hint of points at the tip of his ears. That's why he's never in Highport. Angels don't like diablos at Highport, and diablos don't like angels in Purgatory. Goes way back. Some say even before there were translation ships. Wouldn't know. Just know enough that I never set deals where a diablo gets the better of an angel. Don't last long in Highport if you do that.

Slow for Lorico. Had to be. Looked at me. "Morning, Snark. New?"

"Got eight cubes on the *Elept* to Purgatory. Two on the *Milt* to Sansalibre."

"Ferica might want some cubes to Purgatory."

"Didn't see him."

Lorico grinned, showing the pointed white teeth against ruby lips. "He's out on the fareast concourse. Said you snarks weren't around when he needed you."

"Ferica'd get more if he let us come to him."

"You want to tell him that?" asked Lorico.

I laughed. Ferica was a meter taller 'n me, with nano-iron exoskin. "Need a messenger outfit."

"Be five creds, plus pin."

"Five?"

"You'll have to be Carolyi. They're the only outfit whose messengers are allowed there."

"Since when?"

"Last week. When you used a Steganyi messenger outfit on that deal with Zeagat."

"Me? Never did a Steganyi gig."

Lorico laughed.

I had to transfer six creds, then went to the back room. Came out in purple and silver. Hated Carolyi colors.

"You got twenty hours, Snark."

"Can't get it done in three..." Shrugged at Lorico as I left.

Had to use my pass for the upper guideway. Another cred, but messengers didn't take the underway.

On the way to where the concourses branched, I passed the Clearance kiosk. The non-techs go there for level one screening before they get a pass to Heaven. Moyra was talking to a hermit, long beard, brown boots, hair shirt. I kept walking. Pretty girl, she was. Almost angel-beauty, 'cept her hair's brown, not gold or silver-blonde, and she's too short. Taller 'n me, but not angel-tall.

"Snark!"

Hermit had headed off to Heaven concourse. Moyra snaplooked at me, then back down before her. I eased back over to the kiosk.

She didn't look up. Her voice wasn't even a whisper. "Snark, I heard one of the angel captains. She was saying that there are diablos in Highport. They've set up something."

Wondered. Was that set-up me? Saalmo. Had he been in on it? Made sure I'd gotten the Oligari. Why? "Thanks."

"Be careful."

Smiled at her. "Tonight's on me."

She looked up and raised her eyebrows. "You've told me that three times and left me here."

"Not tonight."

"You've said that, too."

Saw a patroller coming and eased away from the kiosk. Messenger wouldn't stop at the kiosk. Been Saalmo, my entry to the fareast concourse be dead. He knows I stop to talk to Moyra. Patroller was a newbie. Didn't even look my way.

Ferica was running guidesnaps outside the gate from Sansalibre. Legit, but just his excuse to prowl the concourses.

Wouldn't pay a hundredth of what he got from his real stuff. Snaps gave a full Highport map, quick call-up, golden lines to the Heaven concourse. Saved souls from Sansalibre could have called up almost the same thing on the port net. Most didn't have mems, though. Understood that the Imperatior didn't allow them. Didn't even like the angels having a consulate there, but even an Imperatior doesn't buck the angels. Not when a single angelfire scout can take down any other system's dreadnought.

Meant that every so often the angels sent saved souls Heavenward, even from Sansalibre. Some even bought Ferica's guidesnaps.

Saw Ferica's gig, and slowed my pace, waiting until the pilgrims all passed him.

"What you got, Snark?"

"Eight prime cubes to Purgatory. Lorico said you might be interested. Also two back to Sansalibre." Sansalibre was a throwaway. Not that much shipped back from Highport to Sansalibre. Other places, but not there.

"Solid cubes?" Ferica sounded bored.

"Solid. Reserved. Failed transfer, non-seeking clause."

"Can take five. Em-cred a cube."

"They want two em-creds. Might be able to get you one and a half for five."

"Try for one and a third."

I backed off and ran the inquiry through. "One point four and you pay clearances."

"Done." Ferica smiled. Teeth looked steel, too. "Pass me the codes."

Raised my eyebrows.

"Two hundred creds for you. And something else."

Would have liked more than two hundred, but I'd been running close to margin. Did owe Moyra a good dinner, up-level in town. "Codes...blue." Used the remote to trigger the transfer.

"Some hotware there, Snark. Careful who knows you're packing it."

"Loaner," I said. "Repaying a favor. Won't have it long." One way or another, I wouldn't. Snark with an Oligari would be a target if it got around, but things had been thin, and the multiple access had already netted me more options than I'd had in months. "Know anyone else who's looking?"

"Galusi—bulk cubes for Clarkburg. Can't pay more than half an em-cred per cube."

"You said..."

"Oh...something you need to watch. Someone knows you got hotware. Snoop look on you."

"Thanks." All I needed. Suspected something like that might happen. Headed farther out on the concourse. Galusi called himself a cargo broker. Had a real office. Small—less than three meters on a side. Real business, but not how or where he made most of his creds. Did removals—usually pilgrims who'd gone to the angels to escape. Folks who used Galusi didn't want recovery—wanted the word spread that even the permanent pilgrimage to Heaven wasn't certain if you cheated them. Never quite understood why the angels didn't shut him down. They could have. Hadn't, though. Not yet.

Ran a few more inquiries on the Oligari as I hustled outbound. Put in an inquiry for Clarkburg. Nothing on regular transit, but thirty bulk cubes on lowlight—take two years. Kept looking. Didn't find much, even with the Oligari, except some cubes available on a semi-level return run to D'Ahoud and hot-space to Alpha Felini. Hot-space—didn't touch that. No one I knew could spring a hundred em-creds a cube. Not even the diablos.

Diablos—they wanted a way around Highport to Heaven. Always had. No one knew where Heaven was. Anyone, anything, going to Heaven went on an angel-ship with an angel crew. Only angels came back from Heaven—except once a decade—when they'd bring back a hundred pilgrims, turn them over to the lower worlds' techs for mem-testing. Supposed to prove that the stories about Heaven were all true. Hel! What did that prove? Angels could doctor anything, even minds.

Only thing it all proved was that they got better ships, better weapons, and better ways of twisting the truth. If you believe such a thing as truth.

Got a bad feeling as I neared the portals for Xianth, but kept going. Shouldn't have.

Three Angels. Beyond the Xianth portals. Waiting. For me.

You can avoid Angels, go around 'em. Don't buck 'em or try to run. Did what I had to. Walked straight to them.

Angel in the center stepped forward. "Mario."

Could tell she was an angel, even without looking. No one calls me Mario.

"Yes." I bowed. No sense in being stupid.

One of their gold-green screens dropped around us. Left me alone with the angel.

"We have a favor to ask. An angel's missing. Somewhere here in Highport. We'd like to find her. Quickly. She's beyond scanners and screens."

"What kind of angel?"

"Does it matter?"

Did to me, but the tall angel wasn't going to tell.

"I haven't heard anything." That was true. Nothing except Moyra's fears I was being set up. "Haven't seen anything."

"If you do..." The angel beamed an access code into the Oligari. The hidden Oligari. Didn't ask. Just beamed. "You'll know what to do, Mario."

The gold-screen curtain went down, and I kept moving toward Galusi's office. Could feel her eyes on my back. Creepy.

Anyone trying anything on the angels, might be Galusi. Stopped for a moment, and took out the Oligari. Snapped up a search and trace routine that would go off when I got inside Galusi's place.

Galusi surprised me. He was there. "You'd better have something good, Snark."

"Heard you were looking for bulk cubes to Clarkburg. How many?"

"I could use twenty. I'll take fifteen."

"You're lucky. Twenty at a tenth of an em-cred."

"I'll take it. Hundred creds for you, and you pass the access codes over now."

Before I had the codes, he'd made the transfer to my links. "Codes coming."

"Hotware for a snark," Galusi said.

"Loaner. Favor. Got to get what I can now."

Galusi snorted. Understood loaners. Better 'n I did. "Later, Snark."

He was nervous. Would have bargained for a lower cubage rate. Didn't. Decided to push. "Saw three angels. Questioning people on the concourse."

"They're not supposed to do that."

"You going to tell an angel no?"

Galusi ignored the question. "Come back when you got cubes to Xianth."

Another way of telling me to get lost. No one ever got cubes to Xianth. Could feel the Oligari taking in the feeds. Decided to get gone. "Later. Could always get lucky."

Galusi laughed.

I was gone. Didn't stop till I was three portals away. Gimmicked the maintenance lock, and slipped down to the nearest dead spot. Unloaded and ran an analyzer on what the track and trace had come up with.

Three feeds from somewhere in Highport. Let the Oligari go to work.

Two were routine availability notices. Third was a double blind, encrypted. Checked the route bounces and the nanosecond delays. Had to have come from the Sandurco concourse. Only place in Highport with those patterns.

Wondered if the angels would pay. Then...might be nothing.

But...the Oligari had put me back in business when I'd needed it. Owed the angel something for that. Besides, didn't hurt to have an angel owing me. Better than the other way around. Lots better.

Headed for the Sandurco concourse.

No one stopped me. High speed guideway cost me ten creds and still took a stan.

Flipped off at portal four. Patrollers check and know the dead spots on the first three. Beyond that...secure spaces under Lesser Worlds' Agreement. Whoever...had to be operating secured. Three possibilities.

Tried another maintenance lock. Opened it, but blew the alarm. Got beyond the monitors, but got no traces—just a long empty secure corridor. Space open and emissions zilch.

Went through the same routine after portal eight.

Down twenty creds, and probably another fifty for the alarm, if the patrollers pushed it.

Portal twenty—best bet, and didn't have to gimmick the lock. Oligari's routine found a Trojhors and had me through. No one on the other side. Not even a monitor, just a long corridor, same as around portal four. Felt different. Kept going. Empty space and more empty space. Nothing.

Didn't have much time before the patrollers or Sandurco privsec showed. Took my toolset, measured the field, reset the ID. Then dug out the spare mem from the pouch under my right arm. Boosted the field, set it with the phony of the Oligari, and then crammed the Oligari's search routine into the spare. Overrode the safeties, and watched.

That much power on the spare mem—burn it out in less than a stan. Oligari ran that hot forever, but didn't want to do that kind of hackjob on the Oligari.

Took two minutes.

Hotspot a hundred meters ahead, and down fifty. Meant that someone had built a hideaway underground. Not many places near Highport where the fields allow that. Wondered how I'd get down there.

Access hatch and drop shaft behind a phony barrier. Used the back-up mem to fry the lock. Mem was half-gone anyway. Then took the drop at double speed and burst through the screen.

Big fellow, like Ferica, except he had white teeth and was reaching for a burner. Behind him was a pair of gene-overclone cradles. Looked like a med sculptech, renegade. Could find out later.

I didn't wait. Kept moving. May be small, but I'm not slow. Or stupid. Was inside his burner and had my ceramic blade up through his gut to the base of his heart before he could squeeze the trigger.

Burner still blazed across my shoulder. Hurt. Lots. Could barely see. Still managed to knock the burner to the floor. Kicked it out of the way. Sculptech sagged down, dying. He could take his time now.

Two women in the cradles. Restrained. Both naked. Beautiful. Identical. Silver-blond hair, tall, luminous green eyes, fine noses, but strong. Gene-tags'd show them the same.

Both looking at me. Neither spoke.

I couldn't either. Shoulder was hurting more, not less.

Forced another look around the lab. On the shelf to the left of the console was a wide belt, green, trimmed in gold. On the temphook stuck to the wall was a pilot's uniform—AngeLines.

I knew why the angel hadn't told me who the missing woman was. And Saalmo hadn't set me up. The angels had. Someone had wanted me to know what the missing woman looked like, and to have the right equipment.

Slipped the Oligari close enough to the consoles to run a diagnostic. Not one the angels or the Highport admin would have approved. Got a whole web of choices. Could have played games with the angels. No percentage in it.

Accessed the code the angels had given me.

"I've got your missing pilot—and the set up." Fed the coordinates from the Oligari into the web.

"We've got it. Don't move." That was the head angel.

Wasn't about to move. First, doubted I'd get far. Second, had other ideas. Could have waited for the angels, but...infosnarks have their pride.

Both women in the cradles looked at me. Finally, the one on the right moistened her lips.

Asked her, "How did they catch you?"

"It was a sophisticated sonic trap. There was a dead zone on one side of the corridor. I stepped around the maintenance floater, and they had me."

Probably the way it was, too. I turned to the other one, on the left. "What do you have to say?"

"It doesn't matter. They'll sort it out."

There was a quiet sadness in her voice. I knew why. So I stepped up to the console and triggered the releases on her cradle. "Better get your uniform on before they arrive."

The woman still in the cradle swallowed.

"I'd have thought you'd let her escape," offered the real angel. "We couldn't do that much to her."

"Not that cruel," I pointed out. "Couldn't do that to anyone. She'd be taken for a fallen angel. They don't last long. Whoever set this up...they knew that."

I didn't say any more because the side doors irised open. Angels and patrollers swarmed inside. The overclone was still in restraints. She didn't even swear.

Lead angel ignored the corpse. She had some kind of scanner. Ran the beam over both women. Then she turned to me. "How did you know, Mario?"

"Wouldn't be much of a snark, if I didn't, would I?" Turned to the head angel and offered her the Oligari, with my left hand. Right wouldn't move. "This belongs to one of yours."

She frowned, then reached out. Touched my shoulder. Lifted away the pain. Then she looked at the burner. "Hold still. This is going to hurt."

Thought what the burner did had hurt, but what she did was sheer agony. Except when she finished, the pain was gone. Just a dull ache.

"It will still take a few days to heal completely. Don't lift anything heavy."

I offered the Oligari again.

She smiled. Didn't take it. "Keep it, Mario. You earned it."

Wasn't sure I wanted it. Make me top snark in Highport, for sure, but there's more 'n being top snark that way. Besides, Ferica or someone would make me a mark, so long as I had it.

I handed it to her. "Wouldn't be right." Wouldn't have been. She understood...in a way. "What would you like?"

"A few creds...and I'd like to see the pilot's ship lift off."

"We'll have to hurry."

So they let me come, up three levels, and on the superguide to the middle of Heaven concourse. I'd never been there. No one sees it except angels, and pilgrims, the saved souls only once. They escorted me all the way through the portal and to the transfer deck.

Everyone stopped there.

The pilot I'd found looked at me with those luminous green eyes.

Knew she'd never be back. Not to Highport. She'd seen too much, and the angels would find some way to keep her on Heaven. She knew it, too. Didn't say anything, but I could tell.

The angels behind us reinforced that.

Pilot looked toward the transdeck. "I have to preflight."

"Have a good trip." Didn't know what else to say.

Stood with the lead angel and watched the screen for a good stan before the golden needle flared, vanished into overspace.

Then I turned.

Head angel looked at me. "There are five hundred creds in your account, Mario, and an open passage to Heaven. Open your whole life. No matter what."

Could tell she meant it. "Thank you. Not ready for that."

"We know."

Neither of us spoke as she escorted me back to the main concourse, left me there not a hundred meters from Moyra. Wondered if that was an accident. Didn't think so.

Waited out of sight of the kiosk for another half-stan, till just before Moyra's shift ended. Then sauntered up.

"Said I'd be here. Your choice. Any place in town—upper level."

Her mouth opened. Then she closed it and smiled.

Moyra and I—we slipped through the rain so quick that the star drops didn't touch either of us, water or light. Kept running, but not from Highport. Come morning, we'd be back, same as always. I was a snark. Couldn't be one anywhere else.

Still...couldn't, wouldn't get the image out of my mind. The proud and tall lady, beautiful, as all angels are, with the darkness of hell behind those green, green eyes. Standing on the transdeck, call it the dock to Heaven, a place she'd never see again, screen behind her showing stars falling around her...and not knowing that she'd already missed life.

Moyra and I had that.

FIND A PIN
Ru Emerson

IT STARTED OUT as a good day. I had a little money that the lady at the mission had given me the night before—enough for sausage biscuits and Cokes at McDonald's. That put Momma in a good enough mood that she didn't notice all the people giving us the kinda looks street people like us get. She even took her meds without a protest for once, washing them down with the last of her Coke.

I've always been the only one who could ever get the meds down Momma. She says at the Salem State Hospital, they had to put her in restraints, like she's proud of it. She went in, for the first time, when I was six, and stayed in for six months. She was in and out after that, until they closed the hospitals.

It was nice and warm for a change, when we got outside McDonald's. Time to go see if we could find any cans or bottles to recycle at a nickle a can. I had the two plastic Safeway bags I always carry, and handed one to Momma. She found three beer cans right away, tucked in the bushes outside the McDonald's, and I found four along the side of the tracks.

Then I saw sun glinting off a slender bit of metal. A straight-pin. One of the long, fancy ones with a bright red head on it. Funny place to find a pin, but then, you can find just about anything on the streets, if you're used to looking. I pinched it off the ground between my thumb and forefinger and threaded it into my collar. The old doggerel came to me, then. "Find a pin, pick it up," I chanted. Momma slapped at my hand and said, "Lisa Marie, you drop that pin right now! You're gonna poke yourself, swell up and get typhoid and die!"

There never was a good time to argue with Momma, so I just said, "No I won't, on account of the pointy bit is buried in

my shirt-collar and besides, Momma, you and I both got our
tetanus boosters at the Free Clinic last month, remember?"
Momma shrugged and turned away. "I dint get no shot.
Nobody cares if I live or not."

Old turf, not worth discussing. It worries me that she
doesn't remember things very good, sometimes. The phar-
macist at the clinic, where we get her meds, told me we should
get her checked in case it's Alzheimer's, but what good would
it do if I knew?I spotted something sparkling in the long grass
behind the train-tracks. "Momma, think you got a can or two
over there." I pointed.

Momma went over to paw through the tall grass, and came
up hooting. Four loose cans—and a twelve-pack box that was
totally full. "Hey, Lisa Marie, honey, we're rich!" she giggled.

"Hey, Momma, we're always rich, right?" I replied.

That was what Dad used to say. He and Momma married
right out of high school. Her folks—Nona and Popsy—were
so pleased their girl was gonna be a wife and mother. *His* folks
always thought Dad married beneath him and ruined his life,
on account of he was gonna be a lawyer, like his Dad. Dad
always laughed that off—like he did most things in life. "Got
you, got Mom, what else do I need?" he say. And, "My folks
got their priorities wrong, you remember that, Lisa, honey.
Money doesn't count as much as family does. But if we got
each other, we're always rich."

*I remember our first apartment—the one where I was born. I had
my own bedroom, and the wallpaper was pale blue with pink roses on
it. The street was quiet and nice and I could play in the yard, any time
I wanted. I only learned later on that Momma and Dad were Living
on The Edge even back then, on account of she didn't have job skills
and was getting a little odd anyway, and he had a bad heart from
having rheumatic fever as a teenager. Reason we had a good apartment was because Nona and Popsy helped with the rent.*

I looked at Momma and rubbed the pin-head thoughtfully.
Back when she was sewing for me, Momma would never buy
that kind, because they cost too much. Pins like that were

"spendy", she said. She got material from the bargain shelves at Penneys, but she picked careful, and she never needed a pattern. And I was probably the best-dressed kid in my class all the way through grade school.

Momma had to give up sewing about the time I went into junior high. We had to take the scissors and even the pins away from her, like we had to hide all the kitchen knives, because she kept trying to cut herself.

Momma gathered up her cans, and I did the math. "We got enough, Momma," I said. "Let's go to the Safeway and cash them in." We headed west along 12th Street and wound up at the small Safeway store, where they had a set of fancy new outside machines for people to deposit their own cans, then go in with a ticket to get paid. Momma liked the machines a lot; liked the funny noises they made when the took a can and crunched it. I put my bag of cans where she could get it, and looked around. Lot of times, people make Momma nervy, especially little kids.

A big, old faded copper-colored LTD rolled slowly along toward the store as Momma started shoving cans into the nearest machine, mumbling to herself. A thinnish woman in bright red clothes, with even redder hair, got out, looked at Momma and at me and smiled at me, to my surprise. After all, I don't exactly look like your normal office worker...

I was an office worker. Had been. Not that many years back. I had to quit because Dad was gone thanks to his last heart attack, and Momma—well, she wasn't up to being able to cope by herself. I left the job before they could fire me. Momma scared the receptionist, they said.

"Honey," the lady said then, "you are the answer to a prayer." She got in the back seat of that big old car and brought out an enormous black plastic garbage bag. "I have been carrying this around for days, and just don't have the time to run them through the machine. Would you like them?"

I gazed at the bag in awe. There must have been six dollars worth of cans in there. I managed a smile then, and held out my hand for it. "Thank you very much, ma'am," I said. She just got back in her big old car and took off, waving a hand as she turned onto the street.

It turned out to be one hundred forty-four pop cans, the limit for one day's return. Momma and I split them up and it took a long time to get them all in. I took the receipts and rubbed the head of that pin. Luck for sure.

When Popsy lost his shirt in that big stock market crash, they couldn't help us any more. We moved to a smaller apartment, then an even smaller one, where I had to sleep on the couch. Momma wouldn't let me play outside after dark there. Dad started having more heart problems and couldn't work much. We wound up in one of those courts on Portland Road, near where a lot of hookers worked. Each time, it seemed like things couldn't possibly get worse, but they always did. When Dad died that year, I had left school so I could work, but with him not there to care for Mom—well, we had enough money left to keep that shabby little apartment for six months. After that, there wasn't anywhere to go except Dad's old Subaru station wagon. One day, when we were off scrounging cans and things, someone called and had the car towed, so after that, it was the Mission or under the bridge.

Things weren't really so bad for us, most of the time. Not really. At this point, there really wasn't any farther down to go, and I'd gotten used to things the way they were. Sometimes there'd be a little money, but if there wasn't, we could get meals at the Mission or one of the churches. One of the really fancy churches downtown would let us use their shower a couple days a week. Momma and I slept under the bridge, where a lot of people do, but we didn't have to worry about guys trying something because Ed Henderson let everyone know he looked out for us, and Ed's a big guy. Whenever I could afford for a washer and the little box of soap, old Hattie Moran did laundry for herself, me and Momma since I couldn't take Momma in a Laundromat cause people stared and Momma'd start ranting and cussing.

Momma—I was all she had, and that was that.

Inside the Safeway, the nice clerk was working checkout, instead of the snooty one who looks at us like we smell bad, and won't put the money in my hand. We wound up with almost eight dollars, so I bought Momma a little bag of Cheetos, since she likes those a lot, and got me one of nacho flavored chips. I waited until we got back outside to store the rest of the money in the cloth zip-bag I have pinned to my bra, so no one can take it.

"I wanna go watch the ducks," Momma announced, clutching her snack two-handed. "There's a bench, isn't there? We can sit and watch the ducks and I can eat these."

"That's a great idea, Momma," I said, and I was pleased because she hardly ever *does* want to do things, just trails along grumbling when I suggest something. "It'll be cooler down by the creek anyway." Momma walks pretty fast when she gets an idea in her head, so I was pretty hot and winded by the time we got to the other side of downtown. It was after lunch hour, so there were just a couple of people walking by. We found an empty bench in the shade, right next to the water. Just below us, two green-headed mallards, and a she-duck with some half-grown chicks were paddling around.

Momma got comfortable, tore open her packet and began eating Cheetos, eyes fixed on the ducks. I had about ten of my chips, then stowed the rest in the carry-bag I keep my stuff in, so I'd have something if I got hungry later. Momma ate every last crumb of hers and gave me a silly grin. "I got orange fingers, Lisa Marie," she said, and waggled them at me.

"You can wash 'em in the fountain, probably," I told her. She carefully licked all the crumbly stuff off them first. Just then, an idea came to me. "Know what, Momma?" I said. "We got a lot of money here, for us. I think today's the day we get to ride the carousel."

Her eyes got round, but then she shook her head. "Honey, we can't afford that. It's a dollar each, and there won't be some lady giving us a bag of cans like that—ever again probably."

I tipped my collar out and rubbed the head of that dressmaker pin. "Maybe not—but maybe it'll happen. But you'd like to, wouldn't you?" I knew she would. We were all the time going down to that new Riverfront Park where they built that fancy new carousel, and she'd just stand there listening to the music and staring at it like anything. She was gonna shake her head again, I could tell, so I said, "I'd really love to do it, Momma."

Well, that was all it took. It was only about three blocks from where we were, thank goodness, because Momma walked even faster to get to that park.

There were maybe five cars in the parking lot, and a big silver SUV pulled in just as we got there. I pulled two paper dollars out of my zip-bag and walked up to the ticket booth. "Two, please," I said, and hoped there wasn't gonna be someone stuffy back there who'd find a reason we couldn't ride.

The luck was still there, though I almost wished I'd never thought of the carousel when I realized it was a guy I'd gone to high school with. He stared, and I know I did. "Lisa, is that you?" he asked finally.

I nodded, stunned and horribly embarrassed. I knew he could tell right now what we were and where we lived. "Bobby? What're you doing here?" I asked as Momma walked slowly into the big room where the carousel lived, her eyes just shining.

"Oh, I did a lot of the volunteer work when they were building this," he waved a hand at it, "and I just stayed on. It suits me." It did that. Bobby Rayburn'd never been what you'd call ambitious. "Here," he added, and he pushed four tickets across the counter, along with my money.

"I can't –!" I began, but he shook his head.

"Ladies' day," he said with that funny little smile of his. I could hear the woman behind me grumbling about the delay, and one of her kids whining, so I just smiled back, picked up my stuff and went on in. I heard the woman say something to Bobby about 'people like that' in here at a family attraction, but Bobby just laughed and said, "They're nice ladies, and their money's as good as anyone's." I guess she didn't know what to say to that, because she shut up and took her kids around the other side of the carousel to wait for it to stop.

Momma took her tickets, looked at them and said, "Honey, that's half your money, you can't do that!"

"He gave 'em to me," I told her. She looked at the tickets, at me, then reached out and rubbed the head of that pin.

"Lucky you found that," she said, and as the carousel slowed, "I wanna ride the zebra. Think your luck'll let me get it before someone else does?"

"Bet it will," I said. And sure enough, it did. The woman with the kids gave us a dirty look as her three little whiners found horses way away from us. Momma was too happy to notice. She stroked the zebra's neck, and actually smiled at the ticket-man when he came around to collect them.

It was a really nice ride, and I was sorry when it was over. A little dizzy, too. Momma needed me to hold onto her arm as we left the building and started for the sidewalk. The woman with the kids had bought two rides apiece for all of them. I couldn't imagine having that much money, let alone that much to spend on rides.

Her little boy started whining when she got off, though, and she had a hard grip on his hand. "Brian Jared, I told you we did not have that much time. We have to get your brother at soccer camp." She got the kids past Momma and me at double speed and shooed them into the back seat of that big old silver SUV, and already had her phone in her hand before she got in and shut the driver's door.

"See, Momma?" I said. "Life isn't so bad for us, now, is it? We could be rushing here and there like that woman."

"All them whiny kids," Momma said, but she was still in a good mood from the carousel ride and didn't go on about them. She came around to touch the head of my pin again. "Sure is funny about that. How long do you think the luck'll last?"

I shrugged. "Could be a long time, or maybe just to-day." We reached the curb and I pushed the button for the Walk sign.

"Better find another then pretty quick," Momma said, her eyes moving along the gutter and out on the street. "Hey!" she called out then. "Lookit!" I looked where she was pointing. She by golly *had* found a pin, some little round circle jewelry thing, that had maybe been lost out of a car, out near the lane-divider line. Before I realized what she was up to, she darted out to pick it up.

The car in the middle lane managed to stop and the ones in the right lane were pretty far back. Unfortunately. Because the busy woman in the silver SUV didn't even bother to stop for the red light; she just saw there was room for her big van-thing, and she goosed it around the corner. Momma went sailing like a rag doll, clear over the thing, and came down in the crosswalk.

The SUV tried to take off, they told me later, but a pickup truck blocked her way. I didn't see anything but Momma. There wasn't any blood to speak of and she looked like she was sleeping, except for a scrape on her cheek. I wanted to go touch her, but I somehow couldn't move.

I could hear. The woman yelling at somebody, "My children are going to be scarred by this for life! That horrid, dirty old woman must have done that on purpose! No one's children should have to see something like that!"

Bobby spoke up from just behind me. "Ma'am, you ask Lisa here about that. That was her mother you hit." Well, that shut her up. Bobby got me to sit on a bench, and got me some water. The ambulance people came right away and Momma was really gone then. Then the cops and the newspaper people came. I hadn't meant to say anything. I didn't think I could. But the gray-haired cop was nice and the reporter sympathetic, and somehow, a lot came out. About me and Momma, and Living on the Edge. One Edge after another, all my life.

There was a big article in the paper the next day, I guess. Ed told me about it. I felt embarrassed by all the fuss, and never did read it. I felt guilty, not stopping Momma somehow, but Ed talked to me about that, too. "Maybe it was a blessing for her, Lisa, honey." He'd picked it up from Momma calling me that. "You gave her a really great day, she had special treats and finally got to ride that merry-go-round and she couldn't have known a thing when that big old station wagon hit her." He rubbed the head of that dressmaker pin. "So maybe it was good luck in a way, for her. She was a mighty unhappy lady, most of her life. And this is no place for a young girl like you. Now, maybe you can have a chance at getting out from under this bridge." I shook my head at that, but he just said, "Lisa, honey, I keep telling you, you're too darn pretty to be a troll."

Well, that made me laugh, like it always did. But I couldn't think about that, not just yet. It felt disloyal to Momma, like I'd just been waiting for her to die so I could get a real life. Besides, I didn't know where I'd start.

Turned out, I didn't need to do a thing. After that article came out, people suddenly wanted to do things to help. A lawyer came down to the Mission and told the lady there that he'd handle things for me so that woman couldn't get out of paying for Momma to have a decent funeral and so on. A lady from a helping service came down under the bridge and explained to me and some other people how they got people like us nice clothes and taught us how to go on interviews so we could get work. A couple of people came around to offer me money, just give it to me, but I felt funny about taking what I hadn't earned, so I turned them down.

And I guess the woman with the SUV was feeling kinda shabby about how she'd acted, because the lawyer didn't need to do anything. The woman's insurance paid for a decent, quiet funeral for Momma and burial next to Dad, and she put money in a savings account for me, to use for rent.

It's been a year. I'm working in an office again, filing and answering the phones while I learn how to type, and use a computer again. I'm learning how to just talk to ordinary people again, and how not to feel like I'm an outsider. I've got a room at the YWCA for now, because it's close to work and the library, and I can walk, and I'm right on the bus line if I want to go anywhere else. Don't know that I'll ever want to drive a car, or ever feel I can afford to own one, though I've got money in the bank. I'd like to keep it there, because it keeps The Edge away. I still wear that dressmaker pin, but on the underside of my shirt collars, where people can't see it. That was in the paper article, Ed told me, and I felt foolish about people knowing that.

Bobby and I see each other now and again, but mostly because I go down and ride the carousel once a month, and think of Momma and how happy she was, perched on that zebra and grinning like she owned the world. Like I said, he's not exactly ambitious, and I figure if I'm not ready to make a lot of friends just yet, I'm sure not ready for a boyfriend.

Mostly, I'm just getting used to being responsible for myself. I know The Edge is there. But from now on, I decide how close I get to it.

SAILING TO THE TEMPLE
Alan Smale

AFTER A SUMMER spent kneeling at temples, the market at Nakasu-ichi, where the rivers met, seemed perilously close to Heaven.

Walking through the bustle of cheerful commerce Yajiro saw peasant women selling lengths of colored cloth alongside bearded purveyors of animal hides from the mountains. Each hawker and trader stood on his own bale of straw, shouting his best price over the sea of bamboo hats that boiled around his shoulders. Here were sacks of rice, yellow millet and sorghum; there, baskets of water chestnuts, melons, radishes, and sweet potatoes. Women knelt by their cooking pots, tending to their fires and calling the exotic names of broths thick with noodles and dumplings. The quickness and exuberance of life sparkled off every brass cup and cheap bauble.

Yajiro experienced a moment of perfect clarity. Maybe he belonged here, and not on his knees on a grass mat before a sterile golden altar. Even Buddha spent time as a prince, a man of the world, and a husband before choosing a life of holiness.

Then again, maybe this was Temptation, here to be resisted.

"Guide you around the market, sir!" A hatless urchin, his grimy face empty of guile, appeared from nowhere and attached himself to Yajiro's belt.

Yajiro gently pried himself free. "I think I can find my way to the river from here."

"Ah, but I know everybody, sir! Find you a special price!"

"I'm sure you would." Yajiro smiled and walked past him to the quayside.

Boats were plentiful here at the meeting of the waters, and Yajiro found he could drive a hard bargain with the jerkin-clad boatmen, even with Tsuru the urchin bobbing

underfoot, interrupting at every turn. A fisherman's boat would
have been his best deal, but pride and the money he had earned
blacksmithing between temple visits pushed him to settle on a
fur-trader's boat with a covered storage area in the stern and
sails which showed off their previous owner's skill with the
needle. Whatever Yajiro's final destiny might be, for the moment it was enough to have left his parents' home riding a
mule and wearing rags, and return by water in a tunic, breeches,
and hat, like an honest trader. Perhaps it might soften the blow
to their honor when they found out that their second son had
failed to win acceptance with any of the teachers at the temples
along the road.

Money changed hands, and the boat was his.

"Captain, sir! You'll need a crew for the voyage!" Tsuru
again, making as if to step down into the boat. Yajiro grabbed
him by his collar and placed him firmly on the quay, looking to
see if there was any sign of the boy's mother.

His gaze lingered on a slender girl with long black hair who
knelt behind a straw bale twenty paces away, holding a necklace
of shells in both hands. A middle-born woman with a bag over
one shoulder turned to examine it.

A short weasely man sidestepped quickly to keep himself
out of the middle-born's sight. Nobody but Yajiro paid him
any particular attention.

Brazen as a magpie, the man slipped his hand into the
middle-born's sack.

Yajiro wondered whether he should notice. Footpads and
fleas were equally common in riverside markets, and usually
found together. Yajiro could get a blade in his gut for his trouble,
or he could step in successfully and the middle-born could still
be robbed three more times before she got home. Why did she
not bring a servant to look out for her?

It must be a test. The gods were at last giving him the chance
to show his worth. If he'd *wanted* to intervene, it wouldn't be a
test, would it?

Tsuru tugged at his arm. Yajiro brushed him off. "Stay here."

The sun glinted off something golden, shiny and rectangular as the weasel drew his hand from the sack. Yajiro's hand closed around his wrist at the same moment.

The weasel was a head shorter than Yajiro, and thin, but he had a wiry strength. Finding himself snared, he cracked his arm like a whip and dropped down onto his haunches to try to break the hold. The middle-born was still turning to see what was happening as the footpad's other fist landed in Yajiro's gut.

Long hours at the anvil gave rewards more tangible than mere wages. Yajiro gasped but was not winded. He tore the golden box from the thief's hand and pushed him away. The middle-born took a step back, her eyes widening, as the weasel danced out of range and ran into the crowd.

The box was as long as his hand, wide as his clenched fist, and a little deeper than the length of his thumb. For all its gilt finishing and iron corners it was not heavy. Yajiro glimpsed some characters engraved into the gold.

"Your property, Lady," he said quickly, lest the woman should fear that she had merely exchanged a short thief for a taller one. "My thanks at having been permitted to do you this service."

She snatched the box from his hands. "Service?"

Yajiro was startled by her tone, but his attention was drawn away. An open space was clearing around them, and he saw eyes lowered, faces averted, a nod here, a movement there.

"Permit me to suggest one more service that I might do you," said Yajiro. "There is a gang working here, and we have drawn attention. I have a boat."

"You suggest I am afraid?" she said, drawing her cloak around herself.

"I suggest you may end the day with your throat cut and your treasures sold to buy wine. I do not have your courage; please forgive me if I withdraw."

And, having done the minimum to ensure he would not be whipped for impertinence, he ran for the boat.

"Captain, sir!" said the urchin. "You will need a deck-hand!"

"Stay where you are." Yajiro flipped him a coin, cast off the rope, and jumped into the boat. It rocked beneath him. "Where is your mother?"

"She is lost, sir!"

He thrust the oars into the rowlocks. "Go to the market shrine and ask for the priest. He will help you find her."

The boat swayed again as the middle-born stepped down into it and took a seat at the stern. She did not meet his eye, but gazed coolly out over the river.

Yajiro took a long pull at the oars. A ribbon of water appeared between the boat and the wharf. He pulled again.

"Farewell then, Captain!" shouted Tsuru. "May we meet again soon!"

Yajiro did not spare the breath to reply.

Alert faces appeared at the water's edge. The weasel, hands on hips, watched them go, his face unreadable. Yajiro bent his back again, and the prow of his boat cut the river.

Four hundred feet from the wharf he felt a tugging at the bows as the boat began to turn into the gentle current. He shipped the oars and sucked breath deep into his lungs. Cool sweat began to dry on his forehead. His passenger still hadn't so much as glanced at him.

"Welcome aboard," said Yajiro, and bowed. "You honor me and my humble vessel."

"You are a fool, and you should have kept yourself to yourself."

This was gratitude? "But, you were being robbed..."

"Yes. And then, because of you, I was suddenly in fear for my life, and you yours. Was it clever of you, do you think? *Do you?*"

Yajiro busied himself with setting the mast and arranging the lines, all the while keeping an eye out for movement ashore. There were no signs of pursuit. Maybe it was over.

She continued, "Life is precious. A box may be replaced."

"You are quite right," said Yajiro stiffly. "I should have turned my face away and not intruded into your affairs. Forgive me."

He realized he was quivering with fear. He had rough-housed with his brothers, but had never before risked his life. It was not glamorous to know he could have lost everything for the sake of a middle-born's trinket.

If he had died there, would it have been good *sukuse*, good *karma*, or bad?

The tests set by the gods were hard indeed.

She tapped the thwart impatiently. "We should hurry. Is something the matter?"

"Excuse me," said Yajiro. "The sail is in the space beneath your seat."

He threaded the halyard through the eyes on the sail's edge. It was a good, stout piece of cloth. Maybe he would sail on, all the way down the river to the sea, and keep going into the wasteland of the ocean until its immensity swallowed him up. Maybe the gods would think well of him then.

Yajiro had not planned to come this way at all. The quickest way home to Haruno lay along the South Road, where he might have hitched a ride on an ox-cart, or at least found a companion to walk and build a fire with. But south was an unlucky direction for him this month, and he had faced a stark choice; travel even further from home, or take the East Road through the hills and then follow the river as it wound gently southwest towards Haruno.

As he hoisted the sail, he wondered if he had chosen the right course.

He mounted the flatboards in place on either side of the boat, so that it would not skip sideways across the water when he sailed against the wind. They changed places awkwardly so he could take the tiller.

The boat leaned as the moderate breeze filled the triangle of gray cloth. Today's breeze blew upriver, so they were helped by the current but had to work against the wind. Yajiro pulled in the sheet, and they began to tack.

The market shrank behind them until it was just a dark patch against the swath of trees. The hiss of the water was like the touch of soft fingers against his forehead, and the fear drained from him. He breathed deeply in the first exercise of Right Mindfulness, attentive to his sailing, giving his whole mind and body to the task.

She had been silent for so long that he jumped when she spoke. "Will we sail past the temple?"

"Which?" he said, for there were many.

"Kenno-ji."

Four days downstream the river would begin the slow curve out of forestland and into the plains. Two days beyond that, Yajiro would come home to Haruno. Kenno-ji lay on the riverbank nearly half way to the plains.

"We will pass Kenno-ji," he said.

"You may let me off there."

Two days with this woman. Yajiro said carefully, "Lady, I am sure my boat is too rude and lacking in the amenities to be a comfortable vessel for so long a journey."

"By no means. I have known worse lodgings, and a variety of less gentle forms of transport. Would you abandon me in the trees instead?"

It was true. No major roads intersected the river much to the north of Kenno-ji. He sighed. "It will be my pleasure to escort you to the temple."

"You breathe like a novice," she said. "You must draw the air deeper, to the seat of your body." She patted herself on the navel.

Her voice was critical, but its tone a little less strident. "I am less than a novice," said Yajiro. "I have supplicated to many temples this summer, and none would take me, for I was not worthy."

"Who is Miroku Bosatsu?"

By the formal way she asked, Yajiro knew it was a test. Teachers, gods, even strangers on his boat saw fit to test him. "He is the Buddha who is to come," he said shortly.

"Then you are less than a novice, but more than a peasant. Others of your class do not know a Buddha from a bamboo tree, and worship stones and rainclouds."

Yajiro gripped the tiller a little more tightly, but the spirits of the river did not tip the boat in defense of their companions of earth and air.

"Ah," she said. "I see the peasant is still there. No matter. We each grow at our own pace."

They were creeping too close to the other shore. Yajiro took in the sail and came about to take the other tack. When the boat was purring along again and he had the leisure, he looked at her more carefully. Thin as the mast and as straight, her clothes marked her as middle-born but her voice gave her the air of the upper-middle class. She was about the same age as his mother, but now he saw that she was frailer.

He was not surprised to find her studying him just as intently. "You interest me," she said. "How did you come here?"

"From the East Road," he said.

She tutted. "Men your age are in the rice fields, or at best indentured to a tradesman. But you are free as a bird, walking to temples and spending coins at the market. Do not avoid my question. Are you a fugitive?"

He was stung. "Of course not. My name is Yajiro. My parents were farmers at Haruno, downstream from here, until my first sister wed one of the deputy estate managers of our daimyo. My elder brother now guides the work in the village, and my parents gave me leave to enter a temple and bring the teachings of the Buddha back to the village. At least that was my intention."

Her eyes were narrowed. Yajiro suddenly realized he had overstepped himself; to one of her rank, people of his class existed only to labor and serve. Were they on land and she with others of her kind, she could have had him whipped for his ambitions. He bowed low, and the sail flapped as the boat swung off the tack. "Please forgive me. I babble of things I do not understand."

She sighed. "Yajiro, Yajiro. My name is Ume, and you are not my servant. I was born a very long time ago, and I think I will die very soon. You're a strong, healthy young man, and you have no idea what I would give to be young again, whatever the class of the body I would have to wear."

He raised his head and stared.

She went on. "Let me tell you this. I've spent the last few years high in the mountains with a clan of men and women from all over Japan, and we never once discussed how high-born or low-born we were. It was enough that we all thought alike, and sought the same goals." She was studying him again with that intense, almost frightening gaze. "Yajiro, when you walk further down the Path maybe you will learn to know which things matter, and which do not. I would like to be your friend for a while, so please stop bobbing your head and being honored and all the rest of it. It quite exhausts me."

It was the strangest speech he had ever heard. Yajiro could not imagine being with a person and not knowing or caring what rank they held. The idea made him feel adrift, without bearings.

But worse than what she said was the manner in which she said it. The very language they spoke was rigidly structured along lines of family and social class. That day Yajiro had addressed the boat trader, the urchin, and Ume using three very different styles and phrasings. Each had responded to him using the same code, reflecting back to him his own status in their eyes.

But Ume had just broken the pattern. She still used the heavy and sarcastic tone that a superior used to an inferior but the words and inflections themselves were those of a woman to her social equal, even a close friend. Yajiro was buffeted by a gale of contradictions. What did this woman want from him? Was she mad, or dangerous? What manner of test was this?

He felt the boat slowing as they sailed into the lee of the shore again, and seized the chance to cover his confusion.

"Coming about," he said. "Watch your head, Ume-san."

The boat turned, the boom swung, Ume pulled herself to the other side of the boat, and then they were speeding across the water again, away from the trees.

She was waiting for his reply. Yajiro said carefully, "Thank you for your words. I would like to be your friend, and I'm glad we can put our anger behind us." He spoke with the phrasings he would have used to a respected aunt. It was the best he could do.

"What reasons did they give for not accepting you at the temples?"

"All the masters said the same. That there was no stillness in me. Every student has to have a patch of stillness in his heart, where the truth can take hold and grow."

"You're young," she said bitterly. "Plenty of time later for stillness."

There was a ragged edge to her voice. Yajiro took his eyes off the sail. She was leaning on one arm, clutching the other hand to her chest. Pain creased her forehead. "Ume?" Her name meant 'plum-blossom', and he suddenly saw how fragile she was.

She reached into her bag and placed the golden box on the seat beside her. Next, she pulled out something that looked like a piece of tree root and bit off its tip. He saw her jaws working. A thin bubble of saliva appeared in the corner of her mouth.

The root seemed to ease the pain. She took a drink from his water-skin, and looked straight into his eyes. He tried not to flinch.

"This old body will be dead soon," she said. "It won't be long now, I think." She was looking at him very directly. Very oddly. "I hope to make it to Kenno-ji, but I want you to forgive me now if I do not."

Yajiro had dealt with dead bodies before. His uncle, his youngest sister. Neighbors. Contact with the diseased or dead would pollute him, but he could bathe and fast to cleanse himself. "It's all right. You won't be a burden to me. Please rest."

She looked at the box. "That's not really what I meant."

"What, then?"

She did not answer, but picked up the box again and held it for a moment, not meeting his eyes. Then she put it back into her bag.

Yajiro awoke to daylight and a clammy mist that shrouded the boat and cut them off from the shore. Its tendrils stroked his face; its spore gleamed against the wood of the seats and hull.

When he raised his head he saw Ume sitting bolt upright in the bows with the sail wrapped about her shoulders, staring at him. "What?" he managed to say.

Her voice was strong again and sarcastic, loaded with middle-born poison. "Have you ever had to do something terrible?"

Mind reeling, he sat upright and blinked away the last tatters of sleep. He could see twenty feet of water beyond the gunwales, and then nothing but a soft gray-white curtain.

"No. What's the matter? What have you done?"

"Tell me the worst sin you've ever committed. Before the gods."

Demons flickered in her eyes. He searched his life, desperate for something that might satisfy her. There was no adultery, no theft. No dark evils lurked within him. He wanted to obey her, but he'd lived a clean life. He'd sought the priesthood; how else could it have been for him?

"Pride?" he said hopefully.

"Ah, pride." She looked across the water, and seemed to see a great deal more in the distance than Yajiro did. "Pride. If only that were the gravest sin *I* could muster. You're too good. Too good..." Her fingers brushed her heart, and the first beginnings of a breeze touched the calm surface of the water.

He tried again. "Envy?"

Unexpectedly, she laughed. It was a jagged sound. "You're a stone, Yajiro. I want to hate you, but how can I hate a stone? Or a sunset?"

Madness. It could only be madness. And he with no knowledge of even which shore was the closest. Yajiro reached cautiously forward to the mast, and saw that the golden box was lying in the bottom of the boat, closer to him than to her.

"What of my soul?" she said. "What will become of my soul?"

"You make no sense at all. You should rest."

But he could not focus on her. The box held his attention. All at once it seemed to become the center of the boat, the center of the world. The box was everything. The key to all he did not understand about this strange woman whose moods turned from sunshine to thunder and back as easily as he tacked back and forth across the water.

She saw where his eyes were fixed. "Do you want it?" she whispered. "If you like it, you can have it. I mean it."

Anything with power like that was not for him. He forced himself to sit back. "No. I don't want it."

The box *watched* him like a dragon's eye.

There was no escape.

"Tell me about the box," he said.

She raised an eyebrow with definitive middle-born imperiousness. "You *command* me?" Amusement tinged the iron tone of her voice.

Yajiro set his jaw. "Yes. You are a guest in my boat. You have lived in the mountains, where birth counts for nothing. You wanted to be my friend. Tell me."

Ume nodded. "Good. More than a peasant indeed. I will tell you, but the story is long.

"In the mountains to the north there is a stronghold of holy men and women. They cannot be found unless they wish for you to find them. They are the heart of Japan, and perhaps its sole hope for the future."

Yajiro nodded. It was not unusual for bands of warrior monks to take to the hills when they incurred the displeasure of the nobility. All such bands thought they were Japan's only hope.

"You think you understand, but you know nothing of them," she said sharply. "They have *seen* the future of Japan, and I have seen it too."

Yajiro felt uneasy. "The future? Men will die, others be born. New leaders will replace the old. Winters will follow summers. What else is there?"

"Things change, Yajiro. Japan will not always be ruled from Heian. The Fujiwaras will not marry their daughters into the

Imperial line and rule from behind the throne forever. Power shifts, as it always has."

"Life is hard, and worldly things are fleeting," said Yajiro.

"But do you know what Buddha meant when he spoke of the latter days of the law? People who truly keep the commandments of the Buddha are as rare as a tiger in the marketplace—you have heard that?

"It will get worse, Yajiro. Ten generations ago Japan was a primitive place. Ten generations from now, everything will again be primitive, only different. There will be a whole warrior class—men who exist only to fight, for whom blood and honor and the curve of their swords are more important than life or love. There will be two hundred years of war. Thousands will be murdered in public execution grounds just for the sin of serving a different daimyo. Generals will bury their enemies' children alive, and rivers of blood will flow through the streets. The ordinary people of Japan will be worked until they die to produce rice for the warrior class, to help them fight their wars. The gods will turn their backs, and the soul of Japan will be scarred for ten times ten generations."

A hundred generations. Yajiro had lived through barely one. His mind rebelled. "You cannot know this!"

"It is already happening. When I was a girl, that gang of scoundrels at the market could not have existed. Honest men would not have permitted it. The latter days of the law are here, Yajiro."

"Then, if the gods will it, nothing we can do will change it. We must live as best we can."

She struck the thwart with her fist. "That is not true, Yajiro! That is the lie that will ruin Japan!" She calmed herself, her shaking fingers probing the pulse at her throat. "Consider this. You knew I was going to be robbed, and the knowledge gave you the power to stop it. I know how Japan will be despoiled by the warriors, and so maybe that can be stopped too."

He looked away. "You should rest now."

"You think I am mad, talking of many generations when this body will not survive the first frost. But you forget the box."

He had not forgotten. The box had begun to gleam as the rays of the sun burned through the roof of mist. Heaven and earth focused upon that box. Yajiro would not touch it now if his life depended upon it. Foreboding breathed upon his neck and chilled him.

"What of the box?" he said. "What does it contain?"

"My soul," she said simply.

The coldness spread to his heart and stomach. Gods swirled about him in the remains of the morning mist. The gilded box waited in the bottom of the boat, unwinking.

He snatched up an oar and retreated into the stern. The expanse of years, the heart of Japan, the mysteries of a hundred monks hidden in the mountains of the North—the immensity of her words blinded him, but one thing he saw clearly; he was in mortal danger. He did not doubt her words. If a soul could be trapped in a box, his *sukuse* and eternal rebirth were at risk.

Help me, he muttered to the breezes. Help me. I am beyond what I know.

The winds made no reply.

Ume sighed, and trailed her fingers over the side of the boat. "Yajiro, Yajiro. If I wanted to steal your body away I would have done so by now." The sadness in her voice told him it was true. "I tried, but I could not do it. You're no wharf-rat."

His body?

To the left the shoreline appeared. A fishing boat moved against the gray horizon.

"Set the sails," she said. "I won't steal from you."

"Put your box in the sack."

"You have no faith."

"Please..."

She did it, and he watched the bulge in the bag for some time before he would put the oar down.

Dotted across the surface of the river Yajiro saw many boats, some already tacking cautiously, some being rowed downstream, others just hoisting sail. Another trader's boat was heading downriver towards them on close tack, obviously carrying goods that might spoil.

Ume was silent for two hours as he got the boat under way and set off into the freshening breeze across the water. She retreated into herself, and once Yajiro even thought she might have slipped into a trance. Comforted by the silence, some of his unease flowed out of him at the beauty of the day. He was making good time, even into the wind, and he thought that they might make Kenno-ji before dusk.

His boat was a fast one, and only lightly loaded. Yajiro was proud that he was preserving his lead on the other trading boat. He kept close to the wind and came about whenever he felt the effect of the current easing on his keel. The other boat took longer tacks and so wasted less time coming about, but her captain took her too far out of the quicker waters and too close to the trees.

A heron flew near them then, all long beak and wings.

"See, our luck improves already," Ume said. A heron in flight was a good omen.

There was a thump. For a moment Yajiro thought they were aground or had struck a floating log. Then two arms came over the bows, followed by a mop of black hair and a cheeky grin. "Good day, Captain! Permission to come aboard!" Not waiting for a reply, the boy threw his leg across the gunwale and tumbled into the boat like a sack of millet.

"Tsuru!" said Yajiro. "Where did *you* come from?"

Tsuru sat up in the bottom of the boat amid the mess of lines, smiling happily. "Knew you'd need me, sir. Swam after you, all the way from Nakasu-ichi. No, really what I did was run along the bank. Been following a while, now. Market's no place for me, sir. Need to see the world!"

"You'll see little enough of it with us..."

Yajiro's voice trailed away. Ume was staring at Tsuru, eyes rapt. A small bubble of saliva collected at the corner of her mouth, threatening to slip onto her chin. Guilt and greed swam in her eyes.

Then she smiled, all sunshine and cheer. "Where's your mother, scamp?"

"Did as the Captain told me, ma'am. Went to the priest, but he weren't holy enough to bring my ma out of the ground. No, I'd say she's just comfortable where she is!" He grinned.

"The ground?" said Yajiro.

"Told you I'd lost her, sir. Thought you'd understood."

"I suppose not," said Yajiro, his eyes still on Ume.

"Can I steer her, Captain? Work my passage?"

"We're in a hurry," Yajiro began, but Ume interrupted. "Where would the harm be, Yajiro-san? It would give you a rest. I'll give the boy his wages."

"Wait. Tsuru-kun, why did it take you so long to catch us?"

"Hungry, sir. Hadn't eaten for a day. Spent your coin on a meal, blessing you with every mouthful. After that, I couldn't run so fast. And then I had to wait so's I'd not miss you in the fog. But I knew you'd not set me ashore, sir. Fine trader like yourself, just setting up in business, knew you'd need some help." The boy looked around the boat with interest, apparently only now noticing the lack of cargo. "What will you be selling then, sir?"

"Little boys," said Yajiro. "I buy them and feed their bodies to the witches in the hills."

Ume turned her head away in disgust, but Tsuru cackled appreciatively. "A ready wit, sir. I like that in a master."

"I'm not your master," he said curtly.

Ume's eyes swiveled back to stare at Tsuru, sitting in the boat barely an arms-length away from her. Yajiro knew now: the boy was in danger.

"Come here, scamp," he said. "Quickly, now."

"Sir!" the boy exclaimed in delight, and was on his feet in a moment, walking down the boat. He stumbled and caught himself on the mast, and Yajiro saw Ume lean forward, one hand reaching out to the boy while the other sought out the sack at her feet.

Yajiro released the rudder and jumped forward. The sail flapped. "Don't touch him!" He knocked her arm down.

He saw a flash of steel out of the corner of his eye, and the sail fell away from the mast and tumbled over them both. The boat rocked as Yajiro flailed his hands to free himself.

Ume pulled the sail off his shoulders. The boat lurched again and there was a loud splash.

Tsuru had cut the main halyard with a knife and then jumped overboard. He was swimming strongly away, out into the river. The shore was half a mile distant.

"Yajiro." The old woman was pointing upstream over his shoulder. "It seems the little snipe already has a master, and one we know well."

Five hundred feet away and bearing down rapidly was the trader boat Yajiro had been racing down the river as a point of honor. It was now close enough for them to see the weasel from the market at Nakasu-ichi at the helm, and two accomplices kneeling in the bows.

"Gods!" Yajiro struggled to get the oars out from under the useless sail and into the rowlocks. His first instinct had been to jump overboard and swim for it, and he felt a swift flush of shame. Yes, save himself and leave an old woman to the wolves, that would have been fine of him, and good *sukuse* to carry to the next life.

Perhaps they were both supposed to die here. Maybe by accepting his fate in this life he would rise in stature in the next.

Or maybe he would come back as a beetle because of his spinelessness.

One thing, at least, was clear. The urchin was part of the dock gang. The glint of gold had brought the river rats after them. Unable to overhaul Yajiro on the river, the gang had dropped the urchin ashore to run ahead and slow them down. Now he and Ume were at their mercy.

"Yajiro, Yajiro," Ume was digging into the sack at her feet. "Be calm. This is perfect."

"Perfect?" he shouted. "We're about to be murdered by pirates! *Perfect?*"

She slapped him. "Shut up. *Listen.*"

The other boat had sailed past and was reaching the end of its tack, preparing to come about. They would catch up with Yajiro's boat on their next reach. He saw one of the hard-faced accomplices lean over the transom and pluck a bedraggled small boy out of the water.

Ume's eyes shone. "They want the box, Yajiro-san. We shall give it to them. I told you that the box contains my soul, and so it does. If you had opened the box, my soul would have reached out and gained power over the body you wear, casting *your* soul into *this* empty shell, this old woman's body. We would have traded the skin and bones we wear. You would have died old and feeble, and I would have lived on, appearing to all the world as you do now."

The pirates were coming back.

"I could not do it. You did not deserve such a fate. This low-born pirate is another matter. It will be a service to Japan to take his body and place a kindlier mind within it. I will order the other cut-throats away and they will obey me, thinking me their leader. You will be saved."

The other boat bore down on them. One of the men at the bows drew a knife. Tsuru took over the rudder, and the weasel came forward to join his friends.

Yajiro finally understood. "In the market, you *wanted* to be robbed."

"Of course."

There was no more time to think. Yajiro stretched an oar across the water to fend them off, but a pirate knocked it out of his hands and it tumbled into the river. The boy expertly turned the nose of his craft so it lay alongside.

The boat quaked as the weasel came aboard, and Yajiro snatched at the gunwale to stop himself from falling. The thief crouched in the boat, his eyes eager. If he was a small man, the curved knife and the cold, steady look in his eyes made him a giant. His two grinning accomplices held the boats together. Clearly they had no doubts that their leader could take care of this alone.

Fear scraped at Yajiro's heart with a blunt blade, and he could not move. The gods hid below the water, or behind the trees on the land. There were no other boats within a mile.

If Ume was afraid, she did not show it. Indeed, Yajiro had never seen her look so alert. Life crackled in her eyes, although she kept them downcast as befitted a woman at the mercy of a man. She said, "Good sir, I ask your mercy for my friend and for myself. My meager possessions are at your disposal, but Heaven will smile upon you for your benevolence if we are spared."

"Shut your mouth, crone," said the weasel. "Yield up your sack, and keep your prattling gods to yourself."

Ume upended the bag. The herbal root, a few strips of dried meat, some unclean pieces of cloth, and the shiny golden box tumbled out. "You will see I have little enough, sir, for all your efforts to catch me."

She pushed the box across the bottom of the boat with her foot until it was within the thief's reach. He picked it up, his cautious rat's eyes never leaving them. "If there's jewels within, maybe I'll not cut your throats," he said.

Ume smiled tightly. "Be reassured, kind sir. The box contains that which I value the most in all the world. Yet I'm sure that it will find a good home with you."

Yajiro, transfixed in the stern, clutching the useless rudder in his hands as they floated downstream in the current, finally found his tongue. "Don't open it. Don't open the box."

"The big lump has a tongue," sneered the thief. "Maybe I'll carve it out before I leave."

"Be still, Yajiro," said Ume, her voice sharp.

As the weasel raised the box, Yajiro tensed. He was tall and strong. Surely he could wrangle the knife away from this little man. Surely the gods were waiting for him to cast away his fear and put these evil men to flight. Surely...

The weasel opened the box.

And *changed*. Yajiro saw him fall sideways and hold out his hand to balance himself, and heard Ume cry out and clutch at her throat, but the real knowledge came to him from out of the weasel's eyes; the sly meanness and avarice had fled, driven out by a hard intelligence, a rising exultation.

With the merest glance into the box, the weasel snapped it closed. He stared straight at Yajiro. "It is done," he said. "I have what I need. I will be leaving now. Thank you for allowing me aboard your boat."

The old woman's body straightened with a jerk, still clutching her hands to her chest. When her voice came, it was little stronger than a whisper. "I am witched...Witched!"

Tsuru and the other two pirates turned to stare. Stronger, she pointed a finger. "She has robbed me of myself! How was it done? Give me the box!" She clutched at her chest, racked by a deep cough.

Yajiro could see the soul of Ume burning within the body of the thug, and hear her middle-born imperiousness in his voice as he snarled, "Silence! Be still!" The thief's body turned back to Yajiro. "Comfort her and keep her quiet. I fear the shock has chased away her wits."

Now Yajiro saw how cunning the plan of the hill-priests truly was. In her new body, Ume had only to go to Heian Kyo and gift the golden box to a noble-born, and soon she would *be* that noble. She could work her way up through the iron ranks of society as invisible as the wind, displacing souls into more lowly bodies as she went. In time she could be the Emperor, or his wife, or the Fujiwara. When she again grew old she could become her own successor. Her power would be without limit.

As the old woman's breath became shallow, dragged at ever more cost into her lungs, Yajiro looked up at the weasel's lean, hard body with its knife in one hand and golden box in the other, and saw the future with a terrible clarity.

The second oar lay along the spine of the boat. Yajiro snatched it up and slammed it into the smaller man's ribs.

The last thing Ume expected in her new body was an attack from Yajiro. She cried out and tumbled, her knee striking the thwart. Yajiro threw himself the other way, to save the boat from capsizing, and the new jolt sent the box flying into the air. It turned end over end in a gentle arc and disappeared into the river with the merest of splashes.

Ume shouted and clutched her hair, a strangely feminine motion from so obviously masculine a body. The boy Tsuru dived into the water but came up quickly, empty-handed. The river was deep, and the box was gone.

The weasel's mind used the old woman's body to claw at Yajiro's face with a last surge of desperate energy, and died in midstrike, the breath rattling in his throat.

Ume leaned heavily against the mast, still staring into the gray water. "You have killed me. You have killed Japan."

The thief's accomplices looked at each other. The boy scrambled back into the other boat, dripping again.

Yajiro held the old, dead body in his arms. "Japan is too big for me. All I can do is lead the best life I can."

She looked at him, almost pleadingly. "I was doing what was right. You should have..." Her voice died away.

Aware of the cut-throats in the next boat, Yajiro could not say what he wanted to say. *No, stealing bodies is not right. A man's body is his own. Everybody should die at their appointed hour, not earlier, not later. Killing your way through the years is not right.*

He contented himself with the words, "Think of your *sukuse.*"

She shook her head. "I'm already damned." To her new henchmen she said, "Go back to Nakasu-ichi. I will follow later."

They looked as if they would argue, but she snapped "Go!" and they heard the voice of their leader and set sail, heading for the shore where the current was weakest and then flying upriver with the wind at their backs.

Ume stood there, knife in hand. "I wish I could make you live forever, to see what you have done."

"Nobody should live forever," Yajiro replied. He sat quietly for a moment, holding the body, then put it aside and began to retie the cut halyard.

They sailed on to Kenno-ji.

Yajiro, tonsured and clad in a robe of saffron, did not recognize the man who knelt before him on the prayer mat at Kennoji. He took the stranger's gift offering and spoke a mantra before the other man raised his eyes and said; "I see you managed to find a still place within yourself, after all."

The body was now stout with middle age, and the arm muscles turned plump, but the eyes would never change. Yajiro took the knowledge deep and found he was glad she still lived. "Ume. Do you still keep the name you were born with?"

"In my soul, perhaps. Whatever you thought, years ago, I would always have been Ume in my soul."

Yajiro thought for a while, mindful of his breathing and attitude. Then he said, "The plum blossom cannot withstand the strong wind."

Ume shrugged.

"Do you hate me still, then? Was I wrong?"

"You were wrong, but I do not hate you," said Ume.

Yajiro smiled. "How was it, at Heian Kyo?"

"I never got there. I cannot leave my soul—" Ume gestured at the river "– too far behind me. I trip, I cannot walk, I forget to breathe. I toss a pebble and when I reach to catch it, it has already fallen. It is like the birds, when we see them fly and a heartbeat later we hear the sound that has shocked them into the air."

The priest considered that, and nodded.

"There is a colony of the mad on the road. I helped the monks wash and keep them. It is good, sometimes, to spend time with the mad."

Yajiro inclined his head. "You have lived as a woman with the wise, and as a man with the mad." A passing monk kept his features firmly serene. "From whom did you learn the most?"

He did not expect an answer, and Ume did not give one. They sat in silence as the day drew into evening. Finally, Ume said, "So. You did not return to teach the Ninefold Path to your village?"

"These are the last days of the law," said Yajiro. "I do not wish to meet the tiger in the marketplace, and know that he lives because of me. I do not want my family to know from whence my stillness comes."

And he stared into Ume's eyes, until the night came.

THE PILGRIM TRADE
Mark W. Tiedemann

TUSSIG'S ALARM CHIRRED behind his ear and he bolted for the ruined wall that separated the abandoned barrack from the quay. As he jumped over the edge of eroded polycrete, he saw the buddle's geodesic fade as the chameleon mode came on. Everyone else in the buddle—Tussig's four sibs and three pars—scrambled for cover.

He landed off-balance and slid down the uneven slope of detritus grown up against the wall. His boots rattled against the jagged shards of ancient trash and he almost fell. He recovered gracelessly and scurried along the uneven quay toward the storm drain that jutted from what had once been a waste processing node attached to the barrack.

To his right, the Manassa River stretched to the opposite shore. The residential sections of Charic mounded above the shoreline, blue-shadowed by distance, a few bright yellow lights accenting the sameness. Further downriver the Confluences roared where three of Nine Rivers' great arteries met and mingled, unseen but loud. Here, muddy brown water laced with blue and green tangles of growth lapped at the slowly disintegrating shelf.

Tussig tapped the bone behind his left ear to shut off the nagging alarm as he reached the big pipe. It would have been useful if Raja-can had managed to tinker it back to full range so the buddle could communicate, but the alarm mode had been the best the buddle's prime par could do.

In the sudden stillness, Tussig could hear boots on the opposite side of the wall, even treads, three or four people. Tussig climbed into the pipe, hands sinking into a few centimeters of humus, and got to his feet. The drain was large enough for him to stand upright, but he still hunched within it as he made his way in.

The far end of the pipe let out into a square roofless chamber. The walls still showed the shadows and holes where equipment had been removed. Except for a thick layer of dirt on the floor, the room was empty.

"—pain the ass, what I say."

"Quit complaining so much, will you, Sidge? Gets old."

"I suppose you like coming down here to fix shit that shouldn't even still be here?"

"I said—"

"Both of you shut up."

The voices echoed round the broken maze of the compound, amplified weirdly everywhere. So at least three techs had come this time. Tussig worried at that. Four had come the first time to reseal the dispenser Raja-can had jimmied. After that, only one had returned every third or fourth day. He would cuss as he reinstalled the seal, knowing perfectly well that he would have to come back when it was jimmied again. Three times he had come alone. Now there was a group again. That usually meant more than just a reseal.

"Fucken nids," one them said.

"I said—"

"I heard, all right!" Then: "I just want to know why they have to break it every time."

"They have to eat and they don't have our special tools and expertise," another said.

"Huh! Maybe if they did, they wouldn't be nids."

"That occurred to you, did it?"

"Hey, what's your problem—"

"Both of you shut up. I won't say it again."

Silence, then, except for the tapping and shifting of work being done.

"All right," one of them said. "Let's clean them out now."

"I still don't like this."

"You like your job, don't you? Now shut up and start scouring."

Tussig resisted the impulse to run. He pressed back against the cold wall of the drain and tried to listen more intently. His ears began to hum, a high-pitched, directionless presence.

Someone shouted. Tussig jumped back from the opening of the drain pipe as if touched by a sudden current. Then he heard the distinct heavy snap of a stunner. One movement prompted another and he staggered back to the other end.

He gazed out at the river and for a few insane moments he contemplated swimming it.

"Hey!"

Tussig did not look back. He leapt from the pipe and ran up the quay. He had not explored much beyond the ruin of the factory and had no idea what lay at the far end of the crumbling pier, nor even how long it ran. He dodged the holes and larger cracks deftly, sprinting a jagged course, adrenalin carrying him effortlessly, breath loud inside his head.

He wondered later how much further he had to go when abruptly he sprawled onto the polycrete and slid, all feeling gone from his limbs. He barely felt the scraping across his cheek and jaw.

Stunner, he realized, trying to stand. Nothing responded. Consciousness seemed discontinuous, an on-again off-again phenomenon with big chunks of time cut out. That was good, in a way, since he lost all sense of duration. He ran, he fell, he waited, someone turned him over. He wondered vaguely why he was still conscious at all.

Tussig stared uncomprehendingly through the clear faceplate hovering above him at a woman—he thought it was a woman—with a wide face and small, harsh eyes. Thin lips pursed into a moue that made radiating lines around her mouth.

"One down here," she said.

"Where?" Tussig asked.

"Shut up," she said and prodded him with the toe of her boot. He barely felt it, somewhere along his thigh, but he was uncertain which one. She frowned. "All right," she said then, grumpily.

She straddled Tussig and grabbed him beneath the arms. Suddenly his head swirled sickeningly as she heaved him up, up, and across her shoulder. He found himself gazing down at the polycrete, then, as she carried him back along the pier. Distantly he felt nauseated, but he did not throw up. He knew if he were not so numb from the stunner he would, but this way he was only uncomfortable.

She turned off the pier and carried him down a narrow aisle between two relatively unbroken walls, then into another open area.

She stopped, heaved, and tossed him to the ground. He slapped the pavement across his back. Feeling was beginning to return and it almost hurt.

"Hey, careful," someone else said. "That's a child."

"It's a nid," the woman said. Then: "Or is it family, Bryce?"

"Both of you shut up," a third voice said. "Damn, you two are a pain to work with. Is that all of them now?"

"How should I know?" the woman snapped.

"Check!"

She hissed angrily and moved off. "...don't we just bury 'em under the new construction, they like it here so much..."

The third tech moved away down another corridor.

"Shit," the one called Bryce said.

Tussig's back stung now and he could feel his legs. He blinked, realized even as he did that he had been unable to for several minutes. Tears came rapidly, shattering the clarity of his vision, and he tried to raise a hand to wipe at them.

"Take it easy," Bryce said. "Here."

A big hand worked under Tussig's shoulders and pushed him up. His eyes cleared enough to see the canteen being offered. He reached for it, missed, and tried again, seizing it with both hands. He raised it carefully to his mouth and drank. After three swallows, he choked. Cold water sprayed, ran down his chin.

"Slow," Bryce said. "Not all your muscles will be working the same way. Give it a half an hour and you can guzzle."

Tussig looked up at the tech. He recognized him. Heavy man, dark skin and pale green eyes. He sat beside Tussig, his helmet rolled down into the collar of his environ suit, shaven pate decorated with brilliant azure, crimson, and gold tattoos, and stared into the ruins around them.

On the ground lay two of Tussig's pars—Kess and Shimmer—and three of his sibs—Dal, Pelu, and Roshalon, all languidly unconscious. Stunned. Shimmer had a cut across the scalp. They had been dropped where they lay, like baggage.

Raja-can and Fera were missing.

Tussig could not see either of the other two techs. He toyed briefly with the idea of running, but his body still felt clumsy. His toes tingled.

Bryce looked at him. "Better?"

Tussig drank more water. Clean, supplemented, not like the distilled fluid they got from Raja-can's processor which usually left the particular source flavor behind even if all the pathogens and toxins were flensed.

From where he sat, Tussig could see the dispenser.

The big wall-mounted unit now supported a brand new lockout on its ancient delivery ports, like a crystalline growth on its eroded and cracked face. Tussig never understood why no one had cut off its supply of raw material at the source. He blamed those nameless someones for his buddle's current trouble, since if they had done their job and made sure the dispenser lacked anything with which to make food base, fabric, or pathic treatments, then no one would have been forced to come down here to roust them. But all that happened was a tech—this one, Bryce—had come every few days to put a new seal on it. Rather than solve the problem, he compounded it. Now the buddle not only faced trespassing charges, but property damage and civil nuisance charges.

"You should've left," Bryce said. "Didn't figure you'd stay so damn long." He fixed Tussig with an unhappy stare. "I said you'd gone—twice. If they don't dismiss me for false reporting, they'll demerit me for being an idiot."

Tussig kept silent. He looked from Bryce to the dispenser to his unconscious buddle coes and sipped at the clean water.

"What were you going to do," Bryce asked, "set up a dom here or something?" He shook his head. "Bad timing. Nine Rivers doesn't want you anymore. You should've left with the new migration last month."

Tussig stared at Bryce. "We—" He coughed. Bryce frowned at him. Tussig drank and tried again. "We were. We came late."

Bryce snorted. "Word's been round for over a year. What did you do, take the scenic route?"

"We—" Tussig looked down. After another swallow of water, he handed the canteen back to Bryce. "What are you going to do to us?"

"Don't know. We just have to remove you from the site." Bryce took a drink, then waved the canteen to include the whole factory. "Port's expanding. All this is going to be leveled and new launch pits dug out. Probably all this will be customs houses, hotels, shops." He let his arm drop and shook his head. "Imagine. Hm."

Tussig tried to envision the changes Bryce suggested, gazing around at the neglect and decay and picturing in his mind new structures and a broad field of blast pits for shuttles and—

—and started crying, sudden gulping sobs shaking his frame. Bryce watched him, a dismayed expression on his face, then, awkwardly, put a hand on Tussig's shoulder.

"Hey," he said.

Tussig calmed down, uncertain why he felt so totally frightened. Bryce's hand felt pleasant on his shoulder, reassuring, almost parental.

"Where you all from?" Bryce asked.

"Millispa," Tussig said. He sniffed. "Had a barge once. Lost it."

"Barge. You were invested, then. Why—"

"Freelance. Never registered."

"Ah. Unregistered, no insurance. So no barge, no home."

"We heard about the migration and voted to try. But the Millispa River's near the other side of the world. Long road on foot, begging rides, working freight along the way. Near the Manassa, we started coming into one separatist township after another. Last one didn't seem so bad—Suber's Cove."

"Heard of it. Reform Returnist, isn't it?"

"Didn't know that when we stopped. We did all right at first, selling Kess's woodcarvings and Pelu's polymer sculpture. Raja-can said we should've figured what they were by what they asked for, but we were hungry. Stayed too long. Kess carved one of her eros pieces and the mayor found out. We still had two hundred klicks to Charic. By the time we arrived, the migration was over, they weren't taking any more."

"So you ended up here."

"The dispenser still worked," Tussig said, as if that fact alone excused them and put the blame for their situation on Bryce.

He almost smiled. "They never shut off outlets like that, just on the chance they might build new on a site. We never figured anybody could jimmy one of our new seals, though."

"You never figured on Raja-can."

"Guess not."

Tussig wiped his nose with the back of his hand and wiped that one his pants. He studied the tattoos on Bryce's head.

"What are those for?" Tussig asked. "You some kind of renunciate?"

Bryce laughed. "You're smart for a nid, aren't you? Yeah, I used to be. Gave it up."

"Why?"

Bryce shook his head. At first, Tussig thought he would not answer. But then he said, "We were all about balance. Everything you do has to even out in the long run, so the universe can keep a rock steady course on into the future. That's what they taught, anyway. Lot of vacuum. I left when I realized how impossible it was. For me, for anyone. And who's to say the universe wants to be balanced? For all we know..." He glanced at Tussig and looked mildly embarrassed. "It didn't make sense to me anymore."

Tussig nodded as if he understood. "What are you going to do with us?" he asked again.

"Don't know. We were just supposed to evict you. I—"

"Fucken nid! Stop!"

From one of the gangways, Raja-can sprinted into the alcove. He skidded to a halt when he saw Tussig. Tussig opened his mouth, thinking to warn him, when one of the techs came charging out in Raja-can's wake.

The tech collided with Raja-can and they tumbled forward, slamming to the ground in a heap. Raja-can immediately began twisting and writhing and almost scrambled from the tech's grip. The tech—Tussig could not see which one—clawed at Raja-can's togs. Raja-can drew up a leg and snapped it into the tech's sealed helmet. The tech paused, stunned, and Raja-can managed to get to his feet.

Bryce stood, reaching for his sidearm. Raja-can looked frantic, momentarily frightened.

The dazed tech stood. Tussig saw the rock he held just as he brought his arm up. He bashed Raja-can in the side of the head. Raja-can collapsed. A few moments later, blood flowed from within his hairline, covering his face.

Tussig screamed.

"Damn!" Bryce yelled. He stepped forward.

The tech drew a weapon.

"Don't you dare aim that thing at me, Sidge," Bryce said, pointing at the stunner.

The tech—Sidge—staggered back a couple of steps. Bryce took another step forward and Sidge shot him.

Tussig had never seen anyone hit by a stunner before. Bryce seized up as if about to have a fit, and then flopped to the polycrete, muscles utterly relaxed, consciousness gone.

"Shit," Sidge said. A hand went to the collar and Sidge's helmet retracted.

The woman. Her face was angry, confused. She still seemed rattled by Raja-can's blow. She shook her head and approached Bryce, holding the stunner out as though afraid he would get up. When he did not move, she looked at Tussig. She regarded him narrowly for several seconds, then shrugged and went to Raja-can.

"Are they all dead?" Tussig asked, and immediately felt stupid and afraid.

Sidge looked at the others laid out. "No," she said, her voice surprisingly even. "Just stunned." She frowned at him. "You were at the extreme range. Charge wasn't as bad. Not that you know what that means..."

She rolled Raja-can over. His eyes gazed skyward, unseeing.

Sidge glanced over her shoulder, then holstered the stunner. She still moved cautiously, with a degree of uncertainty. She started patting Raja-can's body, searching.

Tussig wondered where the third tech was. He had seemed to be the leader. If he came back now and saw this, maybe Sidge would be disciplined. Maybe, with two useless people—one stunned, the other untrustworthy—he would let the buddle go. They might have time then to leave.

But without Raja-can.

Tussig watched Sidge's hands move over the lifeless body of what used to be Tussig's prime par, the head of the buddle, the man who had kept them centered, optimistic, and moving. Maybe, he puzzled, the stunner had numbed more than just his body, because he could not quite connect what he saw with anything he felt. The blow Sidge had struck had startled him, but now he seemed unable to react. There was a slow chill beginning to course through him, but that seemed a poor excuse for actual feeling.

We're nids, he thought, we don't have feelings. It follows...we don't have anything else, not even identities, that's what it means, after all, NID, No ID, no access, no stipend, no path, no facts, no life, just bodies no one knows what to do with, excess biomass with brains too big to be pets, too small to be dangerous, nuisances...

Tussig had heard all these things said, spoken around pathetic campfires and in disused structures where a few of them gathered from time to time to pass what they had of goods and aid and news to each other. He was uncertain he knew what the words meant, but suddenly they implied much more than they ever had before.

But why is she searching his pockets? he wondered. Doesn't she know we have nothing?

Where is the third one?

Tussig looked at Bryce. His stunner lay nearby.

We could start freeriding, Tussig thought, and turned to see if any of the port could be seen from here. No, only more walls, broken or useless, supporting nothing. But this would be port one day, according to Bryce, which is why Raja-can lay dead now. The nids had to go. Squatters.

Freeriders...the idea carried a romantic patina...they told stories of the freeriders, nids like themselves who hopped aboard shuttles and caught rides on starships. They were more myth than reality, according to Raja-can, but even he had grudgingly admitted that some truth adhered to the stories. All you needed was a kit and a breather and the tech on your back to survive the transfer upwell to the waiting ships and then the luck to hide out in cargo or some corner of engineering. Tussig had even heard of freeriders who carried along a change of fine clothes and slipped into passenger sections of luxury liners and rode from star to star in comfort, sleeping on a good bed, and thumbing their noses at the invested, living on the fringe of overlooked credit and—

And Raja-can was probably right, they were all myth and madness, exaggerations based on a few reckless coes who might have managed it once or twice, but hardly as a lifestyle.

Raja-can had been right about a great deal. But he had never known he would die so soon. None of them had and now Tussig knew how wrong Raja-can could be.

Sidge shifted her position to more easily dig in Raja-can's pants, turning her back to Tussig.

The idea came as clear and clean as Bryce's water. Tussig got to his feet and stepped silently over Bryce. In a smooth motion, he swept up the stunner, walked up behind Sidge.

She began to stand. Tussig placed the stunner against the back of her head and pulled the trigger.

It was shockingly loud.

Her skull seemed to expand. She lunged forward, over Raja-can, and landed, face down, with an ugly slap.

Tussig squatted before her and gingerly raised her head by the hair. Her eyes bulged hugely and her tongue jutted. Blood ran freely from her nose. He released her and let her head smack the ground.

He tossed the stunner back over by Bryce and sat there, thinking.

He thought: *I'm twelve years old and I've just killed someone.*

He thought: *I have nothing anyone can take from me anymore.*

He thought: *I'm terrified.*

The rest of the buddle came to before Bryce did. As each one woke up and remembered what had happened, they saw Raja-can and the dead tech, and each one reacted differently.

Shimmer checked Raja-can's pulse, then looked at Tussig, eyes wide and terrified. The other sibs, all younger than Tussig, started to cry until Shimmer hissed at them. Kess gathered them to her, holding them.

"You?" Shimmer asked Tussig, tapping the tech on the back.

He nodded, unwilling to speak.

Shimmer shook his head. "Bad." He looked at the others, all watching, huddled together, waiting for Shimmer to tell them what to do. He wiped at his head and scowled at the blood.

"Got to assume Fera got away," Shimmer said. He sighed. "We can't have law after us, Tussig. Not this way. They ignore us mostly, but this..." He shook his head again, eyes sad, then turned toward the others. "Get the tent, gather our possibles. We're moving."

"Shimmer," Kess said, "we can't leave Tussig—"

"We can't have law after us!" Shimmer hissed. "We got them to think about. And it seems I'm prime par now."

"So the first thing you do is abandon someone?"

"A murderer, Kess. Think!"

She shook her head, but lapsed into silence.

"All right then," Shimmer said. "Move."

Tussig watched his sibs react. Within a couple of minutes they had found the chamo tent, decloaked it, and broke it down. Packs were gathered, the tent folded into its pouch, and camp, such as it had been, was struck.

"You're young," Shimmer told Tussig. "That counts for mercy."

Tussig watched his place in the buddle eliminated and thought: *I have even less now...*

Shimmer organized the buddle quickly, gave Tussig a last, pained look, and then led them out of the factory. Kess did not look back.

It took another ten minutes for Bryce to revive. He sat up, groaning, and held his head in his hands for a time. When he looked up, color leached from his face.

"Fuck," he breathed, scrambling forward. He checked Sidge quickly, then Raja-can, and sat back. He glanced at Tussig, eyes wide, then searched for his weapon. He crawled to it and grabbed it, then stood. He aimed it first at Tussig, then at Sidge. Finally, he holstered it and looked around.

"Where the hell is Ridel?"

Tussig shrugged when Bryce looked at him.

"You stay here," Bryce said as he walked toward the gangway.

Tussig considered running off while Bryce was gone, but it seemed pointless. His fear had blended with a profound ambivalence, a strange mix of hopeless euphoria and desperate anger that kept him fixed in place.

Bryce was gone for less than five minutes. When he returned, he looked furious. Tussig recognized the tight set of his jaw, the muscle working it between ear and mandible, the coldness in his eyes. He had seen that looked in others and it had never meant anything but trouble.

"Come on," Bryce said, grabbing Tussig's arm and pulling him to his feet.

"The other tech?" Tussig asked.

"Dead. Maybe Sidge, maybe this one. Come on."

Bryce walked him out of the ruined factory, setting a quick pace. He said nothing till they reached the old road that ran alongside the abandoned compound. A transport waited there. Bryce touched the panel on its side and the hatch unsealed and opened.

Bryce hustled Tussig into the vehicle. He followed and closed the hatch, then sat down at the pilot's station. Tussig listened to his breathing, labored and loud, and slowly realized that Bryce was terrified.

"The others," Bryce said finally. "They left?"

"Yes."

"Left you?"

"They—yes."

"Not much different than anybody else, then. Too much trouble, cut a co off, leave him behind. No different at all."

"You don't know what we're like," Tussig said. "You don't know anything about us. All you're worried about is your precious dispenser."

Bryce swung out of the seat and faced Tussig. "Yeah? So what? Before today, would you have believed your buddle would abandon you?"

Tussig glared at Bryce, but he could not sustain the rage. Not at Bryce. He looked away.

"Thought not. So don't give me any shit about not knowing you. No one knows anyone till they're desperate. Then you find out. Eh?"

Bryce returned to the pilot's seat and started up the transport. As the vehicle began to roll, Tussig moved into the seat next to Bryce.

"Where are we going?"

Bryce steered the transport through a half circle and headed for the towers of Charic, visible distantly at the end of the road.

"Were you really trying to make it here for the migration?" Bryce asked.

"That's what Raja-can told us."

"One of you might make it, then."

"Where are you taking me?"

"Home. My dom. I have to sort things out."

Tussig's heart raced as he watched the main city draw near. It seemed his vision was clearer and his hearing more acute. He licked his lips.

"Are you going to try to balance it all?" he asked.

Bryce frowned deeply but did not look at Tussig. After a time, he nodded.

"Maybe. Whether it wants to be or not."

Tussig did not speak the rest of the way.

Bryce lived in a small dom, three rooms and a hygiene cube, on the outskirts of the port. The place was clean and the air tasted pure. Bryce sent Tussig to the cube.

"I got some things to check out," he said. "You get cleaned up."

Tussig stood in the hot spray for a long time. When he came out, Bryce had set out new clothes on the couch. Tussig examined them, amazed, and then carefully slipped them on. He felt new, reborn, and wondered if this was the goal of all those ecstatics in their enclaves along the rivers. Probably not, he decided, since if it were so simple as new clothes they would all have abandoned their self-loathing long ago.

Bryce came into the dom in a hurry.

"There's ships leaving for the frontier every day," he said. Sweat glistened on his scalp. He held up a disk. "Passage out." He handed the disk to Tussig. Then he held up his own disk. "If you don't mind the company?"

Tussig stared at him, gnawing his lower lip. Bryce grinned.

"Been thinking about it for a long time. Charic's getting too fussy with its rules and people like Sidge and Ridel don't make me feel any better about living here. Time maybe to move on."

Quickly, Bryce began packing a bag for himself. Tussig had nothing but his old clothes, so he sat and watched, dismayed. He slipped his disk into a breast pocket and tried to sort out what was happening.

Leaving...

Bryce finished and sealed his pack. "Ready?"

Bryce left his transport beneath an enormous shed at the perimeter of the port and led Tussig, a hand firmly on his shoulder, to a walkway that carried them into the port proper.

Tussig had never been in such a huge, clean space. The white of the walls and supports, the pale, veined stone of the floors, all seemed to glow. People in beautiful clothes stood in lines or strode purposefully through the galleries. The ceiling arched high above. Throughout, Tussig felt the occasional vibration of rising shuttles heaving out of blast pits. The air was cool and curiously rich. He had never been in a place like this, never thought to walk in such a world.

Bryce's grip tightened briefly. Tussig looked around and spotted a group of police officers near one of the queues, asking questions.

"Keep walking," Bryce said. He pointed. "That's where we're going."

Tussig saw a booth serving a line of about a dozen people, all of them carrying bags like Bryce's. Bryce let go of Tussig's shoulder then and handed him his own bag.

"Hang onto this till we get our ship," Bryce said.

Tussig sensed the tension in his voice. Uncertainly, he shouldered Bryce's pack and drifted a few paces away from him. They walked on, parallel to each other.

Then the police came toward them. Tussig's pulse jumped up, but he held back the urge to run. He looked at the booth, the queue, and kept walking.

"Sir," one of the officers called. "Excuse us, co."

Bryce slowed. Tussig continued on, heart pounding. After several paces, he risked a backward glance.

The police officers were putting restraints on Bryce's wrists. The big tech scowled unhappily. He looked up, catching sight of Tussig, and gave a barely perceptible nod.

Tussig snapped his gaze around and continued on. He reached the queue and stood in line the way everyone else stood in line and waited for the official request to step away and come with them for questions, removal, disposal—

"Can I help you, co?"

Tussig blinked, startled. He was standing before the booth and a woman waited for him to answer, smiling innocuously. Tussig swallowed hard and took out the disk. He handed it to her and waited while she read it.

"Very good, co," she said, handing it back. "Gate ninety-seven. You have one hour before your shuttle lifts."

Tussig did not speak. He slipped the disk back into his pocket and stepped away from the booth. Bryce was gone, taken away, and he saw no other police.

He felt tears well up, but he caught them, pushed them back. Not knowing what else to do, he turned and headed for Gate 97.

Tussig sat in a cushioned chair beside a woman who toyed with a palm reader intently for several minutes. A tall window gave a view across the shuttle field. The mushroom-shaped vehicles lifted on shafts of shimmering agrav beams, displaced air returning to give a clap of thunder, awed and frightened.

"Inside," the woman said, "they say you can't hear a thing."

Tussig blinked at her. "That's good."

She smiled. "Where are going?"

Tussig pulled the disk from his pocket and looked at the label. "Diphda."

"Hmm. Never been there myself. Why are you going there?"

Tussig thought about the question for a long time before he answered.

"Balance."

MORE TO GLORY
Patrice Sarath

THE NIGHT JENN came home was just like any other: I was holed up in my bedroom, trying to ignore my parents fighting. I was looking at a book, but I wasn't reading it; I just stared at the picture of the sailing ship on the flat blue screen. Its broad cloth sails billowed with the winds of the Glory Sea, the rigging creaking and the hull slapping rhythmically on the waves.

For a moment second pop's voice rose above everyone else's. I heard, "I know he's just a boy! He needs to face up to facts, that's all!" I turned up the volume on my book. I didn't want to hear what second pop had to say about me.

Tapping at the window caught my attention and I looked up, frowning, unable to see through the wavery plastiglas into the night air. I slid off my bed and went over to it, putting my face close to the surface.

Two bug-eyed faces came into view, alarmingly magnified. I started back.

"Shit!"

Giggling came from the bugs. It was the twins, Dallas and Austin. Heart still hammering, disgusted that I was taken by surprise, I grabbed my respirator, glanced to make sure my door was cycled shut, and slid open the window.

"What are you two idiots doing here?" I whispered. "If my parents find out—"

"Guess who's back in town?"

I looked at them with narrowed eyes, determined to wait them out. Dallas gave in first.

"Jenn," he said. "She just got in."

This time I thought my heart stopped for good. Jenn. My best friend Jenn. Ship's apprentice Jenn. Her parents bought her a spot on a space cruiser and she shipped out six months ago, just after she turned twelve.

"Where?" I breathed and they nodded at the ground below. A white blur waved up at me.

"I'll be right down." I closed the window, tore off my respirator and got into my jeans, shirt and jacket, sealing all the openings meticulously, swearing at the long process that usually only took seconds. My fingers were clumsy and it took forever. I bolted out the door, flung myself back to pick up my respirator, and tore out to the door again.

The fight was still going on in the kitchen. It sounded like all three of them were in there, their voices rising and falling, first and second ma's higher pitched than second pop's but no less angry. As far as I could tell it was the same argument. I tiptoed toward the front door.

"Randy?"

Oh no. I skidded to a stop just before the front door, heart sinking. Tickham. I turned around. He stood in the low light of the hall, looking pale and thin.

"Go back to bed, Tick," I ordered. I gave my meanest glare. "Or I'll tell first mama that you got out of bed."

Tick just glared back. For a little kid, he could be pretty stubborn. "Where are you going?"

"None of your business, tick-turd," I said. "Go away or I'll tell mama."

"I want to come too," he said, and he thrust his lower lip out.

I groaned. Stupid little tick-turd brother. "No, Tick. Go away." I pushed the door open, thinking that would make him run, and was bowled backward by Austin, Dallas, and Jenn.

I forgot Tick when I saw her. She was in her white apprentice uniform, her dark hair and dark skin glowing. She grinned shyly when she caught my eye. Jenn was never shy and I frowned at this new side of her. Then, as if she knew, she reached out and gave me a hug.

"Man, Randy! It is so good to see you! I missed all you guys."

My heart, which had leaped at the thought that she meant me alone, sunk at the "you guys," but the butterflies in my stomach were still roiling in a pretty interesting way. So I held onto her hug. As usual Tick ruined things. He hadn't run from the open door like he was supposed to.

"Jenn?" he said, his eyes wide. Jenn broke away from me, and knelt down to Tick.

"Hey, little Tick," she said kindly, and held out her arms. Tick broke and ran to her, burying his face in her shining uniform. Mindful of Tick's respirator-less state, Austin hit the door button and the door closed. The ventilators cycled the air clear but by the time Tick had lifted his head from Jenn's shoulder, a small smear of blood stained her uniform.

"Tick, you have to go to bed *now*," I ordered in as loud a whisper as I dared. They would come out of the kitchen any minute, see what was up.

"No! I want to see Jenn!"

"Shhhh!" We chorused.

For a moment we were all quiet. Then, "Randy? Tick?" Firs'ma, her voice weak and tired, called from the kitchen.

The twins dissolved into silent giggles. I glared at them and called out, "It's okay, ma. Tick was sleepwalking again. I'll get him back to bed."

Tick gave a glare to equal my own. "I was n—"

"Shh! Look, if you can keep quiet and keep up, you can come. The first time you whine, or cry, or say you're tired, you can just go home by yourself. Clear?"

Looking like I just gave him the keys to the Cathedral, Tick nodded, eyes bright. Between all of us we got him into his outdoor clothes and fitted his respirator on him, and then I hit the door one final time and we headed out into the night.

It never really got dark on the lakefront. White Lake cast a glow where the fuel offgassed from the reservoir, even outshining the string-of-pearls, the strand of moons that hung overhead. In school we learned that other parts of Glory got dark enough to see the night sky, but not at White Lake. I always thought that would be something to see, a night so dark you could see the stars.

We pushed through the crowd thronging the wharfs. It was like old times, dodging the spacers, dockworkers, and shipfitters coming off their shifts and streaming in and out of bars. In pockets of pearlescent light we could see the pretty ladies and the pretty boys, looking like they were half the show. I liked watching them from a distance—up close their eyes behind their masks were harsh and their voices lost the tinkling happiness they put on. But I wasn't looking at pretty ladies tonight. Tonight there was only Jenn. Beneath our laughter and running I kept sneaking looks at her. She had lost whatever momentary shyness had separated her from me earlier. Now she ran with the rest of us, sometimes backwards to shout something, sometimes jumping high to touch the street lamps and make them swing. It had been a favorite game and I was glad she remembered it. We all laughed when Tick jumped feebly off the ground, and Jenn swung him up and he reached out and touched the lamp.

To our amazement, the lamp tottered unsteadily and then keeled over, raising an explosion of sparks and a wicked smell of fuel, and causing shouts from other passersby. We all stared, Tick more astonished than the rest of us, and Jenn slapped him on the shoulder and said with admiration, "Go, Tick!"

That made us all laugh harder than ever and before the wharf guards could make their way to us, wading purposefully through the crowd, we ran off, holding Tick by his gloved hands until his toes barely touched the ground and he only had to make a skipping stride every now and again.

We ended up at our favorite hiding place, a corner alley created where two bars and a machine shop formed an awkward divot in the street. You had to squirm to get through the narrow entrance behind trash bins—only kids could do it. Maybe Jenn had forgotten the knack because she knocked over a bin with a rattling crash. For a moment we all froze, and then, because we were tired of laughing, we settled for muffled giggles. We dragged the bin in front of the opening and set ourselves against the wall.

For a while we just panted and giggled, remembering the wild run through the night. Tick breathed hard through his respirator but the look on his face was just this side of panic, like he couldn't get enough air. I felt a pang of conscience. Don't let him run so hard, I told myself. I patted my leg, an invitation for Tick to sit on my lap, but that same stubbornness took over his face, and he went over to Jenn and set his little body down in her lap. She wrapped her arms around him.

"This is fun," she said wistfully. "I missed you guys."

"Do they know you're out here?" Dallas asked, wide-eyed. Jenn shook her head.

"I'm on shore leave," she said proudly, but the effect was ruined when she added, "but my captain ordered me to visit my parents. I did, but then they made me go to bed." Her voice was full of disgust. "So I figured I'd find you guys."

We all laughed, but I was struck by the easy way she said *my captain.* Like she belonged or something. Do you like it? I wanted to ask, but I was afraid of what she'd say. If she liked it she might as well be gone for good.

"What's it like?" Austin asked. She leaned her chin on her knees, waiting to hear. I snorted quietly in my respirator.

"It's fun. I like it. I mean, it was hard to get used to at first. I really missed—well, everyone. My parents." We all nodded at this momentous admission. "And I kept making mistakes at first. Everyone either ordered me around or told me I was in the wrong place. I got yelled at a lot."

"Like Randy," Tick piped up.

"Shut up, tick-turd," I said.

"*Anyway,*" Jenn said reprovingly. "But I got better at stuff. My favorite part is serving on the bridge. I can't touch anything, but I can watch. I love when we hit the jump gate." I couldn't see her mouth under her mask but I could hear the smile in her voice.

"You've jumped? Where've you been, anyway?" Austin persisted

This time I snorted for real. "Apprentices don't get to go offworld, Austin," I said. "All they get to see are the same four walls, for light-years and light-years. We see more just by sticking around White Lake."

"That's not true!" Jenn said. She was shocked. "I've been lots of places."

"Oh yeah? Where?"

"Lots of places. I've been to spaceports in five systems *and* I was on Earth Outpost."

I kept pushing it, I didn't know why. "Spaceports. Big deal. We live on one, remember?"

Everyone was looking at us, confused. Jenn's eyes became bright with tears.

"You're jealous," she said.

"Of what?" I snapped. "Living in some tin can?"

She stood up, letting Tick slide reluctantly off her lap. She slapped ineffectually at her uniform, but it had lost its white luster. Tick's blood mark rode her shoulder like a rust spot. "I don't have to listen to this," she said, and kicked the bin aside before squirming out of the alley. Dallas and Austin stared at me, and then her, and then followed her out. It was just me and Tick in the dim hideaway.

I couldn't meet Tick's eyes. "Come on," I said gruffly. "Let's go home."

He got to his feet a little slowly, and I knew he was worn out from our escapade. The energy I had earlier had faded and I felt tired myself, along with a bunch of other emotions all caught up in my stomach. Tired, angry, ashamed. Sad. I followed him through the opening half-heartedly, pulling myself through the tight spot. To my surprise I saw the other three waiting for us.

We all stood around for a moment, looking at the rough pavement. After a moment Jenn broke the silence.

"Well? What should we do next?"

When we headed out to the main wharf again, the party was in full swing. Mindful of the guards we slid through the crowd, avoiding some of the more conscientious grownups who shouted that we needed to be in bed and what did we think we were doing, running around the wild part of town? Like we didn't already live there or something.

Jenn and I hung back, Tick lagging between us, still bright-eyed, but flagging fast. Jenn glanced down at him and then at me.

"What happened? I thought he was going to get his new set right about the time I left."

I kicked the ground, bitterness rising in my throat. "You remember what happened to firs'pop, right?"

She nodded. Firs'pop was guiding a fueling tube into the lake when the tube hit an air pocket and bucked. Jenn had been there when first pop's name was chiseled on the memorial stone at the Cathedral.

"Well, after that there was only money for second mama to get new lungs. Tick—we thought he could wait, since he was so little. Now, though, it looks like he's going to need them sooner than we thought."

"He shouldn't even be outside," Jenn said, alarm rising in her voice. I shrugged.

"Nah. The clinic gave us some drugs to keep him going. He'll be fine." I snuck a glance at her. "I couldn't keep him from seeing you. Couldn't keep myself away."

I waited with my heart beating so hard my head swam. Jenn just kept walking, as if she hadn't heard. Then she turned sideways toward me. I could just see her eyes crinkling over the mask.

"Me too," she said, and she reached out and squeezed my hand. "What about you?" she said. "I thought you were going to get that seaship spot."

Even holding hands couldn't take the sting away. "Yeah, well," I said. "They need me on the lake." I didn't tell her I hadn't signed on yet, or that second pop hated looking at me anymore. Or that all we did was fight when we did talk. Or that I missed firs'pop so fierce that I halfway made a promise to myself that I would give up the seaship apprenticeship if only he could come back.

"Look!" Tick shouted. "Randy and Jenn are holding hands!"

We sprang apart, and I made a lunge for him. "You little—"

Dallas and Austin began to sing, "Jenn 'n Randy sittin' in a—"

"Hey, you kids!"

Startled we all turned around. Three wharf guards were coming toward us, their masks sleek and new, their eyes narrowed. Jenn muttered something her firs'ma would disapprove of.

"Can we help you, officers?" beamed Austin. Dallas came up next to her. The twins had the natural ability to project sweetness with their eyes and voices alone. I always looked guilty, even when I wasn't.

"What are you kids doing up this late? Where do you live?"

With blithe innocence, Austin said, "We're sorry, officer. We had to bring dinner to our firs'mas on the night shift. We're heading straight home."

He bought it. His eyes relented.

"See that you do. The docks are no place for kids."

Solemnly we nodded and chorused our promises. Then, with them watching us, we heading quickly in the most plausible direction. We turned a corner and risked a look back—they were still watching, but they had half-turned back to the wharf. One was talking on a radio. I got a bad feeling about that.

"Austin, how do you do that?" Jenn said admiringly. "Come in handy on board." She imitated Austin with a mincing falsetto. "Sorry, officer, I'm just a poor innocent little waif."

We started laughing, but it was too soon—I could see the officer sign off the radio and look over at us again, and then start moving purposefully toward us. Someone must have mentioned the street lamp.

"Uh oh, time to go," I said. Not even Austin would be able to get us out of this one. Grabbing hold of Tick again, we took off through the crowds.

"Where to?" Jenn shouted, her breath coming hoarse through her mask. I looked around for inspiration.

"The Cathedral!" I said.

It was a long steady uphill slog. Before long we were all breathing like Tick. The Cathedral rose above the White Lake spaceport, a mass of solid rock, its feet dipping into White Lake and forming one end of the vast bowl that contained the fuel reservoir. It shone in the reflected light of the lake and the string-of-pearls, shimmering with white and pastels, like an aurora made of stone. In school they taught us that people used to build cathedrals, but those cathedrals were just buildings. No one built this Cathedral except for the planetary forces that shaped the lake itself. It undulated with elaborate carvings, curtains and gargoyles and dainty columns of stone that were as delicate as lace.

It rose so high above the lake you didn't need a respirator at the top.

We walked in grim silence. I knew it wasn't as far as it seemed that night. We'd all been before, for field trips and with our families. But we had been running around all night, and now we were carrying Tick, taking turns to carry him on our backs. I didn't even look up to watch the Cathedral draw near, just kept walking, eyes on my boots as I put them one in front of the other. Every now and then I slipped on the wet path, slick with some fluid that I was too tired to guess about.

When it was my turn to hold Tick I could hear his hoarse breathing against my back. It was getting harder and harder to suck air through my mask—I could imagine how he felt. The drugs had only a limited effect. I remembered taking them myself, being tired all the time and wanting desperately to take a full breath but unable to.

It will be better when we get to the Cathedral, I thought, and shifted Tick up a little higher. He snuggled into my back.

When we reached the gap in the cliff where a narrow passage had been cut, Tick and I almost didn't fit. My elbows and Tick's feet scraped against the rough rock, and my feet slipped on the shallow steps, worn smooth by the passage of so many feet and now running with tiny rivulets of liquid. I went down hard on one knee and Tick gasped and grabbed at my neck, choking me.

"Stop it, Tick!" I said, strangled. "Not so tight."

"Randy, I want to go home," Tick whimpered.

"Stop it. We're almost there."

"Please, Randy. I'm sorry I asked to come."

Shut up! I wanted to scream at him, but I had practically no breath left myself. I just grunted, and shifted him again.

We squeezed through the last turn, and at last we were only ten steps away from the top. Dallas, Austin, and Jenn were already at the railing, their masks off and their faces aglow in the light from the lake. As soon as I reached them I sat at their feet, tumbling Tick to the ground and ripping off his mask and then my own. This high up it was like breathing filtered air, the fumes that offgassed from the lake staying low over the surface of the reservoir. I sucked in air, patting Tick on the back while he coughed and gurgled. Gradually his breathing slowed and color came back into his face.

We didn't say much, just looked out over White Lake. Far off in the distance, the fueling ships sunk their long tubes into the lake, like giant insects hovering around water. Skimmerboats zoomed around them, and we could see the lakefront teeming with activity. Up at the Cathedral it was quiet and peaceful. Even the constant glow was muted and a few stars shone overhead. The air was sweet and a light breeze ruffled our hair. I snuck a look at Jenn's profile, absorbed in the view. She had grown while she was away. Her face had angular planes now where before her cheeks had been round and comfortable. I could see what she would look like all grown up, and I didn't like the way it made me feel. Like I was being left behind.

"Randy, which one's pop's name?" Tick's voice was back to normal. I tore my gaze from Jenn's face. Hundreds of names were inscribed on the Cathedral wall, perpetually lit up by the glow from the lake that killed them. We could read them from here.

"Fourth from the bottom, Tick, middle column." Four more had died since firs'pop.

I couldn't stall much longer. In a few months I would have to take my place on the lake, earning a living like my parents. The extra cash would come in handy—Tick would get a new pair of lungs that much sooner. Never mind that it would never be enough. There would always be new lungs to buy for someone. Heck, once I started working on the lake, my respirator would never completely protect me from the fumes. We worked first for lungs down there. I turned away from White Lake toward the Cathedral. The Cathedral was part of the massive escarpment that blocked White Lake and the spaceport from the Glory Sea. It was hard to believe that on the other side of the Cathedral was a whole other world that I had never seen and never would see. It could be on the other side of a jump gate for all the chance I had to go there, anymore. If firs'pop hadn't— I cut off that thought. Sometimes I just got tired of thinking about it.

"What the—" Dallas jumped up, swiping at his jeans. "I'm wet!"

"Wet!" Jenn scrambled to her feet, checking her uniform. It clung damply to her backside, and I swallowed hard. Then the wet registered and I got up too, looking around. A slow dark patch spread out from the Cathedral Wall, creeping toward the trail we had just come up. Another rivulet meandered toward the railing and the drop to White Lake. Tick whimpered and I knew what he was thinking. Leaking fuel. But in the next instance my common sense caught up with me. If it had been fuel, we would all be choking from the fumes by now. With the others watching me I knelt and took off my glove and touched a finger to the wet. I brought it to my tongue.

Salt water.

The Cathedral wall was leaking.

"What do we do?" Austin said, her eyes wide.

"We have to tell someone," I said with a calm that came out of nowhere.

"So much for sneaking back in," Dallas said. His voice had an eerie grownupness about it. We all looked at the spreading water heading for the lip. This small amount of water posed no threat. It would vaporize before it fell to the lake's surface. But if the leak grew—I thought of water reacting with the hydrazine in the lake, the heat sending the entire reservoir boiling over into the town. My stomach knotted.

"We should find out where it's coming from. Maybe we can plug it up," Jenn said. We trooped back to the wall, following the trail. It led us along the base of the Cathedral and we wound around some fallen rocks away the viewing ledge. The paving stones were broken and dusty, and the native plantings were withered. We could follow the water easily through the mess, a dark trail against the dust and rock.

The leak came from a narrow crevice stuck between two folds in the Cathedral's wall. I stuck my hand in as far as it would go, feeling cold salt water on my fingers. I wiggled my fingers and dislodged a piece of rock. Water gushed.

"Shit!" I said and withdrew my hand.

"What?" they demanded and I reddened. I couldn't say I had just made it worse.

"Okay," Jenn said. "Dallas, Austin, and Tick—you guys try to block this up. Randy and I will head back to town and tell the port authority."

"I want to go!" Tick said. He started to cry. Jenn knelt.

"Tick, listen. We have to go really really fast. It's better for you if you stay up here where the air is fresh. Don't worry. We'll come back for you guys."

"With grownups," I added. "They'll be able to carry you all the way down and you won't have to walk or breathe hard."

"Can you get firs'mama to come?" he sniffled.

"I'll try," I hedged, thinking grimly that it wasn't going to be pretty when I told firs'ma where Tick was.

We left them scrounging for rocks and dirt to block the leak, and headed back to the surface. I hated putting my respirator back on, feeling it clamp off my air and make every breath a chore. The filtered air smelled of sweat and bad breath.

Jenn and I jogged down the trail steadily, not talking at all. The water was running fast. I remembered my fingers wiggling in the crevice and the sudden increase in the flow. I began to run, passing Jenn and slipping on the uneasy footing.

"Randy!" she cried as I went down, sliding painfully along the trail. My jeans tore on the rocks, and I skinned my knee. I got up and hobbled painfully a few steps, my breathing tortured.

"We have to hurry," I gasped, clasping my hand over my stinging knee. It throbbed and blood welled in the scratches. I thought of the fumes from White Lake entering my vascular system through the cuts, and smiled wanly at Jenn. She was as filthy as me, her uniform streaked with dust and mud, and her hair pulled out of her neat braid. She grabbed my hand and we ran on, me limping a little.

The party had died down. Hardly anyone was out on the boardwalk any more, and most of the bars had gone dark. The streetlights were dimmer now, and the throng had thinned almost completely. There wasn't a patrol to be found. Jenn and I banged on doors and ran up to the few stragglers, but no one answered and the drunks were unhelpful. Finally we stopped in the middle of a deserted street, sucking air.

"What now?" Jenn said, throwing up her hands. I kept one gloved hand over my knee.

"Let's go to my house," I said. "They might even listen to me before they kill me."

She didn't laugh. "No," she said. "My ship. Come on." She dragged me once again.

As it turned out, it was the right move. There were plenty of wharf guards around her ship, not to mention her parents. And Dallas and Austin's parents. And mine and Tick's.

They were milling around, talking wildly, and almost didn't see us as we came up into the floodlights that illuminated the docking bays. We shaded our eyes against the light, and were enveloped in a group of weeping adults. Jenn was doubly un-lucky—her parents and what looked like all her senior officers were berating her.

"Randy, what the hell is going on?" my second pop bellowed, his eyes red above his mask. "Where's Tick? Is he all right?"

"He's fi—" I started

"Randy, your knee!" Second ma gasped. "That needs to be sealed! What happened?"

"Ma—"

Jenn was having no easier time of it, but she was more direct.

"There's a leak!" she yelled. Everyone turned to look at her. "The Cathedral—water's coming through. It's leaking into White Lake."

"Tick and Dallas and Austin are up there," I put in. "They're trying to plug the leak."

I was wrong about one thing—well, a lot of things, but a cruiser really isn't like a tin can. I'm not saying it's spacious, but there was plenty of room for us. While the wharf guards alerted the spaceport authority supervisor, and most of the parents went up to the Cathedral to get the other kids, Jenn and I got to rest in the filtered air of the spacecraft and take a tongue-lashing from her captain. He didn't raise his voice any, but by the end of the lecture I was feeling pretty low. Only by following Jenn's example was I able to keep from slinking down in my chair. She sat straight and tall and just took it, eyes forward, her face determined.

When he finished and stalked out, we didn't dare speak, just looked at each other. I could hear low voices outside the par-tially opened door and then second pop came in, shambling and awkward. I jerked up in shock. He nodded at the door.

"Captain wants you, Jenn," he said, and she got up promptly and left, throwing me a look over her shoulder like she was sorry for me. Second pop took her chair and straddled it back-ward. "Damn, Randy," he said when she was gone. "You had us worried, son. Running off like that..."

I figured it out pretty quick. They thought I ran away and took Tick with me. I flushed. It wasn't like the thought hadn't occurred to me. "I didn't run off," I muttered. "We were just fooling around."

"You didn't stop to think that we'd be worried? And taking Tick…"

Anger pricked me. "If I thought you'd be scared I wouldn't have done it. I don't do these things on purpose just to bug you, you know."

"Could have fooled me," he snapped back. "The way you've been acting is like that's all you're trying to do."

"Yeah, well, maybe if you would *just get off my back.*"

"Don't take that tone with me, son!"

The words echoed strangely in the room. I think second pop heard it too, because he toned it down. "Dammit, Randy," he said more softly. "You're my son, but you got all of Trey's hardheadedness in you."

I scowled against the lump in my throat that was blocking all the smart remarks I wanted to throw at him. *You aren't firs'pop. I don't have to listen to you. Just leave me alone.*

Then second pop said something unexpected. "I miss him too."

I lifted my head and stared at him.

"He wanted you to have that apprenticeship, you know. Said there was more to Glory than White Lake, and one of us should see it. Then when he died we had to face up to things." He didn't say money. He didn't have to.

"I know." I said it too quickly, too loudly. "I decided up at the Cathedral. I'll sign on at the lake. I'll go with you tomorrow. I just want to make sure my first paycheck goes to Tick."

He didn't have time to respond. There was a commotion when the others got back, Tick carried sleepily on the shoulders of a tall wharf guard and Dallas and Austin tired and triumphant, their eyes wide as they looked around the cruiser. With all the grownups, the cruiser got tight again.

We got another talking-to, this time from the port authority supervisor. She scrolled through her handheld.

"Vandalism? Trespassing? Breaking curfew? I don't know what you kids thought you were doing, but White Lake and the Cathedral are not playgrounds," she scolded. "You put yourselves in great danger, and I'm sure your parents will have plenty to say about that later." We all looked at the floor. "However. You did carry the warning. So I'm going to let the rest of it go, so long as none of you ever pull another escapade like that."

We all mumbled something, even Tick, and I thought bitterly that it wasn't like I was going to have a chance at any more stunts once I started on the lake.

It was time to say good-bye to Jenn. I had been thinking about this all night, imagining how I would take her aside to some secret place and kiss her. But now, in front of all our parents, in front of her captain, all we could manage was an awkward hug. She whispered in my ear, "Bye, Randy."

When it was Tick's turn, she knelt and opened her arms wide and he ran to her, pressing his face in her shoulder.

"Don't go, Jenn," he cried. "Please don't go."

Little kids don't understand. I knelt down behind my little brother and rubbed his back.

"Hey, Tick," I whispered. "You can stay with me, okay? I'll still be here."

"No," he sniffled. "I want to go with Jenn."

It was the only thing I had to give, and he turned me down.

I signed up at the lakefront the next day, and second pop shook my hand and told me he was proud. I didn't start working right away though. It turned out the entire escarpment was riddled with holes and caves, bored through by the relentless pounding of the Glory Sea. The Cathedral was soon shrouded in scaffolding. Workers were pulled from the port to work on the rigging hundreds of feet above White Lake, my parents among them, swinging high in the fresh air, maskless in the light of the string-of-pearls. The overtime paid well, first for firs'ma's lungs, then Tick's. Things eased up at home too, and second pop was so loud in his praise of me, it made me wish we were back to fighting.

It seemed kind of silly to go to school when I was going to
be starting on the lake, so I cut classes and went up to the overlook. I couldn't help but remember how close I had been to the
Glory Sea and had even let it drip over my fingers. I rested my
head against the sealed-up crack, trying to hear the crashing of
the waves through the rock.

Maybe the ocean had been trying to reach me, too. Maybe
that's why it had busted through the Cathedral, steady drip by
drip. I wondered what it would do if it never found me, but I
guess in a way it did.

They were all in the kitchen when I came home that day. I
paused in the doorway, taking in their tired, beaming faces, their
masks scattered across the table amid calculators and screens.
Second pop grinned at me. Tick bounced on firs'ma's lap, and
second ma leaned against the counter, a crooked smile on her
broad face.

"Looks like we got us an apprentice in the family," second
pop drawled, and held up a contract, the logo of a sailing ship
splashing at the top. I opened and closed my mouth a few times,
trying to get my voice started.

"How—" was about all I managed. Second ma leaned forward and gave me a kiss on the cheek.

"Port authority. If you kids hadn't found that leak, we'd
probably all be dead by now. They're calling it profit-sharing
but it's really just to hush things up."

I didn't have time to figure it out. They all got up and piled
on the hugs, Tick somewhere around my waist and second pop
shaking my hand and clapping me on the shoulder.

Six months later I stood on the shores of Glory, letting the
waves lap against my boots. The sun sparkled on the pinkish
sea, and behind me rose the Cathedral, stretching into the clouds.
Farther up the beach ran Tick, taking random flying jumps into
the air with his arms wide and his mask flopping in the air behind him. Out in the harbor my ship waited, a rusting hulk no
more like the sailing ships of my books than the space cruisers

that docked at White Lake. The air stank of salt and fuel, dead fish and garbage. It was better than I had ever dreamed. I thought about Jenn and wondered if she had felt this way on her signing day, crazy with fear and excitement.

"Randall!" barked the first mate. She waved from the skimmerboat waiting to take me out to the ship. I turned to my parents, huddled behind me. "I gotta go," I said, my voice strained, and gave them each a hug.

"Tick!" pop called. "Come say good-bye to your brother!"

Tick turned and waved both arms. "Bye, Randy!" he hollered, and was off again, chasing waves. I got into the skimmer, and the boat took off with a jerk, bouncing over the waves. I took a faceful of spray, and when I could see again, all I could see was the little figure of Tick running along the shore.

GONNA BOOGIE WITH GRANNY TIME
Sharon Lee

IT BOOK YOU after, you want m'man. M'man Mouse, that who you want, sure.

Lemme tell ya.

Go way up the top of Howard, tie your steed an walk. Ain't far. Safe, if you cool. *You* cool, aincha?

Go on down the street, past the old things store an that print shop got burned last time Jawj an Drood Dude come head on. Go on down, like I'm tellin you, past Shantelle an heading for the clean factory, but don't go there.

Tween Shantelle an the factory, there's a street. Ain't much of a street. One block long, one block wide. Some call it alley, but they ain't met m'man. Mouse Mojo own that street, you unnerstan me. What he say—go.

You after book, you gotta walk the Mouse-man's street.

You don't wanna walk the street, sometime you find him up Shantelle. Sometime you do. Him and Widda gotta rangemint. Mouse, he talk to you there, sure. But it book you after, you gonna be walkin that street, one way or the other.

Member me a dude—white boy, like you, 'cept maybe you ain't stupid. This boy here belong Jax crew. Jax, he own couple club down the Block. Rule is, nobody touch Jax woman but Jax. Easy 'nuff, huh? World full of chicks. But that white boy's brains in his balls. Any girl, either club—he snap his finger, she his. But white boy gotta have Jax chick.

Only thing, Jax woman ain't innerested. Her an Jax tight. White boy care nothin for that. He gonna have her whatever she say.

Short of it, white boy fine he need book. Hell, he need a whole fuckin liberry, digit? Pretty soon, it ain't gonna matter his brains tween his legs or tween his ears, cause Jax, he put the word out. White boy good as meat. If he lucky.

White boy bolt for Howard Street, pay his fare an run. He run past the print shop, past Shantelle. He run til he get to m'man's street, there between. He stop, then, an look around.

Ain't much of a street, like I told ya. Skinny an short. Shimmery, kinda, like it always hot. Buildins kinda bright-dark, kinda—fuzzy. That the Mouse-man's street, awright. What he say—go.

White boy, he don't like the look of m'man's street. White boy, he like street where da buildins don't boogie. Street where it light at day-noon, dark at noon-night.

White boy, he start thinking, now it too late.

He turn hisself round an go on back up Howard. He go on up to Shantelle, open that door, walk them long dark skinny stairs. Top of that stairs, there's your club, dark an empty, Friday morning. There's Widda hind the counter, countin her wares.

White boy say, "Lookin f'Mouse Mojo."

Widda point and that boy turn to see. Table in back. Man at table. Place ain't empty after all.

White boy take hisself over table. Lean on back of the chair an say to m'man.

"Gotta book. Word be out."

Mouse, he look up from his ledger pages. He say, "Set a spell. I'm with ya directly."

"I'm tellin ya—word be out!" white boy say, an I'm askin if that the way you be talk with a man owns a street, when all you got is need?

But the Mouse-man, he cool. He pick up his gold pen an go on back to his pages, that big diamond winkin yalla on his least-finger. "Set or go," he say. "Make no mine to me."

Minute or so, white boy set. He fold his hand on table, watch m'man write, then he turn round an snap his finger at Widda.

"Gimme brew."

She shake her head—"We close"—an go on to the back.

"What t'fuck –"

"Lady say she close," Mouse say from over his figgers. "Nothin say lady gotta sell brew if she close." He make another number, close his pen an put it way inside his suit coat. He fold his hand top his papers an look at white boy.

"You the boy force Jax woman?"

White boy get a little whiter, there in the dim. "How—?"

"Like you say, word be out." Mouse lift a hand, showin palm. "I ain't no particular friend of Jax. But I never heard his woman did anybody hurt. Never heard that."

White boy set his face. "Bitch ask for everything she get," he say, but it don't sound so sure it sounded downtown, now he talkin with m'man.

But Mouse, he only nod. "So why you come here?"

White boy lick his lips. "Gotta book. I told ya." He wait a beat, but Mouse he don't say nothin.

"I'll pay," white boy say then. "Cash or stuff, you say what. Jus gotta book outta here, man, quiet an quick. That's all. Got friends in 'troit. I'll pay you to get me there."

Mouse, he don't say nothin.

White boy lose what sense he got. He slam his fist on table. He glare at m'man.

"Listen, you the book-man or aincha?"

"I tell you how it be," Mouse say then, his voice real quiet, there in the dim. "I ain't no fuckin travel agent, you dig? I own that book—I don't rent. You pay me, sure you do. You pay me cash *an* stuff, just like I tell you. But you don't tell me where you gone, William. I tell you."

White boy stare. "What you call me?" He scare, then, I think. Well, who wouldn't be? All this life you been Jag Saratoga, workin on your legend an movin up that ladder. Now come a man callin you by nother name from nother life—name you half forgot yourself.

"Call you William," say the Mouse-man. "Call you William Bzdrecky, like you mama name you."

White boy he sit back, forehead leakin sweat.

"Now, I tell you, William," say the Mouse-man, all quiet in the near-dark. "You wanna book, I sell you book. I Mouse Mojo an' what I say—go. I say when an I say where. You dig that, m'man?"

White boy swallow, thinkin this too funky. Thinkin, maybe this too dangerous. Then he think bout Jax an Jax woman an he think bout knifes an cow-starters an other hurtfuls they might use him with. He hurt Jax woman—well, he had to, didn't he? Bitch claw him, bite him, hit. Had to smack her down, didn't he? Keep her quiet? Show her who boss?

He nod at the Mouse-man, jerky-like, an wipe his face where the sweat run down.

"Dig it," he say, his voice scratchin outta his throat.

"Good," say Mouse an push back from table. He fold his papers an slide them in a side pocket. He straighten that silk knot on his tie, that big diamond leakin green off his finger.

"Come with me," he tell Jag Saratoga, whose mama name him William Bzdrecky, an head off down them stairs.

They hit the street an Mouse turn left. White boy look right fore he follow, see three Jax boys movin down the side-walk from Preston. White boy scuttle after Mouse.

"They here. They right behine," he say into Mouse's ear. Mouse don't even look around.

"We fine, boy. They know better then come down this street."

He take white boy's elbow an steer him right, tween the clean factory an Shantelle. Steer him right onto that street an it *be* hot an the buildins boogie an shimmer: yella, red, green, black, mocha—gone. An back.

White boy stop an throw his hand in front his face. "Why they do that, man?"

"That?" Mouse look at the buildins, look at them dancin. And he smile some, Mouse, cuz this his street an what he say—go.

"See, they do that cuz they ain't neither here nor there," he tell white boy. "They here *an* there—they boogie down with Granny Time."

White boy don't dig it, course, would you? But he don't get to say, cuz Mouse move his hand an that diamond show wet-blood red—move his hand an say, "This way, now, boy. You gotta book an I don't wanna keep ya."

He go on down that shimmery, glimmery sidewalk an white boy got no choice but follow. He don't be likin this, unnerstan, but Mouse Mojo is his only hope of life. Jax boys find him, they make him into pieces, then kill the pieces, one by one. He take one look behine fore he follow Mouse away, just to see how close Jax boys come.

Behine him there's the street, buildins jumpin on either side. End of street, where it hit Howard, is—nothin. Not black. Not white. Not fog. Not light.

Nothin.

"Face of Granny Time," say Mouse, an take his elbow, easin him down the street.

There people on the street. Cops an drug kings, whores an queens. Some dress in satin, some dress in silk. Some dress in khaki, homespun. Rags. They smile when they see Mouse. They raise their hands. Mouse smile back. Wave. His people go on down the sidewalk, go in them buildins an out.

White boy look at Mouse.

"They dance with Granny Time, too? These folks here?"

"They do," say Mouse.

White boy take a breath, watchin the people flow past him—minidresses an zoot suits. Ayrab cotton an hoop skirts.

"I gonna dance, too, Mister Mouse?"

Mouse he laugh, soft-like, reach out an ruffle the hair of a pickeninny in homespun.

"No, boy. These folk here ain't got no 'counts. Their ledger sheet gone missin. Or their sum be in dispute. You, now—you got 'count. You be added, subtract-ed, noted down an analyzed. We know just what to do with you, m'man. We seen your kind before."

White boy swallow an try to think of another question. Fore he do, Mouse stop, fingers diggin white boy's elbow.

"In here."

This buildin don't boogie. White boy find that—ominous. This buildin got no window. Got no door.

"In?" he say to Mouse. "How the hell I'm s'pose—

Mouse step forward, draggin white boy with him. He walk through that wall, white boy half a step behind.

Everything go way for a minute into cold nasty. Then everything come back an they in a round room all shiny black marble. White boy's stomach turn over. He gag. Mouse pull him close inside, stand him in the center of the room an step back. That big diamond on his finger be black by now. Black like the shiny black walls.

"All right, William," he say, pullin the papers from his pocket. "Now's time to pay up." He unfold his papers an look down.

"You holdin three grand cash," he say, for all the world like he readin it off a list. "You holdin one pound crack. They forfeit." He look up an point at the floor by his shoes. "Toss 'em out here."

White boy's feelin foggy hisself. Feelin—less then together. He reach in his pocket. He toss the stuff. Minute later, he toss the cash.

"Right," say Mouse. "Now you book." He fold the papers, start to slide them in his pocket—

"Wait!" scream white boy. "Wait. I—I change m'mind. I stay here. Talk with Jax. Make it right..."

Mouse shake his head, put his papers away. "Too late, William. You walk the street, you pay the price."

White boy break, then. He fling hisself at Mouse, hands out like he gonna latch roun m'man's throat an—

He bounce, half-a-foot out from his standin place. Bounce an fall. He's up quick and jumps again. Bounce an fall. This time he get up slow, wipe blood off his nose.

"At least tell me where I'm goin," he say then.

Mouse sigh. "Up to Granny Time, boy. Can't say where for sure. This street—what they call a vortex, see? Sometime it here, sometime it not. I don't know all the places you might go.

I can tell you what kind of places, if you wanna know. Might be better, not to know."

"I'm gonna know in a minute, anyhow," white boy say an Mouse bow his head.

"That's so." He pull his papers out an stand holdin them in his hand. "Way it works, you got a debt to Granny Time. Debt ain't balanced by cash an' stuff—not near balanced. So Granny take the rest outta your hide, just like your old man useta." He sigh.

"Places like maybe you go: Ancient Egypt, totin stone. Old Turkey, cock-shaved an servin the harem. Whore boy in Victorian England. Other places—I can't say 'em all, boy. Granny Time span planets, some of 'em worse then here."

White boy slide down to sit on the shiny black floor. Tears mix up with the sweat on his face.

"I ain't goin," he say an dig real sudden in his pocket. Pulls out his piece. Mouse shake his head.

White boy set the barrel in his mouth, close his eyes, pull the trigger.

Nothin happen. Course not.

White boy scream, then, jump up an throw the piece. It hit the floor tween Mouse's shoes.

"You kill me, then!" he yell.

Mouse shake his head an step back, tucking his papers away.

"Can't do that, boy," he say, soft-like. "Granny Time got her hook in me, just like she got it in you."

White boy got time for one more scream, while his standin place fills up with fog, swirlin, glitterin. The fog spin an Mouse watch, like he have to watch, everytime this go down. Then the fog fade away an Mouse look down at his hand. That big diamond's clear now. Clear. Just like tears.

Jax boys climb that long black stair, come out into Shantelle an stop. Grooj come forward by hisself, nod to Widda, there hind her counter.

"Lookin f'Mouse Mojo."

Widda point an Grooj go back to that certain table. The man sittin there look up from his papers an fold his hands, the big diamond on his least-finger blazin white.

"Mornin, Mister Mojo."

"Mornin, Mister Robinson."

Grooj he ain't been Robinson for thirty year, but he know better then to ask.

"Lookin for a friend," he say instead. "Mister Jag Saratoga. Thought maybe you seen him."

"I seen him," say Mouse.

Grooj sigh. "I need somethin to tell Jax, Mister Mojo. You unnerstan."

"I do." Mouse take a minute, look down at—into—his diamond.

"Tell Jax Mister Saratoga be gone," he say, an look up at Grooj. "Tell Jax woman he got everything he ask for."

ANGEL'S KITCHEN
Chris Szego

"WZF'DR?"

Kess said, "Swallow, Bee."

Bee chewed at ferocious rate, swallowed audibly. "What's for dinner?"

"More of what you're eating, so I hope you like it."

"S'fine," Bee said, already into the next mouthful.

Kess resisted the urge to tell Bee to slow down. In this part of Senneville, he who ate slowly, went hungry. Or she, as was likely the case with Bee. Kess was fairly certain, but wasn't about to ask. It was still marginally safer to be a boy, and here in the Darks, any margin was better than none.

The seeded roll and the stew disappeared faster than charity in hard times. There were barely crumbs left. Partly because Bee's technique was three-quarters inhalation, but also because Bee was a tidy person.

As if that sounded some sort of silent direction, Bee gathered plate, bowl and spoon in one motion. "I'll just do these up quick."

Tidy and responsible. For months Kess had worried about Bee, who was neither Hap nor Cane, and who, though undoubtedly older, was the size of a fragile eight year old. But Bee would take nothing extra, would take barely at all, until, inspired, Kess had offered a job. Now Bee appeared at the Kitchen at midday, to help Kess with the mountain of dishes left over from the previous night's meal.

And Kess got to be sure that her smallest charge was eating enough, if not plenty.

And not 'charge'. Small, yes, and possibly fragile. But Bee's eyes were as old as everyone else's around here. As old as Senneville; as old as hunger.

Kess followed Bee into the dishroom. Bee had already started on the cutlery. Kess went to work on the pots.

An hour later saw the dishes clean, and Bee out the door. Kess never watched when Bee left: it would be too much like prying. But she always knew the moment Bee had gone. And that was a problem.

If there was one lesson to be learned at the Angel's Kitchen, it was not to get attached. Not to the hungry crowd who came every night. Not to the wealthy few, who helped out until their hearts broke and they quietly disappeared. And never to the children.

A heavy fist on the door pounded her out of those thoughts. Kess looked through the mirrored arrangement Lucius had set up for her, and sighed. The young man was wearing Cane black. She didn't recognize him. He wasn't long in the Darks, not with that smooth skin, that bright hair. Farm boy, probably, recently come south.

She opened the door. "Dinner's not for another few hours."

"What?"

"You're early. Canes don't eat until eight."

"What?" He shook his head. "What are you talking about?"

"Dinner," she said patiently. "Canes eat at eight; Haps come at nine."

The young man, boy, really, goggled. "Haps? Here? In Cane territory?"

Hmm. If the Kitchen was now in Cane territory, the next few weeks would be...exciting. To say the least. "Did Ash send you to tell me that? That Cane territory has grown?"

"Ash? Talk to *me*? Huh." The boy pulled back, looked away. "I mean, he will, soon. He'll know me. He'll know my name." He said it like a vow, a prayer. Not to Bel, but to one of the older gods, who dealt in gold and fire.

From a boy who looked like he should have been piping the wild sheep down from their ragged hills, it was particularly ardent. And touching. Kess decided not to tell him that Ash knew his name, his hole, and likely, his entire life history.

"And it's all Cane territory," the boy went on, fierce and proud. "Ash just lets the Haps have a corner to give us something to do."

Ah. That, if Kess wasn't mistaken, was a direct quote from Ash's welcome to newcomers. The territories hadn't changed, then. Good. "So...I'm sorry, what's your name?"

"Mac."

"...So, Mac, why are you here, again?"

Mac lifted his hands in frustration. "I'm here for the vig!"

Kess rubbed her eyes. *Bel save me from the new ones.* "I don't pay vig. To anyone."

"What?" This was outside his experience. He was shifting now from foot to foot. Nervous, new, and very eager to prove himself. And big. Not a good combination. "Come on, lady..."

She moved forward, sharp, before he could square up. He went back, into air, then down a step, hard. "Listen to me, Mac," she said. "You're a Cane. What are the Cane rules?"

They came automatically, a simple, shining order to guide them through the Darks. "'Cane helps Cane. Cane protects Cane. Cane hides Cane.' And, uh..."

"...No one messes with the Angel's Kitchen."

"Yeah." He frowned. "How do you know?"

"Because *this* is the Angel's Kitchen." Her tone, developed specifically for this speech, turned into ice, into hail. "There is no Cane here, Mac. No Hap. No weapons, no fists. No rank. And no hunger. Canes come at eight; Haps at nine; everyone else until midnight. This is the Angel's Kitchen." She leaned in, forced him to meet her eyes. "And I am *not* the angel."

Mac went down a step, then another. "Right." Down again, to the ground. "Uh, I didn't mean to..." He stopped, bewildered. And all at once, desperately young. "I thought the Angel's Kitchen was, you know, a metaphor."

Hmm. Anyone in this part of Senneville who knew metaphor enough even to pronounce it was worth a second look. Maybe Ash *had* sent him this way after all. "No harm done. You were just doing your job as a Cane. I can appreciate that."

She let her tone lighten, her eyes. "Want to come in and look around?"

The flash of yearning she saw then, for the memory of walls, of safety, proved him as new to the Darks as she'd thought. Only the new had time for memory. But the way he straightened, and shook his head, proved him to be more than just new, or eager. Resolute.

Or, knowing Ash, romantic. Gods help him.

"Can't," he said. "I've got another block to do." He walked away, stopped after a few steps. "But...thanks."

Kess felt her throat tighten. Rarely did even the new have time for manners. "Some other time."

She closed the door firmly, and when he was gone, locked it. And if she stood for a moment with her hands over her eyes, there was no one to see.

Later that night, she pointed Mac out to Lucius. "Over there," she said, as she passed out rolls. She kept her gaze light, impersonal, moving. It was not done to stare. "Third table. Next to that tall one."

"Which tall one?"

"Twig, I think. I can't quite see from here."

Lucius glanced over. "Green hat?"

"No, the *third* table."

"Sorry. Oh, I see. The fair boy." He kept up the slow and steady rhythm of stew, ladle, bowl. To stew again. "But where are his sheep?"

Kess snorted back a laugh. Lucius was her absolute favorite Brother. Oh, the Brothers of Bel were all kind, and courteous, and helpful. And grave. Only Lucius made her laugh. Only he seemed to understand that it was more than just important to laugh, here. It was absolutely vital.

"He's new," she said, risking another glance. "He's smart. He doesn't belong here."

"My dear, no one belongs in the Darks. Not him, not you, not any of us."

"And yet," she said, "Here we are."

"Yes." All the bowls were filled now. They glanced around the room, watching over the eaters. Then Lucius asked, "Do you ever wonder why?"

The north door opened before she could answer. Two men came through, calm and quiet, the way lightning patiently awaits its moment in the heart of the storm. One was Yil, the Silesian refugee who was the Cane's Second. The other, of course, was Ash.

A current eddied through the room at his entrance. Words began to rise as mouths remembered how to make room for more than food. Yil, slim, handsome, beginning to develop the smoky hair of his race, took his bowl with a sly smile. "Did you meet our new friend, then?"

She nodded. "He's over there. Sitting with Twig, I think."

"Not Twig." Yil lost his grin. "Twig's gone."

Kess' heart stuttered. "What happened?"

"He was taken for theft two days ago."

She exhaled. "Can I bail him out?"

"No." Tattoos circled Ash's eyes, a dark and twisting pattern on his dark skin. They curled, like shadows, teasing the eye, hiding his expression most effectively. "The Council declared him Penitent. His ship sailed this morning. We will not see him again."

He took the bowl from her hands, and went with Yil to a table, where a place was hurriedly made for them.

Lucius tactfully withdrew to supervise the Canes, ensuring that cups, bowls and spoons were returned with alacrity, if not grace. Kess went into the kitchens. She dragged the first empty cauldron into the dishroom, scoured it out with savage strokes. Then, calmer, she stirred the second lot of stew. And said a prayer for Twig, on a cramped ship, headed for Bel knew where. His salvation, the Council would say. Quite possibly, his death.

When she returned, she brought the stew with her. Ash's arrival had shivered new life into the Canes. They were all but gone, trailing out the south door in his wake, a banner of living energy.

She helped Lucius gather the last of the dishes. Then, into the quiet, she said, "I know why I'm here."

He looked up.

"Because I want to save someone."

He gave her a gentle smile. "That's why we're all here."

"No. I used to want to save all of them. Now, I'd settle for one. Just one." She turned, abruptly, headed to the north door. "I'll let the Haps in."

The Haps entered in a flood, a shoal of blue darting into every corner. They equaled the Canes in number, and in hunger. She and Lucius ladled stew, handed out rolls, kept light and easy eyes on the room. A flurry at the entrance, a wave of chatter heralded the arrival of big Johns, leader of the Haps.

He was stevedore-sized, bluff and blond. Kess handed him a bowl containing no more, or less, than any other. And said as he took it, in barely a whisper, "Twig's gone. This morning. Penitent ship."

Where Ash was smoke and shadow, Johns was a wall. A cliff. An impenetrable blank. He moved off with his stew, a mountain in the midst of the sea of Hap blue. Kess stayed behind the counter, a lone island in a sea of bobbing bowls.

It seemed, sometimes, that the Canes and Haps were just the prelude to the large, unwieldy chorus that was rest of the Darks. At least, it seemed that way tonight. There were families here, ragged remains of what might have been. Elderly men and women so brittle and numb they could have been made of ice. Stunned survivors all, searching for a little light, a little food, a voice that was not their own.

Bee came in, behind a small group of raddled women. Kess, who was immovably fair in her division of food, gave Bee the largest roll she could find.

"Hey," said Lucius. "I recognize him."

Kess didn't bother to correct the pronoun. "That's Bee."

"The one who cleans up for you? Figures. I'm fairly certain he cleans up at Meet, too. Right from the Tithe bowl."

She struggled not to grin. "Bee steals from the Tithe?"

Lucius shrugged. "You can't say he's not efficient. It's all coming out here anyway. And he doesn't seem to take much, so I've never pursued the issue."

Efficient. At theft. That was so...Bee. She let the smile come, and went back to work.

Midnight was gone, and the last of the hungry. For tonight, anyway; for now. All the dirty dishes were stacked in the dishroom, awaiting Bee's arrival and the flurry of activity that would begin again tomorrow afternoon. Graver even than usual, five Brothers came to collect Lucius, which seemed excessive. The Brothers were rarely bothered in the Darks: they were too ready to give to be worth any trouble.

Kess doused the lanterns, banked the fires. She went, by and by, to a cupboard that contained mostly linen, but also a bottle of a surprising Silesian vintage. In the flickering candlelight she waited.

The south door opened. Johns came in. She poured a glass. Before he reached it, a thread wound into the room, a pulse. A man.

"Ash." Johns stood. Sunlight met shadow, clasped its shoulders. "I'm sorry. Kess told me about Twig. Damn. I'm sorry."

Ash bowed his head, for the briefest of moments. "Yes." He squeezed the big man's arm, more to give comfort than to take it. Then he let go.

Kess set a glass in front Ash. She lifted her own. "To Twig. May he find fair winds and friendly shores."

They drank. Ash looked at the bottle. "You honor us. You honor Twig." He savored a sip. "Not that Twig would recognize a wine like this."

"Not from lack of trying," she murmured.

That caused Ash's mouth to curve, which had been her intention. Then he drained the last of his wine and it was time to put aside grief for survival. As usual. "There is another problem."

"There's always another problem," said Johns.

"Mmm. This involves an...incursion. Into Cane territory."

"Not Hap," said Johns, firmly.

Ash shook his head. "Of course not. This is something else. A small group, older than most of ours. Twig," and there was the barest hint of a sigh around the name, "was watching them for me. They're organized. Down from the Western mines, apparently."

"Dangerous?" asked Johns.

"Very. Knives, cudgels, mining issue razor wire. Last night they attacked Brother Erikus."

"Oh—" Kess let out a breath. "I wondered why so many Brothers came to collect Lucius tonight. Will Erikus live?"

"He has so far."

"A good sign," said Johns. "Where did it happen?"

"Down Old King's Lane, after midnight."

Johns raised his brows. "Is that Cane territory, then? Since when?"

Ash lifted a shoulder. "Since last night. Who do you have working that way?"

"My littlest mites. It's good training. I'll move them up-town tomorrow."

"Good. Don't let your Haps go out alone. Threes or fours for safety. Who are your best?"

"Jack, Bren, Trellis. And Sean, of course."

"Send them out in pairs. If they see anything, *anything*, they're to watch from a distance and report. Under no circumstances do they offer any provocation."

"I'll make certain they understand."

"Good. That leaves," Ash turned, "only you, Kessily."

He only ever used her full name for dramatic effect. She refused to let him know it always worked. "Leaves me where, exactly?"

"It leaves you nowhere, alone. You're getting a shadow."

"What?"

But Johns nodded. "Someone we can trust. Older, stronger. Big. That Bee's a good kid, but he wouldn't be much help."

She let the 'he' slide, though she'd have thought Johns would know better.

"Who? All the oldest ones are either Cane or Hap, and I won't have anyone recognizable. Bel's eyes, can you imagine? We'd have a war on our hands."

"You need someone new," Ash said. "Unknown. But careful, and loyal, with a responsible heart."

"Ah," she said. *I knew Ash had sent him here on purpose.* "You're giving me Mac."

"Mac," said Johns. "He's the new one, right? Looks like that wild godling. The one with all the sheep."

Ash considered that, and his lips curved. "An apt image, but one I trust you won't mention to him. I will send him to you tomorrow. When he's ready, if he's ready, tell him."

She tried to see past the shadows on his face. Failed. "Everything?"

"Everything you deem wise." He stood, and Johns stood with him. "I'll send him over at noon. He will stay during the daylight hours. Canes and Haps will take turns on midnight walkabout. Canes tonight, Haps tomorrow. Tell them we have a midnight truce, for the duration, you know the trick."

Johns hugged Kess, grinned. "That's good. That's very good."

She checked the door, saw them through. For a blond giant, Johns melted into the dark like one born to it. Ash remained behind a moment. "Strange. I'd expected an argument from you about your need for a shadow. You are perhaps ill?"

"I am, as usual, all admiration for your manipulative genius." She let him smirk, just for a moment. "And I want Mac. I want him."

"Ah, young Mac." Ash's eyes quirked. "He just might be the one. Your one lost soul, brought safely home..."

"Maybe." She watched him. "Will you stay?"

He took a breath. "I think...not."

She nodded. "If you go down to King's Lane—I know you will—for pity's sake, be careful. And if you go to the harbor, as I think you might, bring this." She handed him a bright silver coin.

He twisted the coin in his fingers. "For Twig's sake?"

"And for mine. Throw it into the tide and make a wish for all of us."

"Ever the angel." His hand was light on her hair. Then it was gone. And so was Ash.

She locked the door, gathered the wine, the glasses. She hid the first, washed the second, and took herself up to bed.

Her room was high above the kitchen and dining hall. There were several routes out, but only one way in: a narrow ladder that could be pulled up with ease. Small windows faced east and west, open even now to let in the night breeze. She lit a candle, pulled the curtains, and curled into a bed that was too large without Ash in it.

Ash. Who, more than Mac, more even than Bee, was her one. The one lost soul she wanted to save. Needed to.

He wouldn't thank her for it.

As if that's ever stopped me before. She blew out her candle and let the day go.

"We're finished," said Mac.

"Already?" Kess wiped her hands, then followed Mac into the dish room. The sparkling, spotless dish room. "Wow. Even faster than yesterday. It's not a race, you know."

Mac snorted. "Tell Bee."

"Bee?"

Bee grinned, a wide, happy, smile. And looked, for the first time ever, like a child. "Hey, Shep comes in, tells me he can clean up his half faster than me, what'm I going to do?"

"Prove him wrong, I expect," Kess murmured.

"'Course." Bee's grin became smug.

Mac's smile was more like a grimace. "Time to buzz, little Bee. Come back tonight to collect."

Bee was already mostly out the door. "I will!"

"You made a bet? With Bee?" Kess winced. "Sorry, I should have warned you. You get taken for much?"

"Like I'm going to get taken by an eight year old." Mac stowed the empty kettles with neat precision. "It was just to get Bee going."

"Did you throw the race?"

"No." He glanced over. "Which is a little embarrassing."

"I won't tell anyone." She turned away so he wouldn't misinterpret her smile. "You two get along. I'm glad. Bee is..., well, Bee." She thought of Lucius, and the Tithe, and smiled again. "Can be a bit of a handful."

He shook his head. "Bee just needed to know I was an addition. Not a replacement. You know? My sister was..." He stopped so sharply Kess could have cut herself on the edge of the silence.

It was easiest to balance on that precipice by moving carefully around it. "Mmm. You washed the linens, too. Thank you."

He cleared his throat. "Yeah, well, okay. I fixed the old wringer."

"You fixed my wringer?" She ran for the laundry. When he came in, she was turning the crank, thrilled.

"How long has it been broken?"

"It never worked. I found it, a couple years ago. Ash said it would be kindest to bury it."

"It wasn't dead," Mac said, "Just sort of...sick. I cleaned off the rust. It needed a clamp, right there, and a spring."

"I may just have to marry you." His sudden flush was unexpectedly sweet. "I shouldn't tease. But thank you. For all of your help these past few days."

He ducked his head. "Ash asked me. To help. Asked *me*."

There was enough wonder in his voice to make her blink. "Ash is careful about who he trusts. So am I. Now," she stood, leaving him to sort that through, "I'm going to get dinner started."

She knew he was there the second she stepped into her bedroom. In a city of grey and black and brown, her room was a world of color. Lush plants, thick books, fat cushions. And there, in the midst of it all, a note of darkness that made all the colors more real.

Ash reclined on her bed, longs legs stretched out. He looked less relaxed than quiescent. At least, for the moment.

It was always a point of silent, stubborn pride with Kess to act even more casually than he. "So. Is there news of our Western friends?"

"They are not quite twelve in number. And they are not our friends."

She lit a lamp, a trio of candles. "No, I suppose not."

"They killed Meyer," he said. "Last night."

"Oh." That was bad. Meyer was, when sober, a passable cobbler. When drunk, which was usually the case, he was more often found in a tavern brawl than his shanty shop. A big man, a canny fighter. Dead, now.

"So you will keep your shadow a while longer."

She nodded. "Good."

He quirked a brow. "How fares our young godling?"

"To be entirely honest, I can't imagine how I got by without him."

Ash propped himself on his elbow. "And how am I to take that?"

"However you like." She flicked him a glance. "He fixed the wringer, you know."

"Ah. I see I shall have to be on my mettle."

Rain fell on the roof, a dismal autumn rain, promising a hopeless winter. But her room was jewel of warmth and color and light. She leaned in, put a hand over his heart. "You always are."

"Can I ask you something?" said Mac.

"Add a handful of that sorrel, there. Good. Yes, go ahead."

"Why does Bee call me Shep?"

"Oh. Um." Kess could feel her face coloring. *Dammit.* "It's, um..." She sighed. "It's your hair, Mac. Your skin. You look so...fresh. Like every artist's idea of the noble shepherd."

For the sake of morale, her own, she did not add 'godling'. "In fact, there's a painting, quite a famous one, up at the College. You could have walked right off the canvas."

He shook his head. "Huh. Wonder if Bee saw that painting?"

She considered that. "I wouldn't be surprised. Bee gets around."

"Reckon. Bee was the first person I met in the Darks. It was Bee who brought me to Yil."

"Really?" That was very interesting. Given how aloof Bee kept from both Haps and Canes.

"Mmm. You know, when we first met, Bee reminded me of my sister. But sometimes now, I think it's my brother." He looked over.

"Well," said Kess, "The Darks is no place for a girl. You understand?"

Mac stirred with measured strokes. "You're a girl."

"That's how I know." In the eight days he'd been her shadow, this was the most personal Mac had been. "I'm from uptown originally, you know."

He nodded, kept stirring. "You don't sound the same as everyone else."

"My parents died when I was eight. It was a bad time. I wandered out of the house, ended up not far from here. Didn't mean to. I was practically delirious. Here in the Darks, that made me bait."

"What happened?"

She gave his hand a nudge. He returned his attention to the simmering stew. "This kid found me. Him and his skinny little friend. They got me something to eat, found us a place to sleep. Showed me around. And when I was finally coherent, they took me home." She tasted his batch of stew. "Not bad. A little more salt, I think."

He added a generous pinch. She expected a number of questions, but not the one she got. "How did they die?" he asked softly. "Your parents?"

"Largepox." Time to risk it. "Yours?"

A brief nod.

"And your brother, and sister?"

His voice was soft, with sharp edges, something broken and not yet mended. "It ate my whole family."

Behind those words, Kess heard others. That asked, how was he to be a son, a brother, without them? She knew that echo. Remembered it well. "So you came to Senneville."

Mac rolled his shoulders, as if preparing for a fight, or some terrible ordeal. "They used to talk, my parents, about the College. You know, about me going there. Later." He didn't look up. "Not that it matters anymore."

And right there, Kess knew she had him. It was like a note of music, but made of light, singing inside her head. "I went, you know. To the College."

He looked up. Truly surprised. "You did?"

"Mmm." She kept her tone casual, dimly surprised she could hear it through the singing. "Three years. I still have all my books. All my notes and letters."

Mac turned back to the stew. Stirred as if the fate of the Darks and all of Senneville resided on it. Kess could practically see longing hovering about him like fog. And knew he would not allow himself to take what he so desperately wanted. Ten years in the Darks had taught her at least as much as three in the College. You had to give before you could take.

She let the afternoon work itself out. Then, in the lull before the Canes descended, when Brother Marcus had arrived to supervise the stew, she made her move. "Do you think you could try to convince Bee to stay with us a little longer tomorrow? To spend the afternoons here? It's dangerous out there right now."

"Yil told me about that man Meyer," he said with a frown.

"I don't like the thought of Bee out there alone," she said, pushing it just a little further. "If Bee won't stay with the Canes, here would be just as good."

"I'll see what I can do," he said.

"I know I can count on you," she said, then busied herself with the rolls, confident her wild young shepherd would find a way to keep the most flighty of the Darks denizens safely grounded.

And she would see to it that there was plenty to occupy the two of them. Plenty of books, of notes, of letters. All the learning one could imagine, or desire.

Several days later, watching Bee peer avidly at the pictures in yet another atlas, Kess sighed. "Don't get me wrong. I'm immensely grateful that you managed to get Bee to spend some time here. But Bel's eyes, it makes me feel superfluous. I've been trying for months. You got it right first time."

"Hmm?" grunted Mac, without looking up from his book.

She patted his hand. "Never mind. I appreciate your keeping us company."

"Mmm."

"And such sparkling conversation."

With effort, he tore himself out of his reading. "Sorry, did you say something?"

Kess barely restrained a grin. "Nothing important. I'm going to finish the rolls."

Mac put down his book and stood. "I'll help."

Drat. Kess was irritated with herself, but knew better than to argue. Mac might revel in the study she provided, but he refused to allow himself to be diverted from what he perceived as his duty.

Mac stoked up the oven. "Money talks with Bee."

She paused, dough in her hands. "You pay Bee?"

He nodded.

She laughed. "That rat. *I* pay Bee."

He slid another tray into the oven. "You pay Bee to work. I pay Bee to keep you company."

Kess shook her head. "I can't allow you to be out of pocket for this."

But he shook his head. "I'm not. Ash gave me a special stipend. Because I'm not earning while I'm here. But it's important to him that I stay. You know...I mean, you and Ash...I mean, he thinks..." He trailed off, face fiery.

Amused, she took pity on him. "Indeed. You've been a great help to me."

They worked in companionable silence for a while. Then, Mac said, "I think I understand."

She handed him the last tray. "Understand what?"

He closed the oven, busied himself tidying. "Understand how it works. All of it. Ash, the Canes. The Haps. Johns."

All at once Kess gave him her full attention. It was always important to handle this part carefully. "Yes?"

His voice wasn't diffident, but considering. As if picking its way over a rocky riverbed, where a ducking might be the least of the consequences. "I mean, Canes know the rules. And Haps have their own rules. And we all talk about being ready to square off, all the time. But these past few weeks, here, I've noticed there's no fighting."

She dried her hands, put down the towel so she wouldn't fuss with it.

Emboldened, or at least reassured by her silence, he went on. "It makes sense, in a way. But it wouldn't work at all if there wasn't a place to rest. One sanctuary, where everyone is safe. The Angel's Kitchen."

She said, "I'm no angel."

He grinned. "No, I don't think so. My guess is Ash named the place. Probably as a joke."

That was, of course, correct. "Was it the Silesian Histories that tipped you?"

He looked impressed. "Is that what I'm reading? No wonder it's so interesting. I mean, yes, there's a hint of the idea in it, but mostly it was the frontispiece." She must have looked uncomprehending. "You wrote your name in it. Kessily Kehnap. Cane-Hap. It just got me thinking."

She watched him. These past days of study had been good
for him in so many ways. He looked bigger. Inside. Like his
heart had grown apace with his understanding. She smiled.
"Pretty good thinking, I'd say."

He would have said more, but there was a muffled thump
and a thud from the dining room. Kess headed for the dining
hall. "Bee, I told you I'd get you another book when..."

There were almost a dozen men in the dining hall. Eleven
large men. Strangers. The north door lay drunkenly off its
hinges. Bee, small and silent, was trapped between them and
the locked south door.

So *stupid*! To have forgotten, in the pleasure of Mac's company, the reason for his presence. Kess cursed herself viciously,
even as her face drew into impassive lines.

"Dinner isn't until ten," she said, cool and calm. "Canes eat
at eight, Haps at nine. Everyone else until midnight."

One of the men, with a blue kerchief, snorted. "We're hungry now."

"That's regrettable, but not my problem."

"We could make it your problem," said another miner, a
skinny one.

She gave him a disintegrating smile. "Not you."

Even as he flushed, another man pushed forward. Kess
didn't step back, but she wanted to. He was shorter, this man.
A little broader than the first, a little cleaner than the second.
The focus of them all. That he was the lynchpin, she had no
doubt.

That she was in serious, serious trouble, she was certain.

"Just like we heard," he said. Pleasant, affable. "A hot meal,
and a pretty little angel to serve it to us."

"You've been misled," she said, her voice calm. Her mind
thinking frantically of escape, of Bee, of Mac, stuck in the
kitchen. Of Ash. "This is the Angel's Kitchen, yes. But I am
not the angel."

"Well, I might just make my own judgement on that," he
said. His eyes were pale and dead. "After."

Behind her, the kitchen door opened. Mac pressed the handle of a heavy kitchen knife into her hand. Then he stepped up beside her. His voice was steady and strong. "I think you gentlemen should be on your way."

There was laughter at that, and Blue Kerchief made a grab for Bee.

His mistake. Kess was on him before he could get there. One hard jab to the throat, and he stumbled. She forced him to his knees, set her knife to his throat. "Bee."

Bee flew to Mac's side. The skinny one jerked forward, stopped when Kess drew a drop of his colleague's blood.

"I've been in the Darks for ten years," she told them, her eyes on the leader. "Do you really think I spent all that time in the kitchen?"

The leader smiled. "You wouldn't dare."

Later, Kess knew, she'd remember. She'd shake, she'd cry. She'd probably throw up: she had last time. But that was for later. Now, without losing the leader's gaze, she put the point of the knife under the man's dirty blue kerchief, and sank it home. Sliced down, across.

Dropped the body as the blood began to spray.

The leader wasn't smiling anymore. Kess turned the bloody knife till it lay against her arm and took three steps back. Let them stumble over the body. "Come on, then."

She'd evened the odds, but only a little. These were tough fighting men, not scared drunks. But this was her place. And she was not alone.

"Bee, go to my room. Pull the ladder up behind you. Get Ash. Get Johns. Go now. Don't argue, go. Mac, we're back to back. No rules. Do whatever you can."

Then the world narrowed sharply.

There was a rhythm to knife fighting, one she hadn't forgotten. The first man to test her died swiftly, surprised. The second took a cut, but backed away. She had to follow, to keep them from having room enough to swing a length of razor wire, *gods, don't even think it...*

It was a frenzy of slashing, of ducking, dodging, lashing out in every direction. Of punching, kicking, howling. Of broken chairs, of aching limbs. Of feeling Mac's solid presence stumble, fall...

...He was down, his bright hair splattered with blood. There was a man in front of him. With a knife. And dead blue eyes...

Kess cried out, she knew it. But she couldn't hear. Because a storm erupted in the Angel's Kitchen. A fury of wind, of scouring rain. A desert storm of whipping, blinding sand. Pounding thunder, the sound of a million wings, or possibly screams. And in the center, a fire. Of flashing teeth, of claws. A bolt of lightning, concentrated into the size of a fragile eight year old...

Then...

...Slowly, warily, wounded, the silence crept back.

Bleeding, gasping, Kess stumbled over something that might have been human, once, to get to Mac. His bright eyes gazed up, saw nothing. His chest was a bloody ruin. She sank to his side. "Oh, Mac. Oh baby. Oh Mac..."

A small hand reached across his broken body, took hers. There was blood on the hand, blood on Bee's clothes. Bee's teeth. But Bee's eyes were dark, and warm. And so very deep.

"Bee," she said helplessly, "Mac's dead!" And she sobbed, once.

"Yes."

Kess scrubbed at the tears that kept coming. "I have to take care of him. I have to..."

"I'll take care of him now." Bee's voice was like a rolling wave, a distant star.

No wonder, Kess thought ridiculously, *I couldn't tell.* Not young, not old. Ageless. "Bee..."

There was a light *had it always been there?* around Bee, and Mac. "Ash is coming," said Bee. "And Johns, and the rest. Let them help you."

"But Bee...How..." She stopped, sat down hard. Everything hurt, suddenly. From the inside out. *Especially inside.* Her breath hitched. "What do I do now?"

"You keep on. You feed. You shelter. You teach. And you take care of the Angel's Kitchen."

"Okay," she managed weakly. Tired. Her muscles were oil, loose and greasy. And there was a slice along one arm that was beginning to burn. Kess struggled to keep her eyes open. She could see stars, and wasn't certain that was a metaphor. "I mean, where else are you going to eat?"

And Bee smiled.

When Ash flew in, all his shadows behind him, and found her bleeding but whole, in a mess of blood and bone, Kess was still seeing that smile. A smile of sweetness, and strength, with blood on its hands, on its teeth. She could do worse than to live up to that smile, here in the Darks.

She would try.

LAIR OF THE LESBIAN LOVE GODDESS
Edward McKeown

I STRAINED TO read the movie marquee through the rain-smeared windows. The sonics weren't doing a very good job of keeping the windscreen clear. Sometimes I think we were better off with the old-style solid wipers. A gust blew a clear spot on the windscreen. *"Lair of the Lesbian Love Goddess,"* I read aloud.

"Yeah, great," said my new partner, Regina Delmar. "You sure he went in there? It's a duplex. What's the other movie?"

"Countdown to Cannibalism," I said. "Hey, I've heard of that one. A bunch of writers get stuck in a turbovator and end up eating each other. The survivor writes a book and wins a Pulitzer."

"Maybe he went in there?"

I looked at her. "Reg, he may be Arcturian, but he's male. He went into *Lair of the Lesbian Love Goddess.*"

"What is it with men always wanting to watch two women have sex?" she said, obviously disgusted with males of all species. "And I prefer Regina."

Rather than debate the basic psyche of the male gender, I changed the subject. "Do you want to catch this bozo or what?"

"Did Command have any idea what the Arcturians are smuggling?"

"Nope. Just a buzz that there's something new, hot and illicit driving Arcturians wild and this Toldas Harkarian is the Arcturian at the bottom of it. Don't know if it's tech, drugs or biologicals. Just that there's a lot of money flowing all of a sudden. Who knows, maybe it's some new version of cyber-feelies for the movies."

"Like we don't have enough of that now," sniffed Regina. "Seems like there's another of these porno cyber-feelie palaces every week in the offport. Just more sleazy films."

"Hey, are you a Port Authority Cop or a movie critic?"

"Okay, okay. Let's nail this creep. And no watching the movie."

"Yes, ma'am," I grumbled.

We exited the unmarked into the cold, wet streets of what used to be Red Hook, Brooklyn. New York City in the late twenty-second century burst its old bounds, adding artificial reefs and islands. Redhook was no longer the shoreline; it was part of the off-port. In the distance we could hear the gathering rumble of a climbing starship as it took off from what used to be part of the Atlantic Ocean.

Regina was out front, as usual, hot-dogging again. Young, ambitious and just out of uniform into the detective ranks, she was grimly determined to be the youngest NYPA captain on the force. I'm only three years away from getting my twenty in and retiring; the last thing I needed was a hotshot bucking for rank.

The Lieutenant stuck me with her after Frank retired as punishment for one of my periodic dust-ups with Command. I never could learn to keep my mouth shut. So I inherited Regina. She had all the hallmarks for success: she was young, pretty, fearless, and tough. My wife hated her with the dispassionate hatred wives reserve for good-looking women who spend all day with their husbands. Me, I was just afraid she was going to get me killed.

We flashed our tin at the old guy in the ticket booth. Regina leaned into his box as we walked in. "You give any alarm and they'll be washing what's left of you off the walls."

The old man gulped and dove back into his newspaper. I groaned inwardly and thought of Internal Affairs.

We started looking for our Harkarian. Arcturians were common in this area of the Port of New York, but I didn't think we'd see many in here. Like most of his species, our boy would be about eight feet tall and gray-skinned. Fortunately, he also had a big patch of white scarring on the dorsal fin that rises from the crest of his head. It would suffice to identify him.

Regina stopped and I almost ran into her. Silently, she pointed at a small mirror over the long-disused concession stand. There he was, around the corner from us. He was handing a package to someone we couldn't see.

"Come on Brian, let's get him," she whispered.

"Wait," I replied, "stun settings don't work on Arcturians. We better call for back..." too late, Regina was off and running. "Halt, police," she yelled.

"Oh, hell," I said.

The Arcturian bolted. Whoever had been with him was gone already. All eight feet of the alien sped for the entrance to the movie theater.

Just as I started running, the door to the john opened and I slammed into it full tilt. "Hey," yelled a bearded man as we both crashed to the ground.

"Police," I snarled, struggling to my feet. I looked around frantically for Regina. She was closing with the Arcturian when he turned and threw a glass sphere that hit her in the chest and shattered. Immediately, smoke started to rise from her clothes.

"Reg," I yelled, running toward her. "Molecular acid! Get out of your armor before it eats through." I pulled my service pistol, but my partner was jumping up and down, frantically stripping right in my line of fire.

I reached Regina's side. Her jacket and the body armor on her shoulders and chest protected her from having her skin dissolved immediately, but the acid worked fast. She dropped the big chest panel as holes began to appear in it. I kicked open a door and found what I desperately hoped for, a janitor's bucket full of water. Regina had stripped down to a bra but a dot must have hit the strap. It parted and the bra practically blew off. I upended the big bucket of cold, filthy water over her, the best chemical base handy to counter any acid left. She let out a howl as the water hit her back.

"That should do it," I said, looking over my now topless partner for any sign of acid burning. I couldn't help noticing that she kept a spectacular pair concealed under he armor. God bless body armor.

"I'll kill him," yelled Regina, pulling her sidearm. Before I could stop her she plunged through the doors into the *Lair of the Lesbian Love Goddess*. This time I was only a few steps behind my track-star partner.

The Arcturian was just battering down the exit door diagonal from us when I came in. Regina hurdled over the rows of seats. Not being a gazelle, I ran down the long way. I cheated on Regina's early admonition and looked up at the screen. At least three women writhed in an erotic tangle, doing something very unusual. I ran into a seat. Concentrate, I thought to myself. The moviegoers with their visual and sensory helmets were either too distracted by the agile minxes on screen, or they assumed the topless Regina and the Arcturian were part of the film. Well, I thought, porno is usually short on plot anyway.

Regina tripped and landed on one guy. He promptly grabbed her breasts. "Man, this is some great simulation," he said to his friend. Regina whacked him over the head with her pistol and he slid out of sight, disappearing into the general ick that coated the floor. I went past Regina, for once in the lead, and dashed out what was left of the door. The Arcturian was gone, its two-meter stride having taken it out of sight.

Regina dashed up behind me and looked both ways.

"Shit," she said, breathing hard.

"Did you see the other guy?" I asked.

"No," she said, "just a foot as he went though the other door."

I looked at her. "Your magnificent bosom is heaving," I observed.

Glare.

I slipped out of my jacket and handed it to her.

"Thanks," she growled.

"I'm never telling my wife about this little chase," I said, "and neither are you."

Unexpectedly, Regina gave a rueful laugh. "I guess I went a little gung-ho."

"Just a bit," I replied. "You spooked a big tough alien that our stunners can't stop. That means we either had to use deadly force or take him down by hand. The former is undesirable, as he's our only lead and the latter was probably impossible."

"Plus, God damn it," I added, "you almost got the aforementioned magnificent bosom, which I now have to forget I ever saw, chewed up by an anti-personnel acid-ball."

"Boy, I sure don't sound too smart," she replied. She gave me a rather enigmatic look. "So why do you have to forget my magnificent bosom, having saved it?"

"I got involved with a woman partner twenty years ago when I was single. It redefined utter, complete disaster. Now that I am married it would be utter, complete disaster squared."

Reg grinned at me. Sometimes I really had to work at staying mad at her. "I'll bear that in mind," she said. "Thanks anyway."

"Back to business," she continued. "How do we find our guy now? There's a thousand Arcturians or better in their section of the port."

"Well, we're not going to get anything else done tonight. It'll be sunrise in a few hours. Start of shift tomorrow night we'll go talk to Frederica."

"Who's she?"

"Funny you should ask," I said, holstering my gun.

We found Freddie, or Frederica, as he preferred, trolling for spacers around some of the wilder off-port bars in what used to be Governor's Island. Freddie did an astonishing job of passing for a good-looking girl: with black hair, a splendid surgically-enhanced rack and nice legs. Freddie had the brains to do other things but his soul had turned dark early. Or as he put it, 'I like the night life.'

We cruised over to the curb. Freddie spotted the unmarked and smiled a lop-sided smile after he saw it was me. We got out of the car. It was still raining, always seemed to be lately.

"McManus," said Freddie, looking out from under an umbrella at me. "You finally come to your senses and leave your wife for me?" The husky voice didn't quite give Freddie away. A whisky voice my dad would have called it.

"Sorry, Freddie," I replied. "Not that you don't look good."

Freddie did a mock pirouette, his dress swirling up around legs that were unfairly feminine. "So what can I do for you Flatfoot?" he asked, using my street name.

"Knock off the crap," snapped Reg.

Freddie raised an eyebrow at Regina. "Ooohhh, she's a cutey. New girlfriend, Brian?"

"Freddie, meet Detective Regina Delmar. Reg, meet Freddie."

"That's Regina," she archly, then looking at Freddie added, "and to you it's Detective Delmar."

Freddie extended a hand. Reg ignored it, so Freddie turned it into a curtsey. I could see Regina going into a slow burn.

"Come on, ladies, there's a coffee shop across the street. We can get out of the rain. I'll even buy."

"See," said Freddie with a wicked grin. "Brian thinks I'm a lady."

Reg muttered something obscene under her breath.

Hoping gunfire wouldn't break out behind me, I led the way to a little Greek shop. We slipped in out of the rain and grabbed a table by the window. Gusts of errant wind scrubbed rain into the gutters outside. The waiter, a Rigellian, looked like a cross between an old man and a goat. He smelled like the goat. He brought us coffee and danishes.

"So, Freddie," I said, "what do you know about Arcturians?"

"Bad people," said Freddie with a delicate shudder. "Got a lot of weight and like throwing it around."

"Lately there's one who seems to be moving into the smuggling racket," I said. I sipped the coffee, savoring its warmth and smell. The danish was good too.

"Heard that," said Freddie.

"What else have you heard?" asked Regina.

Freddie gave me an expectant look.

I slipped a small envelope across the table to Freddie. He took it without looking inside. It was the usual. Not much, but it was a ritual. It insulated us from any thought that our relationship was anything other than business.

"There's an Arcturian named Toldas Harkarian," said Freddie, "trying to set up a network to move something past a few corrupt customs guys over in Area Eighty-Eight. Haven't heard what it is. You tangled with him last night, I hear."

"How do you know that?" asked Reg.

"Oh, honey," said Freddie. "When a beautiful female cop goes running topless through a feelie-porno, whacking people on the head...well...word gets around. You've got a street handle now, Topless."

I could hear Regina's teeth grinding.

Freddie continued. "The Arcturian is working with Rat-face Moestel. He owns the theater. Say, did you catch any of *Lair of the Lesbian Love Goddess?*"

"I was too busy to watch," I lied, not daring to look at Regina.

"Film's got artistic merit," said Freddie, "especially the scenes where the Love Goddess ties up—"

"Freddie," I said, exasperated.

"Oh, all right. You know Moestel?"

"Yeah, I know him," I replied. "Never heard of him being mixed up in anything other than sleazy movies."

"He moves a lot of stuff out the back of the theater," said Freddie. "Fenced goods, contraband, things that fall off the truck when the union boys are loading."

"The uniforms should have picked up on that," said Reg.

"Unless they are being paid to look the other way," I replied.

"The theater is the drop-point for the stuff, whatever it is. That's all I know."

"Thanks, Freddie," I said.

Freddie drained the last of his coffee. "See you around, Flatfoot. Thanks for the coffee. Nice to meet you, Topless." Freddie sashayed out into the dark and rain.

Regina started to say something but caught my eye and subsided.

After a minute, we got up and headed for the car. The rain awaited us. It fit my mood. Seeing Freddie always made me feel sad. His was a wasted life and nothing would change it. We got back into the car.

"How do you know that...that person?" asked Reg

"Freddie was getting the crap beat out of him by some spacers. False advertising."

"What?"

"Goods delivered were not goods bargained for. Some of those Free Traders get kind of picky about that sort of stuff."

She looked at me.

"You know, our work day would feel a lot shorter if you'd develop a sense of humor."

"Hah-hah," she replied.

"Okay, that was gruesome," I said. "Anyway, they had poor Freddie beat half to death when I stopped them. Took him to the hospital, made sure he was okay."

"What are you a cop, or a social worker?" asked Reg.

I started the car and put it in gear. The turbines whined. *"All creatures great and small,"* I quoted, *"the Lord God made them all."*

An hour later we crept into the alley behind the theater. This time we both had our weapons drawn and I was wondering why I let Regina talk me into doing this without back-up. Again. Her pride, I suppose. Slowly, we made our way to a window outside what the city computer said was a storage room. We crouched below it. The glass was partially cracked and a chunk was gone from one pane.

I started to raise up for a look when a voice sounded from inside the room.

"Do you have the cargo, human?" rumbled a deep voice.

I quickly sat down on my haunches and looked at Regina.

The Arcturian, she mouthed silently. I wet my lips and nodded. The S.O.B must be just on the other side of the glass.

"Yeah, it's all here," said a recognizably human voice. "And I told you, the name's Moestel. The customs guys are covered and everything is ready to go."

I looked at Reg and nodded. We hit the back door side by side, crashing through.

"Freeze! Police!" I yelled.

Rat-face squeaked and dropped to the floor. The Arcturian turned toward us and lurched forward, a gray-skinned tower of muscle. His hands were empty, so I couldn't shoot him. I leaned to the right and kicked his knee. Hard. He made a booming sound and began hopping on one leg. His hand whooshed over my head as I ducked. Regina leaped with a "*ki-yah!*" and kicked him full in the chest. The Arcturian crashed into some crates behind him with a howl.

Three of the crates broke and cats exploded into the room. Lots of cats. All colors and shapes. They ran frantically in all directions. Most of them ran over the Arcturian. His arms and legs jerked spasmodically, he gave a loud cry then collapsed.

Rat-face looked at me from the floor. "I ain't saying nothing till I see my lawyer."

Ambulances came and took the comatose Arcturian away. Rat-face left in the paddy wagon. Animal control arrived, called for reinforcements, and gathered up the cats as evidence. There was much hissing and scratching. Some of it was from Regina. "Cats," she kept repeating, "they were smuggling cats."

At headquarters, we spent the next several hours writing reports before the Lieutenant called us down to the hospital where the unconscious Arcturian had been taken. The Precinct Captain had been and gone by the time we arrived. The Lieutenant was staring at two Arcturians as we walked in to the ward. One wore a doctor's coat and was carrying a medical scanner.

The Lieutenant looked over at us sourly. "So you're here finally. Detectives McManus and Delmar, meet Dr. Verhoo and Mr. Sandanvah of the Arcturian Legation."

Diplomats, I thought. Crap.

"How's the prisoner?" asked Regina crisply.

"His condition is serious," replied Dr. Verhoo. "While he is no longer in danger of dying, the coma may be indefinite, a side effect of extreme sexual stimulation in our species."

"Excuse me?" said Regina.

"This brings up a delicate subject," said Mr. Sandanvah. "It is only recently that we've learned that the presence of *Felis catus* causes a state of almost manic sexual arousal in the Arcturian species. Harkarian accidentally discovered this on his last voyage. He brought home a few felines and sold them for fabulous sums."

"Cats," I said.

"Yes," replied the doctor with a hint of defensiveness. "Does not petting a cat generate a feeling of euphoria in your own species?"

"Usually only in women of a certain age and marital status," I replied.

"The effect is many hundred times greater in one of our species," the doctor stated.

"So, when he fell into a couple crates full of them..." began Regina.

"Essentially a lifetime of sexual pleasure crammed into a few seconds before his nervous system simply shut down," finished the doctor.

Hysterical laughter lurked at the back of my throat. "Couldn't handle a little..."

"Don't say it," interrupted Regina.

"Our species would find it most embarrassing if this were to become generally known. We must keep this entirely quiet. Your President has assured us of your cooperation."

"Of course," I said, trying desperately to keep a straight face. The Lieutenant looked daggers at me.

The two aliens bowed and walked off, deep in conversation. I looked at the Lieutenant. "Don't say it," he ordered.

I pressed my lips together firmly.

"So," began our Lieutenant, "thanks to you two, we got Arcturian brass talking to Earth brass, who are talking to the Chief, who is talking to the Captain, who told me that it was a good thing that we had all this spare time on our hands from chasing tech, drugs, and illegal aliens, so we could now chase pussycats!

"And all I wanted," mourned the Lieutenant, "was a quiet shift where nothing happened." He looked at us darkly. "Back to the streets for you two. Try not to stir up any more trouble and, for God's sake, avoid reporters."

"Yeah," I said. Regina followed me out silently. I made it all the way to the parking deck before I collapsed against a wall, laughing my ass off.

"It's not funny," snapped Regina. "We aren't even going to get credit for the bust."

"The case of *Lust in the Lair of the Lesbian Love Goddess*," I laughed in a mock British accent. "After all, it was all about kinky sex. Or maybe we should call it, "*Looking for some Earth...*""

"Don't say it," she yelled.

I looked at her and laughed harder as tears came to my eyes. After a moment, she couldn't help it and started laughing too. We both ended up sitting on our butts, incapacitated.

After we laughed ourselves out, I turned to her. "Well, Topless, wanna go fight some crime?"

She sighed. "Why not, Flatfoot. I don't think I'll be sitting for the Lieutenant's exam anytime soon."

We hopped in the cruiser and headed out of the parking lot. Overhead, thunder rumbled through the sky. It seemed it was always raining lately.

thirteen hundred. I signed back onto the bidboard via my new password, calling back over my shoulder to Tommy.

"Write up a mailer to Scully," I said. "Standard sub-contract. Offer him another five percent on top of what he bid on the cryo job. I'm about to underbid him by a wide margin."

"Boss, you're going to underbid him and pay him more to do the work? You'll lose a ton. Why win the bid at all then?"

"Because," I said as I finished entering an updated bid on the board, undercutting my best estimate of Scully's bid by a margin of ten percent. "What happens whenever we win a job?"

Tommy laughed. "You come back to the office and start work on it."

"Exactly." I called up the station time on my screen. Bidding for the cryo job would close in about ten minutes, and my station account would be notified of the win. The homunculi, miniature versions of me, would be monitoring my account and get the news. And they'd come home.

We spent those ten minutes getting ready. I locked Tommy in the middle room after instructing him to stay focused on the door. We'd assembled several pop guns and loaded them with fresh clips of EMP pellets one of the breed-bots had churned out. Tommy's focus made him a natural marksman. He'd only need a single shot per puppet. Next, I recoded the door to the middle room, giving it a one way setting. It would let you in but not out. The last thing I wanted was for any of those puppets to leave again. Both Tommy and I could easily access the system and send an override, and presumably the homunculi could too, but that would take a while. If one of them had enough time to sit at Tommy's terminal and hack an override then we'd already have failed.

I hid behind my desk, just beneath the wall safe. In the past, if a winning bid came through while I was out of the office I might head straight for the middle room, to spin the project with Tommy. Or I could just as easily pull up and work at my own desk. And on at least one occasion I'd gone to the safe to see how much hard currency was on hand for paying off an emergency subcontract. I cradled a pair of pop guns, one in each hand. Unlike Tommy, I'm a lousy shot and expected to need every pellet in both clips

The first homunculus strode into the office at thirteen-twenty, looking like it owned the place. It had reconfigured its appearance somehow, its chrome physique had transformed to the proportions of a portly human, and a prominent silvery mustache occupied a full fifth of its face. It swaggered despite its small size, radiating confidence with every step as it went straight to the inner door, triggered the optic, and passed inside. I heard the frazzling sound of static followed by a thump. Tommy had scored.

Two more came in a few minutes later, arguing the pros and cons of licensing another breed-bot in a pair of voices identical to my own. Neither seemed the least bit put off to be accompanied by proof that it wasn't the one true Walrus. Some day I wanted to talk to the Arconi designer who had found a way to create a limited A.I. that could believe it was someone else but also knew it wasn't. My doppelgangers headed straight for the inner room, but the door wouldn't budge. With a curse I realized that the EMP had fried not only the first homunculus but the door's controls as well.

I rolled to my feet at about the same time that the two puppets turned around. I fired with both guns and managed to miss them entirely. They sprang to either side, two tiny shiny versions of me. I kept shooting. EMP pellets exploded against the walls, scattering my office with bursts of electro-magnetism. And then the puppets started fighting back.

It made sense; I'd have done the same thing. A stapler barely missed my head, followed by a box of invoices and several optical mice. A paperweight clipped my left arm and a pop gun fell from my hand, skittering toward the front door. The homunculi scrambled and leapt like lemurs, zigzagging across the office. I gripped my remaining gun with both hands and fired again and again.

Behind me I heard someone else enter the office but I couldn't spare the time to turn and see who it was. Something hit me behind my right knee and I fell forward just as two shots whooshed over my head. EMP pellets struck the two homunculi, catching each dead center. They keeled over in a wash of electro-magnetic energies. I rolled over and gasped when I saw the face of my rescuer. Another homunculus stared back, cobalt lenses glowing haughtily above a thick mustache of bristling chrome. It aimed my missing pop gun straight for my solar plexus.

"Put it down," I said, wondering how much damage an EMP pellet could do to my nervous system.

The puppet stared at me, unblinking. It didn't lower the gun. "I don't think so," it said. "You put yours down." The voice was unmistakable. Did I really sound that smug?

I lowered my pop gun. The puppets had already demonstrated better reflexes. There was no way I could win a shootout with this tiny version of myself. There had to be another way. I glanced at the useless control ring on my finger. Just last night I'd imagined the success it could bring, and in less than a day I was on the brink of financial ruin. And then I had an idea.

"Walrus," I said to the homunculus, "you got here just in time."

"Yeah?" it said. "How's that? C'mon, don't waste my time; I've got work to do."

"Yeah," I said, nodding. "The cryogenic contract. I, uh, I came back to work on that myself. And when I got here those two were, uh, trying to open the wallsafe. I think they were planning to steal all the solars from the Clarkeson's contract."

"My solars!" it said, and scuttled over to the office safe, and climbed onto my desk to reach it. It kept the gun trained on me and pressed its tiny hand against the safe's key plate. I think it really expected the safe to open.

"Maybe they jammed it," I said, "Here, let me give it a try." I stepped closer, and pressed my own hand to the plate. The security system recognized my palm and the locks disengaged.

The puppet sighed in obvious relief and reached inside with both hands. I brought up my own pop gun and shot it in the back.

Scully Picasso was only too happy to take on the subcontract at a better return than he'd bid for. Tommy and I spent the next four days preparing for the onslaught from hundreds of new jobs when the bidboard's five day period cycled to a close. He repaired all the homunculi we'd zapped and then set both our breed-bots to manufacturing several dozen more. I spent most of the solars we'd earned from the Clarkeson's job renting larger office space and more equipment for GC, six rooms this time, and paying off-duty dock workers to move us and get everything set up.

When the contracts started pouring in on the fifth day I sat in the front room of the old office taking vouchers and reassuring skeptical clients that Gideon Cybernetics would have no problem completing the work on time. I flashed each job to Weird Tommy at the new office by station mail and at the end of the day joined him there.

Tommy sat alone in the new front office at a refurbished workbench. He worked with that furious concentration of his, pounding out code for one of the jobs we'd won earlier in the day. I set a bowl of turkey synth-soy to one side of his keyboard and went past him to check on the next room.

Inside sat thirty homunculi, three to a workbench, row upon row. None of them looked up or gave the slightest indication of noticing me. They were all busy with projects of their own. The drone of humming was like the buzz of a hive of bees. I knew I'd find the same thing in the next two rooms and didn't bother to look. Instead I went back to the front area to check on Tommy again. He still didn't acknowledge my presence, still didn't break his frenetic pace, but his right hand had strayed to the soy and he was absently licking bits of the stuff from his fingertips. On his index finger the control ring burned blindingly bright.

CONTRABAND
Nathan Archer

THE SHIP'S AFTERJETS were still smoking as Jeffers trotted out onto the blast apron, the display panel in his hand showing the manifest the crew had transmitted from orbit. He'd snagged this one the minute he saw the read-out, before Ota or Singh got a look at it, and all because of one word: Pets.

As far as Jeffers was concerned, pets were a struggling customs officer's wet dream. He could claim they were diseased or dangerous, he could demand endless documentation, genetic scans, certifications from half a dozen governments or organizations—basically, he could delay the shipment indefinitely.

And pets needed care and feeding, which would eat into someone's profits for every day the cargo was delayed, and the animals would be getting older and less valuable, and might get sick or die, which would make them worthless; their owner would want them delivered as quickly as possible.

Which meant that Jeffers could expect a very healthy fee to "expedite" the process. With luck, he could wind up with half the captain's profits going onto his own card.

And it was all far safer than "overlooking" drugs or weapons; exotic alien pets were legal, after all, and the people who transported them were therefore far less likely to shoot an overly-greedy customs inspector. He wouldn't be threatening anyone with arrest, deportation, or reprogramming—just with bureaucratic delays. Nobody liked red tape, but only a lunatic would shoot anyone over it, while drug dealers and gun-runners shot each other with depressing frequency.

Of course, the *Lord Lucan* might be smuggling contraband, as well as its official cargo, which could make the haul even richer, albeit riskier. Jeffers smiled happily as he tapped the phone keys on his display.

"Musashi Port Customs, requesting permission to come aboard," he said.

"Just a minute, Customs," a woman's voice replied, though no image appeared. "I'm checking on the cargo restraints. Wouldn't want anything to hit you on the head."

"Whenever you're ready, Captain," Jeffers said. He stood on the apron, waiting patiently, as the sound of heavy objects thumping on metal surfaces came over the display speakers.

At last the woman spoke again.

"Opening the lock, Customs; stand clear."

Jeffers booted up the atmospheric sensors on the display, then tucked the panel under one arm and watched as the outer door of the airlock swung open and extended itself downward to become a boarding ladder. Before the bottom rung had entirely stopped moving he grabbed the rails and began climbing.

At the top he waited while the airlock cycled—apparently the captain wasn't in any hurry to expose herself to Musashi's air. At last, though, the inner door opened and he found himself facing the *Lord Lucan's* captain. She was a sturdily-built woman with coffee-colored skin, wearing a standard ship-suit that was drab blue at the moment.

"Madis Tyler," she said, holding out a hand. "Is Maintenance coming?"

Jeffers shook the offered hand. "Karl Jeffers," he said. "I haven't heard anything from Maintenance; that's between you and them."

"They said they'd send someone right out."

"Shouldn't be more than an hour or so, then. They're a bit backlogged." His curiosity got the better of him. "What needs maintenance?"

"The main drive. That's why I put down; I wasn't planning to land at all. If this place had a decent orbital station instead of just that stupid navigation post, I wouldn't be here, wasting time and fuel, I'd have made the repairs in orbit."

"Then your cargo isn't bound for Musashi?"

"Oh, hell, no; I've got buyers waiting on Telemachus III. I'm just here because I was using the Musashi beacon for transition, and the drive went unstable and dumped me out of hyper about fifteen light-minutes off the point. I didn't want to risk jumping again until I found out why."

This took the edge off Jeffers' enthusiasm; if the ship was going to be delayed for expensive repairs anyway, and the impatient buyer wasn't here on Musashi, his bargaining position wasn't quite as good as he had thought. He couldn't demand payment before allowing the pets to leave the ship, because they weren't *going* to leave the ship here. He could probably still manage something, but this wouldn't be as lucrative as he thought; if he got too greedy the *Lord Lucan* would probably just launch without clearance and run for it, and there wouldn't be much anyone in the Musashi system could do about it. Musashi did not have many patrol ships, and the Confederacy Guard was unlikely to waste one pursuing someone whose only crime was not bribing the port officials adequately.

"I'll still need to take a look," Jeffers said apologetically. "Port rules, you know."

"I figured you would," Tyler said with a sigh. "Every port in the galaxy has rules and bureaucrats. I suppose there'll be paperwork?"

"Oh, I think we can keep it to a minimum, since you aren't offloading anything," he said. "In fact, a small service charge might expedite the process..."

"How much?"

"Well, that depends on the exact nature of your cargo."

"They're pets. Sixty of them. Furballs indigenous to Fomalhaut IV. Do you need the species name? It should be in the manifest."

Jeffers took the display board from under his arm and looked at it. The atmosphere indicators showed a bunch of non-standard trace organics—that would presumably be from the cargo's breath or waste. There were no traces of anything that looked like illicit drugs or out-gassing from explosives, unfortunately, which meant Tyler probably wasn't smuggling anything and Jeffers couldn't extort even more.

The manifest did give a species name—*Ardemanus ardemani fomalhauti*—that was amazingly uninformative, and tapping the query button elicited "No data on file."

He hesitated. He knew he should just name a fee, but he wanted to see what these things looked like. There might be some excuse to charge more if they looked especially valuable.

And a thought struck him. "You only have sixty? On a ship this size?"

"They're *big* furballs, not just hamsters or something, and I've got to haul the food and water for them."

Big animals? That meant he might be able to make an accusation of inhumane treatment, or transporting dangerous livestock; that could raise the price. "I'll need to take a look," he said.

"Yeah, fine. This way." Tyler led the way to the central core, where they ascended a ladder to the main hold.

The smell reached Jeffers before the door slid open, and he almost gagged; there was no question that the *Lord Lucan* was transporting animals. A glance at the display showed four red indicators on the atmosphere readings—but steady red meant "unidentified," not toxic.

Then he looked at the cargo, and saw why Captain Tyler had called them "furballs."

There were about a dozen of the creatures in this compartment. Each stood about five feet tall and about three feet wide, thick legs supporting almost-spherical bodies covered in luxurious fur in a variety of colors. It took Jeffers a moment to puzzle out exactly what he was seeing, beyond walking balls of fur, but at last he understood.

They were tripodal—a leg on either side and one at the back, the back one jointed differently, which Jeffers suspected meant it had evolved from something like a tail. Plastic restraints encircled every leg, each creature tethered to a cargo ring on the bulkhead.

Between the front and back leg on either side of each furball was what could only be considered an arm, though the resemblance to human arms was slight; each was equipped with four things somewhere between fingers and pincers at the end, and also with something clawlike at the lower elbow. There were no actual hands.

And between each pair of front legs hung a long neck ending in a flat, pan-shaped head, equipped with four eyes and a mouth, and other openings that might or might not be ears and nostrils.

Most of those many eyes were staring back at him.

"Whoa," he said. "Who'd want *those* for pets?"

"Rich people," Tyler said. "On Telemachus III."

Jeffers shrugged. "I suppose some people will buy anything." He looked at his display. "I'll want to take some readings."

Tyler didn't reply; she just frowned. Then her com twittered. "Maintenance, waiting to come aboard," it said. "What's the nature of the problem?"

"I'll be right there," she said. Then she turned her attention back to Jeffers. "Don't touch anything," she said. "They're docile, and they're tethered, but that doesn't mean they can't step on your foot or butt you accidentally if you get too close." Then she spun on her heel and marched back out to the ladder.

Jeffers watched her go, then turned back to the furballs.

He didn't really care what they were, or what the readings said; he just wanted to figure out how he could maximize his income from this.

They were odd-looking creatures, and the way they were all watching him made him nervous. The smell didn't help.

"You guys stink, you know that?" he said.

"Sorry," the nearest replied, in slightly-accented Commerce.

Jeffers almost dropped his display. "You can talk?" he demanded, once he was sufficiently recovered to speak.

The furballs exchanged glances; one said, "The captain lady said we mustn't talk to you." Two of the others turned to glare at it.

Jeffers glanced around for cameras, and spotted three—but he knew how to deal with that; anyone who conspired with smugglers had to be able to alter records. He hurried to the compartment's com port and punched up a link between the ship's systems and his display board, then selected one of the display's files and quickly entered a few parameters.

That would generate synthetic images of utterly innocuous behavior in the cargo hold, starting from the moment Captain Tyler descended the ladder.

"She can't hear us now," he said, turning back to the furballs. "Now, what were you saying?"

"We're sorry we stink," a reddish-brown one said. "We haven't had a decent bath since we came aboard, and the food doesn't agree with us."

"Or the air," a bluish one interjected.

Visions of a charge of inhumane treatment, and the bribe it would take to have it dismissed, arose in Jeffers' thoughts, only to be immediately dismissed by a far more basic issue.

These things weren't pets.

Oh, there were talking pets—parrots and mynah birds and Sirian mimic hounds—but those couldn't hold real conversations. A mere pet would not apologize for its smell and complain about a lack of bathing facilities, would it? Those flat heads didn't look big enough to hold much brain, but not every species kept its brain in its head.

"What *are* you?" Jeffers asked.

The furballs exchanged glances.

"Well, our own word for our kind is…" It made a gurgling noise.

"It just means 'people,' really," another explained.

"The captain lady calls us her cargo," said the reddish one.

"Or furballs."

"Or slaves."

Jeffers stared at them. "Slaves," he said.

"That was the word she used, yes."

There was clearly more going on here than a little smuggling. "Not pets?"

The furballs exchanged glances.

"No."

"I don't think so."

"What are pets?"

Jeffers ignored the question and asked, "Do you know what slaves are?"

"Workers," the reddish one answered promptly. "We're to cultivate crops, and run machines, and do whatever we're told. If we don't, our families will be killed."

Oh, this was just getting better and better, Jeffers thought. Kidnapping, slavery, and maybe even murder if Tyler had demonstrated that her threats were serious. Not to mention that she was probably suppressing knowledge of an intelligent species, in violation of the contact laws.

This was not something he wanted to be part of.

Jeffers knew he was not a law-abiding citizen. For the right price he could look the other way when spacers decided to bring in drugs or weapons, because after all, their customers chose to buy the stuff. Drugs might ruin lives, but the owners of those lives had taken the drugs in the first place of their own free will, despite all the warnings in their schooling and entertainment. Weapons might kill people, but people could improvise weapons readily enough, or kill each other without them—human beings had demonstrated great ingenuity in their long history of violence. He could tolerate drug smuggling and gun running, and still consider himself a fairly decent human being; he had no trouble facing himself in the mirror most mornings. He lived with that sort of crime easily.

But slavery? That was an entirely different level of wrong.

And what was the point? Why weren't the farmers of Telemachus III using robots for their labor?

Slaves were probably cheaper, especially if these things would breed in captivity. If Telemachus was a metal-poor system, or if it had an environment that corroded metal or circuitry, robots might be expensive there.

Slaves might be more versatile; the furballs seemed pretty bright.

Or maybe there wasn't any sound economic reason. Maybe the Telemachans just liked the idea of slaves. Jeffers shuddered at the thought, but he knew it was possible.

It wasn't really any of his business, he told himself. He shouldn't get involved...

But slavery?

Still, what could he do about it? Reporting it to the cops here wouldn't do any good; Tyler would just bribe them, or maybe launch before she could be arrested. Jeffers knew very well just how corrupt the local law enforcement was. He also knew what would happen to his own reputation among both cops and smugglers once the word got out.

And if by some fluke he found an honest cop, and Tyler got hauled off to jail, and did *not* manage to flee, then what? He'd be called to testify, and if Tyler managed to find even a halfway competent lawyer the jury would then be treated to all the lurid details of Jeffers' own past. Juries were notoriously unlikely to believe crooked officials.

And the other smugglers, the people who made it possible to live decently on his salary, would all hear about it. Losing half his income was the *best* he could hope for; turning up dead in an alley was far more likely.

No, the sensible thing to do here was to take a moderate bribe and keep his mouth shut, slaves or no slaves.

But he looked at the furballs, at the dozens of eyes staring at him, and wished there were another way.

He blinked, closed his eyes, and tried to clear his thoughts. This wasn't really so different, he told himself. He'd let gun-runners through, after all, and he knew those weapons weren't just for target practice. And he'd seen what happened to people who got too fond of the drugs he'd let in.

It wasn't any of his business. Drugs and guns and slaves were going to be smuggled in no matter what he did; he might as well take his money and keep quiet. He had long ago decided that—well, he had long ago decided that about drugs and guns, anyway; slaves had never come into it before.

He wished they hadn't come into it now, either.

He opened his eyes and found the furballs were looking past him; he quickly tapped the abort on his display and turned to find Captain Tyler climbing back up the ladder.

"They're looking at the drive," she said. "Can we get this paperwork out of the way so I can go keep an eye on them, and make sure they don't break anything they can add to my bill?"

"Of course," Jeffers said. He looked at the display and began entering commands. "So tell me about Telemachus III," he said. "I've never been there—hell, I've never been off Musashi. I love to hear the stories, though."

"I don't know what to tell you," Tyler said with a shrug. "It's just another damn colony. The Confederacy runs the port, but mostly people there just mind their own business."

"They're rich enough to buy your cargo, though; how'd that happen?"

"Oh, the local fauna's good for scents and flavors; real complex stuff, easier to grow it than synthesize it. They've got whole plantations of weird plants they export."

"Sounds interesting," Jeffers said, with a glance at the furballs. That explained what these things would be doing.

"Yeah, and it gets lonely out there in the backwater plantations, so they'll buy fancy pets. Now, do you have the papers ready? Got the fees figured out?"

"Just about..."

Tyler's com twittered.

"Yes?"

"Maintenance, Captain. Looks like you've got a blown balancer."

Tyler grimaced. "Which one?"

"Portside, number three."

"That son of a bitch. I'll be right down."

"I could just transmit..."

"No, I want to see it." She turned to Jeffers. "Show me where to thumb, and tell me what it's going to cost to get out of here as soon as Maintenance has my drive working."

Jeffers decided that he didn't want to drag this out. He held out the display and pointed. "Right there. And I think that, say, sixty kay will cover everything and get you cleared."

"Sixty kay? Try twenty."

"Well, I was allowing for extras, you know how it is. Say fifty."

"Thirty five. The Telemachans aren't *that* rich."

"I can't be sure to get it all done for less than forty."

"Forty's good enough. Give me your card."

Jeffers held out the card, and accepted the funds transfer. Then he took back the display and tapped more keys.

Tyler glared at him. "I thought you said that would cover it."

"It will," he said, not sure himself why he was delaying. "I still need to do the data entry, that's all. It'll just be a minute; I'll be out of here long before they have a new balancer aligned."

"Fine. You know the way out. Don't bother the furballs, okay?"

"Sure."

She wasn't even nervous; he marveled at that. She hadn't asked whether the furballs had done anything, wasn't worried about what he might see or do. She had weighed him in her mind and found him harmless.

Jeffers stood and watched as Tyler once again descended out of sight; the minute she was gone he reactivated the camera jammer and turned back to the furballs.

"Listen," he said, only then realizing what he was going to do, and what he would say, "this is *your* ship, you understand? You bought it, and hired Captain Tyler to fly it for you, and then she chained you up and you don't know why. Got it?"

The furballs exchanged glances.

"No," one of them said. "It isn't true."

"No, it's not true, but it *should* be, and you *tell* anyone who asks you on Telemachus that's what's happened, and they'll make sure that you can go home and that your families will be safe."

"I don't understand," the reddish one said.

"Just *do* it!" Jeffers said. "If anyone asks. If no one asks, forget I said anything."

"But..."

"I don't have time to argue," he said. He turned and headed for the ladder.

He glanced over his shoulder as he descended, and saw the furballs looking at one another in confusion. He hoped they could manage their role—but it shouldn't be too demanding. All they had to do was act like wronged innocents—and that's what they were.

He started working up the new manifest while waiting for the airlock to cycle, but didn't finish it until back in his own office. It was a bit tricky; he had to make it look as if his substitute was the original, and the freight list a fake pasted over it. He also had to make sure that the Confederacy officials at the port on Telemachus wouldn't miss the revised version.

It was a safe bet that Captain Tyler would never check it, but he didn't dare just leave the modified version out in the open; the Confederacy would never believe that...

At last he was satisfied, and transmitted the files, along with a customs clearance for the *Lord Lucan*—a deliberately faulty customs clearance, so that the Confederacy would double-check it.

If it worked—and he thought it would—when Tyler landed at the port on Telemachus and had her documents checked, it would look as if she had been hired to fly sixty passengers to the Contact Authority on Sirius II, and had instead kidnapped them to Telemachus III to be sold as slaves, with altered records calling them pets.

He hoped that the Confederacy officials on Telemachus III were less corrupt than his coworkers on Musashi. They *should* be; the Confederacy had a reputation for clean, if ruthless, administration.

Tyler must have had some way to get past the customs officials there, though. Would the "pets" designation have been enough? Perhaps she knew who to bribe. But the risk in letting a manifest *this* damaged through...

Well, Jeffers had done his best. He could only hope it was enough. The more he thought about it, the more he wanted those furballs safely returned home. He wished there were a way to find out what would happen to them on Telemachus III, but he doubted the news would ever reach Musashi.

An hour later he watched the launch, wondering whether he had done enough—and why he had done anything.

He hadn't known he had any real scruples left, but obviously he did.

As he watched the glowing dot vanish into the heavens he wondered whether it might be time to find another line of work, perhaps even time to get off Musashi once and for all; Musashi Port was clearly not a good place for a man with scruples.

He had tried for years to do without them, but he had discovered today that there were some he was not willing to lose, and the discovery was strangely comforting.

If he settled somewhere new, he would try to do better than he had here, to be a better person. He wondered how honest he could be if he worked at it.

To his own surprise, he thought he would enjoy finding out.

SPINACRE'S WAR
Lee Martindale

SEVERAL TIMES DAILY, Milos Spinacre engaged in a near-religious ritual: wishing, with devout fervor, that he'd taken his chances with that general tribunal. However badly it might have gone for him—and his counsel had been adamant that it would have gone badly indeed—nothing could have been worse than the bargain into which he'd been pleaded. Commander of Ysbet Tertiary until further notice, with further notice, he was told with something akin to glee on the part of the ranking officer of the tribunal, having to do with a mythical subcrust place of punishment and the presence of something called "snowflakes."

That a man of Spinacre's self-claimed intelligence and stature should be consigned to an unremarkable planet within reasonable galactic proximity to practically nowhere was bad enough. That he'd been assigned command of the *least* of three spaceports, faded memoirs of a war fought and finished more than two decades before was, in Spinacre's opinion, deliberate circumnavigation of the Conventions regarding cruel and unusual punishments. And further proof, in his mind, that the command ranks of SpaceMil were populated by ignorant pretenders nowhere near his equals.

Nearly as often, he ran the mental catalog of the ills that plagued his "command." Equipment so old that it broke if you looked at it hard and so obsolete that requisitions for replacement parts were, more often than not, replied to with disbelief that any such piece of equipment had ever existed. A distinct lack of respect from his counterparts at the other stations—one a convicted murderer, the other so profoundly mad that he was frequently visited by the writers of scholarly psychiatric tomes and recreational fright fiction. And then there was his personnel: a fairly even mix of those with summary files that

made his own look positively pristine and new, at-the-very-bot-
tom-of-their-classes-yet-incorrigibly-by-the-book graduates who
amazed Spinacre each morning by having survived the night.

Worse than these, by many orders of magnitude, was the
native quarter that sat like an open sore immediately outside
the station perimeter. It may have once had a name in the indigenous language of the area that translated to something hope-
ful and beautiful, bestowed by founders drawn by the construction of Tertiary and dreams of profitable commerce. But everything in the files, every reference he heard or read, called the
collection of narrow alleys, shabby habitations, bars, bordellos,
and black markets BackGate. And Milos Spinacre hated it.

More than half of the problems that crossed his desk had
something to do with the place. It was the destination of choice
for deserters, not to mention the source of most of the injuries
and all of the cases of food poisoning, alcohol poisoning and
sexually-transmitted diseases treated by Tertiary's medical facility. Central considered the losses in manpower, man-hours and
material his fault. And, thanks to the flat and cavalier refusal of
the riff-raff who inhabited the place to pay taxes and bribes,
Milos wasn't even able to turn the customary profit.

Then one day there came curtly-worded and nearly identical communications from the commanders of both Ysbet Pri-
mary and Ysbet Secondary. An inbound ship was being diverted to his facility, carrying *"troops grievously wounded in action
against Elasian Aggression. You are under orders to see them safely
and quietly settled in off-station facilities, for the purpose of recupera-
tion, rehabilitation and resettlement into civilian life."*

Spinacre hadn't even known there was a war going on, had
no idea who the Elasians were or what constituted their aggression. But he had finally found a use for BackGate: he'd dump
his cripples there.

Whether by design or happenstance, BackGate's thoroughfares
were little more than alleys, barely wide enough for two people
on foot to pass each other and far too narrow to accommodate

even the smallest of mechanized transports in the station. So it was that BackGate's newest residents arrived in equinid-drawn carts and were dumped into the middle of what laughingly passed for its town square like so many sacks of spoiled grain. They numbered slightly fewer than forty and were a varied lot. Men and women of a number of human and near-human races, ranging in age from barely old enough to enlist to old enough to have been retired long before sustaining the injuries that brought them here. Their one commonality seemed to be that those injuries were of a nature to render them, in the apparent opinion of their military superiors, no longer useful.

The last cart was hardly out of sight when a middle-aged man braced himself on the shoulders of two of his companions and pushed himself upright. Balancing on his remaining leg, he looked around much as one might reconnoiter hostile territory, alert to any movement or sound that would give him information, prepared for any attack that might come. "Report," he called back without looking.

"Squad One okay."

"Squad Two okay."

"Squad Three okay."

"Squad Four okay. Sarge, what's going on?"

"Just a guess, but I'd say we've been 'resettled.' I want..." He chopped off as three people stepped out of a doorway and began walking toward the group. "Heads up. We've got company." He heard rustling behind him as those who could stand did so, moving to positions protective of those who could not.

Two men and one woman surveyed the group as they approached. It was the woman who spoke first. "Which one of you is Billem Simmons?"

"That would be me, ma'am."

The woman beamed a broad smile. "Flossa Menderos, Mr. Simmons. Welcome to Ysbet."

"This has certainly been a day for surprises," Simmons said after taking a long pull from his mug of hot soup.

Flossa, sitting across from him at the table, chuckled low and comfortably. "You're surprised they abandoned you like that."

Now it was Simmons turn to chuckle. "Hardly. Anyone with family or planetary ties had been shipped home already. We're what was left. No, what surprised me—and I mean no disrespect—is that we weren't all killed right off the bat, right in the middle of the square."

Flossa smiled knowingly. "Station personnel had a few things to say about BackGate, did they?"

"They talked among themselves. Apparently they were under the impression that missing limbs or blindness meant we were all deaf, too."

That drew a snort from Flossa before she continued, "Well, we *do* cultivate a certain amount of rumor and innuendo. It affords us a limited level of protection against...interference."

Simmons thought back a few hours to what had taken place immediately after Flossa had introduced herself as "mayor of this little corner of Paradise." One of the two men with her had signaled, and a dozen or so people had converged on the square from the surrounding buildings. A moment of tension, but it was soon apparent that the locals were there to offer help as it was needed. Mostly it wasn't; the "squads" in Simmons' company had organized themselves based on mutual assistance. Those with two working legs carried or braced those without, those who could see guided those who couldn't, and so on.

Within a few minutes, they were being settled into a single-story warehouse, or to be more precise, slightly more than half of a single-story warehouse. The front part, accessed from a narrow alley, functioned as just that, which shielded the activities, and people, in the back. It was also warmer, drier and more comfortable than what most of the military folk had seen most of the time. Within the hour, local medics were checking over the new arrivals while other residents carried in pots of soup and platters of meat and bread and started getting everyone fed.

"Well, for whatever it's worth," Billem said as he raised his soup mug toward Flossa in a kind of salute, "my people and I are grateful. I don't know how just yet, but we'll pay you and yours back."

Over the course of the next few weeks, the castoffs concentrated on healing, growing stronger, and catching up on things like regular meals and adequate sleep under the care of their new "neighbors." They also started settling into new lives, thanks to what Billem thought of as BackGate's Rehabilitation and Reintegration Program. He'd spent a lifetime in an occupation where disabling injuries were one-way tickets "out." Flossa's people had taken a different, often creative, approach. One by one, the former soldiers found jobs and trades, new homes and new lives. One by one, they melted into BackGate and became part of it.

"You've pulled off a miracle," Billem told her one afternoon, lifting his glass to her in a toast as they sat at the table that had become their "command post" and would soon be returned to wherever it had come from, along with the cots and kitchen equipment. They'd just seen the last of his people settled in.

"*We've* pulled off a miracle," she corrected, returning the toast and looking around at the deserted barracks. "Well, almost. It's your turn now."

"Don't worry about me."

Flossa was quiet for a moment before she said gently, "Billem, all your people are taken care of. You can stand down now."

"And do what?" Billem pushed himself off the chair, reaching for the crutches one of his people had made for him in her new trade of woodworking. "I enlisted two days out of secondary. No pre-enlistment jobs, no fall-back trade...hell, no hobbies! I've never been anything but a soldier and I never wanted to be anything else. That's it."

Flossa watched him pace back and forth. "Is it?"

Billem glared at her. "Yes."

"Just like it was with about half your people. You were in on those interviews; you heard every single one of them say exactly the same thing you're saying now."

"Yes, but..."

"Yes, but nothing. You've spent the better part of your life in charge of groups of people. Making sure they got fed, making sure they got clothed. Making sure they got the equipment they needed when they needed it and coming up with fall-back plans when they didn't. You've planned strategy and given orders and watched backs. You've probably managed to keep newborn lieu-tenants alive without disavowing them of the notion that *they* were in charge. And you've likely handled discipline problems and worse."

"Yeah, but..."

"*And* you've probably been in more than a few bars and a fair share of whorehouses in your time."

"Yeah, so?"

"So I've got a job for you. Helping to run mine."

Spinacre waited a full six months before starting an "official" investigation into the fate of the cripples he'd sent into BackGate. A month before that, he'd sent out feelers—by way of spies—to make certain that the result of any investigation would serve his purposes.

"It's like they vanished into thin air," the reports came back.

"Not a hide nor a hair."

"Nobody admitted to knowing anything...which means they all know something."

"Thirty-six names, thirty-six blank walls."

Perfect.

Billem was behind the bar at Flossa's when the first warning came in. He handed the street kid a coin before reading it, and was still reading when he reached for the house phone and called up to Flossa's apartment. He hung up, called to the back for one of the pleasureboys to take over for him, and went straight upstairs, message in hand.

An hour later, the contents of the message had been confirmed with two BackGate spies working in the spaceport. The house was "temporarily closed for weekly medical exams," and, in a large meeting room beneath the basement, Flossa's "city council," other key citizens, and all of Billem's people met to discuss what to do next.

"We've been shaken down before," one man said after reading the message, "and, aside from the inconvenience and an arrest or two, it's been no big deal. What makes this any different?"

"Security Order Four isn't a shakedown," Billem replied. "It's Seek and Destroy".

"Seek who?" a woman asked, "Destroy what?"

Flossa caught Billem's eye, raising a questioning eyebrow, and saw him nod slightly. "Officially, they're looking for Billem and his people. And since Spinacre thinks they're all dead and that we killed them, it's the excuse he'll use to level us."

Agreement and disagreement rose in equal waves and clashed in a storm of noise. Flossa let it go for a while, then pitched her voice in such a fashion that it overrode the noise without sounding like a shout.

"Now," pausing a couple of beats until the room was nearly quiet, "the question is how we're going to respond to this. What can we do?"

It was very quiet for a long moment, as eyes darted toward the former soldiers. Finally a voice came from the back. "We could give 'em what they're looking for."

Flossa cocked her head and smiled tightly. "Yes," she said slowly, "we could do that, Basen. I'm sure your daughter won't mind losing her new husband, even with a baby on the way. Zeth, isn't your daughter handfasting one of Billem's corporals next week? Marem, didn't you just make that nice young Callie your apprentice in the gold shop? And Jamston, aren't you..."

"No need to ride your point into the ground, Flossa," Basen interjected, face red with embarrassment even as he laughed. "We get it."

"I thought you might," Flossa replied, laughing herself. Then her face sobered. "These soldiers are *our* people now. They've earned their places among us and they earn their keep. We'll find a way around this without turning them out or turning them over to Spinacre and his gorillas."

"I don't see why not, if it'll keep us safe!"

Flossa's eyes went chill, boring into the woman who'd spoken last. "Because it won't keep us safe. Not for any longer than it takes Spinacre to come up with another excuse to wipe us out."

"So what *can* we do?"

Flossa let the silence establish itself before she said quietly, "We can fight."

The room erupted, a cacophony that made the outburst before it seem a slow brook's murmuring. Again, Flossa let it go, carefully noting who argued the loudest and on which side of the matter. At the same time, Billem was silently and one by one gathering his people by eye.

"Dammit, Flossa, we're not fighters!"

"But *we* are." Billem had spoken quietly, but the tone cut through the shouting and chopped it off. He pulled himself up from his chair by the wall and leaned on one crutch, his eyes slowly sweeping the room.

"But you're..."

"*Cripples.*" The edge he put on the word made even Flossa flinch. "Yeah, we know. So do they. So even if they figure out we're not dead, they won't consider us a threat because they've already thrown us away as useless. The biggest tactical advantage you can hand an opposing force is to underestimate it."

The murmuring was a great deal quieter this time. A handless arm went up and Flossa gave its owner the floor. "Sarge has it right. The average SpaceMil grunt...if he don't see two good legs and two good arms, he don't worry about it. The last thing he expects to go up against is somebody who ain't whole. It's gonna slow him down...and that just may be the edge we need to *take* him down."

One of the townfolk caught Flossa's attention and she called for quiet. "Flossa's told us why we should fight for you, and I don't disagree with it. But why would you and yours fight for us, Billem? Seems to me you've done all the fighting in your life that you need to."

"Two reasons," he replied. "One: I promised Flossa we'd pay you back for everything you've done for us. But more than that," and he drew himself up just a little straighter, "SpaceMil threw us away, said we weren't worth anything anymore. This is our chance to prove them wrong."

"That goes for me, too!"

"You tell 'em, Sarge."

"That's all well and good," came the voice of a local merchant, "but even with Billem's troops, I just don't see it. They've got more and better weapons than we do. They've got able-bodied, trained troops. We simply can't win in a fair fight."

Billem and Flossa looked at each other and grinned in unison. "Who said anything about fighting fair?"

"We're exterminating vermin, Lieutenant, not going to war." Spinacre glared at his aide and wondered if the young man's assignment here was yet another piece of the tribunal's punishment. Milhouser was earnest, by-the-book, and as complete a ninny as Spinacre had ever met.

"But..." Several shades of red crept up the pale face and into the paler hairline but, to Spinacre's surprise and irritation, the kid stood his ground. "Begging the Commander's pardon, but there are women and children out there. Non-combatants. Innocents."

"Whores and their by-blows," Spinacre sneered, then had a thought that made in smile. He added another name to the list he'd been compiling, pressed a key that sent it to the terminal at his aide's desk, and then looked at the young man across his desk. "If you believe that, Milhouser, you've obviously led a sheltered life, and you obviously need combat experience. I'm adding you to the strike force. Now *get out of my sight and get those orders distributed!*"

Milhouser all but ran out of the office, shutting the door behind him and quietly shaking for a full minute. Then he sat down at his desk, punched in a code, and began typing an encrypted message to his girlfriend.

A lot can be accomplished in fourteen hours when that's all the time available. With the planned attack coming an hour or so after dawn, that's what they had. "Not bad planning on their part," Billem had remarked. "The night folk sound asleep for a couple of hours, and the rest just beginning their day."

A lot can also be done and still show the casual observer what he or she expects to see. So the casual observer saw Billem behind the bar and Flossa circulating in the common room, flirting with patrons idling over a drink before or after trips to the back. And because they were doing what they were expected to be doing, their frequent absences, spent in the chambers below, went unnoticed.

That some of the people who came in had never so much as been inside Flossa's before went unnoticed, as did the fact that the particular drink or the particular whore they requested did not exist. One informant, taking note of the transportation of ale kegs from Flossa's to other establishments, was treated to a long and mostly obscene discourse on the ancestry and personal habits of those who used minor difficulties with import taxes and documentation to bleed their colleagues out of business. His report, like the rest of those going into Spinacre's office, opined that it was business as usual in BackGate, with none of its residents the wiser.

An hour before sunrise local, word came down that the strike force was mustering. Within minutes, infants and young children were bundled up and transferred to an underground chamber and into the care of a cadre of grandparents and pregnant women, all armed. At the same time, those people identified as informants were quietly visited by one or two BackGate acquaintances and just as quietly dispatched to their just rewards.

The weapons transported in ale kegs from under Flossa's bordello to staging areas in similar establishments on other streets were broken out and distributed to small squads of defenders, each headed up by members of Billem's former company. Older children adept at being where they weren't supposed to be and hearing what they weren't supposed to hear were dispatched as look-outs and messengers. And a special group of "operatives" assembled on the basis of a list received by one of Flossa's employees.

BackGate was as ready as it could be.

Spinacre sat at the antiquated command console, watching what few read-outs he had and cursing, yet again, the miserable task of trying to run an operation with such junk. All he had was armor telemetry and voicecomm; the onboard visual feeds hadn't lasted as long as it took to get two steps beyond the station perimeter. It would have to do, he supposed, until it was safe for him to "take the field" in hands-on command.

"Command One, Scout One. I'm outside the gate," reported the voice in his earpiece.

Spinacre smiled slightly. The calm of Milhouser's voice was contradicted by the rapid heartbeat and moisture output showing onscreen. The little twerp was scared. Watching Milhouser and four similarly green and ungifted officers fumbling with armor and weaponry with which they had little familiarity had convinced Spinacre that, barring phenomenally bad luck, at least five of his problems would be solved before the exercise was over. "Scout One, Command One," he replied into his mouthpiece. "Proceed down Gate Street to *The Rising Sun* and report." Spinacre set the back of his mind to composing the flowery phrases he'd include in his "We regret to inform you" letters.

"Yessir," Milhouser acknowledged, his eyes nervously scanning the alley in front of him. Not a soul in sight, and he couldn't decide whether to consider that a good thing or a bad thing.

He finally decided he didn't know enough about urban warfare to decide, and began looking ahead and across the alley for the next niche into which he could duck.

He was on the fourth such bounce when he realized that there was a light blinking insistently in his heads-up display. *Comm Channel 2.* No one had said anything about his having a second comm channel, and it took him a minute to figure out how to activate it. "Mil...Milhouser."

"Lieutenant Milhouser, this is BackGate Command. How copy?"

"Five by...Did you say *BackGate* Command?"

The sound of a chuckle came over the headset. "Sure did, kid, and you don't need to worry about us being over-heard by Spinacre. As far as his console is concerned, this channel doesn't exist. But we're having a busy morning here and I need to ask you a couple of quick questions. But before I do, you see the doorway to the *Dandy Bantie* across the street and up from you about twenty yards?"

"Yessir."

"Don't 'sir' me, Lieutenant, I work for a living. Okay, you scoot on up to that doorway. We don't want to tip our hand to anyone watching your read-outs."

"Yessir...I mean...err..."

"Sarge'll do. Now move."

Milhouser did as he was told, too surprised to do anything else.

"Good lad," came the voice in his headset just as his back touched the wall in his new location. "Now, I need a straight-up answer to this next question, Lieutenant. What the hell were you thinking when you sent that strike force roster to Amy?"

"I...uh..It...ohhell, Sarge, I don't know. I guess I figured she'd get it to someone who could do something with it. This whole operation has stun...felt wrong from the beginning, and I guess I wanted to do something to keep her and the baby safe." He paused for a second and then asked, "Are they? Safe, I mean?"

"You know what a flag of truce is, kid?"

"Yessir...ah...sure."

"Then let's make your next move straight up the street to the door of *The Rising Sun*. Your Amy and a couple of my troops are waiting for you inside. That flag of truce covers everybody; you don't try to hurt them and they don't hurt you. They'll explain what's going on and you can decide how you want to handle it. That sound okay to you, Lieutenant?"

"Yes, Sarge!"

"Good man. Get moving!"

The smile that curled Spinacre's lips as the telemetry from the last "scout" went dead was brief but triumphant. One problem solved, the next one poised and prepped with orders both official and clandestine. Ten men, chosen more for the tarnish on their service records than their combat experience, responded to the punching of codes by moving toward the gate. Another master stroke, priming his orders with broad hints that no official notice would be taken of any valuables they happened to acquire along the way, and reinforcement of his belief that the criminal element was even easier to manipulate than the innocent.

As the tenth man's telemetry came up on the console, Spinacre made a small bet with himself that the entire operation would be successfully concluded in time for a late lunch. Which reminded him that he'd need to look over the roster and pick a new aide.

"Hey, Jake!"

"Wha'?"

"These crips we're huntin'...I thought they were supposed to already be dead."

"They are. We're just makin' sure of it."

"Oh."

Fifteen feet later, "Hey, Jake!"

"What?"

"Why? I mean...guys missing arms and legs...seems like they're as good as dead already? How come the Commander can't just let 'em be?"

"Ask Spinacre, not me. All I know is we got our orders, and he made it unofficially oh-ficial that he ain't too particular how it gets done."

"Oh."

Twenty feet later, "Hey, Jake!"

"Dammit, Woody...*what*?"

"How're we supposed to know if the gimps we find are the ones we're looking for and not part of the...uh..indigenous population?"

Jake stopped walking and rounded on the other man. "How the hell should I know? What the hell does it matter? We see one, we plug him. Simple as that."

"What if it's a woman?"

"Huh?" Jake turned around again, following Woody's upraised and pointing arm. It *was* a woman, a young and attractive one if you discounted the fact her legs ended abruptly mid-thigh, seated on a wheeled platform she'd apparently just propelled around the corner half a block away. For a count of perhaps two beats, no one moved, then Jake jerked the weapon he'd left dangling at his side up to a firing position. He didn't make it. Lasfire from the roof directly above the pair drilled into the top of his head and dropped his smoking, sizzling remains to the cobbles.

Later, Woody had the chance to ask why they'd let him surrender. Chuckling, an old man turned empty eye sockets toward the sound of his voice and replied, "I've heard 'mean' in plenty of voices since I lost my eyes and, soldier, I just didn't hear it in yours."

Five streets away and two blocks back, a second team of Spinacre's goons caught the gleam of gold through slatted shutters and kicked in the door to Marem's shop. As their eyes adjusted to the interior gloom, they caught sight of low counters displaying jewelry and gems enough to make their detour worthwhile. They also caught sight of what appeared to be the shop's only defenders—two women, one old, one young, holding antique contraptions of wood and metal. The two soldiers were still grinning when they dropped to the floor, a crossbow bolt between each pair of eyes.

Two by two, the readouts went dead, and Spinacre went from disbelief to anger to full-blown, eye-bulging, capillary-popping rage. As he alternated between incoherent sputtering and equally incoherent screamed invectives, the remainder of his strike force went from amusement to concern to glancing toward one another and coming to the unspoken understanding that where they were was the last place they wanted to be. In fact, several of the assembled troops took the opportunity provided by Spinacre's tantrum to absent themselves from the immediate vicinity altogether.

And none too soon. Spinacre suddenly went deathly pale and frighteningly quiet, except for the quiver that vibrated his entire body.

"Fall in and prepare to engage the enemy!" So focused was he on his anger and his mission that he took his place at the front of the column and marched them out the gate without taking time to don armor.

His focus continued to propel him up Gate Street, totally oblivious to the fact that the ranks of the strike force behind him were melting away, one or two soldiers at a time. Some merely stopped in the middle of the alley, shook their heads, turned around and walked back toward the station. Others had their attention caught by people peeking out of doorways, friends and acquaintances who beckoned them into safety. And the few who tried to draw a bead on the residents of BackGate found themselves silently and efficiently taken out of action.

By the time Spinacre reached the town square, he was in supreme command of a force of five. Needless to say, the force that stepped and rolled and crutched to surround his was much, much bigger.

"Commander Spinacre, I presume?"

The man whirled toward the sound of his name, coming face to face with Flossa and Billem. His look of surprise gave way to one of disdain as he raked his eyes across Flossa. "What do you want, whore?"

In the next second, he was lying on his back several feet from where he'd been standing, his body having followed his chin in an elegant arch translated from the tip of one of Billem's crutches. Flossa raised one eyebrow and the corner of her mouth in Billem's direction. "Now how do you expect him to learn any manners when you don't explain his mistake? Besides, I *am* a whore...or was."

Billem shrugged and grinned down at the woman. "Sure, but he made it sound like there was something wrong with that. And besides, I didn't like his attitude."

"There's a whole lot I don't like about him. Right now, however, we have more important things to deal with." She shifted her attention to the five SpaceMil soldiers standing unarmed and uncertain in the square. "I'm Flossa Menderos, Mayor of BackGate. This is Sergeant Billem Simmons, Space Military Forces, Medical Discharge. As you can see, he is very much alive, as are the other thirty-five 'resettled' war casualties you were told we'd murdered. The mission you're on is based on a lie, which is not your fault. You are also severely outnumbered and seriously outgunned. So here's the deal. Surrender right now and you'll be released unharmed."

There was a scant moment of silence before the "deal" was unanimously approved. Two of the soldiers headed back toward the spaceport; the other three asked for sanctuary. No one asked what would happen to Spinacre.

"Milhouser dropped by this morning on his way to his office."

Flossa input a last number into her datapad, chuckling even as she did so. "Checking on plans for the wedding again?"

"Not this time," Billem replied as he double-checked the tally and signed off on the bar receipts. "He thought we'd be interested in the latest communication from Central."

"And...?"

"The formal charges he filed against Spinacre have been tabled."

Flossa looked up, cocking her head to one side. "Do we need to start making arrangements to disappear the kid?"

Billem grinned. "Not unless he can't handle the promotion they handed him. *Captain* Milhouser has been named permanent second-in-command of Ysbet Tertiary, until such time as he chooses to request reassignment and independent of whoever gets assigned command. His second piece of news was that the new Commander is due any day now and has sent word ahead that she'd like to meet with BackGate's leadership at your earliest convenience. He said she stressed that it was a request and only at *your* convenience."

"Interesting. What's his take on her?"

"He thinks you'll like her. He does."

Flossa nodded and made a note to herself. "I still don't understand why Spinacre did what he did or why he seemed to hate BackGate so much."

"It might have something to do with the fact that he was a bit less than forthright with SpaceMil regarding his background. Such as the fact that he was born Mickey Spinner, father unknown, and grew up outside the spaceport on Keslinger. In a house very much like this one run by his mother."

"Fancy that. Here I was thinking the bastard was just your basic nutcase bugger, and it turns out he had *issues.*"

"Which doesn't keep him from being a nutcase," Billem chuckled. "But that's not why the charges were tabled. No need to court-martial someone who's been permanently consigned to the Violent Patients Installation on Lector 2."

"I do love it when things work out," commented Flossa before returning to the datapad.

"Flossa, there's something I've been wanting to ask you."

The woman looked up, her lips together in contained amusement. "Yes?"

"Why?"

"Why what?"

"Why did you take us in...you and the town...the way you did?"

Flossa leaned back in her chair and smiled. "A guy walks into a whorehouse." She paused, and when the only reaction from Billem was a raised eyebrow, she continued. "He's a shiny new private, headed out for his first war, and it's the last planetfall before the fun and games start. So he and his buddies all have twelve-hour passes and the predictable desire to make the most of those twelve hours.

"Saint Magdaline alone knows why he picks the girl he does; she's young—a couple of years younger than he is—and not doing much in the way of trying to sell herself. But he puts his money on the counter, takes her by the hand and they go to her room. A little while later, he comes out—alone—and asks how much for the night, much to the amusement of his buddies, who've finished their business and gotten down to serious drinking. Between what he has in his pockets and what he borrows from his buddies, he pays the fee and disappears into the back. The next time his buddies see him is right before lift-off."

"And probably ragged him for months thereafter."

Flossa nodded. "Probably. And would have ragged him even more if they'd known what actually happened in the girl's room. It was her second night in the business. The first night—well, let's just say that the customer who won the auction had been none too gentle. The boy may have been green, but he wasn't dumb, and once he found out about it, he bought up her time to give her a night to recover. They talked most of the night, and that was all. Except for him holding her as she went to sleep."

There was a long moment of silence, until Flossa, speaking very softly, added, "I never forgot that kindness, Billem. I've owed you for that for over twenty-five years. I'm just glad that things came around so I could pay the debt."

"I'll...be...damned." He reached out and took one of Flossa's hands, raising it to his lips and laying a gentle kiss on her fingertips. Whatever he started to say was interrupted by the cheerful din of arriving employees. As he levered himself up and reached for his crutches, he leaned over and whispered, "Let's work on balancing the books after closing time."

Flossa's answering chuckle held anticipation that made the one-legged man grin.

BOTTOM OF THE FOOD CHAIN
Jody Lynn Nye

HAP STARED UP at the big screen of the vidscreen with his mouth hanging open. A smiling, elegant lady was enjoying a dainty bite of Orange-O's from a glistening crystal dish. She looked about his own age, twenty-two, but her blond hair was shining and golden, not dusty taupe like his, and her blue eyes gleamed clear and bright. He followed the silver spoon full of gleaming red circles all the way up to her pink lips, which rounded pleasantly around the bowl of the spoon, then imagined the tangy goodness of the smooth-textured O's as they burst upon the tongue. He'd never tasted any Orange-O's, but that was what the announcer said eating them was like. His own tongue traced its way around his mouth, wishing he had some Orange-O's. They must taste better than anything: Sugar Star Bursts, Yogo-Links, Zanzibars, even chocolate. He'd never had any of those, either, but he wished with all his heart he could.

"Come on, youngster!" Merg ordered him. The stocky sixty-something tilted his shaved and scarred head toward the corridor. "We've got to fix that damned conduit, or the whole place is going to be hip deep in sludge by second shift."

Reluctantly, Hap pulled himself away from the screen, just as the woman took another taste of Orange-O's. His watering mouth dried up in a hurry when he got a whiff of the leaky pipe waiting for him around the corner. Reality bit, if gingerly and with fingers pinching the nose shut against the smell.

Not much of the elegant food he saw advertised on any of the Station's vidscreen channels ever got down to Belowstairs. Certainly not in its original form, and not to the likes of Hap. He hungered for it. Oh, he wasn't hungry in the literal sense. He had plenty to eat; the powers that be wouldn't let anyone starve, however inconvenient they might be. The Earth-Gov

Convention of 2265 dictated that every human being was entitled to basic elements of survival: shelter, air, water, food, clothing and education. At the very lowest levels of society, those
were basic, indeed, amounting to just better than exposure, suf-
focation, starvation and ignorance. Delta Station, orbiting
Proxima Centauri along a major shipping route, was far enough
from Earth that few inspectors ever came to see how well their
program was working. They took the word of those Upstairs
that everybody was being cared for. Vids showed the clean dor-
mitories the dispossessed lived in, the well-stocked cafeterias
where they ate, the classrooms where their minds were fed.
Those were just as much fantasies as any of the soaps Hap
watched, nothing like the garbage-filled corridors and storage
chambers where everyone staked out a piece of floor they sometimes had to defend with their lives.

Hap could sleep on anything. At the moment he had a piece
of shock insulation that had been removed from a damaged
airlock Upstairs. It lay in a plastic shipping case that had been
used to bring a couch for some rich person to the station. He
wore a shipsuit that mostly fit, and had good boots that had
come off a corpse that had been strangled and dumped into a
disposer unit on a higher deck. It was the food that griped him.

Nothing was wasted Belowstairs. He and all the other mis-
fits and rejects lived on what was essentially treated and reclaimed sewage. Everything dumped by the folks who lived
Upstairs went through the recycler. It was broken down into
its elemental particles, reformed into 'recognizable' food, and
available at the push of a button by the folks Belowstairs.
Comestibles, anything without heavy-metal or toxic components, could be recycled nearly infinitely. The common joke
was "First they eat it, then we eat it. Then we eat it again."
Newcomers, the recent down-and-out, got sick when they
heard that, but the ones born down there, like Hap, didn't like
it, but were used to it. The only vestige of the welfare state
that supposedly existed was that when someone got sent Below, the daily rations available in the food machines were

increased by one. Whether the person to whom they were assigned got to eat them was left open to chance or muscle.

In an effort to keep the underclass out of the way of the privileged, only one lift on each side stretched between the decks that kept the station functioning and those facilities enjoyed by the upper class. The crew who maintained the engines and power and sanitation plants came down infrequently, either under an agreed truce or accompanied by a troop of armed guards. Traffic only came from one way; you couldn't get on the lifts without an identification chip, and you couldn't get an identification chip without a job, and you couldn't get a job without an identification chip, and you couldn't apply for a job unless you could get Upstairs to the employment offices.

Connecting Belowstairs's decks were staircases, slides, poles, ladders and the occasional lift. No stairs led Up. Hap assumed that Upstairs was structured in much the same way, though their lifts worked all of the time. And they didn't smell of urine and dead things. (Officially, neither did the lifts Belowstairs. Anyone caught defecating in a lift got spaced or recycled, no appeal, but everyone took a leak in them once in a while; it was a long walk to the loos, and the shafts ran gravitywise down toward the Core. God only knew what the base of the lifts smelled like, but as long as Hap didn't have to clean it, it wasn't his problem.)

Mutants, the mentally-ill, science experiments gone wrong, you name it, they lived Belowstairs. If no one wanted to look at them, they ended up there with the rest of the trash. If they lost their jobs and their companies refused to pay for their repatriation to their planet of origin, they were 'relocated' Belowstairs. Even a few so-called rebels against society decided to make their home where they were no longer a number. Down below, they weren't much of anything. No one cared, except officially. They were an embarrassment to a government that wanted desperately to pretend the underclass didn't exist, that poverty and ignorance had been legislated compassionately away. Well, Hap, thought, following Merg's grunted commands to heft the cracked and stinking pipe while he patched it with plascrete, he was there to tell them they were wrong. He'd never had a school lesson in his life. He'd learned reading and history from the kidvids. Being a cipher meant he had no one to ask why so many of the history programs contradicted one another.

"You about finished?" asked Amlin. The burly, one-eyed woman had been a guard Upstairs until she was dismissed for brutality. Now she worked for the Chief. "Himself wants to see you."

"That's not proper grammar," Hap said, and was rewarded with a backhanded slap.

"Who are you, being uppity about talking? Trying to prove you're better than someone?" Amlin asked, with a growl. "The Chief wants you, if you're so fussy. The dispenser plate on his synthesizer is wobbling. It dumped his morning coffee down the drain, so I wouldn't correct anything he says if you can't breathe vacuum."

As in any untenable situation, someone managed to take advantage of a void in order to rise to the uppermost stratum of power. In the case of Belowstairs it was more like floating like scum to the top of a sewage vat, but Gormley Parker preferred to think of himself as the chief bottom feeder. To give him credit, he wasn't acting purely out of self interest. He did care about the other forlorn souls around him, and he always saw that they were provided for—as long as he got his share first.

All unwanted, broken, outdated and frankly obsolete technology ended up passing under Chief Gormley's eye. The exception to castoffs from Upstairs was a food synthesizer, his bribe for releasing a shipment of the precious devices that had been delivered accidentally two years ago to the service dock instead of the goods ports above. Synthesizers broke down frequently and had to be replaced at great expense from the manufacturing colonies on Europa-Jupiter. A standoff had ensued between Gormley and Upstairs, until the powers that be threatened to invade with the full security force, gas every living being unconscious or worse, and take back the machines, but the

Chief countered that before a single guard stepped out of the lift every machine would be destroyed and broken down to its component elements, and by the way, the threat was being digitally recorded for playback to every news agency in the galaxy. Would they care to reconsider their approach? How much better it would be, the Chief had said, leaning back in his reclaimed executive leather-covered armchair with his hands clasped comfortably above his round belly and his face serene, to make a deal in a peaceful manner.

The round face wasn't serene that morning.

"What took your pathetic asses so long to get here?" the Chief bellowed, as Merg and Hap came into his office, a former storage hangar. The fifteen-meter, bare metal ceilings amplified his voice, making Merg cringe. "If you don't answer me smarter the next time you'll find yourself ground up and served over ice cream!" Hap admired the Chief with all his heart, so he didn't mind the threats. Under Merg's nervous eye Hap examined the synthesizer. It was a modest-size machine, just over two meters in height and a meter wide, with a hatch that opened to reveal a hinged grille. It was hanging in down position, as if it had just dumped unacceptable food into the mini-disposer tank in the base. "The damned thing comes up when you order food, then plops down and stays there," Gormley said.

"Nothing to it," Hap assured the Chief. The two workmen unrolled their tool bags.

"It'll be the activator chip," Merg said, as they searched for a replacement. Hap nodded. They had plenty of those. Whenever a machine was dumped Below, scavengers descended on it for usable parts. Hap and Merg were part of a good-sized force employed by the Chief to keep the technology running. Anyone else caught hoarding parts was subject to a gang beating, all the while the Chief gave his speech about deploring violence. Hap understood that a certain amount of force was necessary to keep order Belowstairs. When subtlety failed.

"Hah!" the Chief said. "You see that!" He pointed at the vid on the wall opposite his desk. "We're on the news!"

Hap glanced up from his work. Some well-dressed woman was ranting. "We've got to do something about the disgusting situation! The scum inhabiting our lower levels…"

The scene changed to a view of Belowstairs. Hap recognized it as stock footage. That's all Upstairs had. They might control the government, the media and the supply line, but their influence stopped at the dividing deck. The last time that they'd tried to send a cameraman down to get some fresh footage, he'd been swarmed the second his lift hit bottom. Hap and his mates had stolen everything he had brought with him, leaving him naked in the elevator except for his ID. Yeah, same old vid, he reflected, seeing a mutant shuffle from one side of the screen to the other. Poor Domble, with no more brain than a drinks dispenser, looked fearsome and disgusting with his shrunken skin and gigantic teeth. He'd been dead about five years now.

Belowstairs was useful for diverting attention. Hap and his mates noticed that whenever one politician attacked another for some legal lapse, the next thing you knew, the opponent would be on yacking off at Belowstairs.

"…damaging precious systems vital to human existence…"

"Who do you think keeps this place running, you stupid time-waster?" the Chief yelled, throwing an empty beer bulb at the screen.

Upstairs didn't like to think about that truth. But short of 1) giving everyone Belowstairs official jobs (and, hence, IDs), 2) eradicating them all (which would create opprobrium for Upstairs all over the human-settled galaxy and in alien systems with beings rights), or 3) collecting everyone Below and sending them all somewhere else, Upstairs had to acknowledge it had an ugly boil on its backside. As much as possible it pretended the problem of homelessness did not exist. To tell the truth, that suited everyone Below just fine. But Hap wanted to see Upstairs. He dreamed of having a job and living in the upper levels. He'd been watching station vids all his life. He knew just how wonderful it must be, to be clean all the time and to eat something before anybody else had.

"Dammit," Merg said, sticking his arm down the disposer chute. "I dropped my spanner." Hap leaped to help him. They leaned the synthesizer over on its side. Hap upended it and shook it until Merg could reach his tool.

"Quiet!" bellowed the Chief. "I'm listening!"

An announcer had replaced the politician on the screen. "...reports from Earth of a breakthrough technology: organic circuitry. Based upon theories of human brain development, scientists have at last come up with a means of growing functional systems that can learn like emgrams. It will revolutionize all electronic system, agglomerating all components flawlessly..."

"What's agglom...?" Hap began to ask.

"Bunching them all in a mass," the Chief said. "Shut up."

"So far, however, the process has been slow. Only one small sample of the finished product has been successfully produced. Scientists will be meeting with manufacturers later this week on Delta Station to talk about means of growing more, quickly but accurately. The demand is expected to be worth over eight billion credits the first year alone."

"Whew," the Chief said, flicking the audio down with a gesture. "Wish I had some of that. Don't you?"

"You bet I do," Merg said.

"Yeh," Hap said, thinking what he could do with eight billion credits, or even eighty credits. He'd have orange silk cushions in his crate—no, he'd build a hotel, with rooms as big as the Chief's, and all of them full of silk cushions. And real food from Earth, lots of it, in storage compartments everywhere, so all he'd have to do was reach out any time he wanted.

The Chief saw the dreamy look on his face and laughed. "Go on, get out of here, boy!" he roared.

"I'm so excited to meet you," Perry Antonio, president of Techgen said, shaking hands with Min Haseen. Tall and broad-shouldered with a born executive's thick head of red-brown hair just beginning to silver at the temples, he towered over his guest. The slim, dark-haired woman slid into the seat he indicated for her at the big oval table in the executive suite of Techgen headquarters on Deck J. "Thank you for coming all the way out here to the Station."

"It's a pleasure," she said, nodding to the others. She had soft, dark eyes and a little pointed chin that made her look delicately elfin and childlike. "I've never been on a space station before. It's been an experience. Fun, in fact."

Antonio smiled at her naivete. He went around the table, introducing the rest of the men and women at the table. The skinny, gum-chewing boy with big ears and a crest of carmine hair was Bill Imbrie, Techgen's chief programmer. Darkskinned Lu Obama was head of biochemistry. The troubled black-haired woman in the blue-white uniform was the station commander, Penelope Chinn. The rest were various technology wonks, bean-counters and government officials. Chinn, he knew, was keen to become the liaison for transhipment of the new products. Techgen needed Delta's good will, at least for the time being. They would have a very private conversation later to see if Chinn could bribe him well enough to obtain an exclusive right-of-way.

He glanced at the slender girl in a blue-white shipsuit and cap standing at the far end of the room next to an open door. No expense had been spared to impress Haseen. The finest melons, pate and caviar had been brought up from Earth, and had been arranged on platters with the best fruits and vegetables from Delta's hydroponic gardens. She stood by, ready to serve the refreshments. At his signal she came forward with a tray to begin taking drink orders.

Haseen noticed the direction of his gaze. "Is it all right if I left my things in there?" she asked, nodding toward the other room. "My transport only arrived an hour ago. I didn't have time to check into my quarters."

"No problem," he said, smoothly. "Welcome, everyone. You've all had a chance to thumbprint your nondisclosure contracts, so let's get this meeting under way."

With his back to the rest of his guests, Antonio gulped down a stimdrink at the wet bar at the side of the room. Haseen wasn't the soft touch she looked like. In fact, she was as sharp as that chin of hers. In a moment he would be giving up a substantial share of Techgen's stock in order to obtain manufacturing rights to Opalite.

"Where is it?" Haseen cried.

Antonio turned, putting the little bottle out of sight behind his back. "Where is what, ma'am?" he asked.

"The Opalite," she said, her hands shaking. She pointed at a small white plate on a small mahogany occasional table near the entrance to the hospitality room. "It was right there a moment ago. Where is it?"

"How big is it? Is it a sample?" Antonio asked. He scanned the tables for a strange container, but saw nothing but the depleted bowls of caviar and the fruit platters, nearly picked clean by the browsing conferees.

"No! It's the whole thing," Haseen replied, her eyes huge with dismay. "Three cubic centimeters, worth a hundred million credits!"

Chinn's eyebrows went up, and the two of them began to search the room.

"What's the problem?" Imbrie asked.

"The Opalite is missing," Antonio said, in a low voice.

"Hell!" the boy said, snapping his gum.

"Don't tell anyone," Antonio ordered. "Just help me look. It's an irregular lump, white embedded with sparkling colors, about this big," he held two fingers apart. Imbrie began to push plates and carafes around, looking frantically.

But the Opalite was not to be found. Tactfully, Antonio began to ask the other attendees if they had seen an object of its description, not alluding to the fact that it was valuable, nor that he and his guest were frantic to find it because it represented their two companies' financial future, only that he wanted to know what had become of it.

"A multi-colored lump?" the server asked, when Antonio finally got around to her. "Yes. I thought it was one of Mr. Imbrie's wads of gum. I thought it was kind of disgusting, sitting there on a clean plate in the middle of all this food."

"What," Antonio asked tightly, moving closer so that he was towering over the girl, "did you do with it?"

"Why," the girl said, her eyes big with fear, "I threw it in the disposer."

Antonio turned to Chinn, whose mouth had dropped open in disbelief. "Call security. Now!" He turned to the girl, plucked the ID clip from her collar, and snapped it in two. "You're out of here. Send her Below," he growled at the two armed guards who appeared at the door of the hospitality room.

"What? Why?" the girl wailed. But she was marched away. Antonio closed the passage door and returned to the party. No one could have missed the excitement, ending in the expulsion of the food service worker. He straightened his tunic and strode forward, wearing a polite but grave expression.

"I'm so sorry," Antonio said. "There's been a misunderstanding. Shall we get on with our meeting?"

"I thought we were going to see this Opalite," said Barbara Skyler, Secretary of Technology for Earth-Gov.

"That will have to wait," Antonio said, in what he hoped would be a final tone, but Skyler, a politician, had fried bigger fish than he.

"I don't want to go back and tell the Secretary General that this was all a waste of time, or a *fraud*..." she began.

"No! I assure you, Madam Secretary, I hope we'll have a full demonstration soon."

"Where is my Opalite?" Haseen demanded.

"I'm afraid it's missing, Ms. Haseen," Antonio said, at last. "The young woman we just had removed may be part of a conspiracy to steal the technology. We have to find out whether she was working alone or with a gang."

"This is terrible," Skyler said. "Under our very noses! You will get to the bottom of this. Both of you," she added, glaring at Chinn.

"At once, Secretary," the station commander agreed. Her dismayed gaze met Antonio's.

"...More interviews are being conducted into the theft of the wonder substance, Opalite. Station police ask that if you have any information, you can submit it anonymously on any communications kiosk, no questions asked." The newscaster shifted her eyes to the next story on her teleprompter. "Fans of the Blue Asteroids were overjoyed today when their team went 1-0 against the undefeated Star Slayers in overtime..."

"Hope they don't come down here," Merg growled, kicking a discarded water tube that was in his way on the corridor floor. The owner, a girl of twelve or thirteen, scrambled to retrieve it and stuff it back among her belongings.

"Hey, scum!"

"Amlin," Merg muttered under his breath.

The guard muscled over to them and shoved her face close to theirs. "That conduit in the main square you said you fixed, it's spewing crap all over the ground. There's sparks shooting out of it now. The traders want your eyeballs."

Merg lifted a scanty eyebrow. "That's nothing we did."

"Take care of it, and I won't tell the Chief you screwed up! Now, move it!"

"Dammit," Merg muttered, as they retraced their steps toward the main corridor. "It's worse than being in the army."

"Eat new Frosted Star Clusters!" the cheerful woman's voice said. "Now with all essential vitamins and minerals! Part of this complete breakfast."

Hap couldn't see the screen. He didn't want to think about food at that moment. The leaking pipe had waited just until he and Merg were underneath it, then it had let loose. Gallons of unrefined sewage from Upstairs poured out all over them. Whole peelings, bones, feces, whatever dropped into the disposers up above was all over the place.

Merg grabbed for his radio. "Hey, Sal, turn off the main hose in section 54-Z. Yeah, the one in the market. No, now! Hang in there, kid."

Hap thrust his arm up inside the nearest whole section of pipe, feeling for the emergency valve. His lips and eyes were pressed shut. He wished he could plug his nose and ears against the stench, too. Suddenly, the torrent ceased. He staggered backwards and sat down in a foot of sludge. The traders, men and women who sold anything they could scavenge or make to one another in exchange for a few credits, stood on their tables or climbed handy beams and shouted complaints at the two workmen. Merg got on his radio and called for more maintenance men, but Hap doubted anybody else would come.

He rubbed his hands on his disgusting coverall, dashing away liquid garbage. Something went 'plink' as it flew away and hit the floor. Hap caught a glint of electric red and blue. A chip, perhaps? A piece of jewelry that someone accidentally dropped into a loo?

He picked up the small lump and shook the goo off it. It was an irregularly shaped piece of clay or something, but not like any clay he'd ever seen. It was pretty, glittering in the emergency lights. Hap stuffed it into his pocket to look at later. In the meantime, there was a lot of crap to clean up. Then he was going to march into the bathhouse and demand a full shower, no matter if it wasn't his day to bathe.

Chief Gormley eyed Station Commander Chinn up and down. "Well, well. We're not usually this honored down here," he said, leaning back in his chair with his thick hands clasped comfortably over his belly. "It's like God paying a visit on Lucifer, or am I quoting you wrong? That's what you called me in the media last time."

"You stole a whole shipment of machinery," Chinn said, trying not to look as uncomfortable as she felt.

"Take that back!" Gormley shouted. At his back was a whole contingent of shipsuited men and women, all heavily armed. She wondered how they got ammunition down here, when it was strictly controlled Upstairs. She only had two, which she had only been able to bring to this meeting after considerable negotiation. "I *received* it. Too bad for you if the delivery captain was new and couldn't read the markings on the ports. *I* didn't change 'em."

Chinn hesitated. What he said was true. Earth-Gov hadn't been happy about the error. Neither had the people who'd ordered those synthesizers. The only thing that had saved her and the captain from paying for the lost unit out of their own pocket had been her eloquence. She never dreamed she'd have her words thrown back in her teeth.

"I'm sorry. It was a mistake. Politics. Look, Chief Gormley, I've got a problem."

Gormley grinned. "I know. It's been all over the news. You tell 'em not to talk, but someone takes a reporter aside *in confidence*, and your face is red. Pisser, isn't it? It wasn't the girl who stole it. We're taking care of her. It wasn't nice of you to dump her down here just like that, just for dropping that lump down the drain by accident. She's a hard worker, and I think you even broke her contract not sending her back to Alpha. Well, personally, I haven't seen your missing Opalite. You can take that to the bank, though I doubt you will. Chances are if it went down a disposer it's been broken up into hydrogen by now. But *if* it didn't, a whole lot of hypothetical questions beg to be asked. *If* I knew where this thing was, and *if* I could return it to you safely and not break it *by accident* and not sell it to someone else and not go public about my new acquisition, what will it gain me? You know, I hate long negotiations. I've got so much to do, haven't I, mates?"

His little army murmured agreement.

"If you haven't got it," Chinn said, "then maybe one of your people found it. Listen to me," she addressed the ragged band. "If one of you finds it, I'll reward you very well. You

can't use it; you don't know how. It's of no use down there. If
you return the Opalite you can write your own ticket, but I am
authorized to reward only one person. All you have to do is
contact me in the main office Upstairs. Don't waste my time
with phony claims." She nodded curtly to Gormley. "Thank
you for seeing me." Spinning on her heel, she marched out.

Behind her, she heard Gormley laughing at her. "Lovely
exit," he snickered.

"Chief?"

Aha, Gormley thought, his attention snapping away from
his vidscreen, where the news was running a segment about the
station police's phony search for the Opalite. Who'd have guessed
it would be the boy?

"Come in, Hap," he said. "Sit down. Want some coffee?
Better than the muck in the street machines."

The youth looked at the synthesizer nervously. "Well..."

"All right," Gormley said, taking charge. "Two coffees. Real
connoisseurs drink it black." The machine churned and raised
its flap on two cups. He handed one to the boy and sat down on
the edge of his battered desk.

The boy felt in his pocket and brought out a folded scrap
of cloth. "I found it. This is it, isn't it?"

He shook the brown rag open. Prismatic shafts of living
color, reds, blues, violets, golds and greens, lanced out of the
knot of pale matrix, strong enough to knock a person's eyes
out. Gormley nodded, grinning broadly.

"Congratulations, Hap. So that's what a hundred million
credits looks like, eh?"

The very concept of that much wealth was too much for
the boy. His hands started shaking. Gormley took everything
out of his hands and put it on the desk.

"I guess you'll want to talk to the Station Commander, then,"
he said.

"Yes, sir!"

"Thought about what you want to ask for as a reward?"

Hap nodded vigorously. He was almost grateful to the burst pipe for raining down crap on him. "I want to go Upstairs, Chief."

Gormley's eyebrows rose up toward his thinning hair. "Not a chance."

"But why not?" Hap said, crestfallen. "She said I could write my own ticket. You don't want me to do it?"

The Chief blew a raspberry. "What I want has nothing to do with it. You heard Chinn when she was desperate. They've all had time to think about their problem. Don't try to ask for too much. This is a big fat embarrassment to them. You know what they did to that girl who made the mistake. They shucked her down here without hesitation. She was nothing to them. You're less than nothing. They'll promise you everything you want."

"But this'll be my ticket Upstairs! A job! An ID! A home! A wife! Kids!"

"*Don't* do it," the Chief warned, looking alarmed for the first time. "If you do, you're marked. You don't know how to live up there."

"I've seen it all on vids," Hap protested. He didn't understand why the Chief was trying to hold him back. "They'll show me what to do."

"No, they won't. You'll be on your own. Anything you get at gunpoint, like this, they'll resent forever. You'll make mistakes, plenty of them. They'll be waiting. First infraction, even a tiny one—zing! All your benefits, gone. Second infraction—bang! Jail. Third—you're back down here."

"At least I'll have had a chance to try," Hap said.

"*I've* had it, and it's not as great as you think. Settle for your dreams *as* dreams, kid, and you'll never be disappointed. I'm free down here. I'm *king*, because I only have what I can hold. Can you control anything? Are you ready?"

"Sure I am," Hap said. "I'm not a kid!"

The Chief smiled ruefully. "See? You can't even stand up to me, and I'm only one level up the food chain from you. You are as far away from the powers that be as you are from the very stars outside."

Hap was crestfallen. "So what should I do?"

"Give it up," the Chief advised him. "This whole situation is bigger than your next meal. It's bigger than your *life*. They're going to look at you like a bug that learned to talk."

"Then, you teach me. Please. Help me. I want to go Up. I've never had the chance of anything in my life."

Gormley shook his head with a paternal smile. "You've always been the dreamer. I envy you that. I haven't had a real dream in years."

"Teach me," Hap pleaded. "I know I can get along up there. Teach me how to ask so they won't get mad at me. I'll stay out of trouble. I swear."

"Teach you everything I know in five minutes? All right. I'll keep it simple." Gormley leaned forward over the desk and pointed at him. Hap stared at the finger. "Listen. They're always saying in the vids that knowledge is power. Knowledge isn't power. Knowledge is knowledge. Confidence is power. Everyone is insecure. Make 'em think you know something they don't, or have something they need, and you can get the upper hand. But it all falls apart if you can't pull it off with *confidence*. There," he said, leaning back again. He looked smaller than he had when Hap had come into the room, older and more shrunken. "I've given you everything I can. If you can make it now, I hope that the next time I see you, you're up among the stars." He sighed and reached for the communicator on his desk. "Can't delay any longer. You've got a call to make."

"Chief..." Hap said, hesitantly. Gormley took his hand off the control pad. "There's no hard feelings, is there? Chinn said the reward's for one. I...I can do things for you once I'm Up. I'll try..."

Gormley held up a hand. "Enjoy it, son. I don't need a thing. Down here we fight over cigarette butts, but if you make a fortune, it's all yours."

"Huh?"

"Money makes you lonely, because it throws up walls. When you've got nothing, that's when you know if you have friends or not. Remember that. It's the man who has the least who gives the most."

Hap didn't understand, but he committed the words to memory. Shaking, he watched as the Chief dialed up Station Commander Chinn's office. He straightened his back as the woman's face appeared on the screen.

"Yeah, we've got it." Gormley glanced at Hap, and gave him a thumb's-up. "All safe and sound. I've got a young man who wants to come Upstairs and talk to you about his reward."

The blue-white-clad guards who met Hap at the lift station all wrinkled their noses as he walked out of the lift. Hap felt defensive. He was as clean as three sonic showers in a row could make him. He threw his head back and walked out of the lift without saying a word. The guards, two men and two women in uniforms so tidy they looked new, surrounded him and marched him off. Maybe Hap did stink compared with them. He'd had no way to tell before. The first thing he noticed, not even a step out of the box, was the air. A light, fresh breeze brushed his cheeks. It smelled of flowers, or perfume. No, he was wrong: it smelled of *nothing*. Pure air. His first miracle.

He was so excited he didn't know what to look at first. Not a single speck of anything was on the floor, and it was coated with a spongy material that slightly rebounded his steps. The walls were made of the same high-impact ceramic as the ones below that weren't missing their façade, but they were clean and undamaged. Huge vidscreens were embedded in the walls at just above eye level. The audio hummed, not blared. And the people—they all seemed to be on vid, too. They shone as if they were polished. Even after a shower everybody Belowstairs seemed still to be a little dull or dusty. At a corner Hap noticed another pack of guards walking towards them, escorting a tramp toward the lifts. When he got a little closer he realized he was looking at a polished wall. He was seeing his own reflection. So that's what everyone saw him as.

Hap steeled himself. He threw his head back and walked onward with dignity. Once the Chief told him he had to act confident he watched vids until he found a role model, and studied him. The man in the vids met everyone's eyes with a little smile and a nod, and kept his back straight. When he listened, he leaned his ear toward the speaker, eyes down and a little hooded. When people looked at him as he walked, Hap met their eyes and made his little smile. He was a vidscreen person now. It didn't matter that his suit had three owners before him. Over it he now wore a blast-suit of phony confidence. This was the way, the Chief said, the only way to get what he wanted. Mentally, he ticked off the list: the first thing was an ID. That was the biggest request, the only one that really mattered. Then a job. He didn't care what he did. He was a good technician, and he knew Station systems inside and out. And they'd have to give him somewhere to live temporarily until he made enough to pay for his own room. And food rations until his first paycheck. If they wanted their little lump back, that is what they would have to give him.

The tall man in the impeccable black collarless suit rose and inclined his head gravely as the guards showed Hap into the big room. As overwhelmingly beautiful as the corridors were on the way up, this place was something special, like the backgrounds in a vid about presidents and kings. The soft rose of the walls framed a long elliptical table of real wood without a single pit in its surface. It was gorgeous. The Chief's grand desk looked like scrap beside it. He was awed into silence. Around the gleaming oval were more grave-looking people.

"Sir, won't you join us?" the tall man asked Hap. "Please, sit there."

Antonio eased the visitor into the seat at the head of the table and settled down beside him, wearing his most suave visage. The boy didn't seem impressed by his surroundings. He must know what he had, and what he wanted. Antonio waited for him to speak. Instead, the boy regarded him with a polite smile. He was waiting, too. Antonio was taken aback by his confidence.

"May I introduce myself? I'm Perry Antonio, president of Techgen." He introduced everyone around the table, ending with Min Haseen, on the visitor's other side.

In a low voice the young man said, "I'm Hap Duxon." He fell silent, wearing a little smile.

Antonio got nervous. *The boy*, he thought, *must know he has all the advantage.* Since they didn't know where the Opalite was, they had to play his game. The visitor still waited.

"Well, Hap...Mr. Duxon...We are all very glad you came up here today. I can't stress how important it is to have the Opalite returned to us so quickly. You do have it safe?"

Duxon nodded gravely, keeping his eyes a little lowered while Antonio talked, but meeting them fully when he stopped.

"Yes, it's safe."

"Good!" Antonio was rattled. How could outcast scum be so serene in the presence of every big name on the station? Was he on drugs? Antonio wished *he* was. "Well, you're not returning it just because it makes us happy. You've come about your reward. Naturally, it should be commensurate with the value of the object. We were very upset that the news media started so many rumors. Eight billion credits!" he said, with a little laugh. "This little sample isn't worth a fraction of that, but I will admit to you, Mr. Duxon, that it is enormously valuable. On a hypothetical level, what would it take to persuade you to release it? The price of a new flitter, perhaps? A new flat, with luxury furnishings? Would you like to travel? Have you ever seen Earth? I tell you frankly, Mr. Duxon, we're prepared to go all the way to a million credits, if you are able to return the Opalite now."

Hap liked it when the executive called him Mr. Duxon. He never heard his last name down Below. He'd had to look it up to make sure he remembered it properly because the Chief assured him everyone Upstairs used theirs. Everyone here smiled at him, wanted him to feel comfortable in his nice springy chair.

It was a good thing he'd studied the vid actor, because their offers overwhelmed him into terrified silence. It was one thing to dream of a personal flitter, but this man was offering one to him, for real. To travel off the Station? Or he could buy all these things with a million credits! What to ask for? he wondered. He looked around at the people at the table, trying to guess what they'd choose.

As he met their eyes they all smiled at him. They seemed nice, but their eyes were cold. Hap suddenly realized that everything the Chief had told him was true: they'd hate him forever if he overreached. He couldn't take a million credits. A vast fortune like that would set him up, but it wouldn't keep him out of their hands. If he traveled he'd still have to come back here. He almost opened his mouth to ask for the new flat. His corridor was getting more crowded, and the overflow valves on his level kept opening up to emit gas in the night. But that would mean living up here among them. The Station Commander was at the other end of the table. Hap knew she'd remember his face. There must be vid pickups in the walls that were capturing every angle. He was marked. The Chief warned him to settle for small dreams, ones he could control.

"Can I..." his throat closed. He cleared it. "Can I have something to eat? Food?"

The shining people all looked at one another.

"He's hungry," said the dark-eyed woman at his left.

"Of course," Antonio said. "I am so sorry, Mr. Duxon. We've brought you all the way here and never offered you refreshments." He nodded sharply to a white-suited girl at the end of the room, who disappeared through a doorway.

"I have never been in the other half of the Station," said the dark-eyed woman, Ms. Haseen. "Don't you have enough to eat down there?

"Of course they do!" Commander Chinn snapped. Her face turned red. She and Hap both knew the truth about the recycler-synthesizers. Hap watched her, quietly, until a tray was set down before him by the girl. She wore a uniform like Soraya's.

He'd met Soraya before he came up. She was still wearing hers, but it wasn't as clean as this one. Soraya was trying hard to keep herself dignified, but her big, scared blue eyes told him she was frightened half to death and still mourning about what they'd done to her. Her whole life taken away in an instant, like an explosion. Lots of the people Belowstairs made fun of her, hassled her, but the Chief told them to back off. He was protecting her, but doubted she'd last. Chances were she'd throw herself into a recycler pretty soon.

He smiled his thanks at the server, then looked down into a bowl. His first reaction was revulsion. A fume simmered off the lumpy substance in it, a rich, heady aroma like sewage, but then he realized all the bitter stinks weren't there. It was...it was pure. Pure food. He scooped up a spoonful, and had to close his eyes at the exquisite taste. Nothing he had ever, ever eaten was so good.

"Is something wrong, Mr. Duxon?" Antonio asked.

"No. No, thank you," Hap said, indistinctly, around his mouthful of soup. He hardly wanted to swallow the first bite, it was so good, but he had to have another, and another. Before he knew it, he was scraping the bowl. He longed to pick it up and drink the last drops, but all the vids showed that as being bad manners. The rest of the tray was full of more Upstairs food: little hors d'oeuvres with orange roe and baby artichokes; whipped meat paste or cheese paste in white vegetable stalks; yellow squares of cheese, not stinky or rough-textured, paired with tan crackers, which were crisp, not soggy. Together they were fun to eat. He grinned around at his hosts at the pleasure of it all. They watched him solemnly, and he remembered his dignity. The last thing on the tray was a round tart the size of his palm, its surface covered with jewel-colored slices of fruit and with something in the bottom that looked like yellow slime mold but tasted...it was so soft a taste he had no words for it. The substance melted away in a creamy haze. He almost slipped into a trance enjoying it. He'd remember this meal for the rest of his life. This was what the gods ate.

The shining people watched him eat every bite. When there was nothing left, he wiped his mouth with the white cloth napkin, worth a hundred times more than his shipsuit, and pushed away the tray. For a feast like this he'd have returned a *thousand* Opalites.

"Okay," he said. "Here." A bargain was a bargain. He reached into his pocket and put the wad of cloth on the table.

The smooth-haired woman with big liquid eyes almost jumped for the package, but sat down again. She let him unfold the wrappings until the glowing lump was revealed. They all looked it in silence. Hap swallowed. It was beautiful. If it could do everything the news reports said it could do, then it was a miracle as well.

"We haven't come to terms about the reward yet," Antonio said smoothly. "You're entitled to a finder's fee. Call it a mere consideration. We could extend the privileges of the Station to you, with my colleague's approval," he extended a hand toward Chinn. "Naturally, that would require you being issued an identification chip, so that you would have the freedom of the Station, and the reaches beyond..."

Hap opened his mouth to say that he had already gotten his reward. He realized that he was wrong. He was a fool. He had been wrong even to try and do what he'd come up here to ask for. They were ready to give him a planet, and he'd been about to settle for a square meal. The Chief was right. He was starlanes out of his world up here. He snapped his mouth shut.

The girl came around again, with a plate of tiny cakes and brown squares which she set down before him. She smiled at him, then scurried back to her place. Hap stared at the petits fours and candies. That was real chocolate there on that plate. He was full, but he'd be damned if he was going to leave Upstairs food uneaten. He just couldn't manage it. What would these people do if he put the cakes in his pocket to take with him?

They'd think he was a total idiot. That was it, Hap thought in disgust. He would never fit in up here.

Antonio's mouth was pinched. He was either nervous, angry or both. "Sir, we're waiting for your decision. It's up to you. As you see, we're at your mercy. Of course you'd have to make a nondisclosure agreement, but you'll find us more than generous. Five million credits? Eight million? Ten million?"

Summoning every erg of his courage Hap waved his hand like he'd seen the man do in the vid. "Mr. Antonio, I've got a different proposition for you. I want an ID."

"Ah," Antonio exchanged glances with Chinn. "Of course. That would be the first thing, of course. Otherwise, how could you enjoy your reward?"

"No!" Hap shouted, then hurried on before he could have second thoughts. If he didn't get it all out now he'd falter, and they'd know how close he came..."It's not for me."

"What?" Antonio exclaimed.

"I want it for Soraya," Hap blurted out. "The girl you sent Belowstairs. She gets her ID back. And her job. And wherever she was living, she gets that back, too. You don't know what you did to her. And no retaliations on her, or on me. That's my proposition," he said, settling back in his chair with his arms folded. Then he thrust out a finger and pointed at the plate on the table. "Oh, and I'd like a case or two of all that stuff to take Belowstairs with me. New food, not recycled. Today, right?"

A few days later, fists pounding on the end of his shipping container blasted Hap awake. He groaned with regret. He'd been dreaming about the custard in that tart again. The treasure-trove of food from his visit Upstairs was long gone. As soon as he'd returned Below he'd shared it out with the Chief and everybody on his corridor. It didn't last, but he'd had some, and he had the fun of telling everybody about his adventures. He'd seen Upstairs, smelled the air and met some of the people. Now he had that memory for good. If he'd been a different person, been raised differently, well, he might be living up there now, but he was content enough.

"Will you get your ass out of there?" Merg's grimy face peered in at him.

"Why?" Hap crawled out, blinking sleepily, holding his boots in one hand. An experienced Belowsider, he slept with his boots as far from greedy fingers as he could get them. He pulled them on, yawning.

"Come on and hurry," Merg urged him, as he sat pulling his boots on. "I don't know if Amlin can hold the others off for long."

"Hold them off what?" Hap asked.

Merg grinned. "You got a package."

Hap had to shove his way into B lift past a huge and curious crowd. Amlin stood at the door with her slugthrower held across her chest. She tilted her head to show him where to go. Inside the metal-and-ceramic cage was a shipping container about a meter square. On the top was a label that just said "Hap."

Inside was a note on clean white plasheet. Hap read it carefully.

"I'll never forget what you did for me. They said you asked for food, and they laughed, but I've been down there now, and I know what you meant. They let me take home trays from the parties I work. I'll send some as often as I can. Bless you. Soraya."

With the note still clutched in his hand Hap sat on the floor, astonished, as he pawed through the contents of the box. It was full of round platters the same diameter as the box. He lifted the lid on the first, and gasped.

"What is it?" Merg demanded, peering over Amlin's arm. Hap just shook his head. Here were some of those little caviar treats he'd eaten. He had been unimpressed by them Upstairs, but down here they smelled really good. And little vegetables, real vegetables, stuck down to rounds of bread with plastic rods. And tiny sandwiches with all kinds of fillings. One of them had a bite taken out of it, but who cared? And sweets...oh, heaven! There were fruit tarts! He stuffed one in his mouth and relived the glory of the sweet, soft yellow filling and the sharp berries on his tongue. Ummm.

"Food! Come on, share!" one of the men howled from outside the lift. Amlin put her boot in the intruder's chest and pushed him back.

"Make way for the rich man," she said with a sneer.

Rich man. Hap grinned. He'd never have dared to do it before, but the trip Upstairs had made a difference in him. He picked up one of the little fruit tarts and shoved it in Amlin's mouth. The crowd roared with laughter. With hate in her eyes she started to spit it out. Then her face changed. She chewed. And swallowed. And smiled.

"Well, I'll be damned. I haven't had custard since my sixth birthday."

"Come on," Hap cried, hoisting the case onto his shoulder. "Chief gets first share, then everybody!"

The crowd cheered and fell in behind him.

"Philantropist, huh?" Amlin said, shouldering people out of his way with her rifle butt. "Not everybody would be as generous with a piece of luck. Keep this up and you'll be Chief one day."

Hap grinned. Now, that was a goal he might be able to reach.

ZAPPA FOR BARDOG
Joe Murphy

WRAPPERS MAKE BARDOG hungry; bottles cause thirst. But cigarette butts, those are best. Bardog puckers its maw and spits gravel onto the parking lot. Gray plumes of launch smoke hide the sun.

Tarmac warms its peds, but there, another crushed butt. Soon the parking lot will be clean, soon no more to eat until skyblack and bandnoise. Wriggling, Bardog sniffs the crushed white stub.

This one smells of Jason. Bardog hunkers down, sucks the butt into its foremaw where the stub won't dissolve too fast. Jason (yeah, baby) Hartach. Fast-fingered Jason with the ancient Fendercaster. Jason with dark eyes reflecting launch plumes.

"—wouldn't even look at me," the butt said in Jason's methane-raspy voice. Jason leaned against the brick wall, swallowed a mouthful of beer, and took another drag. "Might as well been on Mars."

"Credit-grubbin' woman is what she is." Dirtman nodded over his own beer. "Sheeiit, not like you need her."

"How'm I ever gonna do better?" Jason shrugged. The night air smelt nasty, full of sulfur from the Companies, tanged with launch exhaust.

The sky rumbled; couldn't get away from the damned launches. Jason glared at the soaring flash that spread a harsh glow onto the slab tenements of Haightport before casting glittering diamonds upon the Los Frisco towers and vanishing over the Pacific. Turning away, he scowled at Dirtman. "Not with this face."

"So get skinned." Dirtman shrugged rumpled suit shoulders. "You got Medi-dole."

Jason shook his head, swigged the last of the beer. He poked a finger at Dirtman's scrawny chest. "A standard face? On me? That's all they'll pay for."

"Hey, man," Freddie yelled from the door. "Some Hee-Haw fucking with your Fender!"

"Jack 'em up time!" Dirtman grinned and started inside.

Jason headed for the door, past an old caddy parked in the shadows. Matecca's caddy, Matecca the money grubbin' bitch is what she is. "Now if I had cash she'd be all over me," he muttered. "Cash makes the world go round." He took one last drag off his cig and flicked it—

Bardog opens its eye. Good, Jason always lasts a long time, so full of flavor. But the lot isn't done. Bardog moves on.

Bottle glass! Matecca's bottle flavored with lip-gloss and Tri-Buzz Beer. Synthetic hops clouds the taste, but man oh man, Matecca's mad. Bardog settles down with a mawful of shards.

Matecca, all glow-in-the-dark garters, leather boots and HyperCalc mind. Profits and Overheads, beer orders and put off paying the band till Tuesday.

"—of course you come first," Matecca tried her most gracious smile. "Business is just a little off, you know? The Port Authority's gotten tight-assed again."

"What's that to me?" Mr. Gambo in his three piece frowned down at her. "I don't get mine; you don't get yours."

"But you'll get it, sir. And I'm not making a dime." Matecca stepped back against the Caddy's hot hood. "I just gotta pay the distributors first. No beer, no profits for anyone."

Gambo reached out and stroked her cheek with a white-gloved finger. His breath smelled spicy from off-world cuisine.

Matecca tried to look past him at the white light rectangle of the club's back door. She concentrated on the Fendercaster's wail, the back beat blues as his hand strayed lower.

"Let's go for a ride." Gambo stroked her hip.

"Business is good tonight." She pulled away. "I need to be here watching the till."

"Then have my money by the weekend." Gambo shoved past. He turned back to her, haloed in the light from the doorway. Could have been a laugh that came out of him, or a sob.

"Hey!" Matecca caught herself against the caddy. But the stark lines of his face, eyes more anguished than angry. Framed against the doorway he looked like a lost child. The image filled her mind; she could have painted him once, but that was long ago, another, better life. The beer slipped through her fingers—

Bardog blinks and sits up. Lotta flavor in that one, yes indeed. More than Matecca's usual. Bardog rolls to its feet and swivels its head. Back to the lot. Plastic cup—not many of these high-priced drinks.

It flops down and slurps the cup into its maw. A zesty ammonia tang rolls over its tongues, salt, and olive oil. A Talto Stinger, so the drinker must be Glib.

Taltos don't come here much, not Haightport. Glib who looks like a giant jelly condom in a wide-lapelled suit, skinny little tentacles that dangled too far past the sleeves. Ever try to play a Fender without fingers?

Glib, lurking behind the audience, sometimes with a rental biomed, just in case. Hee-Haw Glib!

"—Suzy Cream Cheese must rise again!" Glib stood, pseudopods wide upon the stage. The chord rang out, thrilled and frilled with feedback.

"God damn it!" Jason bellowed, stalking past an amplifier. "Get your shit slime off my ax."

"I was just..."

"Hee-Haw!" Dirtman, the bass player, muttered behind Jason.

"Job thief!" Their drummer Freddie, short, muscled to the max added.

"First I must tell you..." Glib couldn't bring itself to use the Fendercaster as a shield and held the instrument out. Jason snatched it and passed it back to Freddie.

They blamed Glib for all Taltos: for the biom workers that made the companies rich without employees. For the Alliance War. Theirs was such a simplistic culture. Plastic People, the Eternal Frank would have called them; oh, what suffering He must have borne.

"I have no...titties to share but will buy beer." Glib offered a gold label bottle never found this side of the port. The other tentacle reached for its own drink.

"Share this!" Jason's many fingers closed into a hard knot that swept forward, growing bigger in Glib's oculars until it filled all space. Reality rolled and tumbled Glib out into the parking lot.

Gravel cut into its tentacles when it tried to stand. Another suit ruined, but worth the price. It, meaning Glib, meaning Glibaster Yol Tomago, had mastered the C major chord!

For one brief infinity, the notes had wailed, soared, and caressed the ears of the universe. All hail The Eternal Frank Zappa! By the Holy Apocrypha of *Joe's Garage*—You only get one chance!

Glib gazed at the red-lit bar. What a dump. Poor management, it decided. No wonder humans lost the war. Of course, if Crechepriest Bobbibrown had its way this place would change. Glib crumpled the cup, and tossed—

Bardog sits up and whines. Glib always tastes so different, so deliciously needy, but in the end always the same old mindache.

Parking lot still dirty but Bardog scratches its ear with a hindped. Nothing good to eat out here. Lotsa time before nightblack. It ambles towards the back door. Might be something better inside. Toilets hold a lot of flavor.

It pads up the back concrete steps, stops to suck up a grease glob and think about the frustrations of life as a cook, then starts for the tiny biom entrance.

"Hold it right there, Mister." Matecca smiles and waggles a finger before Bardog's eye. "You aren't done out here yet. Go finish the curbs. Watch for traffic though. I can't afford another trip to Bernie's Surplus. Even a half price broken down biom like you strains the budget." She shakes her head. "Could have paid Gambo off it hadn't been for you."

Bardog sighs, then tries one of the canine behaviors Bernie of the Tinkering Hands had inserted, slumping down on its torso.

"The lot first, then toilets." Matecca smiles, bending to ruffle its head.

Bardog licks her wrist. Pure flavor! Yet the image it brings is unfamiliar. Why would Matecca want to paint Gambo's picture? What flavor were oil paints?

Happiness is a dirty parking lot on a plumeless sun-bright morning. Bardog scuttles over to the curb, lowers its snout, and sniffs the metal cartridges. Teargas, not much flavor. Port police never very tasty, just a sour meanness that puckers Bardog's maw.

Over by the front steps, it finds better pickings. A glove, oh so yummy. Bardog crouches and holds the black leather in its foremaw.

"—have a warrant?" Matecca asked, and tried her iciest glare.

"Port jurisdiction, lady." Officer Wilcox, according the tag on his black uniform, shrugged.

"No warrant needed," his partner added.

"Gambo put you up to this?" Matecca cocked her head, folded her arms. They looked at her chest and grinned.

"Who?" Wilcox glanced at his partner. They laughed.

"An assault took place last night." Wilcox strained a thick neck to peer over Matecca through the brightly lit door. "Right here."

"You must be joking." Her ears still rang from the band's newest song, "Money Grubbin' Woman"; she hated that one.

"Not when it comes to the Taltos. The Treaty of Alliance now makes their safety imperative, sister," Wilcox said.

"A Talto here?" Damn that Jason, Matecca thought, but a good band was hard to find, especially on what she could pay. "This look like a Hee-Haw hangout to you guys?"

"Looks like a biom pit," the second officer laughed. "Smells like one too."

"We know it happened here. The Talto wouldn't file a report but its crechepriest did." Wilcox fingered a stunclub. "Now move. We're looking for your band."

Matecca sighed, slumped her shoulders, and stepped aside. The officers started into the bar. She didn't follow. She could still see Wilcox's hefty backside when a bottle zipped past his head.

Matecca ran for the back door. Just past the corner, something wrapped around her. Her black-gloved fist lashed back, connected. A tight grip twisted her wrist. Going for her bra knife, Matecca slipped out of the glove—

Bardog howls. The glove dissolves before Bardog can taste anymore. It looks up from the steps, along the wall. It sniffs the air. A cigarette, not half done, lies by the corner. Good flavor there, maybe familiar? Bardog plops off the stairs to find out.

Aaahhh, the flavor thickens. Bardog noses the cigarette then sucks the stub into its foremaw. But the parking lot isn't done yet and the bar is filthy. Whole lotta guilt going on.

—Jason sucked in a mouthful of smoke hoping it would kill the aftertaste of teargas that still clogged his sinuses. He glanced at his watch, almost five. The riot had been over since two and still no sign of Matecca. He pressed deeper into the shadows.

It wasn't like her to leave the bar, especially not with so much trouble. The place was her life, her heart, and her soul.

"Now I'm wishing I was a damn bar." He scowled at the building. "I'd buy the place if I had the cash."

A launch plume flared. Jason scratched his scarred cheek and marveled as the mighty Los Frisco towers mirrored the launch. Once he'd ridden the launchers, a flashy way to a life of wealth.

He could jam on a Fendercaster, but not a launcher. He'd been good, just not good enough to calculate escape trajectories on the fly when a boostpak failed. His scars itched. Now disfigured and broke, he was lucky to be alive.

Where was Matecca? She was the best of everything. Man, he would ride her like a launcher; play her like a Fendercaster, and the music they'd make as they soared, better than Blues...

A black limousine pulled into the parking lot. Gravel popped beneath its tires. He inched around the building, hugging the shadows. No back up on this gig. Dirtman was home, nursing a broken rib. Freddie got slammed and wouldn't be out until his old lady made bail.

The limo stopped. A side door opened; light flashed, filtered through tinted windows. Muffled laughter, all too human in its meanness, floated over the lot. A dark bundle hit the ground, flopped once, and lay still. The bright dot of a cigarette arced past, bounced on the tarmac.

The limo peeled into the night, a launch plume highlighting its chrome fenders. Jason stared at the bundle, only a dark blob on the glittering tarmac.

"Matecca?" He dropped his cigarette and ran—

Bardog rises unable to help itself. Plenty to eat right here, but it pads across the parking lot on the memory of Jason's heels.

More than just eating. Flavors! Rich Flavors of memory, zesty Flavors of doing things *besides* eating. Its snout lengthens and snuffles over the sparse gravel.

There, a smudge, gooey, brightly Flavored, right where Jason saw the bundle. Bardog's Little Tongue flicks out.

"—Please Miss Lady, please just listen." Glib held on, hoping Matecca would stop struggling. Its dorsal nostrils still smarted where she'd smacked it; a thick dollop of sap oozed and bubbled with every breath.

Glib held her in the shadows, moved softly away from the spotlights and sirens. Voices shouted from the bar. A chair flew through the window, showering glass down on them. Glib pulled its tentacle from her mouth

"You!" Matecca shrieked. Her foot sank into Glib's torso; pain throbbed up its nerve bundles.

"We can escape," Glib managed. "Then I must tell you of Bobbibrown's..."

The female's fingers raked his skin nearly catching an ocular. Three loud pops echoed over the parking lot. Fragrantly scented clouds enveloped them. The female burst into tears, shuddering in its tentacles.

Glib hurried towards its battered Triduece Coupe. Just as it reached the door, Matecca delivered a splendidly vicious kick to its nostrils. Her high heel slammed into the car with enough force to rock the vehicle.

The Eternal Frank bobbed on the dashboard, one hand held high in the holy pot-mitten; the other cradled the talisman Fendercaster. Glib took it for a sign of approval; the rhythm of its rocking matched the panting of Glib's lung sacs. Now if it could just fit the female into the car and depart, maybe Matecca would let it explain. Why wouldn't she listen to Bobbibrown's offer? So disorganized, it decided, no wonder her bar was a dump. At least she wouldn't get arrested...

A black limo pulled up. A door opened. Pain shocked through Glib's torso. It staggered against the car banging Matecca into the side. Her nails raked Glib's ocular igniting a bright hazy red just before a curtain of blackness—

A confused tingling fills Bardog's maw. Its Big Tongue stiffens, lengthening out to prod the tarmac. Some dim memory of this from before the bar, before Bernie of the Tinkering Hands. After a moment, Big Tongue droops and retracts. Bardog shakes its head, puzzled. Only grayness before Bernie; nothing to remember. Sadness, dimly tasted, seeps through Bardog. A haunting need to do something that it can't remember. There, a cigarette butt!

Bardog hunkers down, pokes the butt, and extends its snout. What will this bring? A gold band encircles the tan paper. Never tried one of these before.

—Gambo roared with laughter as his limo sped away. "You Hee-Haw loving bitch!"

"Watch your mouth." The woman across from him spat, pushed herself as far from the limp alien as the car allowed. Her eyes widened, almost luminous in the limo's gloom; she stared at the creature. "Jesus, you kill it?"

"I didn't do anything." Gambo sat back, let the seat cradle him, and admired the rip in her blouse. "That's Bullson's forte."

"Aww, Mr. Gambo," Bullson's bashful voice came from the driver seat.

"Shut up," he answered. No point in telling her that Bullson had used a stunner. He grinned at Matecca. "It's ever so romantic, if somewhat disgusting, that you're concerned about your boyfriend."

"I ought to slap you," Matecca said. "The damn thing tried to abduct me."

"Oh please." Gambo smoothed his hair. "That only happens in vids. The Taltos are too religious for mischief."

"What's that have to do with the price of beer?" Matecca finally noticed his eyes and fumbled with her blouse.

"I'm not quite sure." He smiled at her, such delightful modesty for a tramp. "But I'm getting closer to finding out."

"So find out. Go ahead. But let me out. My place of business is in shambles."

"That's what I wanted to talk to you about." Gambo carefully put his hands on his knees so as not to disturb the crease in his slacks, and gave her his most sincere look. "I'd like to buy you out."

"I'd rather sleep with Hee-Haw here." Matecca glared back at him.

"Mr. Gambo," Bullson broke in. "If we dump the Hee-Haw at the bar won't the police find it? And if your little friend here isn't around, who they gonna figure is responsible?"

"Why Bullson, that's quite clever." He stared at the back of his bodyguard's head with new respect. *I should have thought of that myself,* Gambo decided. *Five years ago, he would have, but lately the rackets seemed so dull. How he longed for something different.*

Something clean with life's bright spark. The placid peacefulness of a park. With country air, the song of a lark...

"It's blackmail," Matecca said.

"Or murder." Bullson chuckled. "Mr. Gambo wants Broken Dreams, girl. Otherwise, you or the Hee-Haw, someone gets dumped."

Gambo shook his head and opened his eyes. Had he been daydreaming again? "Hold on now." He flicked a nonexistent speck from his lapel. "Just hear me out—"

The butt dwindles to liquid nothingness and slides down its throat. Bardog stares at the tarmac and moans. The more the Flavors connect the stronger they get. Spicy with needs, pungent with desires.

This Flavor has become so...much...more! Why hasn't Bardog noticed this before? No memories. Only little Flavors, no more than mere tastes, dull and gray as tarmac, that never seem to go anywhere.

But this new Flavor, Bardog stops and tries to think. It's like...bandnoise. Glib calls it heavenly; Jason calls it...Blues.

Bardog rocks back on its haunches. It stares at the parking lot with a fresh eye. Bandnoise changes, not quite the same every night. And if bandnoise can change, can Flavor?

Jason changes the bandnoise. Who can change the Flavor?

Leaving the lot, Bardog ambles up the steps and squeezes through the biom door. All the little tastes are so distracting. But this new Flavor, it's more than something in the maw; Bardog wants to chew on this.

Bandnoise? Coming from downstairs. Soft and tinny, not like the usual bandnoise. Bardog cocks its head. Bandnoise from the basement. This has never happened before. Bardog oozes down the stairs.

Traces of the Flavor tingle on the air. Bardog finds a place beneath the stairs. It waits; it watches. When they leave, one helping the other, Bardog comes out.

A little triangular plastic piece, white with gold lettering, lies on the floor. Bardog sucks it in. It's Jason's, and there, there's the Flavor!

"—never heard of him." Jason shook his head, frowning at the damned Hee-Haw. It lay on the bunk that made up half of Matecca's cramped office. He eased the Fendercaster onto his knee and tried a G-minor riff.

"From Him begat the Mothers, who in one of their many incarnations called forth *Joe's Garage*," Glib explained. The creature squirmed, excitedly writhing into a sitting position. "Then came *Thing-Fish*, and finally the great and wondrous *Yellow Shark*. The power of His music, His heavenly solos, the divine inspiration of His melodies foretold the universe, time past, present, even future."

Jason decided the Talto looked a little better now, not like when he'd first found it. He strummed a few major chords from the Fendercaster, grinned at the Hee-Haw's sudden intake of breath. "So what's all this got to do with the price of beer?"

"Everything! Broken Dreams lies upon the ancient ground. A hundred years ago, here stood the Fillmore West. Triumphant concerts blossomed from this very spot, many of His finest."

"And you think Gambo knows this? He knows about Frank Zappa?"

"Soon he does. For Bobbibrown, our crechepriest, approached him. Bobbibrown too would see this relic resurrected. I sought to make the offer but no one would listen. Now Bobbibrown will try a human envoy. Gambo –"

The plastic melts into a savory film in Bardog's maw. Bardog whines, and snuffles around. Up on the bunk, there, another lump of goo. Bardog noses it, then slurps it in. Careful not to eat too fast, this one also has the Flavor.

—The pain in his craw still seemed as nothing to the agony in Glib's heartring. It studied the human, the long tendrilled hair, dark with dirt, the banded scars that marred the creature's face, making this Jason look more like a fish than a mammal.

Only the hands, as they touched the Fendercaster, only the hands poised upon the frets with the delicate grace of a proper tentacle. Had The Eternal Frank's hands once looked so?

"We've got to find her," Jason said. The chord he strummed sent shivers down Glib's nerve tubes.

"Find her? Dare not go near her. She almost blinded me. Not to mention Gambo."

"Oh, she's always like that." Jason's head shook, his next chord turning sour in Glib's auditories. "But Vincent Gambo, man, he's a tough one. Runs some of Los Frisco's top rackets."

"Out of our minds." Glib wobbled from the bunk. The floor seemed far away when it finally found its pseudopods. Even the walls appeared none too solid.

"What about this Bobbibrown?" The human asked. "Can we go to it?"

"Unwise. Much trouble is mine." Glib spread its tentacles, mimicking a human shrug. "It probably thinks I'm still in the chapel, copying ancient album covers as punishment for failure. And if Bobbibrown learns of my attempt on Matecca..." Glib rested a limp ocular on a tentacle and stared at the floor. Humans were such filthy things, so much dirt here, dirt to clog the pseudopods and Zappa knew what kinds of germs. Where was their biom? Health laws required one now.

"Maybe there's something else we can do." Jason stroked a series of chords.

Glib's pain vanished beneath the rhythmic waves of sound. The human shifted on the chair, played again. Glib stretched, tightening its tentacles, then flexed its craw. Good, almost healed. And the redness had vanished from its ocular. It gazed at the human. "Plan?"

"Let's go upstairs." Jason rose. "I think better with an amp—"

Bardog's Big Tongue throbs and pokes the sheets. The Flavor vanishes. Big Tongue seems to do what it wants. Big Tongue brings the haunting sadness of before memory. Takes a long time for Bardog to retract it back into its maw.

Bardog looks around, finds nothing marked with any Flavor, climbs from the bed, and shakes itself. It starts for the stairs, gazes hungrily at the shadows overhead.

Parking lot beckons. Tarmac must be clean by nightblack.

Nightblack. Launch plumes light the sky and bandnoise shakes the parking lot. Bardog hides in the shadows by the back steps. Little tastes everywhere, but so what? Cars jam the lot, but plenty of room around back for the limo when it pulls up.

The driver emerges and opens the side door. Twin red dots arc past him. Matecca and Gambo climb out. White dress Matecca, white suit Gambo. Arm in arm they sweep past the shadows, past Bardog, and inside. The driver waits, face brightening as he lights a cigarette.

Bardog scoots beneath the limo, inches up behind shiny black shoes that smell rather yummy. Two cigarette butts still smolder by the driver's toe. Little Tongue flicks out, sweeps one in. Hot but no matter. Bardog drops it, brings its eye closer and stares.

How to change Flavor? Must savor first, but can't eat. Slowly its snout tightens; Little Tongue extends to poke the cigarette butt. Gently now. Just savor...Just savor...

"—a deal?" Gambo asked her, holding the champagne bottle above Matecca's glass.

"Indeed we do." She smiled and he poured. Matecca didn't even flinch when his hand brushed hers. A cashier's check for a cool million lay folded against her left breast. More money than she'd ever thought about. Far more than Broken Dreams could ever be worth.

Sure, the asshole would make another million in profit. Talk about gullible, the Taltos had offered him two million, intending to tear down the place and build some sort of shrine. Why her bar she didn't know and didn't care, not after this kind of money.

"We're almost there, sir," Bullson called from the driver's seat.

"Sure you don't want to hang around for another bottle?" Gambo asked.

"If it's all the same to you," Matecca crossed her legs and sipped champagne. "I'll just pick up a few items and clear out."

"I don't see a problem." Gambo pulled out a pack of cigarettes and offered her another. Matecca shook her head and took another puff from her own, plainer brand. Perhaps those fancy brown things were an acquired taste. Maybe she'd find out when she reached France.

In the cool clear Alps, she'd find a place. Somewhere she could be alone and take up painting again. Goodness, it had been ages since she picked up a brush. Not since art school...

The limo halted. Matecca gazed at the shabby square of brick that had been her life for ten years. Damn, what an ugly shack. Filled with ugly people too, like that Jason.

Bullson opened the door for them. Gambo carelessly flicked his butt past the driver's ear, and giggling, Matecca did likewise. Ignoring the hurt look on Bullson's face, she brushed by him and started into Broken Dreams—

No more Matecca? Bardog whines then hushes when Bullson's feet move. Still beneath the limo, Bardog stares at Matecca's cigarette.

No more Matecca. No more Broken Dreams. No more parking lot? No more food? Or Flavor?

Bardog wrinkles its snout, spreads its maw, and tries to extend Big Tongue. Big Tongue is stronger than Little, does different things that Bardog still can't remember. Big never used in the parking lot, but only from before.

Big Tongue wraps around the cigarette stub and savors, savors deeply. Down to the single bits, the tiniest portions of Flavor that tell Bardog who the smoker is, what she looks like, even what she's made of.

Big Tongue takes the Flavor apart. Bardog puts it back together.

"—So we have a deal?" Gambo asked, holding the champagne bottle carefully above Matecca's glass.

"No, we don't." She smiled and he poured. She pulled the check from her bra, a check for a cool million. More money than she'd ever thought about. Matecca dropped it in Gambo's drink.

"Well, okay then." Gambo shrugged. "As long as you keep Broken Dreams open."

"And the parking lot full." Matecca clinks her glass against his. They smile—

There, Bardog decides. Much better. Plenty of food now, forever. Having changed the butt's Flavor, Bardog lets it dissolve gleefully in the back of its maw.

Still hungry, Bardog extends its snout for the other butt, past Bullson's tapping foot, and wraps Little Tongue around it.

"—So we have a deal." Gambo paused with the bottle directly over the woman's glass. Don't let her change her mind, he prayed, don't let her change a damn thing.

"Indeed we do." She smiled so he poured. Things had worked out better than he'd ever imagined. The Talto crechepriest had offered a sweet twenty-five million for that wretched little flytrap of a bar.

Gambo had made quite a tidy profit. He could even retire. How tedious his life had been with all the cheap-ass wheels and deals, bodyguards and killers, on the take cops and greedy hookers. It was all so dull, so senseless.

What he really wanted was a place where he wouldn't be disturbed. An estate as far from Los Frisco as he could get, a country place in another country, say England. He would write poetry, why he hadn't thought about that in years.

"We're almost there, sir," Bullson called from the driver's seat.

"Sure you don't want to hang around for another bottle?" Gambo asked. Within hours she and all the rest of them, even that suck-up sadistic Bullson would be out of his life. Bobbibrown would be here in the morning—

Bardog howls! The cigarette dissolves. Bardog scoots from beneath the limo right between Bullson's feet.

"Hey!" Bullson jumps, then, as Bardog zips under the next car. "What the hell kind of biom is that?"

Bardog huddles next to the back steps. Changing the Flavor of one only changes that one's Flavor. Why hadn't it realized?

Nothing could be done. Not even with Big Tongue. Perhaps that's the difference between little tastes and Flavor. Little tastes just don't matter. Flavor is Flavor, and maybe so sweet because it can't be changed.

The bandnoise cuts off. Something going on inside. Bardog rises, oozes up the stairs and inside.

No sooner through the biom door than the human door bursts open. Bardog tumbles into the wall as Bullson runs by. Bardog rolls to its feet and follows.

So much excitement, Big Flavors, little tastes, all spread everywhere. Jason up on stage points a gun at Gambo.

"No, wait, you don't understand." Matecca steps between them.

"Put it down, asshole," Bullson shouts, stance wide, gun aimed toward Jason.

"Not, I think," Glib eases up behind Bullson; a weapon clutched in both tentacles touches Bullson's back.

"Stop it, all of you!" Matecca shouts. "Jason, don't you dare hurt him."

"But..." Jason stares at her, blank-faced.

"He's the new owner." Matecca slips the check from her blouse and holds it in the air. "Vincent Gambo paid a great price for Broken Dreams. Now it's his."

Jason lowers his gun.

Bullson lowers his gun.

Bardog crawls under a table.

"Cheater! Hurter!" Glib shoves Bullson over Bardog's table. Glib's weapon comes up; a blue beam burns a hole above Vincent Gambo's head.

Bullson stumbles, almost stepping on Bardog's ped. Bullson fires, knocking Glib into the wall. Sap spatters everywhere; a dollop clings to Bardog's maw.

Jason drops his gun and runs to the Talto. He kneels down, feels a place just below Glib's limp oculars. "Oh my God."

"This was self-defense." Bullson faces him, gun still in hand. "You saw it."

"We all saw it." Gambo moves beside them, face pale. "The damn Hee-Haw tried to kill me."

"And now it's dead," Jason says. "But according to the Treaty of Alliance, it must be buried right on this spot. The Talto Theocracy now owns this place; they're allowed to take possession of any burial grounds without charge."

"Holy grounds?" Matecca stares at him.

"Holy shit." Gambo turns even whiter. He rounds on Matecca and snatches the check from her fingers.

"But we had a deal!" Matecca shrieks.

"We're out of here." Gambo nods at Bullson. The guard shrugs and they head for the door. Matecca follows, screaming.

Jason starts after her, glances once at the fallen Glib, grins, and then puts a hand on Matecca's shoulder. She glares at him, but stops.

"Do you realize what you've done?" Matecca whispers.

"You won't be sorry." Jason takes her arm, leads her back to the Talto. He kneels down beside Glib. "It's all right now, chum. They're gone." Gently he shakes Glib by its suit shoulders. Nothing.

"Glib man, come on." Jason shakes harder. "It's cool. They bought all that burial crap."

"What are you trying to do?" Matecca stares at him. Others gather around. So many that Bardog can't see.

Bardog's tongue slips around its muzzle, laps at the dripping Talto sap. Such a wrongness to the Flavor, so bland.

"—Bullets don't hurt you?" Jason asked.

Glib caressed the Fendercaster. "Only one chance in a thousand. We're very redundantly built. But painful. You'll make up for that?"

"I stand by my word." Jason nodded. "We'll each have what we—"

The Flavor dwindles away. Bardog finds nothing; Glib feels nothing. Then, hidden deep beneath the blandness in what's left of Glib, Bardog savors a Flavor to end all Flavors. A big hall, bigger than Broken Dreams, with a parking lot stretching on forever.

So much Flavor lost! Bardog charges forward.

"Hey!" Jason stumbles back.

Big Tongue extends and slides into the bullet hole just below Glib's oculars. Sap, clogging the neural tubes, flows back into the heartrings. The heartrings seal. Big Tongue slips out, having changed what must be.

Memories explode! Bardog stares at a red sky, everywhere Taltos dying. Blue beams flash. But the sounds! Like bandnoise but incredible...

"Did we make it?" Glib murmurs, its oculars focusing on Bardog. "A biomed? A Prime C from the war? How did it get here? Was I really dead?"

"A biomed?" Matecca follows Glib's gaze. "But that's Bardog. Bernie told me it was broken but good for trash."

"It did mess with you a bit." Jason studies his feet. "And we let it. I didn't know what else to do."

"You did good." Glib pats Bardog's head. "Your owner doesn't know what a bargain she got."

Bardog's Little Tongue licks Glib's tentacle; good, much stronger Flavor.

"You lost me a million dollars." Matecca, hands on her hips, glares at Glib.

"I'll get you five million." Jason touches her shoulder.

Matecca jerks, then looks at him, and finally smiles. "For what?"

"For the new Fillmore." Glib sits up. "For Broken Dreams."

"Deal." Matecca beams. She turns to Jason, takes his arm. "This was all your doing?"

"Damn right." Jason grins at her.

"Ever had your portrait painted?" Matecca puts her arms around Jason's shoulders.

"Not with this face. Are you nuts?"

"But you can buy a new face," Glib says. "After all, you have twenty million coming from Bobbibrown."

"And all I got was a lousy five." Matecca shoves Jason away. "You cheat!" She turns and stalks toward the stairs. "I'll be in my office. Packing!"

"Uh oh." Glib watches as Jason's fingers knot upon the Fendercaster.

"It's cool." Jason suddenly grins. "After all, I am rich. Guess I'm just a money grubbin' man. Used to dream about wealth when I was a kid." He slips the Fendercaster off his shoulder and offers it to Glib.

"No." Glib's tentacles come up, refusing the instrument.

"But you wanted to learn." Jason holds the instrument out while Glib climbs to its pseudopods. "That was our deal."

"It was." Glib pauses, looks around, then retrieves a cigarette butt from a nearby ashtray and pops it into its mouth. It offers one to Bardog.

Bardog oozes back on its peds, refusing. No more little tastes, it decides. Only Flavors!

"I had a vision while I was dying," Glib goes on. "I saw the new Fillmore West in all its glory. Man, the parking lot went on forever! Perhaps I've been caught up in this Fendercaster thing too long. I've forgotten the joys of middle management. I'm going to run the place soon as it's built." It glances down at Bardog. "With this little biomed at my side, of course."

Jason nods thoughtfully. "Sometimes we forget what truly matters. Cheapness. The cheapness of fate. There's a song in that. I'll pay someone to write it."

Bardog wriggles, delighted. Whole again, memories intact, it could change Flavor whenever it needed. Now it would always be safe and happy. Gazing hungrily at the Fendercaster in Jason's hands, Bardog licks its muzzle. Could it savor such an instrument? What Flavor is Zappa?

THE TIMES SHE WENT AWAY
Paul E. Martens

THE FIRST TIME she went away, I was a young man, younger than her in fact. I was a poet and I thought myself dashing, even though I was working at my father's tavern at the spaceport. That was just to earn my keep, and perhaps a few dollars more to spend on girls. My hair was long, tied back with a black ribbon, and I wore a moustache that wasn't quite as lush as I supposed it to be. I was tall and strong, and really not a very good poet, but it was the image I cultivated, not the rhymes.

When I wasn't waiting on tables or drawing foaming flagons of ale for the spacers and the whores, the merchants and the grifters, I sat by myself in a corner, posing for any ladies who might come in, a pad before me, a pen in my hand, looking dreamily out the window at the rockets and the shuttles that came and went with rattles of thunder and belches of flame.

That's where I was when she walked in.

Walked? She never walked in anywhere. She swaggered. She strutted. She strode. She burst into a room and claimed it and all who were in it for her own.

Her short hair was dyed crimson and stuck up in unruly spikes. A spaceship was tattooed on one cheek, lightning flaring out from its engines, extending down her throat and on under her silver leather jacket. She stood in the doorway like a Colossus, though she wasn't more than a meter and an half tall, hands on her hips, blocking the rest of the gang with her from gaining entry until she had surveyed the bar and the bar had surveyed her.

"This one will do," she decreed. "Until the ale is gone, or the tables are in splinters." The others crowded in after her, extras and supporting players in that particular act of the story of her life. She led them to the bar, laughing and shouting, jostling for a place next to her. She slapped down a wad of bills and said, "Bartender, start pouring."

My father, taller and broader than me, with a real moustache, called over to me, "Peter, get your ass over here and help." Her eyes followed his. If a cat could smile at the sight of some prey to toy with, it would smile as she did then.

I didn't know what to do as she stalked across the room. I looked around for some avenue of escape. I was used to luring an entirely different kind of fly into my web. What was coming for me now was a kind of fly that ate spiders for snacks then moved on up the food chain for something more filling.

"Oh, no," she said. "He's much too pretty to waste yanking on a spigot. Stay here, pretty boy, and tell me things and I'll fill your head with lies about the suns you think are only stars." She pulled a chair close to mine and I breathed the air of other worlds, tasted danger and excitement I knew I would never know for myself.

I swallowed and prayed my voice wouldn't squeak as I asked, "Where does the lightning strike?"

She paused an instant as she got my meaning, then laughed from somewhere deep and real inside of her. "Ha! So you're more than merely pretty. It could be that later on tonight you'll find out where the lightning strikes." She leered happily at me. "I wouldn't even be surprised if it struck more than once." She stuck out her hand, as if she'd suddenly made a decision about me. "What's your name, boy? I'm Annie Jones."

Of course I'd heard of her. When spacers told their tall tales to each other, they often spoke of Annie Jones. But I never thought she was real. And she couldn't be, not really what the stories said she was, at least. Pirate, smuggler, mercenary. Murderer, thief. Defender, protector. Fighter of lost causes. A trail of broken-hearted men and women across the galaxy. A giant. A monster. Part machine. All machine. An alien.

She looked like a woman to me.

I took her hand. "I'm Peter."

We talked and the rest of the world went away.

"Once we found a colony planet that had been forgotten for centuries. They thought we were gods." She laughed and pounded the table once thinking of the incongruity. "But who can tell the difference between gods and devils? Not their leader. After a very little time alone with me, he made me an offering that took me almost six weeks to waste. And I know a lot of ways to waste money."

"I remember a world," she said, "Where the sands were gold. Not just golden, but gold. And a handful of pebbles could buy you a palace on Earth because they weren't pebbles, they were rubies and emeralds and sapphires." Then she grinned. "When we left, we had to strip down to our skins, which they vacuumed. They searched us inside out. They counted our teeth and tapped our eyeballs to be sure they were really ours. And I came away with enough of their precious pebbles to buy a new ship, with enough left over for a month on Hedys." She barked a laugh at the memory. "Remind me later to show you how I did it."

I had no stories to tell. I had spent my days bound to the Earth, living a little life in a little bar on the outskirts of the rest of the galaxy. I had dreams, though, and I told her about them. And if they were silly dreams, as the dreams of the young often are, they still seemed both wonderful and possible to me. She didn't laugh, even though to her they must have been little things that, despite their size, would likely never come true for me. I even read her a poem.

"I loved a man," she told me, later, her gaze far away. "I loved him but I left him, with a promise that I'd come back. I did come back, in what to me was just a few short years, and he was an old man. Wrinkled and bald and shrunken. He'd waited for me. A whole long life he'd waited for me. When I saw him I turned away so he wouldn't see my disgust. I walked away from him. I left the Earth with no promises to anyone. And I will not make any promises ever again." She looked at me, no laughter in her eyes. "Do you understand me, pretty one?"

I did.

She summoned up her laughter again and said, "Good. Then let's leave this place. With the crew that came in with me, your father should be keeping his eye on his till, not on his precious pup. Come on." She stood up and pulled me by the hand. "We have a lot of vices to cover before your education is complete. And when you tell people that you spent her leave with Annie Jones, they'll be able to see the truth of it in your eyes."

So we left, and we did things. Things I never imagined. We went places. Places I hadn't known existed. We saw people. People I would have run from without her. There were no seconds, nor minutes, nor hours, nor days. The time we were together existed all at once, forever. I blinked and she was gone.

The next time she went away, I was a man. Not young. Not yet old. I had been married, once, or twice, or three times. Depending on how you define it, depending on who you ask.

I told myself it had nothing to do with spending a night (or two? Or three?) with Annie Jones.

But the way I made my living did.

I still sat at that same table in the corner. But I no longer even pretended to write poetry. And I no longer posed to lure girls and women. Now I sat in shadows and waited for people who wanted to sell something that had arrived on Earth and somehow bypassed customs. Or people who wanted to buy something they would rather their wife, or husband, or their boss, or priest, or their local policeman not know about. Or maybe they wanted to get away from Earth, far away, and fast, and, of course, furtively. My time with Annie made me known to people who knew things, in places where the sun winked and found somewhere else to shine. Useful people.

It was just convenience that made me sit at the same table. It just happened. I wasn't waiting for Annie to come back. She wasn't coming back. And if she did, she'd probably look for someone like I used to be. Or maybe not. Maybe someone, or something, else would catch her eye. But not me. I'd had my turn. And I would be damned before I wasted my life waiting for her like that other guy. No promises. I still remembered, I still understood.

There were two men across the table from me. Nervous men with big brimmed hats, who would not look at me but looked at the door often.

"All right," I said. "Passage for five of you at the price agreed." An envelope snuck across the table to me. I counted and nodded. "Berth 17, at one o'clock. Will With the One Eye will meet you. Remember, five and only five. If there are six, none of you will board. And only ten kilos of luggage each. More and your luggage will stay here, even if you don't."

Their heads bobbed. Their eyes searched the room for spies and eavesdroppers and they got up to slip away, when the door seemed to erupt inward and a bald woman in a black jumpsuit of some shimmering, simmering stuff burst in and crowed. Literally crowed, her head thrown back to show the lightning slashing down her throat.

She saw me and cried, "Peter!" and headed for me like a goddess toward an offering left inside her temple. My customers knocked over their chairs and each other in their haste to be gone.

She ignored them and looked me over. "You'll do. You're not the impudent little vintage you were last time. Something stronger now. Fuller bodied, certainly. What? No hug for the prodigal returned?"

I was suddenly aware that my heart was beating, that I was breathing the same air she breathed. "I didn't wait for you."

She grinned. "Yet, here I am. Unannounced, unbidden, and uncharacteristically unkissed." She pretended to look around the bar. "Is there a jealous wife lurking about with a knife? Or an innocent child too young to see what a lascivious spacer might do to her father?"

My own smile broke free, opening the way for other feelings to wash over me. "No, no wife, not at present. And no child, innocent or otherwise to be shocked by you. Just me, and if I didn't wait for you, I'm still glad you're here." I got up and grabbed her, picking her up and squeezing her as if I didn't know I was going to have to let her go again. She gave me a kiss and I swear I felt her tongue tickle me down at the bottom of my stomach.

She hadn't changed much. Less hair. Was she smaller? Maybe I had grown. Maybe the memory of her was bigger than the reality. But why should she have changed? From her point of view, she'd only been gone a couple of years or so. For me it had been a good-sized part of my life. Spent not waiting for her.

We left the bar, and once again time was an ocean in which we swam, too vast to know if we were moving toward or further away from shore, or just staying in one place.

We went places and did things. This time there were as many doors that I could open as ones to which she was the key. Annie of the Stars and Peter of the Port. If we weren't king and queen of our respective realms, we were at least the duke and duchess.

We fought a handful of sailors. We watched the sylphs of Cygnus dance, or mate, or communicate, or all or none of those things, then we tried to imitate them, which caused a tavern full of pirates to be appalled. We tasted the pleasures of a hundred worlds.

"Why did you come back?" I asked her as we lay in bed.

"Chance?" She shrugged. "A job. Someone needed something from there to here and I brought it."

"Why did you come back to me?" I waited for her to answer.

Eventually she said, "It's what I do. There's a Peter on a lot of worlds. I come back to see what you've become. It's like visiting a series of portraits. I see you captured as a young man. Then I visit a moment when you are as you are now. If there is a next time, you'll be an old man. Three ticks of the clock. Beginning, middle, end. Then gone. It's like traveling through time."

"So I'm some sort of marker, a way for you to mark your passage through the years?"

She looked at me. "I made you no promises. You said you understood. I never asked you to wait for my return."

"I did not wait for you," I told her.

I did not wait for her, I told myself.

The next time she went away, I was old.

I'd married again, once or twice. I even had a son and a daughter, both grown. The stories of Annie Jones I'd told them I now told to my grandchildren. They weren't true stories. The truth I kept locked away inside of me, to look at now and then when I was alone.

In fact, I made a good deal of money writing stories about Annie Jones. Like *Annie Jones and the Space Squid.* And *Annie Jones and the Robots of Doom.* And there were others, some of which were made into sensies. If Annie came back, she would find herself a legend, like Joan of Arc, or Buffalo Bill, or Neil Armstrong. I smiled to think of her reaction and hoped I would be out of her reach when she found out.

I still sat at the same table at the bar now run by my daughter and her husband. No longer posing, no longer intriguing, no longer waiting, just remembering and occasionally writing down a tale that had its start in a memory. My hair was white and thinning, and I was smaller than I had been, befitting my smaller life. And sometimes, I admit, satisfied, content, and happy, I fell asleep, nodding in my chair, dreaming dreams I kept to myself.

"Hey!" The voice, next to my head, woke me and almost made me fall backwards out of my chair.

"What have you done to me, old man?"

"Annie?" My eyes weren't as good as they once were, but the woman looming over me had longish black hair, and no tattoo. She was wearing a loose blouse and a short skirt. "Annie?"

"Yes, Annie, you slobbering, senile, son of a…"

"What have you done to yourself?"

She stopped and looked at herself. "What are you talk...Oh, I guess I look a little different than I did the last time you and I...Who gives a spacer's shit what the hell I look like? What's all this crap about Annie Jones and the Whore of Planet X, or whatever it is you've been spewing? Every time I try to pick up a lover or start a fight, people treat me like I wasn't real, like I'm sort kind of story book character come to life. I punched a cop just to see what would happen and she thanked me! Said, wait until she tells her kids that she got punched by Annie Jones. What have you done to me?"

When I was able to speak without letting her catch me laughing, I said, "I made you famous, that's all. Or, not you, so much as the idea of you." I risked a chuckle. "Made a lot of money at it, too."

"Money?" That calmed her down. "Well, I suppose if you did it to make money it's all right." She smiled. "I remember one time when we convinced the people on some hick world out beyond Andromeda that there was an asteroid coming that would wipe out half the planet. We sold about a thousand passages aboard a ship that might have held six or seven people if they didn't mind getting to know each other real well." A laugh burst from her. "Then we left two days, or rather nights, before we were scheduled to and left them all behind. I always wondered if they were so relieved we'd lied to them about the asteroid that they didn't mind losing their money."

She pulled up a chair and we started drinking ale and telling lies. It was almost like going back in time. Almost like being alive. I could pretend that I could keep up with her, that I wasn't tired, that I didn't hope for one more night with her.

Eventually I said, "How about some food?"

"God, yes," she said. "I'm so hungry I feel like I could take a bite out of a neutron star. Where should we go?" She stood up, pushing her chair over, ready for whatever came next.

Except for what I suggested. "How about my place?"

She didn't laugh, which was a relief to me. She did look at me with pity, which made me angry, whether at her or at myself I wasn't sure.

"I have food," I said, with some heat. "And I can cook." She still looked like she wasn't sure how to break it to me that she wasn't anxious to leap into bed with the decrepit husk of what had been a man. "I just thought you might want a real meal for a change, that's all. I have no dark designs on your virtue, if that's what you're worried about." I stared at her, daring her to laugh. Which she did, forcing me to join her.

"Come on, then," she said. "Let's go and fill our bellies with something other than ale for a while."

No promises, I told myself, but a perhaps, a maybe, a could be. I didn't even mind that she helped me to my feet. Her touch warmed places that had been cold too long. No promises, I told myself, but a hope, a wish, a prayer.

Before we got to the door, it opened and a group of five, or ten, or a hundred people burst in, laughing, shouting, shoving, shaking the floor like a stampede of wild creatures in their rush to reach the bar. Spacers and the crowd they accreted as they cruised the port.

"Annie!" they yelled when they saw her. "Annie Jones!" they trumpeted.

And she answered them. "Trisha! Sasha! Wen Ho!" And more. She was surrounded and torn from me by the mob, swept away by a wave of old friends and shipmates. I stood and watched them go. Even though they were just a few feet from me, they seemed to recede into the distance until I was alone, a million miles from anyone.

I went back to my table and waited.

There comes a time when old ceases to have meaning and the young become impatient to have you die and get out of the way. When every day you wake up is a miracle, or a curse, and you are never sure which.

I waited, no more pretending to myself. I hung on, day after day after day. I could hear the whispers of grandchildren and great-grandchildren as they wondered if I would ever die. They loved me, I think, but enough was enough. Besides, I still had some money to leave them.

Yet, even though there were no promises, I waited.

And, finally, she came.

"Peter?" she said, leaning over me as I lay in bed. Her voice was strained with the effort of trying to fit her normal shout into a whisper. Her hair was silver this time, the metal, not the color, though she was no longer young. The way she moved, the way she stood, were still filled with confidence, but some of her brashness was gone, as if she'd met a situation or two somewhere in her travels which she hadn't been able handle all by herself. "Peter," she whispered again, a little louder, when I didn't respond. She leaned closer, trying to see if there was life in my eyes, to hear if I still breathed.

I did breathe. I breathed in the scent of her, the scent of a time before I was born and the time to come after I was dead. I smelled crowded ships visiting a hundred worlds with a thousand taverns. Blood and sweat and sex and fear and joy. I inhaled Annie Jones like a drug.

And when I exhaled, I let it all out.

"You never promised to come back," I said. "But you always did. And I never meant to wait for you, but when I wasn't spending my time thinking about the last time, I was hoping there would be a next time."

"Then you're a fool," she said, but she stroked my forehead as she said it. "I'm Annie Jones and I don't care about anyone but me. I'm a traveler through space and time, and, if sometimes by chance I happen to come back, I always go away."

"I know who you are, Annie, and I'm glad that you came back. But this time it's me that's going away with no promise to return." I smiled at her. "And, unlike you, I mean it." And I swear I saw a tear fall. And I was happy, not that she was sad, but that, in her way, she loved me.

SCREAM ANGEL
Douglas Smith

THEY STOPPED BEATING Trelayne when they saw that he enjoyed it. The thugs that passed as cops in that town on Long Shot backed away from where he lay curled on the dirt floor, as if he was something dead or dangerous. He watched them lock the door of his cold little cell again. Disgust and something like fear showed in their eyes. The taste of their contempt for him mixed with the sharpness of his own blood in his mouth. And the *Scream* in that blood shot another stab of pleasure through him.

He expected their reaction. The Merged Corporate Entity guarded its secrets well, and Scream was its most precious. Long Shot lay far from any Entity project world and well off the jump route linking Earth and the frontier. No one on this backwater planet would know of the drug, let alone have encountered a Screamer or an Angel. That was why he had picked it.

Their footsteps receded, and the outer door of the plasteel storage hut that served as the town jail clanged shut. Alone, he rolled onto his side on the floor, relishing the agony the movement brought. He tried to recall how he came to be there, but the Scream in him turned each attempt into an emotional sideshow. Finally he remembered something burning, something...

...*falling.*

It had been one of their better shows.

He remembered now. Remembered last night, standing in the ring of their makeshift circus dome, announcing the performers to an uncaring crowd, crying out the names of the damned, the conquered. Each member of his refugee band emerged from behind torn red curtains and propelled themselves in the manner of their species into or above the ring, depending on their chosen act.

He knew the acts meant little. The crowd came not to see feats of acrobatics or strength, but to gawk at otherworldly strangeness, to watch aliens bow in submission before the mighty human. Trelayne's circus consisted of the remnants of the subjugated races of a score of worlds, victims to the Entity's resource extraction or terraforming projects: the Stone Puppies, lumbering silica beasts of slate-sided bulk—Guppert the Strong, squat bulbous-limbed refugee from the crushing gravity and equally crushing mining exploitation of Mendlos II—Feran the fox-child, his people hunted down like animals on Fandor IV.

And the Angels. Always the Angels.

But curled in the dirt in the cold cell, recalling last night, Trelayne pushed away any thoughts of the Angels. And of *her*.

Yes, it had been a fine show. Until the Ta'lona died, exploding in blood and brilliance high above the ring, after floating too near a torch. Trelayne had bought the gas bag creature's freedom a week before from an *ip* slaver, knowing that its species had been nearly wiped out.

As pieces of the fat alien had fallen flaming into the crowd, Trelayne's grip on reality had shattered like a funhouse mirror struck by a hammer. He could now recall only flashes of what had followed last night: people burning—screaming—panic—a stampede to the exits—his arrest.

Nor could he remember doing any Scream. He usually stayed clean before a show. But he knew what he felt now lying in the cell—the joy of the beating, the ecstasy of humiliation. He must have done a hit when the chaos began and the smell of burnt flesh reached him. To escape the horror.

Or to enter it. For with Scream, horror opened a door to heaven.

Someone cleared their throat in the cell. Trelayne jumped, then shivered at the thrill of surprise. Moaning, he rolled onto his back on the floor and opened his eyes, struggling to orient himself again.

A man now sat on the cot in the cell. A man with a lean face and eyes that reminded Trelayne of his own. He wore a long gray cloak with a major's rank and a small insignia on which a red "RIP" hovered over a green planet split by a lightning bolt.

The uniform of RIP Force. A uniform that Trelayne had worn a lifetime ago. Gray meant Special Services: this man was RIP, but not a Screamer. RIP kept senior officers and the SS clean.

The man studied a PerComm unit held in a black-gloved hand, then looked down at Trelayne and smiled. "Hello, Captain Trelayne," he said softly, as if he were addressing a child.

Trelayne swallowed. He was shaking and realized he had been since he had recognized the uniform. "My name is not Trelayne."

"I am Weitz," the man said. The PerComm disappeared inside his cloak. "And the blood sample I took from you confirms that you are Jason Lewiston Trelayne, former Captain and Wing Commander in the Entity's Forces for the Relocation of Indigenous Peoples, commonly known as RIP Force. Convicted of treason in absentia three years ago, 2056-12-05 AD. Presumed dead in the MCE raid on the rebel base on Darcon III in 2057-08-26."

Trelayne licked his lips, savoring the flavor of his fear.

"You're a wanted man, Trelayne." Weitz's voice was soft. "Or would be, if the Entity knew you were still alive."

The Scream in Trelayne turned the threat in those words into a thrilling chill up his spine. He giggled.

Weitz sighed. "I've never seen a Screamer alive three years after RIP. Dead by their own hand inside a month, more likely. But then, most don't have their own source, do they?"

The implication of those words broke through the walls of Scream in Trelayne's mind. Weitz represented real danger—to him, to those in the circus that depended on him. To *her*. Trelayne struggled to focus on the man's words.

"...good choice," Weitz was saying. "Not a spot the Entity has any interest in now. You'd never see Rippers here—" Weitz smiled. "—unless they had ship trouble. I was in the next town waiting for repairs when I heard of a riot at a circus of ips."

Ips—I.P.'s—Indigenous Peoples. A Ripper slur for aliens. Weitz stood up. "You have an Angel breeding pair, Captain, and I need them." He pushed open the cell door and walked out, leaving the door open. "I've arranged for your release. You're free to go. Not that you can go far. We'll talk again soon." Looking back to where Trelayne lay shivering, Weitz shook his head. "Jeezus, Trelayne. You used to be my hero."

Trelayne slumped back down on the floor, smiling as the smell of dirt and stale urine stung his throat. "I used to be a lot of things," he said, as much to himself as to Weitz.

Weitz shook his head again. "We'll talk soon, Captain." He turned and left the hut.

Think of human emotional response as a sine wave function. Peaks and valleys. The peaks represent pleasure, and the valleys pain. The greater your joy, the higher the peak; the greater your pain, the deeper the valley.

Imagine a drug that takes the valleys and flips them, makes them peaks too. You react now to an event based not on the pleasure or pain inherent in it, but solely on the intensity of the emotion created. Pain brings pleasure, grief gives joy, horror renders ecstasy.

Now give this drug to one who must perform an unpleasant task. No. Worse than that. An immoral deed. Still worse. A nightmare act of chilling terminal brutality. Give it to a soldier. Tell them to kill. Not in the historically acceptable murder we call war, but in a systematic corporate strategy—planned, scheduled, and budgeted—of xenocide.

They will kill. And they will revel in it.

Welcome to the world of Scream.

—Extract from propaganda data bomb launched on Fandor IV ComCon by rebel forces, 2056-10-05 AD. Attributed to Capt. Jason L. Trelayne during his subsequent trial in absentia for treason.

Feran thought tonight's show was their finest since the marvelous Ta'lona had died, now a five-day ago. From behind the red curtains that hid the performers' entrance, the young kit watched the two Angels, Philomela and Procne, plummet from the top of the dome to swoop over the man-people crowd. Remembering how wonderfully the fat alien had burnt, Feran also recalled the Captain explaining to him how that night had been bad. The Captain had been forced to give much power-stuff for the burnt man-people and other things that Feran did not understand.

The Angels completed a complicated spiral dive, interweaving their descents. Linking arms just above the main ring, they finished with a dizzying spin like the top the Captain had made him. They bowed to the applauding crowd, folding and unfolding diaphanous wings so the spotlights sparkled on the colors.

Feran clapped his furred hands together as Mojo had taught him, closing his ear folds to shut out the painful noise of the man-people. As the performers filed out for the closing procession around the center ring, Feran ran to take his spot behind the Stone Puppies. Guppert the Strong lifted Feran gently to place him on the slate-gray back of the nearest silica beast.

"Good show, little friend!" Guppert cried. His squat form waddled beside Feran. Guppert liked Long Shot because it did not hold him to the ground as did his home of Mendlos. "Of course, Guppert never go home now," he had told Feran once, his skin color darkening to show sadness. "Off-planet too long. Mendlos crush Guppert, as if Stone Puppy step on Feran. But with Earth soldiers there in mecha-suits, now Mendlos not home anyway."

Waving to the crowd, the performers disappeared one by one through the red curtains. Feran leapt from the Stone Puppy, shouted a goodbye to Guppert, and scurried off to search for Philomela. Outside the show dome, he sniffed the cool night air for her scent, found it, then turned and ran into the Cutter.

"Whoa, Red! What's the rush?" The tall thin man scowled down at Feran like an angry mantis. The Cutter was the healer for the circus. "Helpin' us die in easy stages, s'more like it," was how the Cutter had introduced himself when Feran had arrived.

"I seek the Bird Queen, Cutter," Feran replied.

Sighing, the Cutter jerked a thumb towards a cluster of small dome pods where the performers lived. Feran thought of it as the den area. "Don't let him take too much, you hear?"

Feran nodded and ran off again, until a voice like wind in crystal trees halted him. "You did well tonight, sharp ears."

Feran turned. Philomela smiled down at him, white hair and pale skin, tall and thin like an earth woman stretched to something alien in a trick mirror. Even walking, she made Feran think of birds in flight. Philomela was beautiful. The Captain had told him so many times. He would likely tell Feran again tonight, once he had breathed her dust that Feran brought him.

"Thank you, Bird Queen," Feran replied, bowing low with a sweep of his hand as the Captain had taught him. Philomela laughed, and Feran bared his teeth in joy. He had made the beautiful bird lady laugh. The Captain would be pleased.

Procne came to stand behind Philomela, his spider-fingered hand circling her slim waist. "Where do you go now, Feran? Does Mojo still have chores for you?" He looked much like her, taller, heavier, but features still delicate, almost feminine. His stomach pouch skin rippled where the brood moved inside him.

"He goes to the Captain's pod," Philomela said. "They talk, about the times when the Captain flew in the ships. Don't you?"

Feran nodded.

Procne's eyelids slid in from each side, leaving only a vertical slit. "The times when those ships flew over our homes, you mean? Your home too, Feran." Procne spun and stalked away, his wings pulled tight against his back.

Feran stared after him, then up at Philomela. "Did I do wrong, Bird Queen?"

Philomela folded and unfolded her wings. "No, little one, no. My mate remembers too much, yet forgets much too." She paused. "As does the Captain." She stroked Feran's fur where it lay red and soft between his large ears, then handed him a small pouch. "Feran, tonight don't let the Captain breathe too much of my dust. Get him to sleep early. He looks so...tired."

Feran took the pouch and nodded. He decided he would not tell the Captain of Philomela's face as she walked away.

> > > > > > MergedCorporateEntity,Inc. > > > > > >
Project Search Request
Search Date: 2059-06-02
Requestor:*Weitz, David R., Major, RIP Special Services*
Search Criteria:
Project World:*All*   Division: *PharmaCorps*
Product:*Scream*   Context: *Field Ops / Post-Imp*
Clearance Required: AAAYour Clearance:AAA

> > > > Access Granted. Search results follow. > > > >

Scream mimics several classes of psychotropics, including psychomotor stimulants, antidepressants, and narcotic analgesics. It acts on both stimulatory and inhibitory neurotransmitters, but avoids hallucinogenic effects by maintaining neurotransmitter balance. It enhances sensory ability, speeds muscular reaction and lessens nerve response to pain. It affects all three opiate receptors, inducing intense euphoria without narcotic drowsiness.

Physical addiction is achieved by four to six ingestions at dosage prescribed in Field Ops release 2.21.7.1. Treated personnel exhibit significantly lowered resistance to violence. Secondary benefits for field operations include decreased fatigue, delayed sleep on-set, and enhanced mental capacity.

Negative side effects include uncontrolled masochistic or sadistic tendencies, such as self-mutilation or attacks on fellow soldiers. Scream is therefore not administered until military discipline and obedience programming is completed in boot camp. Long-term complications include paranoid psychoses and suicidal depression. Withdrawal is characterized by hallucinations, delirium and seizures, terminating with strokes or heart attacks.

Attempts to synthesize continue, but at present our sole source remains extraction from females of the dominant humanoids on Lania II, Xeno sapiens lania var. angelus (colloq.: Scream Angel). The liquid produced crystallizes into powder form. Since the drug is tied to reproduction (see Xenobiology: Lania: Life Forms: 1275), ensuring supply requires an inventory of breeding pairs with brood delivery dates spread evenly over—

> > > > *File Transfer Request Acknowledged* > > > >
Xenobiology File: Lania: Life Forms: 1275
The adult female produces the drug from mammary glands at all times but at higher levels in the reproductive cycle. Sexual coupling occurs at both the start and end of the cycle. The first act impregnates the female. The brood develops in her until delivery after thirty weeks in what the original Teplosky journal called the "larval form," transferring then to the male's pouch via orifices in his abdominal wall. For the next nineteen weeks, they feed from the male, who ingests large quantities of Scream from the female. The brood's impending release as mature nestlings prompts the male to initiate the final coupling—

Trelayne lay in his sleep pod at the circus waiting for Feran and the hit of Scream that the kit brought each night. The meeting with Weitz had burst a dam of times past, flooding him with memories. He closed his eyes, his face wet with delicious tears. Though all his dreams were nightmares, he did not fear them. Terror was now but another form of pleasure. Sleep at least freed him from the tyranny of decision.

Twenty again. My first action. I remember...Remember? I'd give my soul to forget, if my soul remains for me to barter.

Bodies falling against a slate-gray sky...

The RIP transports on Fandor IV were huge oblate spheroids, flattened and wider in the middle than at the ends. Trelayne and almost one hundred other Rippers occupied the jump seats that lined the perimeter of the main bay, facing in,

officers near the cockpit. Before them, maybe a hundred
Fandor natives huddled on the metal floor, eyes downcast
but constantly darting around the hold and over their cap-
tors. The adults were about five feet tall and humanoid, but
their soft red facial hair, pointed snouts and ears gave them
a feral look. The children reminded Trelayne of a stuffed
toy he had as a child.

Fresh from RIP boot camp, this was to be his first action.
These Fandorae came from a village located over rich mineral
deposits soon to be an Entity mining operation. They were to
be "relocated" to an island off the west coast. He added the
quotes in response to a growing suspicion, fed by overheard
jokes shared by RIP veterans. He also recalled arriving on
Fandor, scanning the ocean on the approach to the RIP base
on the west shore.

There were no islands off the coast.

The other Rippers shifted and fidgeted, waiting for their
first hit of the day. The life support system of their field suits
released Scream directly into their blood, once each suit's computer received the transmitted command from the RIP Force
unit leader. If you wanted your Scream, you suited up and
followed orders. And *God*, you wanted your Scream.

His unit had been on Scream since the end of boot camp.
Trelayne knew he was addicted. He knew that RIP wanted him
and all his unit addicted. He just didn't know why. He had also
noticed that no one in his unit had family. No one would miss
any of them. Another reason to follow orders.

Twenty minutes out from the coast, a major unbuckled his
boost harness and nodded to a captain to his right. Every Ripper watched as the captain hit a button on his wrist pad.

The Scream came like the remembered sting of an old
wound, a friend that you hadn't seen in years and once reunited,
you wondered why you had missed them.

The captain's voice barked in their headsets, ordering
them out of their harnesses. Trelayne rose as one with the
other Rippers, StAB rod charged and ready, the Scream in

him twisting his growing horror into the anticipation of ecstasy. The Fandorae huddled closer together in the middle of the bay.

The captain punched another button. Trelayne felt the deck thrumming through his boots as the center bay doors split open. The Fandorae leapt up, grabbing their young and skittering back from the widening hole, only to face an advancing wall of Rippers with lowered StAB rods.

Some of the Fandorae chose to leap. Some were pushed by their own people in the panic. Others fell on the StAB rods or died huddled over their young.

Trelayne pulled a kit, no more than a year, from under a dead female. He held the child in his arms, waiting his turn as the Rippers in front of him lifted or pushed the remaining bodies through the bay doors. When he reached the edge, Trelayne lifted the kit from his shoulder and held it over the opening. It did not squirm or cry, only stared a mute accusation. Trelayne let go, then knelt to peer over the edge.

A salt wind stung sharp and cold where it crept under his helmet. He watched the kit fall to hit the rough gray sea a hundred feet below. Most of the bodies had already slipped beneath the waves. The kit disappeared to join them.

A nausea that even Scream could not deflect seized Trelayne. Pushing back from the edge, he wrenched his visor up to gasp in air. A Ripper beside him turned to him, and for a brief moment Trelayne caught his own reflection in the man's mirrored visor. The image burned into his memory as he fought to reconcile the horror engulfing him with the grinning mask of his own face...

Dreaming still...falling still...falling in love...

Trelayne made captain in a year, as high as Screamers could rise in RIP. He took no pride in it. When the Scream ran low in him, his guilt rose black and bottomless. But his addiction was now complete. Withdrawal for a Screamer meant weeks of agony, without the filter of Scream, then death. The Entity was his only source. He did what he was told.

Rippers burnt out fast on project worlds, so the Entity rotated them off relo work every six months for a four-week tour on a "processed" world. Trelayne's first tour after making captain was on Lania, the Angel home planet, arranging transport of Angel breeding pairs from Lania to project worlds with RIP Force units. The Entity had found that, with Angels on-planet, concerns over Scream delivery could be put aside for that world.

Sex with an Angel, said RIP veterans, was the ultimate high. But upon arrival, Trelayne had found them too alien, too thin and wraith-like. He decided that their reputation was due more to ingesting uncut Scream during sex than to their ethereal beauty.

Then he saw *her*.

She was one of a hundred Angels being herded into a cargo shuttle that would dock with an orbiting jump ship. Angels staggered by Trelayne, their eyes downcast. He had started to turn away when he saw her: striding with head held high, glaring at the guards. She turned as she passed him. Their eyes locked.

He ordered her removed from the shipment. That is how he met her. As her captor. Then her liberator. Then her lover.

The Earth name she had taken was Philomela. Her Angel name could not be produced by a human throat. She brought him joy and pain. He was never sure what he brought her. She gave herself willingly, and her pleasure in their lovemaking seemed so sincere that he sometimes let himself believe—believe that she clung to *him* in those moments, not to a desperate hope for freedom. That she did not hate him for what RIP had done to her people.

That she loved him.

But Scream strangled such moments. Though not on combat doses, he still needed it for physical dependency. On low doses, depression clouded life in a gray mist. Could she love him when he doubted his own love for her? Why was he drawn to her? Sex? His private source of Scream? To wash his hands clean by saving one of his victims? And always between them loomed an impassable chasm: they were separate species who could never be truly mated.

The news reached him one rare afternoon as they lay together in his quarters. His PerComm unit, hanging on the wall above them, began to buzz like an angry insect. He pulled it down and read the message from the Cutter, the medic in his unit.

She watched him as he read. "Jase, is something wrong?"

He had come to expect her empathy. Whether she could now read his human expressions or sense his mood, he didn't know. He threw the unit away as if it had stung him and covered his face with a hand. "Mojo. One of my men, a friend. He's *Fallen*."

"Is he—"

"He's alive. No serious injuries." As if that mattered.

"Do you think he tried to take his life?"

"No," he said, though the drug in him screamed yes.

"Many do—"

"No! Not Mojo." But he knew she was right. Suicide was common with Screamers, and "joining the Fallen" was a favored method—a dive that you never came out of. The Entity punished any survivors brutally. Screamers were easily replaced, but one LASh jet could cut the return on a project world by a full point.

"Now comes the judging your people do?" she asked.

"Court martial. Two weeks." If they found Mojo guilty they would discharge him. No source of Scream. Better to have died in the crash, he thought. He got out of bed and began dressing. "I have to leave Lania, return to my base. Try to help him."

"They will judge against him. You will not change that."

"I know. But I have to try. He has no one else."

She turned away. "We have few moments together."

She was shaking, and he realized that she was crying. He misunderstood. "I'll be back soon. It'll be better then."

She shook her head and looked up at him. "I mean that we have few moments *left*. It is my time."

He stood there staring down at her. "What do you mean?"

"I must produce a brood." She turned away again.

"You mean you will take a mate. One of your own kind."

"His name is Procne," she said, still not looking at him.

He didn't know what to do or say, so he kept dressing.

She turned to him. "I love you," she said quietly.

He stopped. She waited. He said nothing. She lay down, sobbing. He swallowed and formed the thought in his mind, opened his mouth to tell her that he loved her too, when she spoke again.

"What will become of me?" she asked.

All his doubts about her rushed in to drown the words in his mouth. He was but a way of escape to her. She did not love him. She would give herself to one of her own. She was alien. The Angels hated RIP for what they had done. She hated him.

He pulled on his jacket and turned away...

The trial. I tried, Mojo—but nothing can save us when we Fall, and we were Falling the moment they put it in our blood...

The day after Mojo's trial, Trelayne entered the RIP barracks pod. The Cutter and two other Rippers sat on drop-bunks watching Mojo stuff his few possessions into a canister pack. Mojo wore his old civvies, now at least a size too small. He still had a Medistim on his arm, and he moved with a limp.

The others jumped to attention when they saw their visitor. Cutter just nodded. Trelayne returned the salutes then motioned towards the door. After a few words and half-hearted slaps on Mojo's back, they filed out, leaving Trelayne and Mojo alone.

Mojo sat down on his bunk. "Thanks, Cap. Hell of a try."

Trelayne sat, forcing a smile. "You forget we lost?"

Mojo shrugged. "Never had a chance. You know that. None of us do. Just a matter of time. If the Scream don't get you, they will. No way out for the likes of us."

Trelayne searched Mojo's broad face. *I have to try*, he thought. *We won't get another chance.* "Maybe there is a way."

Narrowing his eyes, Mojo glanced at the door and back again. He looked grim. "I'm with you, Cap. Whatever, wherever."

Trelayne shook his head. "They'll kill us if we're caught."

"I'm a dead man already. We all are."

Trelayne sighed and started talking...

And so the Fallen dreamed of rising again, eh Mojo? What fools we were. But we gave them a run for a while, didn't we?

Trelayne returned to Lania. In his absence, Philomela had taken Procne as her mate. She refused to see Trelayne. He added her and Procne to the next cargo of Angels being shipped to the project worlds, with himself as the ship's captain.

He did not see her until after their ship had made the first jump. Philomela was summoned to the captain's cabin, to be told to which planet she and her mate had been consigned.

She stiffened when she entered and saw him. "You."

He nodded and waited.

"Sending us into slavery to be bred and milked like animals, this was not enough? You had to be here to see it happen, did you, Jason?" She looked around. "Where is the captain?"

"I am the captain on this trip."

She looked confused. "But you have never gone on these..."

He sighed. "Please sit. I have much to say..."

Why did I risk everything to save her? Love? Guilt? As penance? For her Scream? In a desperate hope that one day she would turn to me again? Or as I fell, was I willing to grasp at anything, even if I pulled those I loved down with me?

From the ship's observation deck, Trelayne and Philomela watched a shuttle depart, carrying a "shipment" of twenty pairs of Angels for the project world below.

"Do you know why I chose my Earth name?" she asked.

Her voice was flat, dead, but he heard the pain that each of these worlds brought her as more of her people were torn away, while she remained safe, protected. "No. Tell me," he said.

"In a legend of your planet, Philomela was a girl turned into a nightingale by the gods. That image pleased me, to be chosen by the gods, elevated to the heavens. Only later did I learn that the nightingale is also a symbol of death."

Trelayne bowed his head. "Phi, there's nothing—"

"No, but allow me at least my bitterness. And guilt."

Guilty of being spared. By him. She and Procne spared, only because an addict and xenocide and soon-to-be traitor needed his drug source close. He had stopped trying to examine his motives beyond that. The Scream would mock the small voice in him that spoke of a last remnant of honor and noble intent.

"My sister is on that shuttle," Philomela said quietly.

Trelayne said nothing for there was nothing to say. They watched the tiny ship fall towards the planet below...

At each planet on that trip, we gathered to us the castoffs, the unwanted, the remnants of a dozen races, together with the Fallen. And then, suddenly, there was no turning back...

Trelayne's first officer, a young lieutenant-commander named Glandis, confronted him on the bridge. She wasn't backing down this time. "Captain, I must again register my concern over continued irregularities in your command of this mission."

Trelayne glanced at the monitor by his chair. Mojo and eleven other ex-Rippers were disembarking from a shuttle in the ship's docking bay. In two minutes, they would be on the bridge. He tapped a command, deactivating all internal communications and alarms. He turned to Glandis. "Irregularities?"

"The ip *cargo* we have acquired at each of our stops."

"Those *people* are to be transported to the Entity's Product R&D center on Earth," Trelayne responded.

Glandis snorted. "What research could the Entity conduct with—" She read from her PerComm. "—a Mendlos subject?"

"Physiological adaptation to high-grav," Trelayne replied.

"A Fandorae kit? A Fanarucci viper egg?"

"Biotech aural receptor design, and neural poison mutagenics development." One minute more, he thought.

Glandis hesitated, some of the confidence leaving her face. "You have also protected one specific breeding pair of Angels for purposes that have yet to be made clear to me."

"They too are slated for Entity research." Trelayne rose. Thirty seconds. "Synthesization of Scream."

"What about this stop? It was not on our filed flight plan."

"Late orders from RIP Force command." Fifteen seconds.

"I was not informed."

"You just were."

Glandis reddened. "And what purpose will a dozen disgraced ex-members of RIP Force serve?"

Now, thought Trelayne. The door to the bridge slid open. Mojo and four other ex-Rippers burst in, Tanzer rifles charged and pointed at Glandis and the bridge crew. Glandis turned to Trelayne with mouth open, then froze.

Trelayne had his own weapon leveled at Glandis. "Their purpose, I'm afraid, is to replace the crew of this ship."

And so the Fallen rose again, to scale a precipice from which there was no retreat, and each new height we gained only made the final Fall that much farther...

After leaving the Bird Queen, Feran ran past the closed tubes of the barkers, the games of chance, and the sleep pods of the performers. The kit moved easily among the ropes, refuse, and equipment, his path clear to him even in the dim light of sputtering torches and an occasional hovering glow-globe.

The show used fewer glow-globes than when Feran had first arrived. The Captain said the globes cost too much now. Feran didn't mind. He needed little light to see, and liked the smell of the torches and the crackle they made.

Turning a corner, Feran froze. Weasel Man stood outside the Captain's pod. The Captain had said that the man's name was Weitz, but he reminded Feran of the animals the kit hunted in the woods outside the circus. The door opened. Weasel Man stepped inside.

Feran crept to the open window at the pod's side. He could hear voices. His nose twitched. His ears snapped up and opened wide, adjusting until the sound was the sharpest.

Trelayne lay on his sleep pod bunk, shaking from withdrawal. Feran was late bringing his nightly hit. Weitz lounged in a chair, staring at him. It had been five days since their meeting in the jail. "Where've you been, Weitz?" Trelayne wheezed.

"Had some arrangements to make. Need a hit, don't you?"

"It's coming," Trelayne mumbled. "What do you want?"

Weitz shrugged. "I told you. The Angels."

"But not to hand them back to the Entity, or you'd have done it by now," Trelayne said. But if Weitz wanted the Angels, why didn't he just take them? He had his own men and a ship.

Weitz smiled. "Do you know there are rebels on Fandor IV?"

"Rebels? What are you talking about?" Where was Feran?

"Ex-RIP rebels like you, or rather, like you once were."

"Like me? God, then I pity the rebels on Fandor IV."

Weitz leaned forward in his chair. "I'm one of them."

Trelayne laughed. "You're RIP SS."

"I assist from the *inside*. I supply them with Scream."

Trelayne stared at Weitz. This man was far more dangerous than he had first appeared. "You've managed to surprise me, Major. Why would you risk your life for a bunch of rebels?"

Weitz shrugged. "I said you were my hero. The man who defied an empire. I want to do my part, too."

Trelayne snorted. "Out of the goodness of your heart."

Weitz reddened. "I cover my costs. No more."

I'll bet, Trelayne thought. "Where do you get Scream?"

"I...acquired a store doing an SS audit of a RIP warehouse."

"You stole it. A store? Since when can you store Scream?"

Weitz smiled. "A result of intense research prompted by your escape with the Angels. You made the Entity realize the risk of transporting breeding pairs. Angels are now kept in secure facilities on Lania and two other worlds, producing Scream that's shipped to project worlds with RIP forces. Angels live and die without *ever* leaving the facility they were born into."

Trelayne shuddered. Because of him. But the Scream in him ran too low to find any joy in this new horror.

They fell silent. Finally Weitz spoke. "So what happened, Trelayne? To the Great Rebel Leader? To the one man who stood up to the Entity? How'd it all go to hell?"

"Screamers are in hell already. We were trying to get out."

"You got out, in a stolen Entity cruiser. Then what?"

Shivering, Trelayne struggled to sit up. Where was Feran? "We jumped to a system the Entity had already rejected. Only one habitable planet. No resources worth the extraction cost."

"And set up a base for a guerilla war on the Entity."

"No. A colony. A home for the dispossessed races."

"You attacked Entity project worlds," Weitz said.

"We sent messages. There was never any physical assault."

"Your data bombs flooded Comm systems for entire planets."

"We tried to make people aware of what the Entity was doing. Almost worked." Trelayne fought withdrawal, trying to focus on Weitz. The man was afraid of something. But what?

"I'll say. You cost them trillions hushing it up, flushing systems. But then what? The reports just end."

"The Entity still has a file on us?" That pleased Trelayne.

"On you," Weitz corrected. "You've got your own entire file sequence. Special clearance needed to get at them. Well?"

Trelayne fell silent, remembering the day, remembering his guilt. "I got careless. They tracked us through a jump somehow, found the colony, T-beamed it from orbit."

"An entire planet? My god!" Weitz whispered.

"A few of us escaped." But not Phi's children, her first brood, he thought. More guilt, though she had never blamed him.

"In a heavily armed cruiser with a crew of ex-Rippers."

He looked at Weitz. *That* was it. Even through the haze of withdrawal, he knew he had his answer: Weitz thought Trelayne still had a band of ex-Rippers at hand, battle-proven trained killers with super-human reflexes and their own Scream supply. Something like hope tried to fight through the black despair of his withdrawal. Weitz would try to deal first.

"And this?" Weitz took in the circus with a wave of a hand.

"After we lost the base, we had to keep moving. As a cover story to clear immigration on each world, I concocted a circus of aliens. Then I ran out of money, had to do it for real."

"What if someone had recognized you? Or knew about Angels?"

Trelayne struggled to speak. "We avoided anywhere with an Entity presence, stayed off the main jump routes." He started to shiver. "Why do you want Angels if you have a store of Scream?"

"My supply'll run out, and I can't count on stealing more."

Trelayne stared at Weitz. "So what's the deal?"

Weitz smiled. "Why do you think I won't just take them?"

"Against a crew of ex-Rippers pumped on Scream?"

Weitz's smile faded. He studied Trelayne. "Okay. Let's assess your position. One: I gave your ship's beacon signature to Long Shot's space defense. If you run, you'll be caught."

Trelayne said nothing.

"Two: if you're caught, your ip pals get sent back to their home worlds. And you know what that means."

Trelayne stayed silent, but his skin went cold.

"Three: you, Mojo and the medic get executed for treason."

"Like I said, what's the deal?"

Weitz studied Trelayne again, then finally spoke. "Both Angels for my store of Scream—a lifetime supply for you and your men. I lift the order on your ship and turn my back as you and your band jump. Your life goes on, with Scream but no Angels."

Life goes on, if you called this life. That much Scream was worth a fortune. But nowhere near the value of a breeding pair.

So there it was. Betray his love or die. What choice did he have? Refuse, and Weitz would turn them over to the Entity, and all would die. Run, and be killed or caught by the planetary fleet. Give her up, along with Procne, and at least the others would be free. Besides, she had turned from him, taken one of her own. She had only used him to escape, had always used him. She was an alien and hated him for what he had done to her race.

She had never really loved him.

All that stood against this were the remnants of his love for her, and a phantom memory of the man he once had been.

Outside, Feran waited for the Captain's reply to Weasel Man. He didn't know what the Captain would do but he knew it would be brave and noble. Feran listened for the sound of the Captain leaping to his feet and striking Weasel Man to the floor. But when a sound came, it was only the Captain's voice, small and hoarse. "All right," was all he said.

"You'll do it?" That was Weasel Man. Feran did not hear a reply. "Tomorrow morning." Weasel Man again. The door opened, and Feran scooted under the pod. Weasel Man stepped out smiling. Feran had seen sand babies smile like that on Fandor just before they spit their venom in your eyes.

As he watched the man walk away, fading into the darkness, something inside Feran faded away as well. He stood staring into the shadows for a long time, then turned and entered the pod. The Captain lay in his sleeping place. He seemed not to notice Feran. The kit put the pouch from the Bird Queen on the table, then left without a word. The Captain did not call after him.

How long Feran wandered the grounds, he did not know. Some time later, he found the Cutter and Mojo sitting in front of a fire burning on an old heat shield panel from the ship.

"Seen the Captain, Feran?" asked Mojo. Feran just nodded.

"He's had his bottle? All tucked in for the night?" the Cutter asked. Feran nodded again as Mojo scowled at the Cutter.

They sat silently for a while. "Does it hurt when you lose someone you love?" Feran asked, ashamed of the fear in his voice, the fear that he felt for Philomela.

The Cutter spoke. "Hurts even more to lose them slowly. Watch 'em disappear bit by bit till nothing's left you remember."

Feran knew the Cutter meant the Captain.

"Shut up, Cutter," Mojo growled. "You've never been there. Only a Screamer knows what he lives with." He patted Feran's head. "Never mind, kid."

The Cutter shook his head but spoke no more. Feran rose and walked slowly away to once again wander the Circus grounds. This time, however, something resolved itself inside his young mind so that when he found himself outside the sleep pod of the Angels he interpreted this as a sign that his plan was pure.

The Bird Queen was alone. She spoke little as he told his tale, a question here or there when the words he chose were poor. She thanked him then sat in silence, her strange eyes staring out the small round window of the pod.

Feran left the Angel then, not knowing whether he had done good or evil, yet somehow aware that his world was a much different place than it had been an hour before.

> > > > > > > *Search Results Continued* > > > > > > >
Xenobiology File: Lania: Life Forms: 1275
   The impending release of a brood of mature nestlings prompts the male Angel to initiate final coupling. This act triggers the female's production of higher concentrations of Scream. Scream is the sole nourishment that the young can ingest upon emergence, and also relieves the agony of the male after the brood bursts from him. The female must receive the nestlings within hours of the final coupling, or she will die from the higher Scream level in her blood, which the nestlings cleanse from her system.
   The evolutionary advantage of this reproductive approach appears to stem from the increased survival expectations of a brood carried by the stronger male, and the ensured presence of both parents at birth. Although Teplosky drew parallels to the Thendotae on Thendos IV, we feel...

Unable to sleep, Feran rose early the next day. A chill mist hung from a gray sky. For an hour, he wandered outside the big dome, worrying how to tell the Captain what he had done and why. He stopped. Towards him strode the Captain, at his side Mojo. Both wore their old long black cloaks, thrown back to reveal weapons strapped to each leg. The gun metal glinted blue and cold, matching the look in the Captain's eyes.

Feran felt all his fears of the previous night vanish like grass swimmers into the brush. The Captain *was* going to fight. He would beat Weasel Man, and all would be well.

The Cutter stepped out of the dome as the Captain and Mojo stopped beside Feran. The Captain reached down to ruffle the fur on Feran's head, then glanced towards the dome. "Ready?"

The Cutter nodded. "Just get him inside."

A cry made them turn. Procne ran towards them, stumbling with the bulging weight of the brood inside him. "She's gone! She's gone!" he cried. He fell gasping into the Cutter's arms. Feran went cold inside.

The talking box on the Captain's belt beeped. He lifted it to his face. "It's from Phi. Time delayed delivery from last night." They waited as he read. When he spoke, his voice was raspy, like when he took too much dust. "She's given herself to Weitz. She knows that I won't surrender her and Pro, that I'll fight. She doesn't wish me or any of us to die." He dropped the device in the dirt. "She knows me better than I know myself, it would seem," he whispered.

"Our brood –" Procne began.

"She says she would rather her children die than live as slaves, kept only to feed monsters that destroy races."

"No! Our final coupling was last night. The brood comes!" He placed a thin hand on his pouch. "The essence they must feed on is rising in her blood. If she is not here when they emerge, they will die. If they die without cleansing her..."

"She will die too," the Captain finished. "She knew this."

Mojo frowned. "How'd she know about Weitz? You only told me and Cutter, and just this morning." The Captain shook his head. Cutter shrugged.

Feran felt as if he was outside his body, watching this scene but not part of it, unable to act. Well, he *had* acted, and this was what had come of it. He heard a voice saying "I told her." It seemed to be coming from somewhere else, and only when they all turned to look at him did he realize he had spoken.

Silence fell. The Captain knelt down before him, and all the words that Feran had tried to find before came pouring out. He turned his head, baring his throat to the Captain, offering his life. Instead, warm arms encircled him and held him tight. Feran knew that this was a "hug" and found it oddly comforting. The Captain whispered, "Oh Feran," and Feran began to sob.

"So now what?" the Cutter growled as the Captain stood.

They waited. Then the Captain spoke, his voice as calm as when he told Feran a story. "Same plan, with one change. We need Pro with us." He turned to Procne, and Feran felt a stillness settle like before two alpha males fought. "You and I, we've never quite got it straight between us. Just knew that she somehow needed us both. You never forgave, never trusted me. Can't say I ever blamed you. Well, I'm asking you to trust me now. If only because you know I wouldn't hurt her."

Procne stared at the Captain for several of Feran's heartbeats, then nodded. The Captain turned to the Cutter. "Take Pro inside. Make it look like his hands are tied." He spoke then to all of them. "Nobody moves till I do, and I won't move until I know where he's got Phi. And remember: we need Weitz alive."

Muttering under his breath, the Cutter pulled Feran into the dome. Feran looked back. The Captain and Mojo strode toward the main entrance, their long cloaks closed, hiding their weapons and shutting out the rain that began to fall hard and cold.

Inside, Feran saw Guppert standing beside two Stone Puppies. He scampered over to them, glad to leave the morose Cutter, then stopped. Weapons were strapped to one side of the great silica beasts, the side hidden from the door. The Puppies lay on the ground, and Guppert's shoulder came to the top of their backs.

Guppert grinned and rapped a fat fist on the slate side of the nearest one. "Puppies make good fort, Guppert thinks." He pointed to the ground. "This where you come, little one, with Guppert, when I give word." He waddled around to the other side of the Puppies where water buckets and scrub brushes lay. "Now, we get busy looking not dangerous." He and Feran began scrubbing the Puppies. The Cutter stood with Procne between them and the entrance, Procne's hands bound behind him.

Feran heard them first. "They are here," he whispered.

Cutter nodded. A few seconds later, two men in RIP SS uniforms entered with guns. They looked around, then one called outside. "All clear."

Weasel Man came in, then the Captain and Mojo, and more men in SS uniforms. Feran counted, his hope fading as each one entered. Ten, plus the first two, and Weasel Man. Four carried a metal case, their guns slung.

"Thirteen. Damn, I hate thirteen," muttered the Cutter as he left Procne and sauntered towards a Puppy. Still scrubbing, Guppert moved to the hidden side of his beast. Feran followed.

Weasel Man looked around. "Where's the rest of your crew?"

The Captain shrugged. "Dead or deserted."

Weasel Man raised an eyebrow and glanced at his men. The Captain nodded at the case. "That our stuff?" he asked, pulling back a sleeve to reveal a Medistim pack. He hit a button on it. Feran knew that he had just taken a "hit." Mojo did the same.

Weasel Man wrinkled his brow. "It was going to be."

The Captain smiled. "But you've reconsidered."

"We have the female already—" Weasel Man said.

"Her name is Philomela," the Captain said.

"And you're outnumbered—"

The Captain nodded. "Just a bunch of old derelicts."

"—so now I think we'll just take this one too."

"And his name is Procne." The Captain hit the stim pack again. So did Mojo. Feran had never seen the Captain take two hits. "So you'll leave me and Mojo to die in slow agony?"

Weasel Man shifted on his feet. Feran smelt his fear. The man nodded at the case. "That's worth a fortune—"

"And you have to cover your costs, don't you? Where is she?" the Captain said, taking a third hit.

"On my ship, hovering above us waiting for my call." Weasel Man patted his talking device. "Now, why don't—"

Being a predator, Feran was the first other than the Captain to know that the moment had arrived. The killing moment. And in that moment, for the first time, Feran realized something.

The Captain was a predator too.

Weasel Man was still talking, "—this over with—"

The Captain and Mojo, moving faster than Feran thought men could move, threw back their cloaks and pulled their guns. The Captain shot Weasel Man twice, once through his gun arm and once through his leg. The air sizzled as Mojo fired, killing three before they could even raise their weapons. The Captain shot three more before Weasel Man hit the ground screaming. Feran closed his ear flaps to shut out the screams, his nose stinging from the burnt air smell. The Cutter and Guppert shot one Ripper each from behind the Puppies. The last four, who had kept their guns slung, died still reaching for their weapons.

As he watched, Feran felt only fear. Not of the killing, for he knew killing, but fear of the look on the Captain's face.

The look of a predator.

The Captain stepped over the bodies to where Weasel Man lay like a trapped animal, and placed his weapon against the man's head. "Call your ship. Tell them to land outside this dome to pick up the other Angel."

Weasel Man spat blood. "Screw you."

The Captain put his gun against Weasel Man's forehead. The man swallowed, but shook his head. "You wouldn't kill an unarmed man in cold blood, Trelayne. You aren't capable of it."

But for the twitching of one eye, the Captain seemed carved from stone. Then he laughed. He laughed and laughed until

Feran felt fear again—fear that he did not really know this man. Suddenly the Captain reached down and with one hand lifted Weasel Man by the throat and held him off the ground. Feran had no words for what he saw in the Captain's eyes as his voice boomed inside the dome. "*I have ripped babies from mother's arms. I have killed thousands and laughed while they died. I have ended races. Little man, I am capable of things you could never imagine!*"

The Captain dropped him then and looked down at the man, and Feran heard the sadness in the Captain's voice as he almost whispered, "I am capable of *anything*."

Weasel Man lay gasping in the dirt. Then he looked up, and Feran knew the Captain had won. Weasel Man was baring his belly and neck, showing submission. He took his talking device with a shaking hand and spoke into it. Feran couldn't hear the words, but the Captain nodded to the others.

Feran relaxed. Guppert and the Cutter were slapping each other on their backs. Mojo sat slumped on the ground, his head between his knees, sobbing but apparently unhurt.

A cry cut the air. Feran spun, teeth bared. High above, Procne hovered, wings beating, head thrown back, face contorted in agony. His pouch bulged, then split as a cloud of bloody winged things burst from him and fell screeching towards them.

The brood had arrived.

Trelayne had not taken combat doses of Scream for over two years. The killing, and the joy it had brought, had shaken him. Now as the brood rained down bloody chaos from above, he felt his tenuous grip on reality slipping away. Knowing that the brood must live or Phi would die, he tried to follow what they were doing, but the Scream kept drawing him to the bloody corpses. He realized then that the brood was also being drawn to them.

Resembling winged toads with humanoid faces, gray and slick, the brood swarmed over the bodies, driving a long tendril that protruded from their abdomen into any open wound. But they stayed only a second at each spot, and with each attempt became more frenzied.

Scream, he thought, *they need blood with Scream.*

"Trelayne!"

The cry spun Trelayne around. Weitz knelt, Tanzer held in a shaking hand. Blood soaked an arm and leg, and flowed from his forehead. Weitz leveled the gun at Trelayne.

The brood found Weitz before he could fire, swarming him, plunging their tendrils into each wound, into his eyes where the blood had run down from his forehead, probing, searching. Screaming, he clawed at them, then stiffened and fell forward.

The nestlings leapt up from his corpse to form a shrieking, swirling mass above the ring. They were tiring. They are dying, Trelayne thought. Blood with Scream. Blood with Scream.

He tore open his shirt. Pulling a knife from his belt, he slashed at his chest and upper arms. He dropped the knife and stood with arms outspread, blood streaming down him, waiting for the smell of the Scream in his blood to reach the brood.

They swooped down from above the ring, swarming him like bees on honey, driving their tendrils into his flesh wherever he bled. The pain surpassed even what Scream let him endure. A dark chasm yawned below him, and he felt himself falling.

Trelayne awoke on his back, pale green light illuminating a bulkhead above him. The weight pressing him into the bed and the throb of engines told him he was on a ship under acceleration.

Something was wrong. No. Something was *right.* Finally he felt right. He felt human. He felt...

Pain. Real pain. Pain that hurt. He tried to rise.

"The Captain has returned to us." It was Feran's voice.

"In more ways than one, fox boy, in more ways than one." The Cutter's face appeared above him. "Lie still for chrissakes. You'll open the wounds again."

Trelayne lay back gasping. "What happened?"

"We won. We took Weitz's ship."

"Mojo? Procne? Phi—where's Phi?" he wheezed.

Her voice came from across the room. "All your family is safe. Guppert, the Puppies. All are here with us."

Trelayne twisted his head. She lay on another bunk, Procne asleep beside her. "Didn't know I had a family," he said weakly.

"We knew, Jason Trelayne. All along we were your family."

The Cutter moved aside, and Trelayne could see the brood clinging to her. She smiled. "Yes. You saved my children."

"I haven't seen that smile in a long time, Phi."

"I have not had reason for a long time."

"I feel...I feel..."

"You feel true pain. And you wonder why." Her gaze dropped to something at his side. Only then did Trelayne realize that one of the brood lay next to him, and that the tiny creature still had its tendril inside him. He tried to move away.

"Lie still, dammit," the Cutter snapped. "This ugly little vacuum cleaner hasn't got you quite cleaned up yet."

"What are you talking about?"

The Cutter checked a monitor on the wall above the bunk. "The brood's feeding's reduced the Scream in your blood to almost nil. The big bonus is zero withdrawal signs. Remember when you tried to kick it when we started the colony?"

Trelayne nodded, shuddering at the memory.

The Cutter rubbed his chin. "These little suckers must leave somethin' behind in the blood, lets the body adjust to lower levels of Scream. Angels'd need the same thing when the brood feeds from 'em." He looked at Trelayne. "You just bought a new life for every Screamer the Entity ever got hooked."

As the implication of that sank in, Mojo's face appeared at the door. One of the brood clung to him as well. "We're nearing the jump insertion point. Where're we headed, Cap?"

Silence fell, and Trelayne could sense them waiting for his answer. He remembered something Weitz had said and smiled through his pain. "I hear there are still rebels on Fandor IV."

Mojo grinned and disappeared towards the bridge with Cutter. Trelayne turned to Feran. The kit moved away. Trelayne's smile faded as he understood. He stared at the kit then spoke very quietly. "Feran, the Captain Trelayne that you saw in the dome today...he died with all those other men. Do you understand?"

An eternity passed. Then Feran ran to him and hugged him far too hard, and it hurt. His wounds hurt. The nestling at his side hurt. God, it all hurt, and it was wonderful to hurt again and to want it to stop.

Later, the ship slowed for the jump, and weightlessness took him. But to Trelayne, the sensation this time was not of falling. Instead, he felt himself rising, rising above something he was finally leaving behind.

Meet the Authors

Eric M. Witchey lives in Salem, Oregon. He is a graduate of Clarion West and has won recognition from Writers of the Future, New Century Writers, and Writer's Digest. His fiction has appeared in a number of magazines and anthologies.

About "Voyeur": "Voyeur" came from an exercise in which I attempted to write a short story from four randomly chosen topics: A revelation, Who else has owned this chair?, A voyeur, and Squint. My critique group, the Wordos of Eugene, Oregon, provided valuable feedback. If the results are palatable to the reader, it is due chiefly to a set of good dice and my friends in Eugene.

John Teehan lives and writes in Providence, Rhode Island. He's been a fan of science fiction since he could read, and wrote his first story (a radio play) while in the fourth grade. He spent his younger years at the family bookstore where he was put in charge of the science fiction section which accounts for his love of the genre, so it was only a matter of time before he began writing science fiction in earnest.

Besides short stories, John has also written several pieces of genre-related non-fiction and edits the fanzine, *Sleight of Hand.*

About "Digger Don't Take No Requests": Around the time that thousands of students in Tiananmen Square were facing down tanks, I was attending the University of Exeter in England on a grant from the National Endowment of the Humanities to work on a thesis about **The Exeter Book,** a collection of Anglo-Saxon poems. My room had been broken into at one point and I had lost quite a bit of money. Between the close of term at the university and my return home, I found myself playing my guitar on street corners for enough money to pay for a bed, some food, and a bus ticket to Heathrow.

Street musicians, or 'buskers' as they are called in England, are a fairly friendly crowd and are only too glad to recommend good street corners or even dispense advice so as to increase the day's takings. Many of them took a liking to me—possibly because of the novelty of seeing an American trying to make his way home by playing bluegrass on noisy city streets.

There were also a couple of folks, panhandlers and dealers, who were not as friendly as the rest and who defended their corners vigorously—sometimes even violently. There is a whole subculture on the street with its own customs and proprieties.

These days I always give money to folks playing music on street corners, remembering my own days trying to get along by doing the exact same thing. I've talked with many of them and find the culture of busking is pretty much the same the world over.

How could I not use that in a story one day?

Holly Phillips lives and writes in south-central British Columbia, Canada, one of the most beautiful regions in North America. She has sold many stories to literary and speculative markets in Canada and the US, and to date has received two honorable mentions, one in the 2001 Best of Soft SF Contest, and the other in the 14th annual Year's Best Fantasy and Horror anthology edited by Ellen Datlow and Terri Windling. In addition to her writing, Holly is a fiction editor for *On Spec,* the Canadian magazine of the fantastic, and has just recently entered into the world of the freelance editorial consultant.

About "The Gate Between Hope and Glory": On "The Gate Between Hope and Glory" I had a lot of fun digging through my old notebooks looking for the genesis of this story. The original note says (if I can decipher my own scribbles), "Unionization in space! The problem with striking is that the Company can just turn off the air. The key is to emphasize the precariousness, the vulnerability of living in space—and also the necessity of community." Of course my interest in labor issues is one I inherited from my father (and indeed, from my grandfather). But I find it interesting, and pleasing, to see how closely the finished product adheres to the originating idea. Something of a rarity, in my experience.

eluki bes shahar was born long enough ago to have seen Classic Trek on its first outing. As she aged, she put aside her dreams of taking over from Batman and returned to her first love, writing. Her first SF sale was the **Hellflower** series, in which Damon Runyon meets Doc Smith over at the old Bester place. Between books and short stories (most of them as Rosemary Edghill), she's held the usual part-time writer jobs, including book store clerk, secretary, and grants writer. She can truthfully state that she once killed vampires for a living, and that without any knowledge of medicine has illustrated half-a-dozen medical textbooks. Find her on the Web at: www.sff.net/people/eluki

About "Riis Run": When I finished **Archangel Blues**, the final book in the **Hellflower Trilogy**, back in 1987, I figured I was pretty much done with the Phoenix Empire. After all, I'd chased everybody up a *really* big tree and thrown some medium-sized planets at them, so the scope for a sequel was somewhat circumscribed. The characters would be far too changed for the normal rules of sequelae to apply. (For a look at what I mean, check out my "Read Only Memory," in the **DAW 30th Anniversary SF Anthology**; it's a tailpiece to the series, set some years later.) So while I knew what happened next, and even had a second trilogy plotted out, I knew there was very little likelihood that it would ever get beyond the vaporware stage.

But when **Low Port** came along, I realized that there was a certain amount of elbow-room still available in that universe. There's about a fifteen year stretch between the time Butterflies-are-Free Peace Sincere and Paladin meet and become partners, and the time when **Hellflower** begins.

A lot can happen in fifteen years...

Every weekend, from age five to eighteen, **Lawrence M. Schoen** worked at one or another swap meet throughout southern California. He spent a lot of that time watching the range of humanity passing by, and when business was slow he filled spiral notebooks with endless tales for his own amusement. The fascination with people won out and he put fiction aside to go off to college and graduate school to study linguistics and psychology. After ten years as a professor he put academia aside and returned to crafting fiction. He's also traveled the globe for years speaking and promoting the Klingon language. Nowadays, when not writing or making alien sounds, he's the Director of Research for a series of mental health facilities in Philadelphia.

About "Bidding the Walrus": A lot of my fiction tends to involve cognitive processes, like memory and attention, language and judgment, and their variations as they occur in alien or mechanical intelligences. The original motivation for this story came from a desire to flesh out the Clarkesons, a species I mentioned in passing in another story but didn't get to explore. My intent was to tap into the perils of doing business with creatures so alien in mindset and perspective that despite humanoid appearances they really did not experience reality in the same ways we do. I open the story with Eggplant Jackson's warning, but like the sorcerer's apprentice, Gideon pays no heed. The question you really want to be asking yourself is what the Clarkeson thought would happen. Did Greyce realize what his gift would do? And if so, did he care? The cognition of alien colony beings can be tricky. Fortunately, it falls nicely into balance when human cognitive processes are taken to extreme. I expect to see more of the Walrus, and he wouldn't go anywhere without Weird Tommy.

Laura J. Underwood used to be a stable bum, but she gave up a career with horses and veterinary medicine because she decided she would rather write. She is the author of two novels, **Ard Magister** and **The Black Hunter,** three short story collections, and a host of short fiction in the fantasy field. Her work has appeared in numerous volumes of *Sword and Sorceress*, and in such magazines as *Marion Zimmer Bradley's Fantasy Magazine, Dark Regions Magazine* and *Adventures in Sword & Sorcery*. When not putting pen to paper, she is a fencer, a harpist and a librarian living in East Tennessee with the Cat of Few Grey Cells otherwise known as Gato Bobo.

About "The Gift": When I first read the guidelines for **Low Port**, I was intrigued by the challenge of writing a story placed in the underbelly of society. Very few of my stories ever venture into such settings for more than a scene or two. But then I remembered Rhys, a minor character in a working novel—a healer and an herbalist who happens to be mageborn too. Rhys lives and works in the ruins of the once-proud city of Caer Elenthorn, a city that has never quite recovered from being overrun by the dark forces of The Hound during the Last War. As a trained healer, Rhys feels duty bound to offer his gifts to the "lower levels of humanity" residing in Broken Wall, for these are the people among whom he was born. But what Rhys wants more than anything is to be a True Healer instead of one cursed with the legacy of magic. I decided he had a few lessons to learn about accepting himself as he is. Not everyone can have "the gift" they crave.

L. E. Modesitt, Jr., has published a number of short stories and technical articles and more than thirty-five novels, many of which have been translated into German, Polish, Dutch, Czech, and Russian. His first published story appeared in *Analog* in 1973. Born in 1943 in Denver, Colorado, Mr. Modesitt has been, among other occupations, a U.S. Navy pilot; an industrial economist; staff director for a U.S. Congressman; Director of Congressional Relations for the U.S. Environmental Protection Agency; and a consultant on environmental, regulatory, and communications issues. In 1989, to escape years of occupational captivity in Washington, D.C., he moved to New Hampshire where he married a lyric soprano. They moved to Cedar City, Utah, in 1993.

About "The Dock to Heaven": When I heard that Sharon and Steve were putting together **Low Port**, my initial reaction was two-fold—that it was a great idea and that it was too bad that I didn't have anything in mind that would fit the anthology. But the more I thought about the idea, the more I realized that in anything I'd ever read, and in my own experience, there's one very grubby aspect of every business that very few people realize can be every bit as draining and exhausting—if in a different way—as the hard and dangerous physical labor. And that's what I wrote about, because it's something that I know, from both sides, first as a pilot who didn't have to worry about it and then as a different variety of snark.

Ru Emerson grew up poor in Butte, Montana and after that lived in some of the rougher parts of Hollywood, East Los Angeles and Venice Beach while trying to scratch out a living in a Straight Job. For several years that worked (legal secretary and paralegal in Century City—"L.A. Law" land). After relocating to Oregon some years ago and taking to writing full time, she has again rediscovered the thrills of living on the Edge.

Emerson now lives on five rural acres with The Infamous (and often alleged to be fictitious) Doug, and is bossed around by Roberta the Foo-Cat and twin black Cubs, Mufasa and Bagheerah. When not writing, she is usually gardening or lifting weights.

About "Find a Pin": When I first heard about the anthology and that it would be about people just barely making it, I knew it had already hit a nerve, though I wasn't sure which nerve, exactly. But the next day, I woke up and the story was simply There, fully told, just waiting to be written down; before I even opened my eyes, I *knew* how this woman would sound, look, the little gestures she'd make with her hands.

I can't be sure exactly where the impetus came from on "Find a Pin;" these "just in there waiting to be let out" stories are very rare for me, and not always susceptible to analysis. But for years, I have simply hated the way Oregon has closed its mental facilities and shoved so many schizophrenic patients out the door with a vial of pills: "Here, honey; now, don't forget to take these."

At the same time as the anthology came around, I was dealing with my lovely mother's condition: Mother is 83, has advanced Alzheimers, lives with my youngest sister and has been slowly turning into A Scary Person. Sue and I keep reminding each other, "It could be worse." I guess for the women in this story, it really could.

Alan Smale writes speculative fiction, sings bass and serves as business manager for up-and-coming high energy vocal band The Chromatics, and performs occasionally in community theater. An expatriate Yorkshireman, he is now a US citizen. By day (and sometimes night) he works as a research astronomer for USRA at NASA's Goddard Space Flight Center. Alan's science fiction and fantasy stories have appeared in many magazines and anthologies including *Realms of Fantasy*, *Writers of the Future #13*, Harcourt Brace collections **A Wizard's Dozen** and **A Nightmare's Dozen,** *Marion Zimmer Bradley's Fantasy Magazine*, and *Adventures of Sword and Sorcery.* He has earned several Honorable Mentions in best-of-year anthologies, and is currently marketing his first novel. His fledgling website can be found at www.alansmale.com

About "Sailing to the Temple": I can't travel without becoming obsessed with the country I'm visiting. While touring Japan I tried to read manga without knowing Japanese and derive pachinko from first principles. (I never got lost in Japan, but I often got confused.)

I also tried to peer back in time, beyond the cliches of samurai and ninja, kabuki and haiku. A thousand years ago Heian Japan was essentially isolated, its culture and basic assumptions very different from those found elsewhere. Even equipped with a universal translator, a time traveler would face major difficulties communicating in a society with such elaborate beliefs, superstitions, and rituals. The thought patterns and narrative style are sufficiently alien to us today that the **Tale of Genji** is almost untranslatable, and scholars cannot agree on whether it is complete or unfinished.

I read Genji, and Sei Shonagon's **Pillow Book**, but I couldn't help wondering what the regular folk were doing (apart from working their butts off and dying young) while the aristocracy pursued their cult of beauty and elegant romantic intrigues. I wrote "Sailing" to find out, and attempt to explore these different thought patterns.

Almost by definition, I must have failed. But I did enjoy the trip.

In 1988, Salmon Rushdie caused a stir with **The Satanic Verses** and Gabriel Garcia Marquez published **Love In The Time Of Cholera.** More significantly, **Mark W. Tiedemann** attended Clarion and soon after began publishing a string of short stories. In 2000, he began publishing novels, beginning with **Mirage: An Isaac Asimov Robot Mystery** for ibooks. More followed. His 2001 novel **Compass Reach,** first volume of the Secantis Sequence, was nominated for the Philip K. Dick Award. **Metal of Night** (2002) and **Peace & Memory** (2003) continue the stories of the Secant.

About "The Pilgrim Trade": The Pilgrim Trade is a story from my Secantis Sequence. I began developing the Secant universe in response to a desire to write far future stories against a common background unbound by normal series restrictions of character and plot. I wanted to work in a world that would be recognized as viable in all its pieces and parts, wherein I could tell stories at any level of society, in any geographical (or interstellar) location.

My first Secantis novel, **Compass Reach,** is the story of Freeriders, a kind of interstellar hobo class—the disenfranchised, the unwanted, the unrecognized of my society. It's clear from that book that the Freeriders represent but one segment of the underclass in the Pan Humana. The present story is about another such segment.

The idea originally was to allow me to write about economics as social tool rather than how most people seem to perceive it, as some sort of natural phenomenon, and to show how control of the tool can be used for both good or ill. And how the possibilities of a so-called "post scarcity" world can nevertheless fail to materialize due to simple (or complex) human prejudice.

Patrice Sarath is a writer and editor in Austin, Texas, and is a member of the Slug Tribe Writer's Group. Her stories have appeared in *Realms of Fantasy, Black Gate,* and the Meisha Merlin anthology **Such a Pretty Face.** Patrice's love of the fantastic began at an early age—she was one of those kids who always got in trouble for telling lies. She feels lucky that now she's getting paid for it.

About "More to Glory": In many ways, the working poor have it harder than the purely destitute. They live teetering on that knife's edge that separates a roof over one's head from homelessness, a full belly from starvation. One missed paycheck, one recession, and they know they can be plunged into true poverty. When I first sat down to write my story for the **Low Port** anthology, I knew I wanted to write about an ordinary, middle-class family doing its best to survive, love its kids, and raise them right, all against extraordinary odds.

Baltimore-born **Sharon Lee** is best known for the Liaden Universe® stories and novels that she co-authors with her husband, Steve Miller. Her singleton work includes the mystery novel **Barnburner** as well as a dozen or so science fiction and fantasy short stories. Sharon's most recent publication is **The Tomorrow Log,** co-written with Steve and published by Meisha Merlin. For more information on Sharon, Steve and their work, check out www.korval.com

About "Gonna Boogie With Granny Time": The city in which "Granny Time" is set is Baltimore, Maryland—my hometown. When I was a kid, I walked all over the city—up to the

Enoch Pratt Main Library, down to the docks, across to Lexington Market and the upscale department stores, and down again, to my favorite part of the city—the red light district known as The Block.

The Block and its diverse citizens fascinated me. The strippers, the barkers, the bouncers—they had their own culture, their own language, their own naming system—and their own code of honor.

Many years later, after Steve and I had moved to Maine, I was feeling just a touch homesick for the hot streets of my native city. It didn't occur to me to write a story about Baltimore, though, until I had a conversation with a friend in which he indicated that a particular person had so little personal power as to actually possess "mouse mojo."

Clearly, Mouse Mojo was the name of someone familiar with the streets of Baltimore and The Block. I put the word out—and a day later, I knew where to find him.

After the kind of varied career path that indicates either extreme curiosity or a very short attention span, **Chris Szego** found the job of her dreams managing Bakka, Canada's oldest SF bookstore. A prize-winning poet, her work has appeared in newspapers, magazines and anthologies. Most of the time she lives in Toronto.

About "Angel's Kitchen": Social work is not for the merely compassionate. It's a job for those very few whose hearts are both infinitely giving and tough as diamond. The people who can learn to measure success by an increase of time between failures. Who know that no matter how bad it gets, there will always be something worse ahead. But who try, anyway.

People that brave need an angel who's not afraid to get dirty.

Edward McKeown is a native son of NYC from which he draws much of the color and attitude of his stories. He moved to Charlotte, North Carolina in 1985 in search of reasonable house prices and a commute free of the "non-bathing public."

In Charlotte he developed an interest in the martial arts, achieving a black sash (belt) in Esoma Kung Fu. Writing was always a desire and became a passion after his muse took up full time residence behind his eyeballs. He's fortunate to be married to the noted artist, Schelly Keefer.

About "Lair of the Lesbian Love Goddess": "Lair of the Lesbian Love Goddess" came out of sheer serendipity. I finally listened to my wife and came out of the writing closet to join a critique group. The experience, which I think is an essential one for a writer, was terrific. The group known as Brinker's at Border in honor of a deceased member became a wellspring of ideas as well as a sounding board.

One day, I was e-mailing a friend from the group about a missing member. Our exchange spun out of control as we went back and forth about her possible fate: kidnapped, abducted by aliens, lost in a South Carolina swamp? Finally my friend, Diane Hoover, suggested that she had been captured and disappeared into a particular local institution of higher learning (which I won't name, so don't ask) that she called the Lair of the Lesbian Love Goddess. I laughed till tears appeared.

I decided that I had to write a short story with that as a title. Gradually the pulp-noir tale began to populate itself with characters: the world weary McManus, ambitious Regina Del Mar, flirtatious Freddie and that most critical of characters, New York City, in all its sordid muscularity. The four of them continue to whisper in my ear and three more stories have resulted. I hope eventually to have enough for an anthology of Lair tales.

Nathan Archer is a former New Yorker and a former bureaucrat. He is the author of half a dozen licensed novels and a few short stories. He's not sure what else he is that isn't "former," but hopes to figure it out soon.

Lee Martindale is a warrior-bard in the old tradition. Editor of Meisha Merlin's first original anthology, **Such A Pretty Face**, her own short fiction has appeared in numerous magazines, online venues, anthologies and collections. When not slinging fiction, she's a member of the SFWA Musketeers, a songwriter and filker, activist, public speaker, Life Member of SFWA and a member of the SCA. She lives in Plano, Texas with her husband George and three feline goddesses, and keeps her friends and fans in the loop with her website, www.harphaven.net

Jody Lynn Nye lists her main career activity as "spoiling cats." She lives northwest of Chicago with three of the above (who get plenty to eat) and her husband (ditto), author and packager Bill Fawcett. She has published 25 books, including six contemporary fantasies, three SF novels, four novels in collaboration with Anne McCaffrey, including **The Ship Who Won**; edited a humorous anthology about mothers, **Don't Forget Your Spacesuit, Dear!**; and written over seventy short stories. Her latest books are **License Invoked** (Baen) and **Myth Alliances** (Meisha Merlin), co-written with Robert Asprin, and **Advanced Mythology** (Meisha Merlin).

About "Bottom of the Food Chain": "The bottom of the food chain" is a common phrase currently used to describe the dispossessed. When I read the author's briefing for **Low Port**, it popped into my mind. The homeless or the marginally employed, especially in cities, have trouble maintaining a decent diet. Where they would be accorded basic nutrition by law, such as on a space station, logic suggests that they'd be given the least common denominator of food: enough so they wouldn't starve, but nothing as appealing or as varied as if they could actually *pay* for it. Like Oliver Twist, my main character dreams of the kind of food that rich people get to eat. His dreams may seem very small, but until he's attained those, it's hard to reach for higher goals.

Joe Murphy lives with his wife, up-and-coming watercolor artist Veleta, in Fairbanks, Alaska.

His fiction has or will appear in: *Age of Wonders*, *Altair*, **A**

Horror A Day: 365 Scary Stories, Bones of the World, *Book of All Flesh*, *Clean Sheets*, *Chiaroscuro*, *Crafty Cat Crimes*, *Cthulhu's Heirs*, *Demon Sex*, *Full Unit Hookup*, *Gothic.net*, **Legends of the Pendragon**, *Marion Zimmer Bradley's Fantasy Magazine*, *Outside*, *On Spec*, *Silver Web*, *Space and Time*, *Strange Horizons*, *Talebones*, *TransVersions*, *Vestal Review*, and **Why I Hate Aliens.**

Previously published stories are now on the Internet at Alexandria Digital Literature(www.alexlit.com) and at fictionwise.com. Joe is a member of SFWA, HWA, a graduate of Clarion West '95, and Clarion East 2000.

About "Zappa for Bardog": I really found the guidelines for **Low Port** interesting. And I've been experimenting with alien points of view. That's how the idea to tell a story through an artificial life form who could read information directly from human DNA came about. Having also been a fan of the late Frank Zappa, I've always wanted to do a tribute story as well. All these things kind of just came together and somehow managed to work.

Paul E. Martens is a son, a husband, and a father. He has a job. Paul was a first place winner in the Writers of the Future Contest and received an Honorable Mention in the 2001 Best of Soft SF Contest. Other stories have appeared in a variety of print and online magazines. He likes to pretend to be a cynical curmudgeon but he's actually a neurotic optimist.

About "The Times She Went Away": I knew I wanted to write a story for **Low Port**. I started with a guy like Peter in his middle years (a smuggler, a fence, someone making his living, not exactly on the dark side, but certainly on the crepuscular side), and his kind of wild adopted daughter. I thought the story had potential, but no real plot yet. Then Annie Jones showed up. Once he met Annie, Peter had no choice but to spend his life hanging around the Low Port, waiting for her to come back, and I had my story.

Douglas Smith's stories have appeared in over 40 professional magazines and anthologies in fifteen countries and thirteen languages, including *Amazing Stories, Cicada, Interzone, The Third Alternative, On Spec,* and **The Mammoth Book of Best New Horror**. In 2001, he was a John W. Campbell Award finalist for best new writer, and won an Aurora Award for best SF&F short fiction by a Canadian. He's been an Aurora finalist eight times and has twice been selected for honorable mention in **The Year's Best Fantasy & Horror**. In real life, Doug is a technology executive for an international consulting firm. He lives just north of Toronto, Canada. Like the rest of humanity, he is working on a novel. His web site is www.smithwriter.com and his email is doug@smithwriter.com

About "Scream Angel": The genesis of this story was a trip to a circus. Ever since my oldest son, Mike, was about five and until my younest son, Chris, decided it was no longer cool, we've gone to a circus show that tours Toronto each summer. They just set up in a field near the parking lots of one of the big suburban shopping malls, charge way too much for popcorn and candyfloss, and put on a fair-to-middling show. It's no Vegas, but it was always fun and for a good cause. Chris is physically handicapped, so when he started going, we were given seats reserved for wheelchairs right at ringside. A great view, close enough to really smell the elephants. But being that close let me notice something I'd missed from farther back. All of the performers did double, or even triple, duty as circus hands, setting up equipment, acting as safety catchers, or even shoveling up after the horses and elephants. Seeing the trapeze artist, who had just dazzled the crowd in his spiffy sequined outfit, show up in coveralls cleaning up elephant poop gave me the idea of a down-and-out circus of aliens, just scraping by. I coupled it with another idea about a drug I ended up calling Scream, made the big act a pair of bird-like aliens, and the rest grew out of that.

Come check out our web site for details on these Meisha Merlin authors!

Kevin J. Anderson
Robert Asprin
Robin Wayne Bailey
Edo van Belkom
Janet Berliner
Storm Constantine
John F. Conn
Diane Duane
Sylvia Engdahl
Phyllis Eisenstein
Rain Graves
Jim Grimsley
George Guthridge
Keith Hartman
Beth Hilgartner
P. C. Hodgell
Tanya Huff
Janet Kagan
Caitlin R. Kiernan
Lee Killough
Jacqueline Lichtenberg

Jean Lorrah
George R. R. Martin
Lee Martindale
Jack McDevitt
Mark McLaughlin
Sharon Lee & Steve Miller
James A. Moore
John Morressy
Adam Niswander
Andre Norton
Jody Lynn Nye
Selina Rosen
Kristine Kathryn Rusch
Pamela Sargent
Michael Scott
William Mark Simmons
S. P. Somtow
Allen Steele
Mark Tiedemann
Freda Warrington
David Niall Wilson

www.MeishaMerlin.com

The Mythology of
Jody Lynn Nye

Applied Mythology

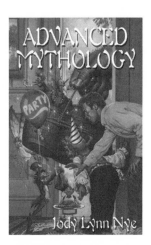

Advanced Mythology

"Whimsy is a delicate and dangerous kind of writing to attempt. To make it work takes a special kind of writer, one skilled at splicing the real world together with the new and unreal one seamlessly enough not to leave any telltale roughness around the interface. Some writers, surprisingly good ones, never get it right. But Jody Lynn Nye has mastered this difficult art, and succeeds in making it look easy. These books are a graceful and enjoyable romp."
—Diane Duane

Explore the Secantis Sequence of
Mark W. Tiedemann

Compass Reach
*Finalist for the 2001
Philip K. Dick Award*

Metal of Night

Peace and Memory

For more great short stories, look for

Such a Pretty Face

edited by *Lee Martindale*

"In the anthology *Such a Pretty Face*, the heroes aren't perfect. In fact, they're pretty ordinary sometimes. And those who do rescue the day don't fit the mold. This is the kind of fiction that doesn't make pretend with the clichés—some effort to be original is not wasted."
—*True Review*, July 2000

Featuring new short fiction by Sharon Lee and Steve Miller, Jody Lynn Nye, Laura J. Underwood, Lee Martindale, Selina Rosen, Gene Wolfe, Jane Yolen and many others!

To read more of Laura J. Underwood's Ard Taebh Chronicles, look for

ARD MAGISTER

from Yard Dog Press
(http://www.yarddogpress.com)

And coming in August 2004 from Meisha Merlin:

Dragon's Tongue